Ival spun around and backed against the door...

The stranger was on the loft, and momentarily Ival wondered how he'd managed to get there so quickly without the creaking sounds of the ladder. He watched as the stranger pulled on Ival's spare tunic and leapt down lightly to the floor, landing on the balls of his feet. Ival shrunk against the door as the stranger walked straight at him, seeming to grow in the room, casting a huge shadow behind him. *I was wrong before. He's bigger than the soldiers.*

"Not you, little man. I hunt them."

With a huge laugh, the stranger lifted Ival aside like a child then set him down, and flung the door open. Taking a deep breath with closed eyes, he stooped beast-like and uttered almost a growl, then was off, running along the road the truck had taken; running faster than Ival had seen a man run before.

Ival sat on the slightest edge of his chair, not looking, and slumped to the floor, shaking so hard his teeth chattered. Would either one be back?

Which was worse?

Also by Christopher Taylor:

SNOWBERRY'S VEIL

OLD HABITS

LIFE UNWORTHY
by Christopher Taylor

KESTREL ARTS
http://alphawolf10.wix.com/kestrelarts2

LIFE UNWORTHY

Christopher Taylor

Print Edition

Printed in the United States of America

Life Unworthy/Christopher Taylor

ISBN 978-0-9838176-9-7

First Edition

No werewolves were harmed in the writing of this book.

For Loren
Whose books always teach me I have more to learn, but lift me up to strive harder. Thank you for decades of reading.

"Remember that all through history, there have been tyrants and murderers"
-Mahatma Gandhi

CHAPTER ONE

Outside the sky was bright and sunny, one of those clear days that made Poland seem even more green and alive than even an ordinary spring day. Under that sky the flowers bloomed, the birds sang, and the grass grew as it all had for untold ages before, unchanged by man's doings and struggles. Another train rolled across the rusty metal of its tracks singing the rhythmic chant of the steel wheels over the joints as it slowed. Within was another load of cargo, so overloaded some had been lost on the trip over the long miles. That didn't concern the owners of the train especially; the cargo was all going to be dead soon enough in any case. The closer the train drew to its destination, the more awful and dead the countryside became; muddy gray with ash and dirt that spread across everything from its dread center in uncertain patterns driven by wind and rain.

Within the barbed wire-topped mesh walls of Birkenau stood stark, utilitarian buildings. The train slowed as it passed through the main entry between bleak rows of long bunkers for the cargo to live in briefly beneath towers scowling down at them, towers filled with bored guards not fit for normal duty on the front. One of the crematoriums belched smoke as the train came to a halt, raining ashes down like snow onto the camp and nearby village, the smell unlike anything most arriving had ever known. New arrivals passed a mound of hair shorn from the frightened and confused Jews, Gypsies, and others who didn't fit the plan of the Reich. The eyes of the cargo showed sudden realization that hope was gone, that the chance to make a break—to hide—was over. The guards were impassive, and even the distinct charms of some of the naked women generated no interest; no more than watching cattle herd by as they were processed. They were all eventually going the same place, no reason to pay them heed.

Nearby was a partially sunken building, a sloped concrete ramp leading down to locked iron doors. "Showers," the sign over the door read in German, a simple word. That word spiked some of the arrivals with strange fear through the haze of shock, having heard dread tales where water didn't come from the nozzles. True or not, recent events had them certain almost anything could be believed. The ones already in the camp didn't look up, it didn't matter where new arrivals were going or who they were. Survival in this dread place meant not being noticed, not making friends, not caring, not hoping. The ones who had the most spirit and fought to have hope were the first to die: give up, give in, forget life, and just exist. The fact that more came in at all was the only surprising thing, were there really that many more people that needed to die before the Reich was placated?

Within the showers stood naked men and boys, huddled together in fear and confusion, not knowing what would come out of the nozzles. Even more unnerving were the scratches in the iron doors, as if dozens of desperate fingernails had shattered on the unyielding metal. The air was stifling hot, and having the room crammed with naked bodies made the room reek even worse than the train car had. Children clung to older men, young men lost their fierce pride, weeping and watching, chewing nails. A young blond man sat against the wall, repeating the name of a lover he'd never see again, as an older man watched the youth with sorrow, thinking that his own life was almost ended, why must theirs be cut off? One man tried to console the others in thick Polish accented with a strange tone. It might be water, the tales might not be true, be strong, be of good faith. Others cursed him, cursed God, cursed the Nazis, and most of all cursed the rest of the world that sat by as they were ruined.

Sounds creaked through the pipes, aching with rust and use; they shuddered with something passing through them. Something moved along the iron, around the joints, and to the nozzles, as one man felt his heart erupting with pain and pressure like a hog squatting on his chest. A heart attack? Angina? Did it really matter now?

Outside the guards chatted, lighting cigarettes. Olaf had drawn the duty this time; none of them liked handling the Zyklon, even though the scientists told them that it was perfectly safe in the cans. Before the war it had been mostly used to kill bedbugs, now it was used to kill other creatures deemed unworthy of life. It was the short time the cans were opened with a chisel and dumped into the six vents on the roof that were nerve-wracking. Six kilos per load in the shower was a lot of exposure, even if it they had done it so often before. Olaf held his cigarette in shaking fingers; the muffled howls of the people inside weren't helping his nerves settle any. He hoped the others didn't notice, they seemed so calm and unaffected. After a while the screams and sounds ended, but the guards sat around talking and smoking to make sure the air was cycled out. Supposedly it refreshed every 3-4 minutes, but why take a chance? Getting a whiff of almond in the spring air didn't help ease the soldiers' nerves either. And they had made a lot of noise this time in the showers, different sounds than before.

2

Ordinarily the Sonderkommanden would deal with the cleanup, prisoners tasked with the dirty work and given a dubious SS title. But the sounds had been so strange this time that the guards had been called in to investigate. Olaf stood up and checked his MP-40, delaying a bit longer then slung it around his back. The first few times into the showers the Sonderkommanden had been given gas masks but they were stored away once the ventilation system proved effective. Olaf wished he had one, just in case.

The Soldiers looked at each other and headed down the ramp with the boldness of company. The doors were unlocked and with a metallic bang swung open. The stench of sweat and feces and vomit filled the air, the worst part of the job. *They never died clean*, thought Olaf, the *dirty Jews couldn't even have dignity at death.* The bodies were piled on top of each other, pink and pale, choked out by the gas. It was fairly quick and efficient, and the system cleaned up the ones most likely to cause trouble, along with the sick and the old. They weren't any use in a work camp anyway, and they had no future. Better to end them fast. There was something wrong in back, though. Dark liquid was on the walls, some of the bodies were torn apart, limbs scattered, ripped open. The lights were all out in the back, casting deep shadows in the showers, one nearer light flickering irregularly showing glimpses of more but not long enough to recognize anything.

Something dark in the back moved, and Olaf started at the sight. A growl shook off the walls of the concrete bunker, a tone that resonated with the iron piping overhead. Some... *thing* was alive in there. It was an eerie sound, nothing like the young farm boy Olaf had ever heard in the wild—like some huge hound but deeper, louder, something unearthly. It reminded him of a thing he couldn't place, like a long-forgotten nightmare. The dark shape moved, suddenly across the room in an instant, and with a roar that shook Olaf's bones and passed him—stiff fur scraping across his uniform. Wetness splashed over his side, and turning he saw Hans looking at him with surprise in his bright blue eyes. Then Hans' head fell, landing on the floor with a dull crack, followed shortly by his body pumping crimson from where his neck used to be. Olaf turned, swinging his Mp-40 off his back as he watched Gunter fall beneath a huge dark form, the sound of crunching hidden by a furry body, a sound like branches cracking in a wet bag. Blood hit the walls with a slick sound, and Olaf wondered why Gunter didn't make any sound.

Arie was the first to fire, the sound deafening and painful in the enclosed concrete room. The smell of gunpowder and the flash of his rifle were shocking and comforting at the same time as he saw creature's body shake from impacts of the bullets. Even in the stark bright flashes of rifle fire the form was still shadowed, black, bristling with stiff hairs. One stray shot ricocheted off the wall, showering concrete chips and dust over Hans' body, but even in that short burst of time Olaf felt something was wrong. Arie went down in another instant, the sharp explosion of his rifle firing into the body of the beast, then a sound like when Olaf's dog went under the wheels of his father's tractor. He felt sick and terrified; there was only him left, where were the others outside, hadn't they heard the gunshots? But it had only been seconds, portions of seconds.

Olaf's hands trembled, fumbling with the safety on his machine pistol and tried to keep the muzzle on the dark form as it moved forward at him slowly. Its fur was black, with reddish tips like it had rolled in rust. The eyes of the beast burned red from within like a coal fire was inside its skull, and its muzzle was matted and wet with blood, all across the whole head. Its ears were back, lips pulled over blood-streaked ivory fangs and black gums with with deep, chilling growl that made Olaf feel colder over his whole body, a sound that shook his bones, that rippled his guts—a sound that paralyzed his soul.

It was a wolf, a great wolf, bigger than any Olaf had ever seen. It stood nearly as tall as his chest, the shoulders hunched and high as it moved slowly forward. Olaf fired into the beast, holding the trigger down for a stream of leaden death straight at the horror in defiance of his training to use short bursts. Terror gripped him, as his body let go in his uniform, soiling himself. The bullets hit the beast, but had no effect. They shook it slightly; he could see its fur ruffled where they hit. He watched a trail of these dents up its body and shot the ceiling as the barrel of his gun climbed from the recoil.

The gun sounded a metallic click empty as the last brass rattled off the concrete ramp in ringing wind chime-like sounds. The wolf shook its self a moment like it was wet, and then leapt. As his bowels released, all Olaf could think of is how he'd die with all the mongrels on the floor behind him.

CHAPTER TWO

Captain Jogl Venderben looked at the carnage in the shower, the camp guards standing around him with rifles at the ready. In the heat the blood was already dried—caked and flaking on the walls, thick like pudding on the floor in puddles with flies swarming. The stench of the chamber was making him uncomfortable and queasy, but as a good German officer he could show no weakness in front of the men. Venderben looked at the bodies of his fallen soldiers, crumpled like they'd died on their feet suddenly. Three he could not identify, one in fact had no head at all, as if some titanic jaws had taken part of his chest and all of his head in one mouthful. One had his head lying at his arm. Hans, it looked like. The final soldier was not in enough of one piece to really identify; chunks were strewn around the room, most no larger than a fist. All that was really left to know what the meat had been was a nearly bare bloody skull that still had most of the face on it, frozen forever in a scream of terror and pain. Jogl swallowed back hard, trying not to vomit as he tried to take it in. This was no escaped gypsy or Jew, something *else* had been in the showers with those wretched mongrels.

Without a word he turned and left, knowing that the soldiers would have to deal with the mess. They would put some of the prisoners on cleaning it up,and it would disappear like the mist this morning. *Put a crew on the fence to repair the tear. Get back to business as usual.* Venderben looked into the ash- drifting blue sky and realized with a sinking feeling he would have to call headquarters in Krakow about this. What would he say? Better to let the new commandant call. The other soldiers milled around uncomfortably, wanting to say something but too disciplined to until Jogl spoke.

CHAPTER THREE

Spring in Berlin was still snowy, the clouds low and heavy, which made the city relax more. There had been few raids since the previous fall, and those long-range British bombers could not bomb what they could not see, but the memories were still strong. The snow was old and dirty, piled up beside the roads to slowly melt and it was warm enough that water stood between the cobblestones rather than ice.

The flags over the Reichstag were barely stirred by the limp breeze, crimson showing on the flagpoles. A tall, thin man dressed in a black coat walked up the steps briskly like he'd been here dozens of times. In truth, Vladimir Czerny had seen the building only briefly, in passing. His small round spectacles flashed reflecting the cloud-covered sunlight, and his bowler hat covered a completely bald head tattooed with startling designs in old black ink. Czerny stopped for a moment and consulted what looked like a pocket watch for a few moments, unmoving in the cold air. German men dressed in suits and overcoats stepped by Vladimir with barely a sideways glance, busy with the regimen of life. After a few moments, Vladimir snapped the device shut and tucked it into a pocket inside his woolen coat, then briskly walked up the steps and into the building.

Inside, Reichsleiter Martin Bormann waited impatiently. True, that Romanian consultant wasn't late yet, but a good man was always early. Bormann hated to wait; he hated to be at a disadvantage to any man. Best to make the foreigner wait outside before seeing him, yes, perhaps a good cigarette first.

The folders sat on his desk mocking him with their absurd notions and faerie tale words. How could any modern leader of the Reich believe any of this, discuss this nonsense? Aryans were not afraid to admit that there were more things than dreamt of in the philosophies of lesser men, but there were limits. Whoever wrote these papers clearly had read entirely too much of the old tales for Bormann's liking. He'd heard all the legends of course; Thor and Frey, the dark elf Svirfneblin, the dwarves, the dragons. Tales from the ancient honored history of the Aryan race. Tales to stir the heart, to make the soul sing with heritage and connect to the strength of ancestors. But to believe them?

It was true that the Fuhrer was fascinated with these things, ever seeking more power from the occult, ever sending men to find rumored artifacts, hinted objects of arcane might. There was a crack team of chemists, the best that Germany and Poland had to offer, working in Berlin on the Philosopher's Stone – turning lead to gold. But still... werewolves? Bormann finished his cigarette and stubbed it out, deciding on the proper course of action and tone with this Romanian. He began to reach for the intercom button and his door opened revealing the tall, thin man.

Behind him was Helga, young, lovely Helga with the shining blonde hair looking worried with her hands clasped.

"Oh, I'm so sorry Herr Bormann, he just walked up to the door and ... well it opened before I could stop him!"

Bormann allowed himself a rare smile, awkward and unfamiliar on his face. He couldn't ever stay mad at Helga for long, she was even more charming and lovely than her predecessor. Helga would never have to be sent to a camp. Well, probably not.

"I was expecting him. Close the door Helga." Bormann said, trying not to scowl. Everything relied on being in charge, in never letting anyone see you confused or unready. There was could be no weakness in the Reich.

"Be seated, Herr... tserrny is it?"

The thin man's eyes were cold as Russian winter through the round spectacles, a pale ice blue almost indistinguishable from the whites of his eyes.

"Cherrny."

Bormann turned his back, facing a wide window overlooking Berlin. *A Slav, perhaps not a Russian but still, one of those people,* thought Bormann. *More Asiatic than European even. You could teach them to speak and act properly but they were still barbarians inside.*

Martin Bormann held against his back with both hands a folder with photos and graphic descriptions of the Auschwitz Shower event, *Die Auschwitzer Duschefall.* His eyes were on the window, looking outside at the glory of the new Berlin, future seat of the world's capitol. Bormann waited a moment; deliberately slow to speak to build tension for the visitor. But when he turned, Vladimir Czerny had not changed expression in any way, still sitting patiently and quietly like he'd rehearsed this again and again and was simply filling a role. Bormann sneered.

"When the Third Reich has subjugated the lesser countries, we will have a more standard language. For commerce and to teach the children, you see."

If Czerny had any thoughts on the matter, he did not betray them, as if willing to let Bormann lead the conversation to a point he felt important enough to respond to. The Reichsleiter frowned and turned to the window again. What would shake this man, he couldn't have blood as icy as his gaze suggested.

"You have been briefed on this... statement, I trust?" Bormann said to the window.

Vladimir Czerny's expression remained totally unchanged, the light outside from the sinking sun now reflected off his spectacles, obscuring his eyes entirely.

"The soldiers at the work camp at Auschwitz have discovered and been attacked by a lycanthrope, which then fled into the countryside nearby. It apparently was among the men placed in the shower there for decontamination."

Bormann glanced back and watched Czerny's face for any hint of sarcasm or judgment regarding Birkenau or the showers. He could read nothing; it was as if the man was indeed made of ice, or stone.

"And you believe this report to be, shall we say, accurate?"

The Romanian responded in a calm, neutral tone. "The details, the creature's actions and the deaths of the men, the report of the tower guard describing a dark shape tearing through the fence seem consistent. It is possible, but unless I visit the site I cannot know. I was told to report to you for papers and instructions on how to proceed."

"But surely you do not believe such nonsense! Monsters in the modern age, what are we, children reading tales of Fafnir?"

"Apparently not everyone in the Reich is so skeptical. Do you have the full reports for me?"

Bormann turned to the window again, feeling vaguely ashamed. *Damn this icy Romanian, damn his calm. Martin Bormann has no superiors! Other than the Führer, of course.* He gestured vaguely at the desk without turning.

"They are in the folder for you, as are your instructions, straight from the Fuhrer's office. You are to proceed to the camp and examine what evidence is left. From there you will track this creature and find it; I am told that you claim to have faced such things in the past in your home land."

"Such creatures are rare—even in Romania—but I have faced one before," Czerny replied to his back.

"You will leave immediately. There is a car waiting that will take you to a plane. There are a few marks in the packet for your discretion, but the Reich will not tolerate waste. Heil Hitler!"

We shall test his loyalty, thought Bormann, and he waited for the response for a time but heard nothing. Turning with a savage look, he found his office empty, the door closed.

CHAPTER FOUR

A simple man with a simple life, Ival Piotrowski lived on a small farm at the edge of woods that had seen history unfold for millennia. He still plowed walking behind oxen, he still got water from his well, and he still rode a horse, even though he had a motor car under a tarp in the barn. He'd gotten the car right after the Great War; fresh out of the military with some gems he and his friends had managed to 'borrow' from a chateau in France. The car had sat in the barn ever since, tires flat, undriven. A relative had lifted the engine out for his own auto years ago, but Ival didn't want to get rid of the machine.

Ival ran a hand through his thinning hair and looked out over his oat field carefully planted around that enormous oak in the middle. He considered sitting under it with a cold beer and relaxing in the abundant shade, but the fence needed mending and his roof leaked in heavy rain, plus the chimney should be cleaned before autumn, and the horse hadn't run for a few days; he should get Mishka out for some exercise. And the slowly drifting ashes from above would fall into his hair, into his beer. Ival tried not to think about the ashes, what they represented, where they came from. It was downwind of him most of the time, on the other side of town. But sometimes the wind blew toward his little farm. The wind blew the ashes, the stench, and sometimes as he lay alone in his simple bed at night, Ival imagined it blew moans of the damned.

They all ignored it, like a boil on the face of your lover; you tried to act like it really wasn't there and go on with your life. It sat in what was once a boggy area, among the trees, hidden from sight but not from the conscience of the locals. They'd cut down the tree on which Ival had scrawled his love to Misa, cut down enough for a huge flat area using miserable bald slave labor that died under the crushing need of the Third Reich.

One could not fault their efficiency, and the German war machine seemed unstoppable. Certainly it was impossible for a simple

9

farmer to do anything about the conditions in the camp. They must be criminals, why else would anyone do that to people? The Germans were a lot of things, but they weren't monsters. The soldiers that had visited his home looking for food were just young men like Ival had been in 1916, hungry, dirty, homesick, tired. But he'd gone by the camp once, seen the skeletal forms, the star of David on so many arms, and doubt rode him like an evil thing.

Ival saw movement in his barn, a shadow in the shadows, and was glad for the distraction. Last time it was a deserter, and the time before that just a dog, but it spooked the horse and it never hurt to be sure. There hadn't been wolves in this area for decades at least; he remembered his last hunt with his father in the cold of a snowless November day late in the last century. His father had been more worried than Ival, who was simply full of youthful excitement. Ival never had understood the concern, the breath of relief when the wolf died from a ball of lead spat by the old man's muzzle-loading rifle.

Ival opened the barn door and peered inside, his breath a cloud around him. The familiar smells, dulled by the crisp air greeted him; dust and straw smells, mixed with the animals. The barn looked familiar, with its usual contents in their proper place including the mounded shape of the automobile under its old stiff canvas. Ival pondered yet again using the canvas elsewhere, a single piece of sailcloth stained with salt water from years on the ocean long ago. It would make functional curtains in the bedroom, the lace ones in place were crumbling from age, hand-crafted by Misa's mother as a gift at their wedding. They needed repair and cleaning but Ival didn't dare try his thick, dirty fingers on them for fear of damage, and the curtains were the most visible thing he had left of his wife.

A breeze stirred the dust and ashes slightly near the door, swirling around Ival's feet as he stepped into the barn quietly. Mishka whuffled softly, shuffling his hooves as he saw Ival enter, but didn't seem nervous. Perhaps he hadn't seen anything at all, just ghosts from his conscience. Mishka moved to the edge of his stall and hung his long brown head over the edge, hoping for a treat.

The small forge in the back stood cool, the hammer on the anvil where Ival had left it before.

The hay stood stacked in a heap in the loft overhead.

Somewhere a mouse was chewing away industriously, making tiny crunching noises.

Under the mound of canvas he heard a sound, like a cough or a throat clearing. Ival stood still in the shadows of the barn unsure if what he had heard was real or his imagination, and unsure if he really wanted to know what was under the tarp. An escaped prisoner, a soldier run from the army, perhaps someone escaping the German secret police; Gestapo, wasn't it? What if it was just someone who needed food? The bombing and war had created thousands like that, homeless, foodless, alone, wandering refugees. What if it was him under the tarp, would it matter why he was there? He would just need help.

Ival lifted the edge of the tarp and looked under, into the car's window. Crouched on the seat he could see a figure, curled up and naked.

From the camp, thought Ival. *Escaped and hiding here. Put the tarp down, pretend you didn't see him.*

There was blood on the man, but he looked strong and healthy, very healthy. His skin was darker than most poles, with dark hair covering almost all of him. A gypsy? The man looked up, eyes yellowish with pupils dimly reflecting light almost like an animal's. Ival felt a chill run over his back but knew he couldn't ignore the man any more. Their eyes had met, there was a human connection. The two men looked at each other, Ival swallowing and holding the tarp, unsure what to say or do. The hairy man looked back, calmly assessing the farmer.

"I ... do not speak the pole muchly... you know *Romani*?" The man asked, his voice deep and strong, almost causing the wood of the car to vibrate.

Ival shook his head, not sure what Romani was, Italian? The man's Polish was heavily accented, foreign in a way Ival had not heard before. *Probably a gypsy. Trouble. Tell him to leave.*

"Come on inside," Ival heard himself say, "I have some clothes and food for you, you can't stay here."

Misa would have wanted to help. Perhaps her spirit is with me now, guiding me. Ival crossed himself. The man looked away with a grunt, but climbed out of the car and stood unashamed and naked by Ival, towering over him. Ival led him to the house, wondering. This man was not just in good health—he was a colossus. He was huge, strong, muscled like Ival's brother, but a full foot taller, and radiating confidence and control. Ival felt like he was standing near a king. Perhaps he was a gypsy ruler of some sort, did they have kings? But the huge figure was splattered with blood, someone else's blood for there were no wounds on his body, like someone had died badly near him.

The man followed easily behind Ival and ducked under the doorway, looking around impassively at the old dusty home. Ival pushed the curtain to his room aside and looked through the rough wooden wardrobe he'd built for something the giant could wear. Not a giant, Ival thought, for he knew men this tall, but the stranger seemed even bigger than his stature. Ival stepped back into the main room with some old worn clothes. The man took them without a word and pulled on the pants. They fit him like a boy's trousers, barely longer than his knees and tight against his legs. The man looked down and growled, or grunted, he seemed annoyed, but not at Ival. The tunic fit better, it was long and baggy on Ival, whose shoulders were broad from hard work.

Ival busied himself in the home cutting bread and cheese, and dishing out cold stew from the night before. The man would need food

11

now, and it took time to start the fire up again. He set the food at the table and watched as the man sat and ate quietly, ignoring the bread entirely. Ival checked the bread subtly, was it moldy? He should have scraped it off just in case. *It wasn't that old, maybe he just didn't like rye. It was good bread, everyone thought so--*

"The clothes do... fine. I must go so to not trouble yourself."

Ival shook his head. "No, friend, it is late, you must stay, sleep here, you can move on tomorrow. But you can stay in my root cellar if you are concerned about being discovered. No one comes out here, I am a humble farmer, no one cares about me."

The gypsy king looked carefully at Ival, trying to understand his words like he was reading unfamiliar text on a page. After a moment, he looked down. "Yes, rest is good, I..." he paused and seemed to choose a word, "weary"

The gypsy king didn't look weary, but Ival wasn't willing to press the point. So he probably wasn't a king but the name was as good as any, and Ival did not care to know any more about this man than he absolutely had to. The Germans had only come here once, when they first took over and ate all his food. He understood why they did, armies never were fed enough, but it still had been a pretty rough month or two. Even the patrols just drove by his little farm, either he looked dull or safe—he could not decide, nor care. Being unnoticed by the army was good.

The gypsy king climbed into the loft with a few quick, powerful movements and lay on the wooden floor near Ival's bed. Ival busied himself putting away the few dishes and built a fire for the evening. It was already cool in the room and the night would be bone chilling. The gypsy king would need a blanket.

CHAPTER FIVE

Ival stood paralyzed at the base of the ladder extending up to the sleeping loft. He had jumped when a powerful fist hammered on the old wood of his door, shaking loose small puffs of dust but now he couldn't move. Someone shouted in heavily accented Polish to open the door, and Ival trembled, then like a puppet pulled by strings stumbled to the door and just before opening it, jerked his head around for one final look at the loft and the source of his doom.

As he swung the door open, Ival remembered his youth, as a noble of some sort had come to the door. He recalled his fathers downcast eyes, obedient actions, and humble tones. *This is how you deal with authority*, he remembered thinking as a child. Filling the doorway was a blond German officer wearing a uniform he'd not seen before. It was not the slate gray of the German military, but was jet black, with a design new to Ival. Behind him was an old German army truck, with a small group of men climbing out of the back.

With an absolute assumption of authority and power, the German roared in the same tone and accent as he had outside the door: "You, farmer, have you seen any strangers in the area? Anything unusual?" The officer's grey-blue eyes were dead, as if Ival was no different from the chair behind him. Insignificant.

Other than you? thought Ival, but swallowing hard as he concentrated on the stomach of the officer.

"Strangers, sir?" Ival mumbled, trying not to stammer or seem guilty, "why would anyone come to my little farm?"

"Stand aside!" he was commanded, and without waiting the soldiers shoved past him, turning his body back away from the door. Ival felt the room turn darker, as his death moved closer, a tomb closing in around him as all light seemed to fade away. *They will find him, they will take me to that camp, and I will die as one of those wretched skeletons. I will see you soon, Misa.* He turned without thinking to stare at the loft as the soldiers moved into the room, searching roughly. They loomed over him, five men filling the room, younger, stronger,

13

and larger than Ival. *Taller than the gypsy king,* thought Ival. *He seemed so big but he really wasn't much taller than I was.* He with his back straight and prepared to face his fate, crossing himself and swallowing hard as one of the men climbed into the loft.

Oberleutnant Sigfried Koenig of the SS watched as the guards detailed to him from Auschwitz I searched the shabby little one-room cabin. The table was clear, the bed was rumpled but empty. *Sloth, waking up so late in the day, small wonder the Poles were so easily defeated* Koenig thought. The little wretch at least understood his place, cowering before the might of the third Reich. He commanded a soldier to search the root cellar and noted one of them tucking a rough jar of liquor under his coat. Later, he would reprimand the idiot and destroy the stuff; probably make a man go blind.

As the officer stepped out of the building, Ival dared peek around the room. The soldier in the loft had stabbed his bedding with a bayonet, but was coming back down. There was nowhere to hide up there among the sooty rafters. Was the gypsy king a ghost? Ival felt the chill in his gut clench tighter. Outside went a soldier and he heard the root cellar open with a bang. One of the soldiers broke some of his crockery and Ival winced at the loss. They were taking his food and wine as well, no surprise there. The officer had left the little home; apparently he didn't care what happened inside.

Finally, the soldiers stepped out of the building one by one, the last sneering at Ival, a wordless promise that they were far from done with him. Ival looked up toward the heavens to thank Saint Stanislas when he saw, up in the rafters, in the darkness above the door a figure clinging to the ceiling like a spider. A half-naked, hairy figure with black eyes staring down at him, not as a warning, not begging him to stay silent. Like a predator looking at prey, a wolf staring at a lamb. Unconcerned, but waiting out of sight to strike. His feet were on the edge of a small projection on the inside of where the front porch met the front wall, his back against the peaked ceiling, hands against the surface with fingers spread and clawlike. His eyes were shiny black, but still Ival could see them in the dusty gloom. Ival blasphemed, for the first time in his life, and one of the soldiers looked back and laughed.

As they drove away, Ival heard a soft sound behind him.

"Now I am refreshed. Is time to hunt."

Ival spun around and backed against the door. The stranger was on the loft, and momentarily Ival wondered how he'd managed to get there so quickly without the creaking sounds of the ladder. He watched as the stranger pulled on Ival's spare tunic and leapt down lightly to the floor, landing on the balls of his feet. Ival shrunk against the door as the stranger walked straight at him, seeming to grow in the room, casting a huge shadow behind him. *I was wrong before. He's bigger than the soldiers.*

"Not you, little man. I hunt them."

With a huge laugh, the stranger lifted Ival aside like a child then set him down, and flung the door open. Taking a deep breath with closed eyes, he stooped beast-like and uttered almost a growl, then was off, running along the road the truck had taken; running faster than Ival had seen a man run before.

Ival sat on the slightest edge of his chair, not looking, and slumped to the floor, shaking so hard his teeth chattered. Would either one be back?

Which was worse?

*****

First Lieutenant Sigfried Koenig sat in the front seat of the Opel Blitz, bouncing with the rough road. With more rank and status he could get a sedan, but this ten-year-old rusting trash was the best he could get from his seniors. The soldiers sat petulantly around him sharing unhappy looks, still angry that the Oberleutnant forced them to give up their booty taken from the farmer. It was one thing to force them to give up the wine, but pouring it out on the ground while lecturing them on the dangers of rustic liquor was too much.

The trip to the next farm was made in silence as each man stewed about their ill treatment by superior officers. Sitting between Koenig and the driver Berthold, corporal Dieter studied the map of the farms they were to check, scribbling a note by Ival's that he had a horse of dubious quality in case the cavalry or artillery teams decided they needed it. As the crow flies, the next farm was not far from Ival's - perhaps half a mile - but the roads wound more than two miles around hills, ponds, and fields over rutted dirt and potholes that jarred his teeth. If they'd been given a halftrack they could do this in half the time and have no worse a ride, he mused. Straight across the fields and over the creek. Probably a better officer than Koenig would have gotten one instead of needing to ride with flags flying on the front bumpers like he was important. Dieter looked up briefly with the irrational fear someone could read his mind and would tell the SS officer of his disloyalty.

Overhead the clear evening sky was surrendering to dark, heavy clouds that obscured the setting sun and the temperature began to drop. Lieutenant Koenig pulled his coat closer around his throat and steeled himself against the cold. No Polish peasant would see an officer of the SS show discomfort or human reaction of any kind due to the weather. Unconquerable, superhuman, that's how the world must see the Aryan soldier: hopeless to oppose.

The roof above the men caved in with a terrific bang, shocking the men so much that several in the back cried out as the windows on the sides exploded in a shower of glass to the sides of the road. Over the side of the car a man's fierce countenance showed, beard and long hair tangled like a wild savage. A hairy arm reached in and grabbed Berthold by the throat, yanking him through the broken glass. Dieter grabbed Berthold's legs and tried to hold him but the pull of that arm was inexorable. Hiss pants tore and pulled partly off, a shoe came loose, and Dieter lost a fingernail, but Berthold was pulled out the window with glass shards slashing his arm and thrown spinning into a field nearby like a sack of grain, dozens of feet away from the road.

The driverless truck coasted to a halt on the dirt, turning sideways on the road as Dieter grabbed the wheel and tried to control the Blitz. Heavy laughter echoed through the lonely countryside as lieutenant Koenig began shouting orders. The men rolled out of the back of the truck, clutching rifles and cursing as Berthold staggered to his feet, shaking dirt out of his hair and face. They spotted the figure running toward the wood between Ival's farm and the next on the list, running with incredible speed as the soldiers opened fire at him. Koenig fired his Luger, knowing that he was at best unlikely to hit, but it helped express his frustrated fury. After a barked order, Koenig and his little troop took off after the fugitive, watching dirt kick up around the fleeing man from bullet impacts.

Only Berthold looked at the truck again before running off, looking to see the roof caved in to the level of the seats, wondering how on earth the man had hit so hard. He had felt that steely grip, the impossible strength that flung him out of the car to crash like a rag doll into the hard dirt and inside him he felt the chilling fear of the unnatural. His left arm felt numb and useless, like it had been dislocated, so he picked up his Karabiner with his good hand and stood a moment watching the others as blood from the gash dripped off his fingers. Berthold considered lying in the field, knowing his arm would start hurting badly soon. Who would know he had not passed out? But the strength of that man filled him with dread, and he felt strangely alone and exposed in the cold empty field. Berthold gritted his teeth and followed the others, cursing.

The soldiers slowed as they neared the wood, as Koenig warned them it could be an ambush of partisans. Although rare in this part of Europe, there still were pockets of resistance, ragged and poorly equipped, and he did not wish to be another victim of Armia Krajowa, the Polish resistance movement. The man was easy to see in the forest, his ragged gray pants stark against the dark woods, but he was ducking past birch trees and soon was out of sight as the soldiers entered the wooded area.

The soldiers crouched as Koenig scanned the forest. There were dried leaves and debris on the forest floor covering any obvious footprints and he could see no sign of anyone other than the fugitive ahead. He motioned to the men to spread out and search for their attacker. The men set out in a loose pattern and began to search the forest. The guards split up and became increasingly isolated, relying on occasional checks to see where the nearest soldier was. Koenig became worried that one of them would shoot another and called for them to form up closer.

Although the wood was not more than a few hundred yards across, it was thick enough that soon all sight of the fields around them was lost, and the quiet became even more oppressive. No birds sang, no horses rode by. Each man could only hear his heart and the soft footsteps across twigs and leaves as he searched. With nervous eyes they scanned the trees for movement or a human figure.

A burst of automatic fire shattered the silence, with shouting and as Karl and Lars trotted to the area, they found Dieter standing over a bullet-riddled dog, his fellow soldiers laughing and congratulating him on shooting an escaped canine. Koenig ran up and stared at the dog, then looked around the forest. He counted quickly—five of his men, where were the other three?

A scream sounded in distance, shuddering and jerking then cut off with a horrible sound. Koenig's eyes narrowed. That hadn't sound like any of his men, it barely sounded human. Then the laughter started again, echoing in the wood, powerful and long, and moving through the forest, confusing the source. The four men caught up with the place they'd heard the scream come from and discovered Berthold. His body had been twisted in an unnatural position, curled backward as if some horrendous force had seized head and pelvis and pushed them to almost meet. Berthod's face was etched with agony, straining to breathe as blood misted out his mouth onto the forest floor, chest spasming. His eyes moved, wide and desperate like a dying animal, pleading with the men for release from his agony.

Koenig stopped and stared several seconds before looking up and around. *What had done this?* Berthold gave one last groan and stopped breathing.

The laughter started again.

CHAPTER SIX

Still feeling somewhat weary from the loud, lurching military flight from Berlin to Krakow, Vladimir Czerny stepped out of the gleaming staff car as snowflakes began to fall from a low, leaden sky over the camp. He had been briefed on the drive over by commandant Friedrich Hartjenstein; Auschwitz was divided into two camps, the second more properly known as Birkenau. Auschwitz had been built on a Polish military base named Oswiecim, designed for "undesirables and lesser races" who were sent to work for the Reich, yet in less than a year Herr Himmler had issued orders for the extermination of the lesser races and a Birkenau had been built to focus on this task.

Commandant Hartjenstein had joked with Czerny about early attempts to follow Himmler's orders, using wool filters soaked in sulfuric acid and thrown into a room of prisoners, but noted that it was inefficient and dangerous. The guards hated working with the poison, even if it was almost instantly lethal to the prisoners. Bodies had been burned on an iron grate in the open air, but it soon became obvious that there was no way to handle the workload in this manner.

A series of showers had been built, sunk beneath round level and the pipes leading into them could be used either for water or to issue cyanide gas into the chamber. The bodies were then taken to a series of crematoriums where they were quickly reduced to ashes. Hartjenstein proudly said that Herr Himmler admired his efficiency, although he'd gotten the design and ideas from a man named Eichmann.

Confidentally, Hartjenstein had leaned over and shared how Commadant Höss of the first Auschwitz camp initially was squeamish about shoving screaming women and children to their doom.

"He doesn't talk about it much, and I suspect he feels ashamed of this weakness of his." Hartjenstein smoked a moment, reminiscing. "Adolf Eichmann set him straight, though. He explained to Höss that it was especially the children who have to be killed first, because where was the logic in killing a generation of older people and leaving alive a

18

generation of young people who can be possible avengers of their parents and can constitute a new biological cell for the reemergence of this people?"

Hartjenstein seemed to agree, or at least was willing to buy into it for the time being. In his office, Czerny removed his leather hat revealing the stark tattoos on his bald head. Hartjenstein tried not to stare, but could not help himself from peeking on occasion. Czerny ignored it, face still implacably calm and almost bored looking, used to the reaction of others to his appearance. Commandant Hartjenstein leaned back in his chair and looked at the paperwork Martin Bormann had issued him. Vladimir Czerny quietly spoke as Hartjenstein read.

"So your recent attempt to use the showers revealed something other than one of the usual prisoners?"

Hartjenstein nodded grimly, picking up a carbon-copied sheet. "Yes, it was batch... 2501, yesterday morning. A group of male prisoners deemed unworthy of life were separated from the workers and escorted to the shower, and the Zyklon B was introduced into the system. Death is almost instantaneous when the canister is administered, yet in this instance apparently it was ineffective on one of the prisoners."

Czerny was confident in German paperwork and efficiency; they would have impeccable records of who was in that shower and why. "You have his name, then?"

"It was... Cezar Alexandru was the only prisoner unaccounted for, when the pieces had been put together," Hartjenstein said after consulting a file. "Doctor Mengele was most helpful in this effort."

"Yes I have heard of Doctor Mengele's skills," Czerny responded in a flat tone, devoid of judgment and emotion.

Hartjenstein stood up and poured himself a cup of coffee without offering any to the strange Romanian. "I have sent a group of guards out with an SS officer to check nearby farms and hiding places. I am confident they will find him without delay, but my orders are to extend you all assistance," he sounded somewhat amazed that such an order would be given. "So if you wish to tour the grounds or speak to guards - or prisoners - I shall make it so."

Czerny stood and went to the door quietly, thinking *yes, I'm sure they will find him - or he, them.* Any minute now the commandant would heil again and Czerny preferred to be out of the picture when that took place. Replacing his hat against the cold, he turned and nodded. "I shall go and do just that, thank you for your cooperation."

Outside, the temperature had dropped below freezing, leaving no memory of the previous clear sunny day. Snow was beginning to accumulate in a thin layer, drifting out of the sky in large, slow falling flakes mixed with slightly grayer ashes which fogged out the distance and strangely altered the sounds of the camp. Waiting on the porch was the SS liason Czerny had been assigned, Major Karl Ritter.

Czerny could feel the misery of the place like a weight pressing down on him. The spirits of this area were restless, angry, and lamenting almost audibly. The prisoners were silent and only visible as wraiths in the distance, shuffling as if in a dream. How many people had suffered and died here? Czerny was briefly amazed, did the nazis not know what would happen if this continued? He shook his head and walked to a barracks building. Behind him, Ritter followed, and Czerny knew that he was here more to keep an eye on him and report to his superiors than to ease his work. It was irrelevant, and completely predictable. All tyrants played the same games, and he'd seen them come and go.

The officer's quarters was surprisingly warm and well furnished for such a bleak place. There were only a few men present, and at seeing Major Ritter immediately they jerked to their feet at attention. The men were not in high spirits; six of the guards were out on patrol and four had died in the showers, which left them short-handed and working longer shifts. Some had friends who had died that morning. They were somewhat surly and unwilling to work with a strange Romanian, but with the pressure of an SS officer standing by had answered the questions without commentary or insult. Czerny learned little, few of them had even seen the event; only a pair who were in a tower and one who looked out a window had caught a glimpse. One of the tower men insisted he'd hit the creature at least once with his MG-42 but it didn't even slow down.

Czerny next went to the shower and sighed, for the first time looking upset. Major Ritter sneered, misunderstanding Czerny's reaction. The fools had kept using the shower, hundreds had died here since the event, and now uncovering any impressions and information from the jumble of deaths and souls enraged by their treatment would be nearly impossible. Ignoring the towering blond SS officer, Czerny opened up his little black medical bag and pulled out odd-looking instruments and items. Setting up the materials in the sloped concrete tunnel leading down into the showers, Czerny hoped that the strongest impressions of the creature could be found there, unmuddled by the deaths in the showers.

Ritter watched as the strange Romanian drew designs on the concrete in chalk, set up incense burners and strange devices with colored optics and brasswork, and shook his head. The acting camp commander of the guards leaned over to Major Ritter and muttered "How long is this shit going to take? We have a schedule to keep, and I'm undermanned already."

Ritter rolled his eyes and shook his head. He offered a cigarette to the commander and gave him a helpless look. "Berlin orders me to give him every assistance and let him do his job, whatever the hell that is supposed to be. If we shoved him into the showers we'd be up against a wall tomorrow. Still, might almost be worth it."

The two men shared a laugh and a smoke as Czerny worked, barely aware of their presence. As he entered a meditative trance, he could sense their malice and frustration, but pushed it aside, seeking something else. In the mists of his mind, he sensed the teeming hordes of the dead, their impressions and emotions released to tear apart the spirit world around the camp. Not truly ghosts, they were merely souls of the dead, temporarily trapped by the concentrated hate and death in such a small place. Yet in them he found something else, something more potent and almost solid. A darkness, raging and clawing at the spirits, rending them apart as it moved closer. The beast, so potent a supernatural force it left an imprint on the area far more clear than Czerny had expected.

It neared him, a darkness that pulled all light nearby into it, an endlessly hungry maw of rage that surged and crashed against the wards Czerny had established before trying to make contact. The angry spirits were a nuisance, but combined with their rage and fear a presence this powerful could be lethal even as a mere spiritual echo of the monster's departed physical presence. Czerny studied the horror carefully, learning how it felt and how it affected the spirit world. Such a tearing, raging force could not hide; it would be far easier to track than some others he'd encountered that were far more subtle and clever. This was no sinister creature of seduction; it was an enraged force of hatred and destruction. And it was a force far more potent than he had anticipated.

Although, Czerny thought, *it might be calmer once it gets away from the immediate attempt to murder it and scores of others in a foul concrete bunker.* It was a start. Czerny pulled away from his trance and the images and spirits faded, leaving them to their uncertain, gauzy world. He put the materials away without a word and rubbed out the chalk patterns. Ignoring Ritter and the other soldier, he walked back to the main office building for word on where this Cezar Alexandru had been captured. Efficiency and recordkeeping, at least you could rely on the Germans for that, even if their hyper-rationality ignored a significant part of the world around them. Commandant Hartjenstein did not disappoint.

The horse that the Major Ritter had requisitioned from a nearby farmer was thin and swaybacked and old but steady, but it seemed happy to be out on the road rather than in the old drafty barn in which it lived. Major Ritter, of course, had a beautiful stallion to ride; magnificent, powerful, and probably not much good as a runner. Vladimir Czerny was under no illusions that the horse would be returned; he doubted the owner was still alive. Yet in a car he'd be moving too fast and be too distracted to maintain an awareness of the spiritual energies the monster had left behind, and while it was easy to trace at the moment, as its rage and fear diminished, it possibly would become more difficult to track.

Czerny stopped the horse and concentrated. The spiritual path was leading back to the farm the horse lived at. Should he follow the trace in and almost surely lead to the farmer's capture, or claim he lost the trace and search around for it in the area? The creature almost certainly had moved on, yet perhaps it was hiding in the shack. It might be injured and crouching somewhere, healing like an animal. Snow fell slowly and silently around them, flakes smaller now and the air even colder.

Vladimir Czerny's implacable expression changed slightly to resignation and he nudged the horse toward its home. The horse seemed reluctant but obedient and the soldiers followed on foot, hoping to get a moment out of the cold in the old farm house. Herr Ritter's stallion stamped its feet and snorted, apparently concerned it would be forced into the stable as well. The snow had laid down a carpet of a few centimeters already, softening the contours of the farm and disguising its old, run down appearance. Smoke drifted from the farmhouse's chimney, suggesting that the farmer had been alive earlier that morning, at least.

"You believe the prisoner has come here?" Major Ritter refused to call Vladimir by name or even "Herr," which would be too respectful.

Czerny sounded distracted as he concentrated on the trail: "the impressions move in this direction, I cannot tell yet whether it stopped or simply moved past."

Ritter ordered the men to fan out and search the farm. At this point, even if the monster had not sought refuge here, the farmer would be taken in for questioning. Czerny wondered why the creature had spared him; clearly the soldiers who took his horse would have spoken to the farmer earlier and did not report him dead at the time. Czerny suspected that they likely felt the death of a polish peasant did not warrant mentioning.

By this point, about half a mile from the camp, its impressions were somewhat calmer, it probably had cooled down enough that the berserker rage was faded. Perhaps it changed into human form again somewhere on the farm.

Major Ritter stared into the distance. Just through the snow he could see a truck, sideways on the dirt road, gathering snow. The patrol sent out hours ago had taken just such a truck, and they had not yet reported back. Ordering one private to take the farmer to the camp for questioning, he gathered his troops and set out on a quick march toward the vehicle. Vladimir Czerny followed, confident he knew what the wreck meant as he picked up the trail of the monster once more, bright with hate again.

The horizon was close in the snowfall, a few hundred yards before it was too white to see any further. The snow was in smaller flakes now, but coming down in greater quantity. The horses blew clouds of vapor as they stepped through the snow layer, the men breathing smaller clouds. All was silence, interrupted only by the footsteps of the men and beasts and their breathing. Soon a line of trees could be seen, dark under a layer of fluffy white lying quietly on the budded branches. Then a scream was heard, clear and long, choked off horridly. The soldiers looked around them nervously, guard duty was easy and safe: the prisoners were no danger, nobody was invading Poland. They had been stationed at Auschwitz because they weren't very good soldiers to begin with, this marching around in the cold with frozen toes hearing screams was not to their liking.

Major Ritter dismounted and left his horse with a guard. Czerny looked at the force he was with: down to six men. He volunteered to hold the horse and Ritter just sneered at him, turning to move into the forest. *Coward*, his expression shouted, too filled with contempt to even speak the word.

Fool, Czerny thought, his expression blank and unreadable. He wiped the condensation from his breath off his glasses and waited. Distant, deep laughter began, echoing over the forest. They weren't hunting the monster, *it was hunting them*.

Major Ritter found First Lieutenant Koenig first, impaled on a broken branch seven feet off the ground. The branch was jagged on the end, frozen with smeared blood and protruding from Koenig's back several inches. The wood had clearly piercing the lieutenant's spine and possibly his heart. Something had rammed him against the tree with terrific force, punching the branch entirely through his torso. Ritter picked up Koenig's Luger and checked the load. *Five bullets fired*, he thought as he mechanically replaced the magazine and drew his own pistol. Two guns ready, he moved into the forest, quietly.

Major Ritter had been a hunter and a woodsman even before the previous war started, and those skills had not left him. Even encumbered with the winter coat he still moved easily through the forest with little sound, watching for movement. Stopping, he crouched, looking at a dark form on the forest floor. The snow had not penetrated much here, only a light dusting. It was starting to form on the back of a prone guard, lying still on last autumn's leaves with his pale pink intestines strewn on the forest floor in a pool of dark blood.

Nothing moved ahead of him, although he could hear his men stamping around and muttering behind him. He smelled tobacco; some guard had lit up a cigarette like a giant beacon to alert the enemy with. He missed his old squad; they were soldiers, not like these fools. Fat, undisciplined, some clearly idiotic. *Prison guards*, he sighed. *Still, a good commander works with what he has.* Cautiously, he moved up to another body and found the fallen soldier lying, chest on the forest floor, face staring up at the sky with eyes still open. Lying under him was a Karabiner 98k rifle, another in his grasp. Slung around his shoulder was an MP-38 and brass from spent cartridges ejected from the rifles were scattered all around the young man's body. The young man's face was still warm, his face pink in the cold. He was dressed in a corporal's uniform but Ritter could not remember the name from the roster he'd been given.

This young man must have been the one who screamed. The last kill, alone and hunted in the forest for hours. Ritter stared at the body.

It must have taken incredible force to turn his head completely around like that. What is it we're after? Ritter scanned the trees with cautious eyes. *This not the handiwork of some wretched gypsy.*

Ritter turned and looked behind him to where Czerny was standing, yards away at the edge of the forest.

The SS Major turned back to the young soldier, looking down at his Aryan features. *Maybe the Romanian is not such a coward after all. He knows more than he's saying, but I wouldn't have believed a word of this five minutes ago.*

All nine of the party sent to find the prisoner were discovered, each one killed. Spent casings of bullets were scattered around most, little blood was found anywhere but at the bodies. In the distance, the laughter rang out again, becoming more distant.

Vladimir Czerny and Major Ritter shared something, finally: a shiver of fear.

CHAPTER SEVEN

The morning sun came through the windows onto Doctor Stoffel's bed, gleaming off of the brass headboard and illuminating the bodies of the doctor and lovely young Helga. Doctor Konrad Stoffel looked down at Helga's face, beautiful even with her hair tangled and her lipstick smeared. She would be upset that he let her sleep this long, but it was paradise to have her in his arms. She even smelled wonderful, still. Lying here helpless in his arms she made him feel like some glorious knight of old, Siegfried reborn. The sun painted highlights in her blonde hair, making her even more lovely than when she was dolled up the previous night at the club.

Still, he'd never have another chance at her considerable charms if he made her too angry. With a sigh, Konrad kissed her awake and she drug out of her dreams with little murmurs like a cat, pawing at his face. "Liebchen you must awaken it is almost seven o'clock."

For a moment Helga almost slipped back into a wonderful luxurious dream of that young man she had seen at the market, shirtless, moving crates off a truck, but the reported time dug into her consciousness. "What?" Sitting upright in the bed she stared around panicking.

"Seven! Damn you, Konrad, you know I have to be at work in an hour, how in the hell will I be ready by then? If Martin even has a hint of where I've been —" she couldn't finish the sentence. Throwing the covers off, she gave Konrad Stoffel one last glorious glimpse at the dimples near the base of her spine then rapidly dressed.

"He's already in a terrible mood because of some fool Romanian that barged in his office yesterday, I don't need to make matters worse by being late because I was in some other man's arms!"

"Romanian? What on earth is he seeing someone from that wretched country for?" Konrad muttered as he too started to dress.

"God in heaven, don't get me started. Supposedly in one of the camps some guards were killed; they said it was some sort of monster that tore them to pieces."

Konrad stopped buttoning his shirt. "Monster?" He tried to sound amused, keeping the excitement out of his voice.

"I read the reports. One of the gypsies to be eliminated lived through the process somehow and turned into some gigantic wolf, if you believe the guards. It tore four of them to bits and ripped through the fence. This Romanian is supposed to be some sort of a monster hunter. Martin is furious at the whole thing, he's been in a mood ever since. Have you seen my hat?"

"Turned into a wolf..." Stoffel stared at his face in the mirror. *Was it possible?*

He turned to Helga and handed her the dish-shaped black hat. She stared at him angrily then her frustration broke down. He was so handsome even if he was a little scrawny, she couldn't stay mad. With a brief kiss, she fled down the stairs to catch a taxi to her home to dress for work as Herr Professor Doctor Konrad Stoffel sat on the side of the bed and thought.

Turned into a wolf. Those old myths... could they really be true? If I could just examine the creature, find out how it happens, what causes this... A special legion of werewolf soldiers, prepared by myself exclusively, they would demolish and terrorize any possible enemy. Almost unkillable, stronger, faster, brutally lethal, so the legends say. The morale effect alone would be devastating. Let the Americans invade, they would scatter like sheep. And I alone would gain the glory, the notice, finally, he thought. *Women like Helga would claw their clothes off to be with me.*

Doctor Stoffel finished dressing even more swiftly than Helga had. There was much to be done.

CHAPTER EIGHT

Aniela Wisniewski was a pianist. She knew how to play the piano, but it was a different sort of keys that gave her this name, and a different sort of tune that she played. Aniela had a device that was the size of a heavy typewriter that she could type messages into, coding them with garbled nonsense, which then were sent by a burst over the radio and would be decoded in England. What they did with her little reports, she didn't know, but Aniela hoped that it would be some small measure to fight the German occupiers.

She puzzled over the rumor she'd gotten from her cousin. Mirela had first reported that the Nazi troops had found and rounded up a portion of her tribe and sent them on a train to a prison camp. Nobody ever came back from those trips, and that wasn't really news but Aniela had sent it anyway. Although she wasn't living in the gypsy community any longer and had married a *gadje*—a non-Gypsy—she kept in touch with her Romani people and was concerned about them, even if nobody else seemed to be. After her husband had died in the bombing of Krakow she was no longer tied to that *gadje* world but she never would truly be of the Romani again.

Then came a second report: one of them had escaped. And what's more he'd killed several of the guards in the process. Rumors of escapes from the camps leaked out every so often but this one was different. The troops were out looking for him, and someone had flown down from Berlin to ask questions about the event.

And there was something odd about this report; something about a beast that escaped as well, or with the prisoner, or *was* the prisoner. It didn't make sense, and Aniela wonderd if she report that as well? Aniela didn't know, and didn't *want* to know how Mirela knew this; she suspected that at least one of the guards was friendly with a gypsy girl. When the Germans swept in, the Rom community swiftly went underground. No more camps, no more distinctive clothing, no more schemes, for now. They had to hide and move around carefully, yet still many were being rounded up. The Rom were remembered by the locals, by people they'd scammed, by those who remembered the palm readers. Yet still, the Gypsy girls were often beautiful and skilled at deception, and they could get very close to the enemy without being detected, for a time at least.

Aniela felt a chill of fear crawl down her spine with icy skeletal fingers, like she did every time she opened up the back of the cabinet and pulled out the heavy machine. Just having one was a death sentence, after torture to find who else she knew was a pianist. Carefully she signed on and typed out a brief message to the men across the water. What they could do with this was anybody's guess. Aniela just felt proud to do her part, however humble. She put it away again carefully, closing the hidden compartment and stacking her clothes in place again.

*****

In the small English village with the odd name of Bletchley, the locals studiously ignored the cars that came and went and the men who showed up from the government at odd hours. It was something to do with the war, and loose lips sunk ships; pay them no heed. Sure, they never came to the pub, but they probably didn't have time. Some of them were a bit odd looking; academic types. *Busy, busy, good for them, we'll beat that Hitler chap yet.*

In a facility known as Station X in Whaddon Hall, the radios were constantly busy, picking up reports from all over Europe: France, Poland, Czechoslovakia, yes, even Germany. Pianists from all over the continent and all walks of life contributed small pieces of information, even gentle children's writer Princess Noor-un-Nisa Inayat Khan. They slipped bits of information, sometimes trivial, sometimes unbelievably vital, to this central location where the machines decoded their messages and the whole was pieced together.

Combined with radio traffic from the German ENIGMA code system, these reports gave the Allies key information about troop movements, activities, and the intentions and plans of the Germans. ENIGMA hadn't been fully decoded, but the gist of the message—particularly in context of other messages—could be coaxed out. The British Spymaster known as INTREPID was particularly proud of the Polish intelligence officers who had managed to capture and smuggle out an ENIGMA machine, complete with all the code wheels, for the British intelligence services to examine.

Brent Whitley looked at the strip of paper the decoder had given him. He looked at it again, for a long time. The pianist who sent it—codename BANGLE—had always been reliable and useful, pulling in information that few even had access to because of her gypsy connections. But this?

"Commander..." Brent began, then trailed off, unsure what he was going to say.

"Whitley?"

When Brent Whitley stammered and didn't respond, the watch commander strode over to his station impatiently. This wasn't like Whitley, usually so dependable and sober. "What is it, man, out with it!"

"Sir, this message from BANGLE, ah, well I'm not quite sure what to make of it."

"Very well, let's take a look eh?"

The two sat and read the message at Whitley's cramped station, piled with cutting-edge tube-driven electronic equipment. The message was longer than BANGLE's usual offerings:

Gypsy prisoner taken to Auschwitz camp escaped, four guards killed, fence torn. Prisoner had been put in execution chamber with others, survived. Prisoner being hunted by soldiers, specialist sent from Berlin to investigate. Specialist a Romanian supernaturalist. Prisoner reported by guards to have become enormous wolf.

The two British men stared at the last sentence.

"Check the decoder, see if it is functioning properly. Has she used code like this before?"

"I'm not sure it's code, sir. She's a gyppo sir, they tend to be a bit more accepting of the spooks and goblins, as it were."

The watch commander nodded. Maybe this should go to someone higher up.

*****

The snowfall was becoming thicker, but the flakes were larger as the temperature began to rise again. The man known as Cezar Alexandru ran through the snowy fields with tireless, powerful strides, moving toward Krakow. While it was true the city had a very large German army presence, it also had a lot more people and a lot more places to hide, and was only 50 kilometers or so distant. Cezar wasn't afraid of being caught, he was afraid of being overwhelmed and having no peace. Something inside him wanted to find a dark corner and wait for things to calm down as well, something animal and feral. *Get into a cave, lie low, pick your moment.*

As he ran, Cezar also thought of Marisol, her hair in a pile on the ground, her lungs filled with poison, her body burnt in an oven. His rage began building again, and his eyes slitted. Now wearing only the old farmer's ragged pants, Cezar ignored the cold, even his bare feet on the snowy ground and rough terrain caused him no discomfort. But the pain in his heart at learning Marisol had been taken still ached inside and filled him with hate. It had only been a few days ago, when he stole

29

back into Krakow to see her, against her father's wishes. They were together but a few hours, then Cezar had to flee again, curses ringing about his ears as Marisol's parents discovered them. It would have been so easy to destroy them, but Cezar had long ago sworn never again to kill any more Romani.

Marisol, how she had captivated him. He had first seen her shuffle by his hiding place in the basement of a ruined building in Bytom. She had been bundled up in clothes to hide her beauty, in an old scarf to cover her raven hair, but the smell; she couldn't hide her scent. She was intoxicating, and Cezar's senses crackled with the mere presence of her. Her face was dirty and covered up as much as she could manage, but he could see how lovely she was. Just sixteen and in a nightmare, living in fear of being discovered, denounced, destroyed. Cezar had spoken to her a few times, and when he drew near, he could tell she was attracted and excited and frightened all at once. He was used to that, women usually responded the same way, but this was different. She was not merely some bitch to mount, she was something greater, an angel in the misery and hell Poland had become.

It did not take long for Marisol to give in to Cezar's advances, it rarely did. Even running away from her family, Cezar was laughing and filled with a joy he'd not felt for so very long. Yet when he returned that night, the troops had taken her. Stupidly, in a daze he'd run about to Gypsies he knew, trying to find out about her, what had happened, who had tipped them off, where she'd gone.

The Gypsy community had long ago declared Cezar *marime*, an outcast. He had no friends, no family. Hated by the *gadje* world and shunned by the Gypsy, he was alone in the world. They did not wish to speak to him, not even be near him; they feared his curse and his power, they sensed the darkness in his soul. They knew his dark past. Yet he tried, and in those tries, he was among them when the soldiers came. He could have escaped, he could have killed them all, but what would happen to the poor family he was with? Marisol had gone to Auschwitz, he learned; she had been taken to the prison camp where no one left alive.

In misery he crumpled in the boxcar, overcrowded and stinking beyond imagination to Cezar's incredibly heightened senses. He waited, for in Auschwitz, he could find her, and they could escape together. Then the scent went cold; he could barely, faintly sense it. She had been there, maybe a day before, but there was no fresh scent. And when they shoved him into the shower, he could smell her there, her terror amid the stench of the underground chamber. Her death. The showers came on and the gas poured into the room, and then... the beast had come out.

Cezar was nearing Krakow now, the outlying homes and buildings scattered in the budding trees, and everything covered with a thin blanket of white. The snow had almost stopped, a few large flakes falling, and the streets were wet with melt. Cezar closed his eyes. The beast, he'd almost gotten it under control after all the years. He only changed when he wanted, except when the moon compelled him. It snarled inside him, mocking. Cezar knew that it would never be controlled, not completely. A moment of fear, anger, even unguarded passion and it could be free once more.

Cezar moved through yards and the wooded areas, avoiding the roads now. There would be guards, soldiers moving through, police, checkpoints. He knew how to get into and out of the city safely, but circumstances might have changed since his last visit. He cursed the Germans in Romanian; they were even worse than the Russians. Pausing at an apartment building, he caught a whiff of German soldiers–their equipment or food or something gave them a distinct smell–then he heard their language. His hate grew once more, the beast within him twisting and clawing at his soul.

Let me out. Let me deal with them. Let me have their flesh, it growled.

Cezar pushed it down, again. The fierce joy of the slaughter and dominance raced in his veins a moment and then he calmed.

Kill them all and the war ends, he thought, *but who can kill them all? And the more they know of you, the more likely they'll find something that will actually hurt you. Only in secrecy can you exist, there is safety only in being unknown.*

It had become a law to him, a steel-clad part of his nature. Gypsies had to live in secrecy and stealth, Cezar knew he must live even more so. At least before the war Gypsies could travel and live in relative openness. He never could, not anywhere. As far as Cezar knew, he was the only one of his kind; he'd been exceptionally careful to not let his curse spread. It had happened once, and the hunt to end his hellish offspring had taken months.

Kill them completely so they cannot change. No more of my kind, he thought.

Fill the world with our kind, the beast within him snarled.

Cezar leapt up to the tiled roof of a second story building. On the rooftops there was a sort of safety, for few people looked up when they traveled on the ground. Yet there was a greater danger as well; anyone from higher up would be more likely to notice someone on a rooftop than on the ground. He did not look particularly distinctive when clothed, and Cezar knew he needed better clothing to blend in with the city. He growled, without realizing it. The home beneath him had several families; he could pick up the scent of at least three related groups, eighteen people or more. There were no pets; no one could afford a pet except the Germans. Dogs were terrified of him, but that was more of a problem than a benefit. The hounds would cringe and cower and whine and run in terror, but that told the Germans at least as much as barking and growling, told them that something was there which did not belong.

31

Behind the house hung a clothesline left unattended in the snow, and Cezar stole a few pieces of stiff, frigid clothing. He'd get shoes later, but for now it was time to find a safe spot. Looking over the city, he broke into a grin. He knew just the place.

The Krakow headquarters of the Security Police was in the Silesian House on the corner at an intersection where the streetcar swung by at regular intervals. A rounded six-floor building at Inwalidow Square, it was cleaner and more reputable-looking than the informants and tipsters who slouched in as secretly as they could to turn their enemies for in cash, or to pay the secret police to leave them alone for another week, or day, or hour.

Cezar lay quietly in the building, listening to the Germans busy below, talking in broken Polish to the locals, interrogating people, doing paperwork, arguing and discussing matters. The typewriters clacked, the phones rang, and the cars came and went. Somewhere he could hear screaming and sobbing, deep in the building, probably from the basement. Here Cezar found his den, in a section of the upper floor that had a false ceiling, giving him several feet of clearance between the rafters and the dusty, cobwebbed roof. It was warmer there than his last hiding place, and his presence was very unlikely to be discovered at the heart of darkness in Krakow.

As he lay there, trying by force of will to not think about Marisol, Cezar listened to the Germans. His Polish was very poor but he knew German well enough, and the same words kept coming back over and over. Jew. Gypsy. Spy. Undesirable. Traitor. Camp. Confess. He learned that the German Security Police and Security Service were every bit as corruptible as the police in his native Romania, but less reliably so. You could buy the Germans, you just couldn't rely on them to *stay* bought. They would take money from one man, then from another find out where the first man kept his wealth, and raid him for all of his cash. They would take a bribe for a week's protection and then get an order to round up the protected person and do so.

Cezar was torn; part of him felt despair and emptiness, wondering how this could possibly be fought. The Polish people and army had waged a desperate fight to stop the German invasion, and paid a horrible price for their resistance. Earlier, Romania had fallen even more easily, and while he had no real home, he'd spent his youth in that beautiful wooded land that it was the closest thing for Cezar. The Nazi forces seemed unstoppable and their dominance inevitable.

Another part of Cezar, however, admired the Germans, snarled inside him that he was weak and foolish, that the only thing they were doing wrong is that they were too concerned with paperwork, with appearances, with order. *Take what you want. Devour the weak. Rape their bitches. Destroy.*

As always, Cezar slept fitfully. For too many long years now he'd been this way; the only time he really remembered and knew what he'd done while the beast took him was in his dreams, reliving in disjointed glimpses the horrific moments of slaughter and blood and screams and worst of all the soaring sense of power and joy as he killed and killed. In a way he felt it was a blessing that he didn't need much sleep since the curse took him.

The curse had its benefits, despite the evil in his soul. Cezar was tremendously strong, was very difficult to harm, healed very rapidly, had senses keener than any man, could literally see in the dark, and could track by scent. He never became sick, he only was briefly weary after tremendous exertion, the cold and heat of weather Cezar could feel, but they lacked discomfort.

Were it not for the beast within him and the lack of control, it would have been a wonderful life. He had not aged for decades, watching the new century come with the same vitality and appearance he had when he first had been cursed, save more black hair. His body hair was growing every year, a little more, subtly shifting his face to be more lupine and feral. Wiry, dark hair that grew on his back and chest and limbs, his beard thicker and growing higher on his face, even his eyebrows were bushier and met in the middle as his hairline slowly crept downward.

Then there was the anger. His rage was almost constant now, a fury against the world, against anyone who crossed him. People who were friendly to Cezar were weak and trying to appease him. People who were indifferent were hiding fear and to be despised. People who were hostile were adversaries to be destroyed. Was it the times, the war, or the beast within? Or had he always been that way?

Marisol... she had been the only one he had ever shared his dark secret with. She listened, afraid but willing to face anything with him and treating it all as part of life's merry lark. He growled again, quietly, eyes filled with hate.

They took her. Go below, tear them like sheep, empty this building of everything but screams and blood and terror, the beast snarled within him. *Let go. Let me free. I will make the pain all go away.*

Cezar forced it back down into the depths of his consciousness and finally slept. Later he could hunt, but for now, he must rest and wait. It never occurred to Cezar that he'd surrendered again to the demands to hunt, kill, and destroy... just not right away. It wouldn't be a full moon for two weeks, and the beast was patient, ageless and confident. Even if the fool would keep him caged up for now, for those three days *nothing* would.

Now if only Cezar could be lured to another weak, simpering family to destroy again...

*****

Shopping was always an adventure in Krakow those days. Aniela Wisniewski dreaded running out of supplies, but supplies always seemed to be low. Her work at the ladies salon was regular and had a steady paycheck, but it didn't pay very much and everything cost so much in the market. They said the Great Depression had ended, but there was little sign of it in Poland.

Aniela put on her winter coat and scarf and stepped out into the slushy street where mud and street grime was splashed on the melting snow along the sidewalk, turning it filthy and black. The clouds were tearing apart in the sky, revealing glimpses of blue once more as winds drove high above the city streets. The trees were still mostly bare, but green buds and a few early small leaves were visible, peeking out to see if winter was really over. The people Aniela passed kept their heads down as she did; drawing attention was never a good thing. Don't talk, don't look, don't stop, go about your business and stay out of trouble. Whenever possible, stay in a crowd, so you don't stand out.

For the most part, it was easy—there were hundreds of thousands of people in Krakow even after the Jews had all been walled off in the ghetto, and there were only thousands of German soldiers and police. They couldn't watch everyone, and they didn't want to. They only wanted the troublemakers, the leaders, the thinkers, the people who stood out and questioned.

For a woman, being attractive was a particular risk. Rape was not unheard of; some poor girl dragged into a room or alley by a soldier for a few moments of humiliation, terror, and pain. Technically it was illegal, and the Germans made a big show of executing publicly any such soldiers caught, but they didn't catch many. And even if one was caught, well justice was not so blind in Krakow. A few banknotes and the right contacts and you could walk free; you could get away with more than murder. Aniela didn't expect much more from the German invaders. She expected more from her own fellow Poles, but they were an even bigger problem.

Have an apartment someone else wants? Get denounced and disappear. So pretty that some jealous girl's boyfriend pays you too much attention? Get denounced and disappear. Anger someone? Buy the last coat in a shop? Have a long-standing grudge against you? All it took was someone in a moment of anger or especially petty disposition and you could vanish in a storm of boot heels and German commands. Aniela checked her papers, keeping them close and neat inside her coat. Supposedly her work at the salon was essential, at least her boss paid plenty in bribes to convince the Germans it was so. The carefully typed and stamped paperwork in her coat ought to protect her; it had in the past.

She walked, saving a few złotych by not taking the streetcars. Besides, it was too easy to get into trouble with a soldier on the streetcar, there was nowhere to run as they let their hands get a little too free. There was a line at the butchers, again. There always was a line. Two lines actually, with two men working feverishly to meet the demand. The butchers seemed to be doing good business, assuming their taxes, fees, bribes, and incidental payments to the German government weren't eating it away too heavily. Nobody asked what kind of meat it was.

Aniela's calves were aching, and her feet hurt. Her old shoes weren't as comfortable as they once were, and they never were especially so. The heel on the left one was coming loose, which forced Aniela to correct her walk making her left leg even sorer. She looked discreetly in the direction the wall that contained the ghetto, over the river. *I'm still better off than they are.* If there were any people left behind the wall.

When she looked back, she saw the man to her side in the other line looking at her. His gaze was bold and relaxed, with the powerful confidence of someone who has no fear and does not care how the other person reacts. He was fierce looking, but his eyes were compelling and powerful. Amber colored, with a ring of orange at the edges, they were like nothing else she'd ever seen. His brow was dark and met in the middle and his beard grew high on his cheeks; usually that was terribly unattractive, but for some reason it only made him more compelling.

"I am Cezar," he said, voice deep and rich, clear over the short distance though he spoke quietly. Aniela blushed heavily and looked quickly down again. She'd been staring, she had not even thought about it, thinking only of his eyes. She broke the rule, she got noticed. He wasn't a Pole, clearly, neither was he German, just as clearly. He was darker skinned; with a bit of cleaning up and shaving he might look suave and handsome. Even though he was just as ragged as the rest and his beard was untamed, he still was handsome. Aniela nodded, swallowing hard. Looking steadily at the dirty sidewalk, she saw his golden eyes still in her mind.

"Lets hope the horse meat isn't so old this time, eh?" His voice was rich with humor. "The last steaks I bought were from before the invasion, I think."

It was only then that she realized: *he was speaking Romani. In public, out loud.* She cringed, trying to hide within herself. Was he an idiot? Did he not know what they did to the Romani? Even hearing the language would be enough to be taken to the camp, why did she respond, what was she thinking? How did he know? Then terror gripped her even more powerfully in icy tentacles: *what if he's Gestapo, testing people by speaking our language?*

She waited for the iron grip of the soldier on her shoulder. They would learn it all, they would find out she had a cypher machine, her whole family would pay the price. Why did she agree to do it? They would take her to Plaszow or Auschwitz, and she'd never be seen again. They would torture her, she'd talk, they'd learn the codes. She felt a despair and hopelessness she'd never known, paralyzed, unable to run or hide, she could not think of anything to do.

The hand never came. She could hear him talking still, quietly, but the words made no sense as fear scrambled the sounds in her mind. Why wouldn't he shut up? *Go away, walk away, come to the market later. Go away now*, she thought furiously, trying to will her legs to move, but she was unable to take a single step.

"I have frightened you," he murmured. "I am sorry lovely one. I did not mean to, it is only that I have not seen the such beauty as only a Romani can have for so long. Please, forgive me. I shall leave you to shop, but know this: I am here, and I will remember you." He turned away and pulled a hood up over his head. With this simple gesture, he seemed to blend in. Without that powerful gaze, without seeing his face, he became just another tall local in the line. The gap ahead of her widened as customers moved on and the line moved up. Behind her someone bumped into her, a subtle hint to move forward. Finally, she took a step, then another, trembling like a newly born fawn.

The trip home was a blur; she could almost hear the steps of the Gestapo behind her. She wanted to look around, see if she was followed, but then she would look suspicious, she would stand out, she might be noticed. Doing so would break the rule, again. When she locked her door and put the package down in the kitchen she broke out crying, uncontrollably sobbing and shaking. Her uncle ran into the room and took her into his brawny steelworker arms, not saying a word.

He didn't need to know why, he didn't even care. There were so many reasons to cry these days and Aniela was always so strong to hide her emotions. She couldn't keep it in forever.

Aniela thought of the cypher machine hidden upstairs. It was like a horrid burning thing that threatened them all, a disease that would inevitably doom everyone she loved. Yet at the same time it was her only weapon. To live like, this to constantly feel the oppression of fear on them every moment, was infuriating; she could not stop. It was her only way to fight, her only way to defy the German invaders. She was no soldier. She was only a pianist.

CHAPTER NINE

That night when Aniela checked with the machine to see if there was anything for her, her fingers shook and she wept again, but she kept working. She felt ashamed at her weakness, her cowardice, she just knew the others around Europe were stronger and more courageous. They would not feel this awful terror and the desire to destroy this machine, she was certain. If any of them were left. The message printed out for her, and she read it through tear-distorted eyes.

Investigate camp escape. Name of escapee Cezar Alexandru. Make contact and report.

Aniela stared at the paper, although she'd already memorized it. She forgot to be afraid, she forgot the machine, she forgot her tears. She even forgot to burn the paper immediately, staring at it. *Cezar... could it possibly be?*

Burning the decyphered paper, Aniela watched the little fire on her desk as the paper blackened and curled. Her mind was elsewhere, split between Cezar's amazing eyes and the demands of the paper. Gone was the fear of capture, gone was the worry that someone had overheard the conversation in Romani at the market, save for one thought: had she responded in Polish or Romani? *Did I even say a word?*

Find the escapee, even if it was Cezar at the market, how was she to find him? There were over two hundred thousand people living in Krakow, and a man like that would be even more cautious than an ordinary citizen, although he seemed bold enough when standing in line.

He was Rom, that seemed clear. That must be why the British had wanted her to do this, with her background and ties she might have an easier chance than anyone else. Were there others in Krakow with the heavy machine? How many could they have in a city this size?

Aniela felt alone again, against a vast army of unconquerable soldiers in the Reich. There was always Uncle Rys, the king of the clan. She was technically not part of the clan any longer, but Uncle Rys was always cordial and even welcoming. His wife Marta had never forgiven Aniela for marrying a *gadje*, but Rys seemed to understand with a twinkle in his eye.

It was late; she would have to go tomorrow or risk being caught out after curfew. And it never was wise to head out of the home too often on a day off; the more trips you made, the more the neighbors saw, and the more likely the Security Police would see and wonder why you left and where you were headed.

It was not easy to go to sleep, she lay awake in her soft bed with the warm blankets staring at the ceiling for hours thinking about the day and trying to calm down. Her heart was still pounding from fear and excitement and her mind whirling with how to deal with this new adventure. And the memory of that man clung to her like a layer of sweat on her skin. When sleep finally came it was light and fitful.

As she dressed to go out again the next morning, Aniela felt regret. She had never taken this part of her life to Uncle Rys, and he had been so successful at fooling the Germans for so long, this might endanger him. Yet, what choice did she have? If anyone would know something about this man, it would be Uncle Rys, and she had to know. If only just to see Cezar's eyes one more time, to see if they matched her memories.

And to get the information to the British, of course, Aniela thought.

The trip to Rys was across town, too far to walk. Aniela had just one day off before she had to go back to work again, but there was no real way to contact Rys except in person. She took several streetcars across Krakow, listening to the electrical crash overhead as the car moved along. It was a Sunday and the car was not as filled as usual. Aniela took the ride to watch the scenery and look around her. The snow had all melted by now, and it was bright and sunny again; already the trees looked more full and the leaves were growing rapidly. It looked beautiful, other than a few buildings in rubble as the Nazis tore down old structures to rebuild.

She stepped off the car and head down walked to the bookstore. It was a sad affair now; many of the books had been pulled out of the shelves and burned when the Nazis had taken over. Uncle Rys survived by out-Germaning the Germans, with only the finest and most proper books and art, a Nazi flag flying out front, free coffee to any Aryan, and the snappiest salute. His store had a proud display of Nazi posters in the window with copies of *Mein Kampf* prominently visible, which probably explained why the glass was still intact.

Uncle Rys wasn't in the store, of course. There was a pretty brunette at the counter who Aniela knew once had a crystal ball in a shabby part of town before the war. Maria was her name, she could look as young as 20 and as old as 40 depending on her makeup and her hair. She was openly beautiful and radiant, not hiding it as most women did in Krakow, which meant she was protected by someone powerful, at some cost Aniela did not care to ponder. The little bell tinkled as Aniela came in and Maria looked up, her smile empty and unrecognizing, although Aniela was sure she knew her.

Aniela browsed her way to the back and carefully looking around slipped into the back room where the books were sorted and priced. In the room sat an ancient looking man, bent and bespectacled, writing prices in the books with a pencil. He looked up at her with frustration in his eyes at the interruption, then patience as he waited quietly for Aniela. She wrote on a piece of paper that she must see Uncle Rys, and after looking the paper over, he put the paper into the flame of a candle while looking Aniela over carefully. After a time, he nodded. Many of the Romani did not care for her after the wedding, but Rys had evidently left word that she was to be allowed to visit him.

His name was Fonso and in his youth he had been deadly with a knife and devastating to the ladies, dark and charming and dazzling with his manners and style. He was still deadly but the ladies had begun passing him over for younger men decades ago. Unlike many Rom, he was able to read, and used that for some very audacious schemes with the more educated and wealthy of Poland. Now he was a bent old man in a musty bookstore, deaf in his old age, and hiding from the Nazis like the rest of them. Still, in its own way, surviving and hiding from them in Krakow was a wonderful game of its own. The payoff was life, not just for yourself, but your family and friends and clan.

Fonso scribbled something on a piece of paper and tucked it into a book, handing it to Aniela. She turned and peeked through a hole in the door, then stepped out quietly and after a few more minutes of browsing carried the book to the counter. Maria made pleasant small talk, going through the motions of selling the book and as Aniela looked up, she saw that the flags and the posters on the front window actually concealed almost all of the workings inside. Looking back, she saw that Maria had handed her the book with a complimentary bookmark and a well-practiced smile; the one she used on friends, not marks.

"Its too bad you cannot make it at 2:00, we'll have a special guest then to sign books."

"Two? Oh no I'm afraid I won't be here then, I hope it goes well," Aniela said, looking properly disappointed.

"I hope so too," said Maria, her tone hinting a warning.

Aniela left the store and did not open or look at the book until she was at a little cafe several blocks away. Sipping something hot that was supposed to be coffee, but tasted more like burnt bread crumbs, she opened the book. The front of the bookmark bore the bookstore's sailing ship logo, but the back had a few scribble on it like someone had been doodling.

In rural areas, or when Romani would meet in the country, they would leave signs that only they could read. A crossed branch with a leaf the direction to go, a mark on a tree trunk, stones in a pattern. These marks told the traveler where to go and when, leaving more information than the uninitiated could imagine or understand, even if they noticed them. The practice was very old and beginning to die out, but every young member of a clan still learned the meanings and how to use them because who knew? You might need them some day. A day like today. A meeting at 2:00 at a location noted in the scribbles.

Aniela read the book for several chapters, warming herself with the awful tasting brew and buying a pastry to take with her. The pastry was wonderful; apparently sugar and flour were not as critical to the war effort as coffee. Perhaps an officer liked the shop and made sure they were well-supplied. The book was a silly romance that Aniela struggled to stay interested in, then finally gave up. She took another streetcar to an apartment building just by the Planty on Gertrudy street, and stepping out like she knew the area and had been here often, she walked straight into the apartment and up to the third floor. On the floor there was a German soldier standing guard by the elevator, and Aniela's heart stopped. Was this it?

"What is your business?" He asked in horrible Polish. His blonde hair was cropped almost to the skull on the sides with a short brush on top, and he wasn't bad looking for being the enemy.

"I, I have come to speak to my Uncle Rys" Aniela said, trying to conceal her fear.

"You are Aniela Wisniewski?"

Aneila nodded. It was pointless to deny, she had papers on her that proved it.

"Come with me."

She followed the soldier meekly, knowing that to run was futile and clinging to a tiny hope that this was not her doom after all. The soldier led her to a door with a nazi flag on it, and knocked. The door opened and an enormous blonde man opened it, filling the door. He was taller than anyone Aniela had ever seen before, broad as the doorway. The soldier said something in German and the giant nodded, gesturing for her to enter. The soldier walked back to the elevator and Aniela stepped into the room.

Behind the giant the apartment was huge, with a wall of windows in the back overlooking the Planty in the oldest part of town. It was furnished with fine paintings, draperies, carpets and furniture, a fire in a huge fireplace warming the room.

Sitting in a plush, overstuffed chair with his slippered feet on an ottoman was a well-dressed man smoking a cigarette. He had white hair and weighed more than two Anielas combined. His face was fat and smooth and happy, and his name was Rys Radescu. Aniela ran to him in relief, wrapping the fat man with a hug as he laughed and hugged her in return.

Uncle Rys smile broadly and held Aniela by the shoulders so he could look at her. "My angel, it has been so very long, you never visit enough! I am sorry for the reception, but the Germans insist I have a guard, since my life is in danger from desperate characters in town!" Rys didn't quite wink but somehow with a smile and a glint in his eye, he managed to convey one.

Aniela had not had to play a part like this since she was a girl, but the old patterns returned, and she stepped into her role comfortably. "Uncle Rys, no, who could hate you?"

"Ah, dear girl, too many people see the new government as wicked and evil, they do not see the corruption that it cleans from our fine city, the old and the failed it replaces. Yes, it was hard in '39 but the governor-general has brought us food and jobs. He's even repairing the roads! Sometimes change can be difficult on those who are too used to the old and the familiar." Rys looked sad, then his face changed "But these things are too sad for such a pretty girl, come Aniela, why do you visit? Wait, no first, I must have coffee."

Rys struggled out of his plush, comfortable chair and waddled with an exaggerated walk into the next room where a bright modern kitchen awaited, with a powered refrigeration unit humming away. Aniela suppressed a giggle at Rys' playacting and then looked around at the room with its gadgets and conveniences with wide eyes. "Uncle Rys, you have an electric icebox, how I wish we could afford one!"

"Well, it's convenient, but there are drawbacks as well. It is noisy, it it takes regular cleaning and it doesn't keep things quite as well as the old icebox, but at least I don't have to dump the water out or replace the ice." Rys started a pot of coffee perking on the stove, filling the air with the roast smell of ground coffee beans. "And the electricity bill, you wouldn't believe! All these lights, and the radios and the electric stove and the icebox, such a cost."

Aniela stared at the coffee pot. *Uncle Rys certainly was doing well to have fresh coffee*, she thought, eyes half closed at the wonderful aroma. Rys chuckled and got another mug down from the cupboard for her. He stood close to her and lowered his voice.

"I got your message Aniela, what is it you wish? You know I can deny you nothing."

Aniela looked around nervously, and Rys smiled again, eyes crinkling with lines of perpetual use "It is safe my angel, that hulking fellow is a German but he is loyal to me. And he cannot hear us from here, especially while he listens to the radio so loud" He looked out the batwing doors that divided the kitchen from the other rooms, where the sounds of a jazz band played some energetic song Aniela did not recognize.

"And Mariska, should I say hello to her first?" Aniela said, cringing inside at how clumsy her ploy was.

Rys chuckled, benevolently watching her nervous look. "My wife is away shopping, angel, I knew you'd both be more comfortable that way."

Aniela visibly relaxed, feeling dizzy. *This is too much stress for one day*, she thought.

"Uncle Rys I need you to help me find a man."

"Well, Aniela, now perhaps isn't the best time but you have been alone too long, I agree!" Rys said with a grin, watching Aniela for her reaction.

"That's not what I meant!" *I mean, mostly*, she thought. "I need to find one of our people. We met at Stanley's meat market, and I have to talk to him." Her voice lowered almost to a whisper, and Rys had to bend closer to hear. "It is about an escape from a camp, his name is Cezar, Cezar Alexandru, please Uncle Rys I need to find him."

Rys straightened up suddenly, spilling coffee from his cup, and his face became wary and thoughtful. He began to speak slowly, carefully.

"This... Cezar, tell me about him."

Aniela flushed at the memory of him. "He is tall, and broad-shouldered," she began, and thought a moment. The picture of Cezar was still strong in her mind. "His eyes are very light brown, almost golden in color. They seem very intense, even when he is trying to seem at ease. He has a strong face, with a lot of whiskers. Usually I do not find such a face attractive but on him I think it was a good look."

Rys was silent a moment, arranging his thoughts, his eyes staring into the past. She had been trying to seem detached, objective, but he could sense her attraction to the man and concern grew great in his heart. Rys started to speak, then was silent again. Aniela started to worry again as the moments grew longer and Rys said nothing. Finally he spoke, quietly but urgently.

"Angel I can refuse you nothing but you must listen to my advice, both as your Uncle and as the King, even if you have strayed from our camp.

You must not seek this man, you must listen to me," Rys said quickly, as Aniela started to speak. "You must stay away from him."

Rys looked so stern, so unusually unhappy and urgent that Aniela took a step back.

"But, I must, you need to trust me, I cannot explain why!"

"Aniela. Please listen to me, I know when a girl has her heart set on a man, even at twenty-four such as yourself, she will listen to her heart and not her wise elders, but you *must listen*. This man is dangerous, he is unspeakably dangerous; you *must not see him again*." Rys began to pace, his voice rising louder than the quiet murmur they'd been using. "He is *marime*, child, he is forbidden. He is... he is dangerous, he is cursed."

Aniela stared at Rys feeling uncertain. Never before had she seen him like this, he was forgetting himself, the man outside might hear, and he was speaking of the ways of the Romani too loudly. "Uncle please, you must calm yourself I was just curious, please!" She looked about nervously, meaningfully staring out the doorway then back at Rys.

Rys composed himself then knelt before Aniela, looking up at her. "Angel, please, child, as I love you and your dear departed parents," he crossed himself and bowed his head a moment, "you must promise me to abandon this matter, you must promise you will *never* see this man again."

"Uncle Rys please do not kneel so, I promise I will not seek him out; for you I promise, but I met him at the market, what am I to do? I cannot stay in my room all day!"

Rys nodded, awkwardly standing back up and brushing nonexistent dust from the spotless linoleum floor off his knees. "That is all I can ask, my angel. God send he will not come after *you*."

Later, as they sat in the room and drank coffee, Aniela noticed the huge German casting shy glances her way and cursed the war once more after so many previous curses. All the power of the Romani was no good against this vast world conflict. There was word that even the Americans far across the ocean would become involved. In another time, this man would have been handsome, and even exciting. Now he was frightening, and the thought of his touch made her stomach curdle. He represented oppression and evil, and Aniela felt a twinge of guilt that his mere nationality was a horror for her. The coffee was wonderful, and the stay with Uncle Rys was relaxing, but one look from him and she felt like a fist closing up, clenching tightly.

Rys was a Nazi Party member; he was well regarded by the new government and the military leaders in the area. The glint of sunlight through the window off the small swastika pin on his lapel helped tell the lie. He had established himself firmly and carefully and was known as a strong patriot of the new Reich that extended across what was once Poland. In short, he had pulled off the greatest game of his life, and was reaping the benefits of comfort and safety. Of course, all it would take to tear it down was one false move. One word, one hint of his true nature and it would crash down in death and suffering.

Yet at the moment, Uncle Rys was secure and Aniela knew this was the safest place she could be. And because she had married a non-Gypsy, Aniela was safe for Rys to have in his home as well. She wished she could come back, he had such a collection of new records, he had such wonderful food, it was a paradise. He was thieving from the Germans and they were helping him do it, truly this was a great moment for all the Romani of his clan. Yet for all his comfort and security, he could do nothing to help his people when they were caught. No bribe would get a gypsy out of the camps, and anyone who tried would be at best suspect. He could protect at most a small few that worked for him, and the rest he could only watch as they were captured, beaten, tortured, and killed with precision and order, all the correct paperwork filled out and carefully filed.

The sadness of his position showed in unguarded moments behind the smiles Rys presented to the public. The helpless frustration he felt was in some moments evident even in his greatest triumphs.

I shouldn't have come here, Aniela thought. *I've endangered him and made him even more upset and nervous.*

Reluctantly, as curfew drew near, Aniela said her goodbyes and took with her a package of coffee, sugar, and nylons under her arm. Uncle Rys gave her a final stern warning to listen to him, and she nodded meekly and obediently. On the streetcar she thought of how she'd word her refusal to the British. Then she realized all she had to do was simply not even attempt to follow their orders, instead simply send in regular reports about other issues. They needed her far more than she needed them, and they were over a thousand kilometers away across enemy territory. They were powerless to do anything if she refused a request, for that was all it could be.

She would just forget bold Cezar and his beautiful, powerful eyes. Maybe. At least she wouldn't look for him. Perhaps they might meet again; she felt a thrill inside at the thought, then wariness. What was he that filled Rys with such dread? A murderer? A rapist? It took a horrible crime for someone to be thrown out of the camp, to be declared *marime.* Was he a collaborator with the Germans? Fear crawled along Aniela's back on spider legs once more.

Yet he seemed so kind, nothing like the horror that Rys said he was. Maybe it only showed up at some times, maybe he was a good man except in bad moments. It was foolishness to think of romance at such a time anyway, who could find love amongst such horrors? Fumbling, clutching sex out of fear and desperation, a need for affection and love finding its self in physical action was common enough, but love? Your lover might vanish the next day and you with him if they wanted. It was not the time. Yet the heart has its own priorities and knows nothing of reason nor history. The heart knows only the endless longing for love, to somehow fill that yawning emptiness within.

Aniela showed her real Uncle Aleksy and Aunt Joanna the presents Uncle Rys had given her, and talked with them about her visit, omitting the real reason for it. Everyone loved Uncle Rys, he was just one of those people one could not help but admire and enjoy. Lights out came and Aniela carried a carefully shaded candle to her room. She sat on the bed looking at the heavy covering over the windows to conceal her light, and sighed. It was like being a child in school, standing in line, obeying orders, to bed at a certain time, turn the lights out at a certain time, rationing.

It was the way of the tyrant, she supposed. Treat everyone as a child so they depend on you, control them with rules and guidelines so it is easy to find the people who do not follow the rules, to single out the independent, the thinker, and the troublemaker. People became accustomed to the most awful things if only given regularity and order. The constant layer of fear over everything and the promise of a better tomorrow if only you will do what the government says was wearying, like a heavy weight. Some seemed to thrive under it though, appreciating the lack of freedom and the need to think. Some were buried under the weight of it until they simply died, or were crushed to death deliberately by the pitiless Reich.

Aniela started to change into her nightgown and then froze. In the corner was a figure, a man, standing quietly and watching. *In her room.*

"Aniela, I heard them call you. It is a beautiful name. Angel, it fits you well. Under those rags you wear you are even more beautiful than I thought." The man stepped out closer to the little candle.

It was Cezar.

CHAPTER TEN

Following the trail of the monster became more difficult as the creature's passions faded and the dominance of the beast within Cezar Alexandru lessened. Yet at the same time, Vladimir Czerny found it easier to find the spiritual residue of its passage because the path he took was largely uncluttered by other travelers. Czerny was loath to explain his work and his learning to anyone because it was obscure, arcane, and usually met with no small level of skepticism. There were so many charlatans in spiritualism that he couldn't blame the skeptics, but it was frustrating to be a proper professional in a field strewn with liars.

Yet when Major Ritter and he left the forest, the tall German SS officer had a different attitude toward Vladimir Czerny, one of at least begrudging respect and the camaraderie of two men who have faced the unknown and walked away.

They returned to the camp, frustrating Czerny with the delay, but Ritter insisted and the Romanian knew it was pointless to argue. Papers had to be filed, reports made. And the dead men had to be identified to the authorities. It took hours, and by the time all the necessary work was done, it was too late to head out. Czerny did not sleep that night. The swarm of rage and frustration and fear around him in the camp were so strong that he could barely lie still in the bunk provided him with the guards.

In the morning, it was frigid and overcast but the snowfall had ended in the night and a warmer breeze blew over Auschwitz. Three miles of riding over the slowly melting snow passed before either man spoke, and Ritter sounded almost apologetic in tone.

"You... are able to see the passage of this creature, somehow."

Czerny's face was unchanged but the pale ice in his eyes softened somewhat. He suspected that it had cost the Major a great deal to speak publicly about the events and admit that perhaps the Romanian was not a madman or a fool. He had the attitude of a god had admitting that maybe a mortal was not *entirely* wrong. Czerny nodded, relaxing part of his concentration, but still sounding distracted.

"In a sense, yes. I do not see with my eyes, but with my mind."

They rode on along a trail that led through small clumps of trees and fields, across the land toward Krakow. Major Ritter looked at his map and compass and confirmed it: almost a straight line to the city.

"And this ... this sense, you can trace the creature, track it?"

Czerny took a deep breath and sighed. The truth was usually the best policy, yet with the SS, saying what they do not want to hear rarely ended well. Still, for the moment he was protected by the German high command and ought to be safe while he was useful.

"It is more difficult with more people in the area. I... this may be boring or unwelcome, do you wish me to explain?"

Ritter hesitated, then nodded, unwilling to actually say the word aloud. He looked back at the soldiers tramping through muddy snow and melt without comment. Discipline would prevent them from speaking up in his presence, but later? For now marching the miles across fields and farms was all they were concentrating on. That and the memories of what they'd seen in the forest.

"Then I shall make it as brief as I may," Czerny continued. "Each of us as we pass through the world leave... traces, shall we say, of our passage. It is like the scent a hound follows, but is instead a residue of our passions, our emotions, our spiritual state. It is as if you leave a piece of your soul behind like a cloud that follows a horse on a dusty road."

Czerny slid his eyes sideways to see the Major's reaction so far. Ritter was impassive, watching ahead. *At least he issn't visibly amused or repelled*, thought Czerny.

"The more violent or extreme these spiritual conditions, these disturbances of the soul, the more 'dust' is left behind in the air, so to speak, yes?"

Ritter nodded, this made sense, even if it was absurd fancy; it was consistent and understandable.

"So when a monster of this sort passes through an area, it leaves a considerable 'dust cloud' and is easy to track. However, the more the beast calms down, the less the cloud is visible. And in a city, there is more of this... 'dust' being kicked up by everyone who passes by. A spurned lover, a thief fleeing the police, a man angry at his children, and so on. It can become difficult, even impossible to track."

Ritter nodded again.

"The creature we track has... has two natures, a duality of soul. There is the man, who can be of any sort, but often is what would be called wicked by the more religious. And there is the beast, a monster within him that struggles to be let free, a horror that slowly over time consumes the man and becomes his all, kept back only by an incredible strength of will. While the beast is dominant, the trace he leaves is distinct and quite obvious. While the man is dominant, the trace becomes more ordinary, not as distinct." Czerny paused as the

47

concentrated to keep the path ahead clear in his mind. "He is calming, becoming more the man, and thus the path is more difficult to follow. It is possible he even knows this and hopes it will hide him."

Ritter stared ahead across the wet farmlands as he rode, listening to the men tramp behind them. He had more questions but felt foolish and uncomfortable, on unfamiliar ground. The further they got from the forest, the less real the destruction of those men seemed, or at least the more plausible realistic scenarios of how they died became. Perhaps a man could have done it all, an exceptional man, but a mere man. Yet in the back of his mind, at the most basic, primal level, he knew better. The image of that corporal lying dead, surrounded by all the weapons he'd collected from his hideously slaughtered fellow soldiers kept returning to Ritter's mind. They rode in silence.

*****

Herr Professor Doctor Konrad Stoffel was frustrated. It had been a day since he heard about the prisoner's escape, and while the information about the event had been carefully collected and regularly updated with efficiency and attention to detail, his plane trip to Krakow had not been. Delay after delay prevented his travel for hours, and each step was the more frustrating for Dr Stoffel knew that sufficient backing by a party official or the willingness to pay larger bribes would have sped things up. Dr Stoffel was a man of few morals, but bribes and deliberate corruption was something he was a purist about. It was not to be tolerated, a stain on the purity of the Aryan race, and the thought of it enraged him that the men surrounding the Fuhrer kept him so busy and distracted he was not able to address this problem directly. Clearly, it had to be the case; Stoffel was certain the beloved Fuhrer would not allow such corruption otherwise, and obviously *he* had to be aware of it.

Just as he was about to board a dubious looking He-70 passenger airplane bound for Krakow, an official car pulled up with an impressive escort of cold and miserable looking soldiers on motorcycles. Dr Stoffel restrained his rage with great effort; it would be typical that after four missed flights, some party official decided he'd take the last seat on the last commercial flight out of Berlin that evening. Then he realized that a party official would have a much better plane ride than this one looked to offer. When the door was opened and Heinrich Himmler stepped out, Dr Stoffel's anger slid into cold fear.

Himmler, Reichsführer of the Schutzstaffel, head of the SS and in command of the most feared military force in the world stepped out of the car, a little stiff from the ride. With a word, Himmler could make an entire city disappear into the camps. One of the most powerful men in the Reich, and thus the world - as Dr Stoffel saw it - Himmler terrified him. For all his power, Heinrich Himmler was not very impressive to look at. He had a weak chin and a thin moustache, matching his slight build and short stature. His hair was shaved into a small patch at the top of his head and his thick spectacles covered sleepy eyes. Yet a chill presence accompanied the man, the certain knowledge of his power and influence.

Himmler personally directed Dr Stoffel into an office, ejecting all of the airport workers who fled as if the building was full of wasps. Rubbing his hands together for warmth, Himmler looked unhappily at the surroundings. Clutter filled the little office, with pictures of scantily clad women hung on the walls, stacks of forms and paperwork in disordered piles on the desks, a bottle of cheap Schnapps lay empty in the trashcan, and cigarette butts overflowed ashtrays. The split leather on the best seat revealed the horse hair stuffing from inside, pushed out like a burst baked potato. Himmler brushed off the seat and leaned back in it, gesturing for Dr Stoffel to sit in the other, wooden chair.

"Sit please, Herr Doctor, we must speak and there is little time."

Dr Stoffel sat down with a mixture of confusion and relief. What under heaven could pull such a powerful and important man to such a place, to talk to him? Was the SS involved? No, he wouldn't ever see Himmler then, he'd see a draft notice for the Russian campaign, or a soldiers' rifle butt in his face then a firing squad.

"I have been informed of some inquiries you have been making regarding a Polish prisoner," Himmler waved his hand in dismissal. "No, do not be alarmed, you have been a loyal National Socialist and working hard for the Reich. This is not a reprimand, nor is the SS interested in you. As it turns out, this is an... opportunity, a chance for greatness for the Reich."

Dr Stoffel nodded. He was certain it was best to let Himmler continue speaking and respond when he was directed to, like back in school.

"Your inquiries have been very enlightening and well-ordered, suggesting an organized, scientific mind. I looked into your dossier and found that you are a brilliant and dedicated scientist. I understand your paper on genetic anomalies in epileptics was very well received; it was partly what formed the Reich's policy regarding these madmen."

Dr Stoffel nodded again. "Madmen" was a bit inaccurate, but far be it from him to correct the Reichsführer.

"It seems you are taking a bit of a different approach toward the stories out of Auschwitz; explain."

Time to talk, thought Dr Stoffel, *keep it short and to the point*.

"Herr Himmler, I am flattered and delighted in your interest in this project. I was not sure I had enough information to take this to an official capacity, but your question proves that I need not have worried so."

It was Himmler' turn to nod; *we know everything* his gaze seemed to say. *Not quite*, Stoffel thought, and plunged in swiftly, as if afraid of interruption.

49

"In my previous examinations of genetic anomalies and mutations I have read about studies in the past of various very strange atavistic throwbacks, men who have become more bestial, even monstrous. There was a case recently in Dusseldorf of a criminal who drank the blood of his fellow man to survive, as his body was unable to generate certain required chemicals. This lack was seen in short order while in prison, causing his gums to recede and exaggerate his canine teeth, causing his eyes and skin to react violently to sunlight; all classic characteristics of Nosferatu, or the "vampire" of Stoker's novels and many previous legends."

Dr Stoffel slid a plain silver cigarette case out of a coat pocket while he spoke and lit one, offering Himmler his last cigarette. Himmler shook his head, but did not seem bored or annoyed, yet.

"Some older records, particularly those seized from the southeastern European states, have some indication of a different sort of mutation, causing increased hair growth, growth of fingernails, teeth, and ears. The kind of mutation that would be portrayed in decadent American cinema as a wolf-man, no doubt. Yet in these studies there was a hint of something... more."

Dr Stoffel hesitated. This was the precipice that divided between an awful plunge into mockery and disregard, or heights of glory and achievement. He took a deep breath.

"There were some studies done that suggested cases where the mutations were more extreme, more radical. That hinted at someone who could seem ordinary - aside from some hints in their physiognomy - but in times of stress or certain periods in their life change into a more bestial form, a 'monster.' Such mutations would result in greater strength and agility, an unbelievable level of healing and resistance to harm. This sort of creature was called *lycanthrope* in the ages past: the were-wolf."

Dr Stoffel stood and began to pace as he spoke, waving his cigarette in the stale air of the small office as he gestured, emphasizing points by stabbing the glowing end in the air.

"Fascinated with the possibilities, I have been watching decades for just such information. Could such a thing exist, was such radical change possible, so rapidly? What could it mean for science? Could these healing properties be as great as they were said to be? Most modern science scoffs at the old stories, the tales of monsters and witches and magic, yet the modern *Aryan* scientist knows that in these tales are the seeds of reality - the witches brew brings us penicillin, the vampire is a diseased man drinking blood to survive. What secrets of the jungle and the superstitious past are we abandoning while we seek modern science and reason? What strange adaptations might evolution have resulted in over the millennia, hidden from sight by rarity and fear?

"The French philosophers laugh at such ideas, yet Nietzsche wrote of monsters and of reality beyond that which we can reason and discover through ordinary scientific observation. We Germans know better of the world, that beyond the veil of science there is much more that must be known and studied. Our Fuhrer himself leads the way with archaeological studies of the past, bringing artifacts and information to the capital to learn from - not out of superstitious fear or religious nonsense, but the need to know not simply the accepted and studied by lesser men, but the whole world as yet unknown. For how can we master the planet without comprehending it all? How can we consider ourselves men of reason and understanding without learning and knowledge that which has previously defied reason and science?"

Dr Stoffel stopped, realizing he was rambling and likely to annoy Herr Himmler. He glanced briefly at Himmler but saw no immediate signs of frustration or annoyance, rather a sort of fascination and interest. Dr Stoffel pressed on, wanting to capitalize on the moment.

"The old stories were written in ignorance we no longer suffer from, struggling under the burdens of religion and superstition; yet with proper discipline and method, we can peel back the layers of myth and lies and reveal the reality - more than reveal, exploit it! What could be accomplished with a man who can shrug off bullets and heal grievous injury in not weeks, but hours? What sort of front line soldiers would berserkers in wolf form be, when guided by German genius and tactical brilliance? In short, Herr Himmler, what sort of gain would the Reich enjoy from the capture, study, and duplication of such a creature for our benefit? How much more swiftly would the needs of the Reich be met with a soldier of this sort?

"And so I began to dig into this story - just a hint of some wolf monster in a work camp - hoping dimly that I might have finally found what I've wondered about all this time. And the more I studied the more I realized it *must* be what I seek.

"I was hoping only to get to the scene of these incidents, to study, to gather evidence, and to hope to see the creature. What great things could be accomplished, if only I could gain access to this creature, alive?"

Himmler sat and thought, his head tilted slightly. What he thought was hidden in his features, but his eyes showed respect for the doctor's ideas. Finally he spoke.

"What indeed?" *Put a German in charge and something useful could be done.* "You see, Herr Doctor, I came personally because of a request you sent trying to procure a flight to Krakow. I was intrigued by the report, and by the paperwork you requested, it appeared you were interested in something that was a concern of mine as well.

"The creature is being hunted by a Romanian specialist. As you say, the high command has seen fit to send this man to track him down, but they wish this beast destroyed. Yet the more I thought about this case, the more I realized that this would be an opportunity squandered. How did he accomplish what he did? What let him survive the liquidation process? How did he escape? These are questions that we must answer, and killing the prisoner would not do so.

"There is much in the past that we do not understand, and which transcends modern sciences, Aryan or otherwise. I have personally taken a great interest in the myths and legends of the past and recent discoveries..." Himmler paused, weighing his options, "let us say merely that they are less myth than we had once believed.

"I wish this creature captured, studied, and his powers understood, his strength harnessed for our righteous cause. Destroyed he is of little use. Alive..." Himmler's eyes flashed up to meet Stoffel's. "Alive, he may be of service to the Reich, even if he does not wish it. Yet, even one such as I am limited as to what I may accomplish openly. I cannot give you orders that contradict what the Fuhrer has commanded, yet... I may help you reach the Romanian and work with him, provide you with troops and passes, with paperwork that lets you move.

"This is between you and I, you understand..."

Himmler trailed off and Dr Stoffel understood very well. If something went wrong Himmler would be completely unconnected and Dr Konrad Stoffel would be all alone. If he succeeded, Himmler would be there to take credit. So be it. The scientific community would know, and the Fuhrer would as well. His reward was assured.

"Yet I will do what I can," Himmler continued, "'behind the scenes' as the thespians say, to assist you in your efforts. Go now; the plane is waiting for you. When you arrive in Krakow you will be met by my men. Find the Romanian, and the rest is up to you.

"I will not tolerate failure, Herr Doctor, but I will greatly reward success. You are an Aryan, there is no limit to what you may accomplish. Make your people proud."

And, thought Himmler, *this would bring me greater acclaim and access to the Fuhrer, and trump that brutish thug Bormann.*

Dr Stoffel nodded nervously and saluted. *What have I gotten myself into?*

*****

Aniela stared at the form of Cezar, the flickering candle barely lighting him across the room. He seemed larger than before, a massive presence in rough-spun clothes in the corner where she hung her coat and scarf. She shrank against the wall holding her blouse, arms crossed over breasts with an overwhelming sense of vulnerability and that naughty feeling of having been caught like a child with her hand in the cookie jar. Fear, and a whisper of excitement. *He saw me undressing.*

Cezar's eyes were barely visible in the candlelight, a gleam against the shadows of his bearded face. He looked so serious, but not worried or eager. She might scream, or she might run, or she might rush to his arms, none of it seemed to concern him. He didn't seem bored, he merely seemed confidently ready for whatever came to pass. Aniela felt her heart pounding through her chest, telling herself it was fear, and knowing it was more.

"You shouldn't be here!" she whispered at him, frozen against the wall.

"I shouldn't be anywhere."

"What are you doing in my room? How did you get in? What do you want?"

"Please, calm yourself, Aniela. I am here only because I wish to speak to you, in a place you were not so filled with fear. When I saw you at the market I knew I had to know you better, to spend time with you. But it seemed you believed that merely speaking to you would bring the hordes of hell upon you so I let you go.

"But you never left my mind, Aniela. I have been thinking of you." Cezar said. *Your scent was simple to track through the city,* he thought.

Aniela swallowed hard, a mad thought flicking through her mind that he knew of her thoughts of him over the last day. Then she became angry, forgetting herself, she put her hands on her hips, blouse in one fist.

"You spoke Romani you fool, in public, what were you thinking? How did you know I would understand?"

Cezar moved one step away from the wall and smiled, his eyes becoming softer and kinder, with little crinkles at the edges that Aniela noted and stored in her memory without thinking.

"I could sense you were one of the People, and who else could have such beauty and fire within them? The world can hate the Romani, but love and sense of family cannot be broken by their hate. No one would bother you with me there, Aniela. I would keep you safe." Within Cezar, the beast snarled *like you did Marisol?* and Cezar winced slightly and hung his head. "Yet... you are right, it was rash. I should not have done so. But would you have spoken to me otherwise? There is so little time to meet someone in these days, I... forgive me Aniela. I did not mean to frighten you."

Aniela rebelled a moment - *he thinks of me as a mouse* - yet she remembered the stark terror and helpless feeling in the market line and shuddered, missing Cezar's moment of sadness with thoughts of her own fears. *I'll show him I'm no frightened child!*

"It was foolish, and rash. You know the slightest hint is enough for any of us to disappear. Never do so again!"

Cezar smiled; was she even aware she implied they'd speak in public again? Aniela caught herself then became angry again.

"Ah! You know what I mean! Why must you be so frustrating?"

"I could have waited a bit longer before speaking, if I was so unconcerned with your dignity," Cezar said, eyes crinkled at the edges again.

"I saw you before you spoke!"

"Because I let you see me, angel."

"You have no right to call me that! My name to you is Mrs Wisniewski!" Aniela said with fierce pride, louder than before.

"Ah, Mrs Wisniewski, where is your husband? I saw no ring upon your lovely hand." Cezar sounded disappointed.

"He..." Aniela stopped. *Should I lie? He would only find out*, she thought; *He might go away*, a deeper voice whispered. "He... died in '39; our home in the country was bombed while I was away. "

Aniela hung her head, the empty pain in her heart still there, as an echo of the staggering agony dimly clutched her soul. He would always be there, a ghost that could not fill the gap of his absence, just enough to remind her and haunt her with his love and memories. It had been years yet the emptiness would not go away. Poor Alexander, the poetic soul crushed under tons of stone and wood by German hate.

"I am sorry for your loss."

The two stood as they were, Aniela looking at Cezar's eyes in the flickering candle light, Cezar looking at Aniela's yet taking in everything else. In the darkness he could see the whole room as if lit by bright moonlight, for darkness was never all that deep for him. Aniela was not wearing her rough coat and clothes from earlier, her slim body was not covered by layers of heavier cloth. Her bare feet made her look younger but her face was worn by care and sadness beyond her age. He looked at her wavy black hair, her large dark eyes, her full lips, and dragged his eyes down her body. The woman was thin, like so many in this time, but still had pleasing curves. Aniela felt his gaze and her arms twitched slightly as she reflexively almost covered herself again, then stopped. She did not care what he saw, and she was wearing more than she did at the beach. Only, it felt tighter now.

"Who are you, to move so freely through the city? How did you get in here?" Aniela demanded.

"I am a refugee, like yourself."

"A refugee? From where? Your Romani sounds like the local tribes."

Cezar's gaze moved from Aniela to the wall, unwilling to explain.

"There's word a big gypsy like you escaped from..." Aniela whispered "a camp."

"I've heard that, too."

"How is it possible? Can anyone get out?"

"I've heard of others who escaped, that fled to the English."

"Always someone who heard from someone else, though. No one ever meets an escapee."

Cezar shrugged. "I expect they try to avoid being seen."

"Who are you?" Aniela's eyes narrowed slightly. Handsome and somehow physically compelling as Cezar was, Uncle Rys' desperate warning sounded in her ears.

Cezar tilted his head slightly, looking at Aniela again but with more respect. Most women would roll over and pant when he spoke to them, but while he could sense her interest, she was cautious, thoughtful.

Outside, a car sped by and backfired, causing Aniela to jump and cover her chest with her dress. Cezar turned his head slightly and looked toward the window then back to Aniela. Her nervousness was back, with a dread in her eyes greater than a mere startling sound should have caused.

"Aniela, I had to come to speak to you once more where you would not fear so for the stamp of German boots. I will speak with you again, at another time. Until then, remember me and I shall think of you."

Aniela nodded, swallowing hard. Her toes curled a little as she watched him cross the room to her window to open it, moving like some great cat; all muscles and smooth, athletic grace. Cezar turned back to look at Aniela once more as he pushed the heavy curtain aside, her pale body in a white bra and slip, blouse in one hand dangling at her side. He smelled the air like a connoisseur of cognac and grinned a wicked grin at her, then with a single movement dove out the window.

Aniela gasped, rushing to the window. She forced the curain aside to look out and down to the brick road two stories below. There was no sign of Cezar, as if it had all been a dream. She clutched the blouse against her chest with both hands, over her heart. The room felt so warm despite the open window and the cold breeze through it. She closed the window and pushed the heavy cloth over it again to shut out the light of her little candle.

Cezar moved through the streets in a trot, running on the balls of his feet and making little noise. His eyes darted about, watching for movement and the shape of trouble, avoiding the main streets and ducking through alleys. He leapt over fences and across yards, covering the distance of several times his height without effort. Cezar ran, and leapt, and fought a battle within his soul.

Take her. Go back and take her, she's in heat for you, the beast growled within him.

Cezar shook his head, as if the beast was watching him.

Mount the bitch! She's probably on her back now, thinking about you.

Cezar gritted his teeth and ran harder. The lust was strong on him, making his senses keener and his skin prickle with heat. It would have been easy, he knew. She would have yielded to him. In these times of danger and fear it always was easy. There was something about his raw, feral nature that women were almost helpless against. *Not this time,* he thought fiercely. Aniela deserved more respect than that, more than simply another conquest. There was an intelligence and a fire in her that even Marisol hadn't shown.

Cezar slowed, then stopped in a small wooded area in Krakowski Park. The beast was feeding off his desire, weakening his will. It would take him soon, if he did not find something to distract it. He crouched and sniffed the air, unaware of how much the beast was in control already. He smelled squirrels, a cat, mice, a nesting bird. There were lovers in the park not far away, hiding from curfew and prying eyes in a glen. The smell of the city and the nearby water washed over him, telling him thousands of tales in each individual scent.

Not far away was the Silesian House, mostly empty this time of night. One scent out of the mix, faint from distance, reached out to him.

CHAPTER ELEVEN

Chief of the Krakow Security Forces Hauptsturmführer Hans Sturmberg put on his cap and straightened in front of the mirror. Other officers had an aide de camp who would help them dress, but Sturmberg rejected this as weakness and vanity. He wanted to look presentable and give the proper image of a German officer, not to primp like a schoolgirl. The the face in the mirror looked weary, with a somewhat prominent nose, deep blue eyes with bags under them. The scar he'd gotten from an American bayonet in the Great War showed more prominently when he was ill or weary, and it was visible along his forehead beneath the hat band.

As he pulled his gloves on, Hauptsturmführer Sturmberg watched his fingers. They shook again, as they always did at the end of a long day. He held his hand out and willed it to stop quaking, and eventually it did. Interrogating the wretches and traitors who came into this building was always stressful. There was no danger from them, only a battle of wills until the prisoner cracked, as they almost always did. Some were strong and refused to give in; those were the first to die in the camps, he knew.

Sturmberg looked up and saw Peter Klein looking at him in the mirror, a few respectful strides back. Klein, always puncilious and precise, always on time, and never making mistakes. *It is appropriate of him to be behind me*, thought Sturmberg, *always breathing on my neck, always ready to take my place.* The slightest error and Klein would send a memo to Berlin. The slightest failure to follow procedure, and another letter went out. Sturmberg knew he was not able to catch them all before they reached his superiors, and enough of them would one day pile up enough for Klein to take his place. Yet he was effective as an officer, and useful in his place. Who knew what tricks his replacement would attempt? Better an enemy with familiar methods and habits than the unknown.

Klein would run the department poorly, Sturmberg knew. He only thought of exact following of orders, obeying the law and

57

producing perfect paperwork. Deals such as the one with that gypsy Rys were too useful in gathering more critical information and dealing with spies and troublemakers than rounding up one more gypsy. Right now the Rom community was complacent, hiding and obedient, and Rys was said to be a leader. Drag him off to a work camp and his followers would almost certainly join the resistance in full strength. Clever for an inferior race, the gypsies could present a signifcant annoyance. Once the Jews were dealt with, there would be time for the rest of the Gypsys, and he knew where they were. So Rys stayed in place and was useful to Sturmberg. And the resistance had all but died out in Krakow and the surrounding area.

That was the essence of good leadership, in Sturmberg's mind. Use the resources you have wisely and in their place. Results mattered more than procedure, something Klein would never understand. And while he continued to produce results, Sturmberg was confident Klein's contacts and conniving would never topple him, unless he made a serious error.

Sturmberg snapped his heels together and straightened his back, with a smirk. Turning, he disregarded Klein's farewell and stepped briskly out of the office, past the dowdy secretaries and underlings working the night shift. A walk to his apartment was always exhilarating, particularly on a cool evening such as this. Pushing the doors of the Silesian House open to the street, he paused a moment to take a breath of the cold night air. It smelled of rain, the night air, a distant rain. He looked at his driver waiting patiently by the door with a long black Mercedes and waved him away. How Karl was always ready when he left he was not sure, although he suspected that his secretary Gretchen called his driver. He suspected they talked more than just about when to pick up their superior, more than talked as well. Sturmberg thought it none of his business, but he faulted Karl's taste in women.

As Karl drove away, Sturmberg looked up at the clouds. They were heavy but did not seem likely to rain. He felt proud in his sound judgment. Something caught his eye on a rooftop, a shape. Looking directly at it, he saw nothing there. Had there been someone? Sturmberg crossed the street to that side and strode along the sidewalk. If there was a sniper, he would find the shot at a target straight beneath him challenging. There had been no word of any attempt on his life or any other resistance activity lately. It was unlikely that the shape had been a sniper, but it was always best to be cautious. The streets were conspicuously empty, as they should be after curfew. The soldiers knew him by sight and knew to not bother Sturmberg on his irregular nightly walks, so it was always a peaceful trip.

The city was so quiet this time of night, almost as if it were abandoned. The windows were all darkened, no radios or conversations could be overheard in the buildings he passed. This pleased Sturmberg, who knew order and obedience was a sign of security and of his success. Somehow, this night the darkness was deeper than usual and more ominous, as if it hid something sinister.

Sturmberg liked Krakow. The Polish people had fought hard against the German forces, but were hopeless in the face of superior arms and discipline. Now they had given up, bending to obey their masters. But Krakow had never fought; it had merely given up when the Wehrmacht approached, saving the city from artillery and bombardment. Sturmberg had been there when the mayor had personally met the invading German troops to surrender the city, and no shots had been fired. The Captain's face betrayed a rare smile, a small one at the corners of his lips that turned slightly downward, and then the smile vanished.

His brisk stride slowed, and then faltered. Something... was following him? Sturmberg turned to look behind him. Nothing was there, only the feeling of eyes on him, of something behind him. Who would dare? None in Krakow. After a moment, Sturmberg turned and continued. It was just a feeling, stress from too many long hours this week. His mind drifted back to an interrogation earlier in the day.

The old Moravian preacher he had questioned was bald and bent, a man who looked almost like a skeleton in his simple clothes. Caught harboring Jews, the Moravian had been dragged in to see what else he knew. After days of questions and time in the cells, Sturmberg knew he had just tried to help the subhuman wretches from their proper fate. Gloating, he summoned the old man up for one more session of questions before shipping him off to a quick death.

"So, priest. Your weak faith teaches forgiveness of enemies, to turn the other cheek."

The priest waited, his eyes half open with weariness and hunger, saying nothing.

"Do you... forgive me... priest?"

After a long moment, the Moravian cleared his throat and coughed a few times, then with a wavering, weak voice said "It is not my forgiveness you must concern yourself with, Herr Hauptsturmführer."

Sturmberg scowled. Why had that memory risen again? Followers of that pathetic dying Jesus were all the same, all ready to forgive and help and lend aid, but without any backbone or strength. Had not the Fuhrer said the Christians had no place in the future of the reich?

Germany would show them a better way, after all, where was that priest's Jesus now? He probably wouldn't even survive the trip to be shot. The wretch was probably not a priest anyway; Moravians didn't have priests. *Like the Lutherans that way*, Sturmberg thought, *but just as pathetic as the Catholic priests*. How easily they'd bowed to the Reich, their grand notions of love and peace forgotten in the rush to survive this new era.

The wet cobblestones were less a dark river between the sidewalks than a chasm yawning between the buildings on either side.

Sturmberg listened to the echo of his footsteps off the walls, imagining the families cringing from the might of the Third Reich inside the apartments he passed. But the thought gave him no comfort and he pulled his coat closer around his throat.

Behind him, he heard the clicking nails on the street, some stray dog out looking for trash or its home. Sturmberg looked back to see the hound and saw only an empty street. The curve of Plac Inwalidów behind him showed a dark alley like a black wound in the walls of buildings, shadowed and unknown, and for a brief moment, the Captain saw a glimpse of red, like eyes in the tomb-like depths of that darkness. He faltered in his step slightly, then saw only darkness where the eyes had been. Too many late nights at work, perhaps a day or two off would be wise, as his wife kept insisting.

Sturmberg strode down the lane again at a brisk pace, and heard a sound echoing in the streets behind him, a hideous spine-clawing sound like laughter – but the laughter of a huge hound, as if some great beast was chuckling as it growled. The deep, chilling sound faded and Sturmberg began to walk more swiftly. *Just a few blocks and home*, he thought. What could it have been? Sturmberg gripped the folded leather flap covering his Luger in its holster.

Turning the corner to Stanislawa Konarskiego, Sturmberg jumped back in alarm as he came face to face with a patrol of three soldiers.

"Good evening Hauptsturmführer Sturmberg, are you all right?" One of the men asked. The soldier was a round faced, ruddy fellow, young enough to be his son.

Sturmberg looked behind him and faltered. "I – I am not sure, for a moment it seemed... I think something is following me." Sturmberg felt foolish, his cheeks hot as the soldiers looked at each other. Two of them turned the corner and looked around.

"I think it was a dog, perhaps it is rabid. It didn't sound... right."

"You have dinner in your pocket, Hauptsturmführer?" the tallest soldier asked with a bright grin.

Sturmberg shook his head as if to break out of some sort of trance, and strode off without answering. The soldiers spoke quietly behind him as he walked away, making him feel even more foolish. *Just a dog, no doubt Klein will hear about this and make another report.* Above him, something sounded, like an object landing on the tiles three stories up on the rooftop. The growling chuckle echoed off the quiet buildings, somewhere behind the row of homes. Sturmberg didn't look, bending his head down slightly and walking swiftly toward his home. It was just ahead; he could see the steps to his door. His back felt vulnerable, like when he was a child and the thunder raged outside. He would crawl into his father's bed and press his back against the strong back of poppa, broad and muscular and safe. Sturmberg fought the urge to look behind him, feeling his skin creep under his jacket, both chilled at hot at once.

Reaching the door, Sturmberg looked around nervously, one hand on his pistol as he dug in his pocket for keys. He fumbled at the door, cursing his hand for shaking as the key chattered against the lock, then finally slid in and engaged. *This damned blackout*, he thought, *I can't see to open my own door.*

The door of his home rapidly closed behind him, Sturmberg felt comforted in the dark hall leading to his rooms. Ahead, he heard his wife say "What?" then a ripping sort of sound. Sturmberg put his keys and hat by the door on the little table with a familiar clash of metal on the lacquered wood and locked the door against the fears of the night. The house felt cooler than Inge usually kept it. Then ahead there was a series of soft thumps, like parts of something slumping to the ground in a fabric bag, quiet but clearly audible. Sturmberg cocked his head slightly, puzzled.

"Inge, I am home late again." He walked forward.

The arch leading to his sitting room by where the fire and the radio kept he and his wife company was dimmer than usual, stretched with unfamiliar shadows. On the floor, as he came closer, it seemed as if one shadow was reaching out from the room, spreading across the wooden floor. Sturmberg stopped. The shadow was wet and dark, glistening in the dim light of the sitting room, a steadily expanding pool. He pulled his Luger, stepped around the corner, and froze.

Sturmberg began to scream, but was cut off in a gnashing of jaws.

CHAPTER TWELVE

"Silver Bullets." Ritter said.

The Romanian rode his tired old mount, head down a moment, before responding.

"That can be effective, yet..." he began.

"Sir!" one of the soldiers interrupted from behind them. Ritter brought the ragged column to a halt, Czerny's horse sagging beneath him with deep heaving breaths. Vladimir looked down at his mount impassively as the soldier trotted up to Ritter's side. It had been so eager to be out of its stall earlier, but after several hour's ride the wretched creature looked near death.

"Report," barked Ritter. The ride had worn on him even more than march had the men, his spine and thighs aching from the saddle. After years of ease as an officer he now regretted avoiding the physical conditioning the infantry were forced into by the military.

"The men need a break, sir, for a meal." It was Sergeant Klontz who spoke, a withered man so browned and thin he reminded Czerny of a mummy. *Still a sergeant at his age,* thought *Czerny, either a man who loves his job... or a man unfit for promotion.*

"They will rest when I do," replied Ritter, quietly between his teeth. Rest seemed dearer than treasure to him, but he had an image to uphold, especially to this rabble. "There are many long miles before we reach a proper place to stop."

The trail was still strong, amazing Czerny. He concentrated and could sense it stretching in front of him into the distance, between trees like a twisting pathway of reddish smoke. Here and there it would blaze brighter as if the creature had a moment of increased rage or perhaps frustration and other places dimmed, but always was there for the Romanian to follow.

Ritter gritted his teeth as he rode, each step by the horse sending jolts of ache through his back. His eyes slid to the side the Romanian rode on. The bastard showed no sign of weakness or even discomfort. His mind danced back around the images in the wood, the

62

horrors of his men, mangled and slaughtered. Still, it didn't have to be some mythical monster, did it?

A raw recruit in the Great War, he had fought in Marnes and seen men blown to pieces and horribly dead, but even that evil time had not compared to the death in the forest. At least in the trenches he had an enemy to kill; they were human, they died and bled like his friends and fellow soldiers. Lying in the filth and mud and blood he knew he was at least putting the French through the same hell. But this... monster. It didn't even seem to be harmed by rifle fire; it obliterated an entire squad of the Reich's soldiers. Granted, the several thousand SS troops at the Auschwitz camps were sadly not the finest of the army. With his own men and his leadership, it could have been much different, *would have been*, he told himself. And he would replace them with better men once he reached Krakow. But something inside him cold and sharp knew better.

"The trail is starting to diminish," Czerny said quietly.

Ritter looked up from his reverie, the sounds of the French and British guns echoing in his memories as he thought of that scrambling retreat in 1914. He looked around, forcing his thoughts to the present. "We're not far from Krakow; he must have run to the city. Can you track him there?"

"It is difficult; the more souls are in an area," Czerny answered, "the more cluttered the trail becomes, especially as the creature calms. He is nearly indistinguishable from an ordinary man at this point."

"You will not lose him in the city," Ritter insisted.

Vladimir Czerny made a grim face, for the first time displaying emotion and humanity. "There is... a way to find the creature even though it is hidden in the mass of humanity, but it is... not a manner I enjoy using. I hope that it will not become necessary."

Major Ritter looked over at the little Romanian with imperial loftiness. "You will use whatever means you must to obey the Fuhrer's orders."

Czerny reluctantly nodded. "Yes, I will do whatever I must to find and destroy this beast." He was silent a few minutes riding steadily. "Perhaps you seek vengeance or to stop a rebel threat. You do not yet know the horror that it might unleash upon the land, upon all of us. You do not understand how the curse can spread in a city, out of control. The creature must be stopped, though the cost may be very great. There are," he looked straight at Major Ritter with a severe gaze, "greater terrors than your science are able to unleash."

Ritter rode in silence as they approached the outskirts of Krakow. *There are things that lesser men ought not question in this world as well*, he thought. *Perhaps this arrogant Romanian will soon need a reminder.*

Herr Professor Doctor Konrad Stoffel rode into the town of Oświęcim in the back of a long, black Mercedes-Benz convertible. He wasn't sure what the model was, all he knew was that it was fast and comfortable, taking the rough road more smoothly than his little old BMW Dixi. Beside him in the rear seat was an SS officer and in front were two more. Doctor Stoffel was not comfortable with the men in their black and red uniforms; he had never been comfortable with military even when he was a medic in the Great War, but the SS filled him with a sort of uncertain dread. He'd heard the Gestapo were even worse, but he had only seen one officer at a distance, and he was merely dressed like an ordinary man. These SS in their special uniforms were somehow more intimidating and felt more dangerous. Stoffel again regretted his rash decision to pursue the were-creature, but his curiosity burned like a living flame. And the rewards if he were right, those were a powerful motivation as well.

The men were content to ride without speaking, which was just as well as the car's engine and the wind were loud enough to make conversation nearly impossible. Even with the convertible roof up, the car whistled and blew as it raced along the road.

When Dr Stoffel's plane had arrived at Krakow, the SS were waiting with a car, full of courtesy and military discipline, apparently informed by Himmler about the doctor's mission. Doctor Stoffel didn't remember the men's names but he understood they were at his disposal, which made him feel better about the trip to Auschwitz. He knew little about the camps or their operations but had read some reports by a Dr Mengele from the work camp Auschwitz I and they turned his stomach. The reports were fascinating from a clinical perspective, although the man's conclusions were absurd and Stoffel secretly suspected the man was a lunatic.

Dr Stoffel was a patriot, a man with a deep abiding love for his country, his people, and his German heritage. He saw Adolph Hitler as a great leader and man of vision, a genius at the right time when Germany was at its lowest ebb. Hitler brought a clarity and focus to Germany that was now working great modern wonders of science and technology, but the racial theorizing of men such as Alfred Baeumler and Josef Goebbels sickened and disturbed Stoffel, privately. Early in his education he had encountered the wild speculations of Count Joseph Arthur De Gobineau and his hierarchy of humans based on their physical characteristics, but Stoffel had found in his studies that humans were all but indistinguishable at the cellular level. Recent science made outward physiological differences laughable. True the Aryan man seemed to have a greatly superior culture, but as a human all were the same.

Still, it didn't serve his country or Dr Stoffel's best interests for him to be the lone voice of reason in a symphony of racial superiority conducted by the gifted, if ignorant, Goebbels. With the SS guard, Stoffel felt protected from any slips or expressions he might betray at the camp. They were a sort of blessing from the Fuhrer, or at least Himmler, to sanctify and allow any quirks he might display.

Through the simple brick entry into Birkenau, Dr Stoffel found the place simply horrifying. Bad enough the entire complex had been built on a swamp, but the stench of rot and unwashed human bodies nearly more than he could bear. How anyone could possibly endure the atmosphere, almost certainly swarming with pathogens, was beyond Doctor Stoffel's understanding. Although Auschwitz I had been constructed as a work camp for the IG Farben factory, Birkenau was simply a death camp and the stench of death lay over the complex like a fog. The commandant had sneered openly at the handkerchief Stoffel held over his face, but the SS troops accompanying the doctor seemed to understand.

Doctor Josef Mengele had traveled to Birkenau to meet Dr Stoffel, a fellow man of science in a sea of fools. The man struck Stoffel as oddly upbeat for such a dreary place.

"God in heaven what a stench," Stoffel mumbled through the handkerchief.

"In time it becomes less intolerable," Dr Mengele said with a cheerful voice. "I insist on bathing the inmates but they are idiotic and slow to respond. I have created a special dormitory exclusively housing twins, which are kept cleaner."

Stoffel nodded. "I have read several of your reports, it is a unique... opportunity."

"It was when I served with the Waffen SS in Russia that I first formulated the theory; there were twins in my troop, and it occurred to me that this presented an opportunity to learn more about the nature of humanity, with a control subject for the most pure and specific results." Mengele looked sadly at his mud-caked boots. "When I earned both of my Iron Crosses, the Winkler twins were with me. It gave me the germ of an approach, a possibility for study.

"There will never be another chance such as this, to study the lesser races, to understand their weaknesses, their tolerances. What we might learn about human evolution here is immense!"

"So many lesser races in such a small place, a thousand per housing structure. It is inevitable they should reek with their corruption," Commandant Hartjenstein said defensively.

Mengele continued as if the commandant had not spoken. "The Winkler twins were such fine soldiers; it occurred to me that were the women of the Aryan race able to bear twins or even more young each pregnancy, it would more rapidly build up the master race and provide warriors, engineers, scientists, and leaders for the next generation. We must always look to the future."

The three stood at a section of the fence surrounding the camp, a cluster of SS troops behind them. Stoffel was silent as he examined the section of fence the creature had burst through. The damaged length had been repaired and electrified, but the removed sections that had been torn were lying in a tangle on the ground, ready for removal. The wires were thick enough to require tools to cut, but according to the reports he'd read, the creature had slashed through them like cobwebs. Dr Stoffel's eyes widened as he examined a section. Carefully using tweezers he gathered tufts of blackish fur from the wires, tucking them into a paper bag he folded carefully into his briefcase.

"The soldiers who were slain, where are their bodies?" He asked.

Josef Mengele spoke then, his voice bitter; "burnt."

"There was concern of contagion, we did not wish any infection to spread," Hartjenstein said hastily. "The men were cremated and their ashes buried."

Doctor Stoffel looked up for a long moment at the commandant. *Superstitious idiot.* He felt a moment of sympathy with Mengele, who was scraping his shoe with a piece of wood.

"I was denied an opportunity to examine the bodies, and so you have been as well, I suppose," Mengele said with a voice dripping with barely-restrained fury.

"All was according to standard procedure when dealing with infectious disease!" Hartjenstein insisted.

"Acerbum est circumveniretur cum tot stultorum," Mengele grumbled, his voice still edged with fury.

"Talia facinora superstitio habet causatur," Doctor Stoffel responded sympathetically—it is painful to be surrounded by fools; what crimes superstition has caused. Stoffel pulled a notepad from his coat and consulted it.

"Was there anything particularly notable about this... Cezar?" Stoffel asked in German.

"Not according to the officers in charge of processing the prisoners. He did not stand out in my examination; I focus on racial anomalies and hereditary defects. I do not even remember this man." Mengele said, sounding cheerful again. He bounced in place on the balls of his feet. "It is too bad, I would have relished the opportunity to study him in greater detail; how would he have responded to electricity or dismemberment? I have injected caustic acid into some of the younger inmates to document their physical reaction, what would this creature's body be able to survive?"

Doctor Stoffel tried to hide the horror he felt and decided he had reached the limits of his endurance of the camp. He nodded to his SS driver. "Very well I have learned all I can here. Thank you for your assistance."

Commandant Hartjenstein clicked his heels and they all saluted Hitler. Josef Mengele left without a wave and Stoffel watched his back a moment. Were it not for this camp, this war, what would this man have become? What evils were unleashed in such a setting, dormant and unknown in men's hearts until the right opportunity or setting arose? Although the SS driver visited the small farm where the creature supposedly passed through, there was nothing of interest there and Doctor Stoffel rapidly lost interest and patience, as if the stiff black hairs in his briefcase were burning in his memory. The sooner he could get to a lab the more he could learn. The Mercedes headed back toward Krakow where Himmler had promised a laboratory had been made available to him.

*****

Cezar woke to a scream. It was louder and closer than most, just beneath him in the office, but different from the ones in the basement, or in his dreams. It was a squeal of delight, one of the girls happy about some occasion. She jabbered in a nearly incomprehensible German dialect, but the tone reminded Cezar of a girl talking about a beloved; some welcome news about her boyfriend, no doubt. He stretched and yawned. The beast within him was quiet, lazy from its slaughter the night before. But in its place he felt a gap, an emptiness.

Several floors beneath Cezar, Peter Klein looked around his new office. The position meant an increase in pay and authority but more than anything else it meant a vindication of years of effort. Years of work behind the scenes finally were paying off. He could afford to ship his wife back to Bavaria and live with his mistress here, and no one could question his use of resources. He could run the office efficiently and effectively. He had already sent a hand-written note of thanks to the men responsible for his promotion, but a gift would be appropriate. He made a note.

The office was spare and orderly, as he preferred, but it still felt like Sturmberg's office, somehow. It would need to be rearranged, changed to be made his own. The reports of Sturmberg's death were disturbing, according to a nightly patrol he'd acted strangely on the way home, then he and his wife were found torn literally to pieces in their home. Some resistance group trying to spread terror, no doubt.

Klein's first task was to contact the Fuhrer's special duty squad that had just entered town. Sealed top-level orders from the Fuhrer himself had commanded him to extend Sturmbannführer Ritter and all with him full courtesy and advise him of any unusual occurrences. Ilsa was already at work copying the reports from the Sturmberg killing. That would be sent out immediately.

Another packet of notes had informed him of a scientist sent to the city on special orders, this one from Himmler's personal office. Klein wondered how Sturmberg had been able to deal with all these troubles in his haphazard, disorganized way.

Peter Klein ran down the daily list of tasks he had prepared the night before. It was his regular ritual, without fail, to arrange each day before sleep the previous evening. Klein prided himself on being able

67

to create an exacting schedule that was able to shift and adapt to the unexpected such as fool orders from his former superior. It had taken three hours to get the office safe open; Sturmberg had never told anyone else the combination. Within had been the usual paperwork and petty cash, legers, and files, but several of the folders within were on persons in the city Klein had suspected were used by Sturmberg to maintain security and order.

Looking through the files on Sturmberg's desk, Klein examined work unfinished from the night before. The Moravian preacher file he put away; the old man had died in the night. There were several other open prisoner files, including one authorized for release. A notation was at the bottom: King. Klein curiously looked at other release orders, and several shared the same notation. Was this a code word from high command, one he had not been told? Who was the "King?" Poland had no Monarchy under the Reich, and his position had been largely ceremonial after the great war. Klein began to read through the old notes in Sturmberg's desk.

*****

Major Ritter sat at the tavern, separate from his men at the table. A girl sat with him, leaning close with one leg against his in warm familiarity. At first, he had welcomed the distraction but now he was thinking of a way to get rid of her. She smelled stale of sweat under her perfume and he suspected she had been entirely too familiar with too many men before him. Although he had a supply of condoms, he despised the things and the filthy diseases that made them necessary. The girl breathed alcohol into his ear, whining that he was ignoring her in awful Polish-accented German.

"Go find someone else, slut," he roared, louder than he'd intended and shoved her. She sprawled on the floor awkwardly, her skirt rising up to show skinny legs without stockings, to the amusement of the soldiers in the bar. Two of them helped her up and Ritter ignored her venomous glare. Ritter was furious with himself for shouting, and pushed the Schnapps bottle away from him on the table. It was too early to be drinking anyway, but what else was there to do in this worthless Polish town? It had been spared destruction by the German armies when Poland was conquered, yet Ritter felt out of place. German high command called the city "ur-Deutsche," some primordially German center of Aryan culture in the east. But to Ritter it was dreary and cold.

The little Romanian had lost the "scent" in the city, assuming he'd ever had it to begin with. *Was he making a butcher's mess with us?* The Romanian could claim anything, even be leading them directly away from the escaped gypsy's path. The troop had arrived exhausted and sore late the previous night, with the Romanian on foot when his old mount had finally collapsed, its heart destroyed from the effort.

Ritter still was sore from hours in the saddle. Billeted in a seized home, the Romanian was under careful guard, sleeping according to the last report by Corporal Jaeger.

How was this Romanian better than a few German Shepherds on the trail? The Birkenau commandant claimed the dogs refused to follow the trail, whining and cowering, pissing themselves, but maybe they just had worthless dogs. *Well that seems unlikely, they're trained to hunt down and kill escaped prisoners*, Ritter thought. The Schnapps wasn't helping him feel any better about the job, he just felt stupider and more the target of some cruel joke.

A courier stepped into the bar from the outside, letting in another cold blast of wet wind. He looked around the bar and stepped up to Ritter with rigid discipline, snapping his heels in a crisp salute.

"Sturmbannführer Ritter?" The courier asked, his voice cracking.

Ritter looked up at the boy, who appeared barely old enough for recruitment. "Yes?"

The boy paused and swallowed, the prominent Adams apple on his thin neck bobbing. "You are Sturmbannführer Ritter?"

"Yes, yes, I am he, what is it?" Ritter demanded, letting his frustration show again with a twinge of regret.

"I have papers for you, sir."

Ritter waited, eyebrows raised.

"Ah, yes, here, please yes, ah, sign this," the boy stammered, holding out a paper on a clipboard. Ritter scribbled a signature and took the papers away from the boy, turning to open the package. The boy turned immediately and hurried out. Another burst of wet cold blew across the back of Ritter's neck as he read the paper.

It was a local crime report, short and methodical. Captain Sturmberg in charge of local security in Krakow and his wife murdered late last night. Ritter's annoyance began to increase. Why had the local authorities troubled an officer of his stature with such a...

Torn to pieces in their home, dismembered by what appears to have been a wild beast.

Ritter read the report slowly, squinting in the dim light of the café.

Door locked...

...windows closed and locked...

...Sturmberg's keys missing, nothing else stolen...

...bodies horribly mangled...

...captain torn in half, his wife with her throat mostly missing...

... as if bitten by gigantic jaws...

...no visible point of entry...

...no sounds heard by the neighbors...

...in the blood were the tracks of some gigantic hound...

...reporting "unusual animal activity" to Sturmbannführer Ritter as per orders...

Ritter sat back heavily in his chair, the cold feeling creeping down from his neck through his spine.

It was here.

CHAPTER THIRTEEN

Aniela felt comforted and relaxed in the salon. She knew that the women who came in were all locals and safe; none were going to have a husband order someone to the camps for a bad haircut, and besides she felt experienced enough to not ruin some poor woman's coiffeur. She chatted with the plump woman in her chair as she trimmed her graying black hair.

"I heard we're going to get some new movies into the theaters finally, can you believe it?" The woman asked. Aniela knew her from many previous visits, Oliana Sankevich. "Years, its been, except for the German films. Maybe they're good, but I can't speak a word, how can you enjoy a film you can't understand?"

Another woman spoke up, someone Aniela didn't know. "Oh, I speak some German, but it's hard to keep up in a movie. We went and saw that *M* movie last week, the Kino Sfinks has run it for weeks now. Such a creepy movie, so awful with that strange little man killing children, it made my blood chill."

"Oh yes, we saw that before the war, Gregor and I did. Except that was dubbed in proper Polish then. My husband loved it but I thought it was just a nightmare."

"It's been so long since we had a new film from America here..." began Oliana, then faltered as the other women in the room threw her a warning glance. She had brushed too close to criticizing the German occupation, and one never knew who was listening. Aniela busied herself with her shears. She was glad Oliana had given up coloring her hair. Before the war many women dyed their hair, but the supplies were hard to come by and the vegetable dyes never seemed to give good results.

Aniela cocked her head to look at her client. Oliona didn't look much like Greta Garbo, but she now possessed almost the same hair as the actress had shown in *Anna Karenina*. Out of the corner of her eye,

Aniela spotted a man standing outside, looking through the lettered glass at the front of the salon. Cezar.

For a long moment Aniela and Cezar looked at each other, separated by a few strides across a hair-littered floor and a sheet of glass with carefully stenciled words. Aniela felt as if the room had faded, and only they two were there, his eyes dominating the entire world. Cezar lowered his head, turned, and walked away. Aniela took half a step, as if to follow, then realized where she was.

"What was it?" Lucja asked from the next chair over, working on the other woman's hair.

"Someone... I thought I recognized him, but he's gone now."

Lucja nodded sadly. "I know the feeling."

The room was silent in shared sadness and loss.

Cezar walked away from the salon with his head down, hitching up his collar against the cold he didn't feel. The beast inside him was quiet now, sated after last night. He'd heard about the killing but had only vague memories of a hunt. Now he walked the streets alone, without even the monster within to keep him company. The city felt closed in, as if the buildings were leaning toward him. Families walked by him, couples hand in hand even in this atmosphere of oppression and occupation. Businessmen spoke quietly by their shops, children in small groups led by an adult passed by Cezar, parting briefly as they moved around him. Life went on swirling around him and he felt like a stranger to them all. His life, his experiences, no one of them could possibly understand or know them.

The smells on the wind were a distraction, something he usually was able to ignore. The stink of unwashed bodies, the dust of bricks crumbling in the elements, the smell of soap and warm water in a bath, a few flowers beginning to bloom, meat being cooked, all of it swept by him on the slight breeze. He closed his eyes as he walked, letting his other senses guide him. He had no papers, but that was of no concern. He was confident that a battalion of soldiers couldn't stop him.

Would Aniela possibly understand what he was, how he had lived? His mind went back over the years, stretching into the distance of time. The things he'd done, Marisol simply did not care, did not want to know. But Aniela, so much quicker in her mind, she would need to know. After so long, Cezar felt little shame or regret, only a deep weariness, like he'd been carrying a heavy weight for all his life.

Cezar looked up. Above him towered St Mary's Basilica, the ancient church in the center of Krakow. It's twin reddish stone towers pointed at the sky, one taller than the other, drawing his gaze further upward along their height. Cezar felt no religious awe or comfort; he was convinced he had been damned long ago. Yet he opened the smaller door in the huge main gate to the building and stepped in. Cezar's footsteps only echoed slightly as he moved smoothly over the hard stone floor. Everything in the building felt hushed and reverent, and for a moment Cezar felt like a stain in the basilica's clean rooms. No one noticed or stopped him as he stepped into the tower and ascended its steps. The doors were already unlocked for the afternoon ritual, and Cezar made it all the way to the top, then stepped out of the tower through a window and climbed easily and comfortably to the higher tower's central spire.

A bulge near the top was still plated with leaf gold, and he crouched on it, staring down over the city radiating outward from the church. All these people, so crowded together, so busy, so noisy. He missed the quiet forests and mountains. He could not see the peaks of the Carpathian mountains through the low clouds, but he felt their loom to the south. They called to his soul, a lonely place he could be unhindered by others, to roam free and hunt when he chose. Cezar felt that he did not belong in this city – nor any city – but Aniela was here, and he could not leave, yet.

There was no one else, now. Marisol had made him feel less alone with her bright eyes and ready giggle. She had been so willing to love, to give herself without any concern for the future or what the consequences might be. When he told her he was *marime*, she had laughed and said that made him even more exciting. When he had told her his darkest secret, who he really was inside, she had stared at him with huge dark eyes and then kissed him again and again as if she could love away his curse. Now she was gone, forever, and he was all alone in the world. No other of his kind existed, that he knew of. Cezar had looked for years, decades, and found no trace of any other cursed as he was. In all the world, there was only him, alone in the many millions of people, alone in the masses of lives in Europe.

Staring down at the city he felt a building resentment at the scurrying figures. Their families, their loved ones around them like a warming fire, and him alone in the world, more alone than anyone. He could leap from the tower and slaughter them all, killing them until they felt alone as him, as oppressed by the city and its stark buildings. Cezar sighed heavily, knowing it would not help, and worse would only drive them to each other's arms for the comfort he could not know. They would only share their terror of the monster and become closer.

Cezar heard footsteps and voices beneath him in the tower. An older Polish man was talking in his language to someone with a German accent as they entered the highest room of the tower beneath Cezar. He could hear them clearly but strained to understand their language.

"Each day now, for centuries, one or more trumpeters will ascend this tower and play the Hejnał Mariacki. Before the war, it was played four times an hour, each time changing direction out of the four windows. Now, of course, the song is only played once at noon time, the same time Polish National Radio plays it for the whole country."

"Yes, yes" the German said, sounding impatient. "But why this song, why not bells like every other church? What is the meaning of the trumpet, and why is the song cut short when it is performed?"

"It is an old story, a legend. Perhaps it is true, I do not know." The older man cleared his throat and went on. "Long ago, the Mongol horde rode out of the steppes to the east under General Subotai, the greatest of their generals. They had conquered and pillaged their way all across Asia, nothing could stop them."

"Genghis was a mighty man, for an inferior species," said the German. "I have studied his conquests."

"By this time," the older man continued, "Genghis had died and his grandson Ogedai was khan, but Subotai was still the general who served the khan. Subotai's armies crossed the Carpathian Mountains and rode for Krakow, the greatest fortress in the area. Having faced defeat by the Mongols twice near Krakow, King Henry the Pious brought his armies here to face the Horde and had a man watching out from a tower on the wall, with a bugle to call out if he saw the army approaching.

"In time, this brave soldier saw it, and began playing the Hejnał Mariacki as a warning, perhaps thinking the Mongols might not recognize it as a signal. Yet one of their extraordinary archers saw the lookout and launched a barb toward him. Before the trumpeter could finish the song, an arrow claimed his life, cutting off his final note. Perhaps it was the warning notes of this trumpet, but whatever the reason, the Mongol horde was turned back here, and never returned to Europe."

When the German spoke again, his voice was quieter, more respectful. The power of legend and tradition made sense to him, a loyal Nazi.

"I understood Krakow had been sacked by the Mongols under Genghis' grandson Baidar, and it was Breslau where they were turned back."

"Ah, well you know how legends are. Perhaps it is all a myth, but the legend serves to bring great pride and honor to the Polish. It leaves us some shred of national pride yet, and brings us together as a people. It helps us feel... less alone, perhaps."

"The Polish people have much to be proud of, priest. It is sad that they foolishly resisted German troops."

The old man was silent a moment, then quietly said "Pride, it is said, goes before the fall."

There was a minute of silence, and then a lone trumpeter began to play the song. Hejnał Mariacki was a somewhat sad song, and it was not very long. Almost a bugle call, it was made up of only five different notes. Cezar clung to the spire above the music with his eyes closed. Below him the city was quieter, the Polish people listening to the song as a sort of comfort and regularity in their lives from before the war.

74

They felt a kinship and pride in their history, united in their blood and ancestry.

The trumpet player continued, facing out the window, then stopped abruptly, before the final notes, as it had long ago in the legend. He slid the window shut swiftly and turned away, then stopped, looking around him in alarm.

Just as the final, abruptly ended note sung over the city, a long, deep howl rang out echoing off the quiet streets. The lonely howl was almost as long as the song had been, even louder and clearer than the trumpet had been. All the dogs in the city became silent and cowered, low to the ground, and the people of Krakow felt a deep sense of emptiness and isolation as the echoes died away. A child looked up and saw a glimpse of a dark figure on the roof of the basilica, but then it was gone.

CHAPTER FOURTEEN

Doctor Stoffel examined the tuft of fur he'd collected at Birkenau as he waited for his supplies to be unpacked and set up. The lab had not been prepared as swiftly as he had hoped, but the workers were diligent in their efforts, and with German efficiency he knew soon he would have his workplace. The SS soldiers seemed unhappy with the labor they were doing, but each knew to do his duty without grumbling. Stoffel and his superiors agreed on using only reliable German labor for this project; local workers presented too much possibility for sabotage or spying.

The location was good, not far from the amenities of town and yet away from prying eyes in a residential area. Apparently the building had belonged to some tailor, probably a Jew, but it was almost empty when the workers had first arrived. All the clothing and goods had been looted, first by soldiers removing the owner, then the locals taking whatever was left over. The Fuhrer had argued that this was proper, as the Jews had stolen so much from everyone through high prices, unequal business practices, and excessive interest on loans. They had to give back what they had stolen. Stoffel wasn't convinced, but it served his interests in this case so he was willing to ignore the circumstances.

The tuft of black hair was slightly reddish at the tips, like rust. It was coarse and thick, without any hint of a softer undercoat often found in animals. There were small tags of skin at the base where the fur had been pulled away by the barbed wire, which delighted Stoffel. It wasn't much to work with, but it was a start, and the sooner he could send a report to Himmler, the safer he felt in his position. The Reich could tolerate failure in science, but not sloth or a total lack of results.

Doctor Stoffel's thoughts drifted, as he waited for an area to be cleared so he could start work. He requested a microscope be set up with a table and good lighting, not feeling confident enough in his position to order these men to do anything. They had stripped off their

76

black jackets and were working in rolled up shirt sleeves, but still were intimidating in their size and obvious physical competence. He imagined Helga probably preferred men like this to him, although she seemed affectionate enough. It was of no account, she was far away in Germany and he had plenty of women here to find company with. It was simple biology; women sought men of power and position for safety and provision, so they would take him into their beds. And Stoffel had been told often enough he was handsome to believe it himself. The Polish women were said to be very lovely in their youth, according to talk among the soldiers, and the doctor loved beauty.

One of the soldiers interrupted Stoffel's thoughts, informing him of the area set up for him. Herr Doctor Konrad Stoffel prided himself in being able to work around any distraction, and he rushed to the table, pulling off his jacket and set to work. The table had been placed near a window and two lamps had been set on either side for increased light. The chair was an old wooden one, pulled to the table until the more useful stools could be unpacked and set up. It creaked slightly as Stoffel sat, setting about the task of separating the hairs and applying a few of them to a slide with a drop of water.

Hours later, the lab had been unpacked and set up around Stoffel, largely unnoticed by him. Books stacked on the desk, some lying open to a page, bracketed the notes scribbled on a pad and the microscope. Stoffel rubbed his eyes. Some time during his work he had transferred to a stool, but he had no memory of it. His stomach complained about lack of food, and his hands felt somewhat shaky. It was dark outside, the light-blocking curtains over the window before him, and Stoffel wondered how long he'd been at work. The last time he'd eaten was at the airport before he drove to Auschwitz, and he felt weak and light headed. There was no time for food yet, he reminded his body, and bent to work again.

Sample after sample gave the same results, and they were ambiguous. The fur had the scale pattern and ovoid structures of dog hair, but the fragmentary medulla of human hair. It was very dark, almost opaque even underlit in the microscope, with pigment taking up most of the hair structure. It was only near the reddish tip that the medullae were visible. The root of the hair was spade shaped like a dog's, not a standard rounded club shape as humans typically have, but the few scraps of skin tag at the base were very similar to human skin cells.

Stoffel had noted that the result was almost as if dog and human DNA had been somehow mixed or fused, creating a hybrid with characteristics of either. And even more frustrating, the samples were rapidly decaying, already starting to become brittle and crumble just days after being torn from the creature's body. When exposed to weather, it took years, even decades for hair to decompose, but Stoffel estimated in a matter of weeks the hair would be dust.

Doctor Stoffel straightened his back, hearing it crack along the spine. He could prepare a report based on this information but he wasn't getting very far with only hair, especially hair that wouldn't survive long enough for rigorous peer research. He had to have more, and all that was available to him at this point was vague eyewitness description and crumbling fur. There had to be more data, someone had to know more. He stared at the dark woolen curtains over the window.

Someone had to be hunting the escaped prisoner, someone who had more information. It wasn't a matter of state security – yet at least – so the Gestapo would not be involved. It was highly likely that this someone would be SS, men trusted by the Reich to do their job without questions or talking too much about it. Stoffel racked his brain trying to think of the name of one of the SS men assigned to him, but drew a blank.

"Excuse me, officer?" He called out. One of the men, blonde, tall and broad like the others, stepped into the room. He had his black jacket back on and looked even more brushed and groomed than normal.

"Yes, doctor?" The soldier's German sounded northern to Doctor Stoffel. *From Schleswig-Holstein, probably*, he thought.

"I regret to say I do not recall your name, please accept my apologies."

"Markus Kohler, Doctor Stoffel." The soldier did not show anything in his face, but Stoffel felt the slight reproof in the use of his name. The soldier hadn't forgotten *his* name. Well there was only one of him and many soldiers.

"Thank you Untersturmführer Kohler." *If I can't remember your name, at least I can show I know your insignia and rank*, Stoffel thought. The SS had its own special ranks; the regular Wehrmacht equivalent rank "Leutnant" was easier to remember. "I wonder if you could help me identify one of your fellow soldiers. He's on special assignment from the Fuhrer as I am." Stoffel judged it wouldn't hurt to remind the man of his position and connections.

"Any way I can be of service, doctor." Markus clicked his heels stiffly.

"I do not know his name but he should be on detached duty seeking an escaped prisoner. He probably will have a Romanian national with him, a strange looking fellow."

Markus almost smiled and nodded. "I know that squad. I believe they are commanded by a Hauptsturmführer Ritter. I was on my way to a pub nearby where they are stationed in Krakow, if you would accompany me?"

Stoffel grabbed his coat, his mind racing.

*****

Vladimir Czerny woke from a dream of a hilltop execution remembered long ago, and reached for his glasses without conscious thought, an automatic gesture every morning for years. He sat on his bed and meditated six minutes exactly, then checked the odd device on a chain shaped like a pocketwatch. Waiting for something, he sat motionless for another minute, then snapped the device closed and rose from bed. The room was dark, and Czerny had only a dim light from under the door but seemed unhindered by the gloom as he dressed with rapid precision.

He tried the door and found it unlocked, with an SS soldier standing at attention outside.

"When Sturmbannführer Ritter returns, please let me know immediately, we must begin work as soon as possible."

The soldier merely stared at the Romanian as if he was a fly hovering nearby. The Nazis ranked slavs nearly as low as Jews in their racial hierarchy, Czerny knew, but he knew that Ritter would want to get this over with as quickly as possible as well. The soldier didn't have to respond, only do what he was ordered by the major. Czerny had requested a map the previous evening and spread it out on the bed in the dim light. He pulled a small irregularly shaped candle out from his baggage and lit it, waving the match with a complex gesture before touching the flame to the candle's wick. From his baggage he pulled several books and scribbled notes on loose pages and began to study them.

In the flickering light a simple map of Krakow was revealed, not sufficient for military use, but good enough for travel to noteworthy parts of the city. Pulling a black wax pencil from his bags, Czerny began marking the map in specific areas, and drew a line between each of them, forming a triangle with St Mary's Basilica in the center. Then he rolled the map up, put away the pencil and notes, and snuffed the candle. From his bags he assembled the strange device he'd used at Birkenau's shower just over a day earlier and began meditating himself into a trance again.

After ten minutes the Romanian shook his head and showed a flicker of frustration on his placid face, and put the device away. All he could do now was wait, it would be morning before he would likely be able to act again. Czerny laid back on his bed and rested, remembering the long years of his life.

*****

A light rain had begun to fall by the time Kohler and Stoffel reached the Boneslaw Restauracja. At the hotel where Stoffel's unit was staying, they had told him that the Major was eating dinner nearby. Stoffel handed his hat and coat to a thin, elderly man in carefully brushed but clearly aged dress clothing and was shown to the table where Major Ritter sat eating by himself. Ritter appeared to be in a very foul mood, stabbing his steak with more force than needed and chewing with harsh, jerky bites. Rather than focus on his food, the Major stared at a point beyond the chair opposite him, eyes cold and blue.

"I beg your pardon, Sturmbannführer Ritter, I am Herr Doktor Professor Konrad Stoffel, may I have a few moments of your time?"

Ritter stopped chewing and was still for a moment, then took a deep breath and let it out. His eyes flicked upward to take in Stoffel and then he sat back and his face softened slightly.

"Yes, please do sit, and excuse my mood." Ritter nodded at a chair. "It has been a... challenging few days of late."

Stoffel sat in a creaking wooden chair and ordered a bottle of Mosel Riesling from the hovering waiter and turned to Major Ritter. He suddenly found himself unsure how to begin, worried that his theories and hopes of capturing a monster would be absurd to a professional, lethal-looking soldier such as the SS Major.

"I have been sent to this city by high command," began Stoffel, hoping the credentials would lend him plausibility. "I believe our tasks are related in Krakow."

Ritter glanced up from his plate at Stoffel and took another deep breath, letting it out in a huff through his nose. He couldn't get away from it. Ritter focused on eating and hoped that the doctor would be brief.

"If you wish to see my credentials, I have brought them with me, but I assure you I am well qualified and cleared to speak on this matter. It involves a... an escapee from the camp in Auschwitz."

Ritter speared another piece of steak and chewed on it, savoring the flavor. He had not expected much from the small restaurant but the chef had surprised him with an excellent cut perfectly prepared. He finished the tender piece of steak and cleared his throat.

"I am here on the Fuhrer's orders, direct from Reichsleiter Bormann. My mission is not to be interfered with in any way."

"I understand, yes," Stoffel replied. "And I have no desire to interfere with you or your men. All I seek is some information, data so that I can move ahead with the work that I have been tasked with by Herr Himmler."

Ritter hesitated a moment before placing his fork on the tablecloth. Probably before the war the cloth would have been of finer material, but the restaurant had done well by trimming it carefully and edging the rough cloth with lace. Stoffel's comment changed things; if Oberführer Himmler was truly behind this man's work, he was worth listening to. Not only was Himmler Ritter's senior commanding officer, but a man Ritter personally looked up to and considered a model of German soldiery.

"Perhaps I should see those papers," Ritter said quietly.

Stoffel swallowed hard. The papers were very complete, but they were quite vague on the exact details of his mission, deliberately avoiding specific mention of any monster or lycanthrope. He had hoped that a bluff would be enough, the mere mention of Himmler and paperwork sufficient to impress the officer. Stoffel reached into his jacket and handed over the small packet.

For long minutes, Ritter examined the papers, reading carefully. The only sound at the table was the occasional rustle of papers as the Major read and the quiet clinking of silverware from other diners. Ritter hoped his squint was not too obvious, in recent years it seemed like there never was enough light for him to read small print clearly. The doctor was clearly an educated man of letters and would not be impressed by a man who could not read well.

Ritter folded the paperwork up neatly and returned it to the packet, sliding it across the table. The papers were not very specific but they told enough that an experienced officer knew what they meant. He'd received orders of their type before, the kind that made sure his commanding officer would not suffer any ill effects should he fail to carry them out properly.

"And what is it you need from me, Herr Stoffel?"

"I too seek this, this escapee, for different reasons than yourself. I believe... the evidence suggests that this person is... is more than simply some escaped gypsy." Stoffel felt even less confident and thought furiously about how to continue.

"Yes?" Major Ritter prompted.

"Er, yes." Stoffel looked down at the packet of papers as if notes were written on the cover. "The... the reports Himmler has received and passed on to me demonstrate an unusual array of abilities, which the Reich would benefit from greatly were I allowed to study the, the subject."

"I have been ordered to find and liquidate the fugitive, then return the body to Birkenau," Ritter replied.

"Yes, yes, and as I said I have no interest in interfering with your orders. However, my study would greatly benefit from any insights, information, anything you have witnessed or discovered."

Stoffel waited as the thin waiter brought the wine to the table and poured two glasses full. When the old man left, he sipped the Riesling and nodded appreciatively.

"I'm glad not all life's pleasures have been cut off by the occupation," the doctor chuckled.

"Indeed, it is up to we Germans to bring civilization even to countries such as Poland," Major Ritter said, "ancient home to many Teutonic Knights."

Ritter made a resigned sound and put his glass down.

"Very well. Yes, I have some observations to make, and from your hesitation I suspect you may not be particularly surprised to hear them. This prisoner, who I shall not name in public, has shown himself to be quite exceptional." Ritter looked around the room, which was nearly empty and the few others were carefully ignoring the SS officer and his clearly distinguished dinner guest. The major continued quietly, "he is extraordinarily strong, and the guards at the camp say that their rifle fire did not seem to bother him. He ignored... a gas attack... and destroyed a small squad of guards sent to recapture him.

"His systematic and brutal slaughter of those soldiers indicates not just great strength and speed, but a level of intelligence beyond a mere beast. The men fired nearly all of their ammunition in the forest, but I found no signs of a single wound or blood trail from the prisoner.
"

Ritter stopped and stared at the remnants of his steak, deep in thought. The memory of those young soldiers in the forest had chased his appetite away; the events were too reminiscent of the ghastly trenches in the Great War. He pushed his plate back and looked away from the meat.

"Herr Doctor, I have someone I'd like you to meet."

CHAPTER FIFTEEN

Aniela sat at the table with Uncle Aleksy and Aunt Joanna, eating the meat Joanna had to pick up at the market after Aniela fled meeting Cezar. It was getting easier to find food now, although the rationing was still in place. Governor-General Frank was despised by the Poles, but he had overseen rebuilding the nation and the economy was doing better.

The roast was tough and stringy and Aniela grinned slightly at the thought of it being some old horse as Cezar had guessed. She looked up to make sure no one had noticed her, but Aleksy and Joanna were looking at their door, hearing footsteps come to a halt outside it. A look flashed between them, and a chill was shared. Then came the hammering knock at the door that they had feared all these long months since the Germans had taken over. It was their time to vanish.

Aleksy silently said a short prayer as he stood and walked to the door, pulling the napkin from his shirt with a shaking hand. The door opened to an officer in the "Blue Police," holding a clipboard. The Blue Police, properly known as the Polnische Polizei, were the official law enforcement of Poland under German control during the occupation. Formed of former Polish state police and Polish-speaking Ukraines, the Blue Police were the hand of the Germans in controlling the population.

"Aleksy Sawiki?" the officer asked. Behind him were standing several groups of German soldiers with full packs and dufflebags, looking bored and talking quietly to each other.

"Yes, that is I," Aleksy answered drawing himself up tall, determined to face his fate with dignity.

"Your home has been selected to quarter a squad of German soldiers. You will be compensated for their presence each week." The soldier tore a piece of paper off of his clipboard and extended it to Aleksy. "Present this to the paymaster at the address shown each week for your stipend."

Aleksy looked at the paper in confusion and relief as the soldier turned and spoke in German to the others behind him. They pushed

83

past Aleksy roughly, six of them carrying dufflebags and packs jutting with weapons and tools. The police officer with the clipboard turned and walked away with the remaining soldiers, leaving the street empty as Alesky stared at the paper, not reading it as his mind whirled.

Joanna stared in confusion and fear as the men bustled into the room, eyes darting from the soldiers to her husband and back. Aniela shrunk behind the table, pulling her sweater around her closer. In the comfort of her home, she wasn't covered up enough and felt exposed to the eyes of the soldiers as they looked around the home.

Aleksy closed the door and took a deep breath.

"Do... any of you Polish the speaking?" He slowly worked out in German.

The men chuckled and nudged one of the men.

"I have some of the Pole, old man," replied a thin, tall soldier with hawk eyes and a sharp thin nose. "My name Abel Hoffman, I will speak for us."

Aleksy nodded. "It was good, my German is... is... falling."

"Poor," corrected Abel.

"Yes, yes poor."

"We will need a room to sleep and separate room for Sergeant Franz when he showing," Hoffman said.

Aniela listened with her head down. Just communicating was going to be a nightmare let alone any privacy. *Privacy*. Terror rolled down her like a wave of ice as she thought of the machine in her room. She must destroy it, throw it out. *They will find it.*

Abel nudged Aleksy "hey, tell your girl she stop shaking, if she thinks we look bad wait til she sees Franz."

Joanna put her arm around Aniela, pulling her close. It was true, Aniela was shaking as if she was caught in the snow, her face pale and drawn with terror. *Such evil times*, Joanna thought, kissing Aniela's soft blonde hair. She whispered comfort to Aniela as if she were a little girl again, rocking her softly.

The men dumped their packs and dufflebags heavily on the floor and started exploring the house, leaving Abel to watch over their gear. Aniela began to quietly cry.

*****

Vladimir Czerny was sitting in a chair by the fire, hands steepled when the doctor and the major entered the room. He watched with calm brown eyes as they pulled out of their overcoats and hats.

"I thought it was spring," grumbled Ritter as he pulled his gloves off and stuffed them into an overcoat pocket.

Konrad Stoffel said nothing, still feeling uncomfortable and awkward around the soldier. He had been home studying medicine during the Great War and felt a coward beside the taller man, although Ritter had done nothing to indicate he felt that way. His coat was expensive and he hadn't noticed much of the cold, but the Major's uniform apparently hadn't been as warm.

"Yes, this is the man. Sherrny," Major Ritter gestured at the Romanian. "He is the one assisting me in finding the fugitive."

Czerny stood and waited. Doctor Stoffel crossed the room and looked at Czerny, curiously. *Such an odd-looking little man,* Stoffel thought. He had little patience with slavics of any sort, especially Romanians. The stories from that backward land were wretched with superstition and nonsense. Ritter seemed convinced this man was helping him but Stoffel was sure it more than water dowsing with a pair of sticks than any real assistance.

"Assisting the major, are you?" Stoffel asked, looking down at the Romanian.

"Where I am able, yes."

Ritter was surprised at his clear, unaccented German. "And you believe this fugitive is what?"

"A lycanthrope, Herr...?"

"Herr Doktor Professor Konrad Stoffel, of Heidelberg University."

"Herr Doktor, thank you." Czerny nondded. "The fugitive is apparently a Gypsy by the name of Cezar Alexandru, and he suffers from lycanthropism."

"And what is the nature of this... affliction, in your opinion?"

Vladimir Czerny tilted his head slightly, the light from the fire reflecting off his glasses instead of showing his eyes. "I am not exactly sure. There are many causes of lycanthropism. Without knowing more of his history and how he changes, I cannot say. There is, as a man of science would say, insufficient data."

"I see." Doctor Stoffel sat in another of the chairs by the fire. Ritter pushed Czerny aside and sat in the one he'd been when they entered. "I speculate that this condition is a genetic anomaly, a sort of throwback to an earlier time, perhaps an undocumented sub species of man predating *Homo Erectus.* You speak of a change?"

"Just so. The man Cezar Alexandru appears to be much as any other of his kind, perhaps somewhat more hirsute than others."

"Gypsies are not known for their sleek and shaved appearance," Ritter said.

"Indeed, and he would possibly be more so, depending on the duration of his...affliction."

"So you believe this is something he contacted, a disease of sorts, then?" Stoffel asked.

The Romanian stood between the two chairs with his hands behind his back, facing toward the fire so his back was to neither man. "It is something which he was not born with, more than likely, although I admit there are other possibilities. In my years of research and experience, there are several sorts of lycanthropism. It is said that one sort may be passed on through birth but I have not read or heard of such a case occurring since medieval times, so one must be hesitant to give the reports too much credence."

Stoffel grunted and chuckled. *Indeed.*

"Other sorts are transferred by the attack of a lycanthrope, such as in the American film of a few years ago. This is of course a very old legend in our lands as well."

"My son adored that movie," said Ritter, "although he cried every night for a week after fearing the wolf-man's attack. I found it silly."

"The film was inaccurate in its portrayal of the lycanthrope in many respects, yes," Czerny continued. "Another possibility is someone who through some mechanism or effort contrives to grant themselves the ability to change."

Stoffel lit a cigarette and breathed out smoke as he asked, "this 'change' you speak of, what do you speculate is happening with the fugitive?"

"The camp guards spoke of the escape being by a huge creature, like a wolf. Yet no wolf entered that shower, and the missing prisoner was a man. Thus, one may reasonably conclude that Cezar Alexandru at least in some circumstances 'changes' from a human into a beastial form, perhaps that of a wolf."

Ritter and Stoffel looked at each other, feeling less confident. The strange little Romanian made Stoffel feel as if he were back in school.

"The 'fugitive' as you refer to him is someone who may have the appearance of a normal man and yet can display unusual strength, swiftness, senses, and even resilience to harm."

Ritter thought back to the laughter in the forest and the dead young men on the equally dead leaves. "How...resilient would you say?"

"Legends speak of such a creature being virtually impossible to kill, without certain sorts of attack."

"Yes, yes, silver, perhaps fire, I know the legends," snapped Doctor Stoffel. It was time to assert his authority again. "Absurd. Even such creatures as the starfish take days to regenerate a missing arm, and resilience to a bullet would take ridiculous bulk and weight like a tank. One must read the stories of the old days in the light of modern science and achievement."

"Perhaps you are right," said Czerny. "Perhaps the camp guards missed their target as it tore through the steel fence, and all those soldiers in the forest were unable to aim as well. But perhaps there is more, as the English writer Shakespeare wrote, than is imagined in your philosophies."

All three men looked at the fire and watched the flames dance and flicker as it devoured the wood.

CHAPTER SIXTEEN

"The troops have all been quartered in local homes, as you commanded, Herr Sturmbannführer. There were no problems with the families, and we were able to choose homes with enough room for the troops. A weekly stipend of 10 złoty has been authorized by the paymaster. Here is the list of addresses and the proposed patrol assignments."

Ritter looked up at the young lieutenant with the spectacles. His own son was about the same age now, serving in France. Fischer, that was this soldier's name, volunteered because he spoke Polish. One of the many Germans living in the Danzig unified to the fatherland in 1939, Ritter guessed.

"Very well, thank you. Report to your commander."

The lieutenant clicked his heels with an impeccable salute and left. *So much energy, these young men*, Ritter thought. A map of Krakow lay on his desk, marked with locations and lines. The Romanian was confident that he could locate the escapee with his plan, but it seemed so absurd. The deeper he was sunk into this scheme the more Ritter could feel the ridicule and contempt of his fellow officers. *What would my old squad back in the trenches think of me now?* Ritter bitterly thought.

Yet each time the implausibility of the Romanian's claims arose, Ritter could only think back on what he'd seen and heard. And Stoffel, a prestigious professor of medicine at Heidelberg University had spoken of the hair taken from the prison camp and its odd nature.

Well. Orders are orders are they not? How many times did I charge over the top when told to by a superior officer? I cannot question the judgment of Herr Bormann, he thought, grudgingly. Clearing the papers off his desk with unhurried precision, Ritter folded them into a satchel and carried it out of the small office he'd been given. Outside, Stoffel and Czerny were waiting, still debating. They had discussed the case late into the night and started up again in the morning. It was giving Major Ritter a headache.

"No of course we cannot let this one live, it is a gypsy and entirely unreliable."

"You must not let *any* of his kind live, I assure you."

"Nonsense. The Reich will be strengthened by their genetic material, these are weapons, not monsters."

"And yet, professor, how often are the two not the same? What horrors have the wonderful advancements of science wrought over this century already?"

Ritter gestured toward the car, waiting with the orderly holding a rear door open. He'd had more scientific advancements in warfare than he cared to in the Great War and the blistered scars on his back from gas to prove it. Stoffel and Czerny stepped into the car, still talking. Stoffel rolled his eyes.

"Yes, and mysticism was so positive in the past. Perhaps you argue for the return of the inquisition and the rack for those who argue against a dead Jew rising from the grave?"

"No indeed, these things in the past are warnings for those of the present and the future. Knowing the unintended and awful consequences of well meaning people's brilliant schemes should serve to caution us today, should it not?"

Doctor Stoffel slid to the far end of the seat and scowled as the others pulled in beside him and the door closed.

"So in the fear of something being misused, you believe it should never be attempted? Such an attitude would have us living in caves, fearful of building a home that may fall down."

"There is a certain point at which the drawbacks and dangers of technology and advancement might begin to outweigh its benefits." Said Czerny.

"And *you* would be wise enough to know this limit, of course."

"I believe that there will come a day when we look back and realize that the evil of mankind that was once restrained by the limits of his reach becomes uncontrollable with technological advancement. Where a monster was once restrained by his limitations, technology allows him to reach far beyond those limits.

"Our weapons and communications give greater reach to the worst sort of person with even the meanest intelligence or education. That horrors may be released on the world does not take special foresight to imagine."

"Nonsense," Stoffel replied. "You are speaking as someone from the previous century, like a fool. Modern scientific man has made order and sense out of the world which seemed like mystical chaos to lesser peoples. The New Man is not bound by religious or superstitious nonsense, no categories of good and evil. We make the world what we wish, through science and proper technique. Our will shapes the world, not our faith or our fears."

Czerny removed his glasses and cleaned them with his handkercheif a moment before responding. "I speak not of faith, merely of human nature. Consider the slaughter of the Great War, with new devices unleashed without thought or understanding of their consequence. The machine gun, the chemical weapon, the tank, even aerial bombardment. And now you wish to replicate a monster you cannot even understand, to experiment with something far worse than these technological terrors."

Stoffel shook his head. "Blaming those horrors on technology is like blaming bad food on fire. There will always be abuse of everything man puts his hand to, from weapons to... to bad art. Have you seen this man Picasso's work? A child could paint better. "

"And that abuse becomes easier each day, does it not, as we grant man greater and greater reach?" asked the Romanian. "A man abusing a rock harms one man. A man abusing nitroglycerine can kill hundreds, thousands. A man abusing water can drown a man. A man abusing mustard gas can murder an army."

"It is the abuse that must be targeted, not the devices. You speak of humanity as corrupt and weak; you are correct. As the Fuhrer has noted, such must be culled from our society and our gene pool. The New Man is stronger, wiser, and better able to handle the wonders of science."

"There are horrors no man should ever add to his arsenal," Czerny replied, "and you are toying with one of them."

"What exactly do you believe will take place should my experiments prove successful?" asked Doctor Stoffel.

"You do not understand the nature of these creatures, Herr Professor-Doktor," Czerny said quietly. "One of these things can infect dozens in a single night. Within a month, those infected can each, individually, infect dozens in a single night. One incautious monster in your armies could result in a cataclysm that would make the black plague insignificant in history."

"Ridiculous. If this creature is as you say, the world would already be full of them!"

"One such being, if cautious, could prevent any more of their kind from being created, with care. One. And yet there is always the chance they might not catch them all, that another might be created, then another. But dozens of these creatures, scores? An entire battalion of these creatures? You do not have the slightest conception of the horror that would be unleashed upon the world! You believe you can control them but you cannot."

Stoffel pulled out a cigarette and lit it, frustrated. "Sturmbannführer Ritter, what would you say to this?"

"I'd say you're arguing with a Romanian as if he's a German," grumbled Ritter.

The driver sighed, enjoying a quiet ride the rest of the way to the first destination.

The long black Mercedes pulled to a halt in front of an ordinary-seeming structure with a squad of Germans in front of it.

Before the car had pulled up, they were lounging on the steps and windowsills, but as it stopped, the jumped up and snapped to attention. Even without clear markings, they could tell this was an officer's car. Behind the structure, the newly-built wall around the Jewish ghetto loomed.

Ritter exited the car first and nodded to the sergeant.

"Franz."

"Sturmbannführer. The building is clear and secure. It seems to have been abandoned, perhaps even before the invasion. All we found are rats and dust."

Sergeant-Major Martin Franz was a terrifying looking man. Horribly scarred by a gas attack in the Great War, he returned from the hospital just in time to be damaged even more by shrapnel from a bomb dropped out of an airplane over Somme. Now half of his face looked like melted wax had been poured over raw skinless flesh, leaving patches of angry red and colorless, misshapen streaks. The shrapnel had taken an eye, and the Sergeant rarely covered the empty socket. Several teeth had been removed on the left side from his injuries, causing his cheek to cave in giving the damaged side of his face a frightening skull-like appearance.

Major Ritter was familiar enough with this kind of injury but it took all his willpower not to stare at or look away in horror from the man's ruined face. Ritter peered through the small squares of glass forming the front window.

"Odd, it seems a fine enough location."

"I believe this property has an ill reputation," said Vladimir Czerny from behind him.

Ritter turned to see Stoffel taking a breath to launch into another argument.

"One moment, Herr doktor. What leads you to this belief, Romanian?"

"There is an old legend regarding this place. "

Sergeant Franz nodded. "They did not seem to know why, but nearby shopkeepers seemed to think the place was unlucky."

Stoffel sighed and lit a cigarette, restraining himself. Ritter had treated him with respect but he did not wish to antagonize the soldier, still not confident in his standing with the SS.

Ritter nodded to the sergeant and raised an eyebrow at Czerny. Vladimir had already spoken far more than he ordinarily was comfortable with in his debate with Stoffel, but the intellectual challenge had been refreshing. And the tales of these locations fascinated him. He stepped closer to the door and turned, taking on the role of the teacher once more.

"As you can see this is a very old structure, although it has clearly has undergone renovation to modernize it; lights, and such. The tale is of a man in the 12th century named Twardowski, who was an alchemist and inventor, some say wizard. It is said that he sold his soul to the devil so that he could learn the secret of the Philosopher's Stone."

"The stone which could allegedly transform metals into other metals, in alchemy," Stoffel offered, seeing Ritter's look of annoyance and uncertainty. His demeanor did not change much.

"The devil told Twardowski that he would claim that soul when the alchemist went to Rome, so Twardowski wisely avoided the city; a simple enough task. However, one day he took a walk after a particularly difficult experiment damaged his laboratory, and visited.." Czerny turned to gesture at the door, "this building, so it is said."

All three men and several of the soldiers looked at the building again. It was a simple enough brick structure, typical of the old buildings in Krakow with squared windows and little adornment. The stones looked very old and worn, with grime deep in their rough surface from centuries of coal and wood smoke. The three men entered the building and walked through an empty room strewn with pieces of wood and broken bricks in the dust. Behind them, the soldiers trailed with blank looks as the officers talked to the strange little Romanian.

"This building at the time held a tavern and Twardowski came to rest and dine in the courtyard formed by the squared building," Czerny continued. The men walked with him to the central square of the building.

Here, the building rose three floors above the worn cobblestones, growing grass and weeds between the rocks. The gray sky hung low overhead like a lid on the courtyard, without feature or movement. Around the courtyard were arched sections and columns along the ground floor, supporting a balcony that ran around the second floor.

"And it was here that Twardowski encountered the devil a second time, or so the legend says, for the alchemist did not notice that the name of the tavern was the 'Rome.' It was here that the devil demanded his payment."

"And the devil took him to hell through a crack between the paving stones, eh?" asked Ritter, scuffing the ground with a boot.

"The legend claims he escaped by transforming a rooster into a huge size and leaping on its back to fly away. Apparently the increase in size enhanced its ability to fly considerably, for it is said he now lives on the moon, continuing his studies. One can only speculate that the effort surprised the devil into inactivity."

Stoffel looked up momentarily, then cursing inwardly brushed his hair back and pretended to look at the balcony. *Rode a rooster to the moon, such an insulting story.*

"And you believe here is one place you will be able to work toward finding our fugitive?" prompted Ritter.

"One of the three I indicated, yes. This will take a while, if you wish to find somewhere to sit."

"Could use a drink from that tavern," murmured Ritter.

"I understand the Rome closed soon after; terrible plague." Czerny opened his satchel and began taking out various implements.

Stoffel stared at the little Romanian in growing disbelief. Out came chalk, a candle, a small jar with dust in it, a strange implement with lenses and brass structures, and a bellows. Did the man think he was a magician?

"What exactly do you believe you are going to accomplish here?" He demanded.

Ritter put a hand on his shoulder. "Perhaps we should take a walk; one of the men can keep an eye on the Romanian."

But Stoffel was not to be moved. "Hey, Romanian, what do you think will happen here? Do you plan to summon the devil? How much of this ridiculous story do you believe?"

Czerny looked up at the professor. "Very little. However, it is plain that something of great import and supernatural significance did take place here. And I intend to harness that to find your quarry. Think of it as... setting a wheel into a stream to turn a millstone, a source of energy."

"This is ridiculous, for modern men of German enlightenment to turn to this superstitious nonsense, how can you..."

"Do be patient, professor. It should take about a full day to finish my work in the city and then we shall see if it is of any success. If I fail, all you have done is visited a few curious spots in the city and you can have me taken out and shot earlier than is planned. If I succeed, then we are no worse off and you can find some plausible reason I was lucky. Either way, you have lost nothing."

Ritter managed to move Stoffel back into the building, directing a soldier to stay and guard the Romanian. "Lost our dignity..." mumbled Stoffel as they walked away.

Czerny looked around the courtyard as he assembled a device on the paving stones. There was not much of the event left, only small shifting shadows, a slight movement where the sun did not reach, a sibilant hissing of spiritual energy slithering between the cobblestones. But it was there, as he had hoped. The darkness of this place, its fell energy would serve as the guiding force to the darkness in Cezar Alexandru's soul. He set to work, ignoring the corporal leaning on a pillar with his MP 40 leveled on its strap at his back.

*****

They hadn't found the machine yet. Aniela had been able to keep her own room, as the building was large enough to house the soldiers comfortably. A Jewish family had lived in the adjoining building and initially Aniela had wondered why the soldiers hadn't been put in the empty house, but at breakfast she saw why. For a few extra złoty a week, the host family was expected to feed not just themselves but the soldiers as well. It was cheaper and easier for the Wehrmacht than feeding the troops or leaving them to fend for themselves, and the soldiers all expected Joanna to do their laundry as well. Aniela vowed to help when she returned from work, but the strain was already showing on her aunt's face.

Aniela had not slept much that first night. She could imagine the machine calling to the soldiers like a squalling child and all of them being pulled off to the Silesian House for questioning as spies by the Gestapo. She was afraid she'd forgotten to turn it off, so that it would suddenly receive a message and everyone would hear it. She was afraid to get up and check it, for fear one of the soldiers would come into her room just as she pulled it out.

She lay in her bed curled like a fetus, blankets pulled tight against her in the cold the way she did as a little girl when a nightmare would come. She faced the window, thinking about taking the machine out and throwing it onto the street below. But it was so heavy she did not think she could throw it far, it would lie on the street just outside her window, shattered from an obvious fall. Everyone would hear it. They would know.

Once, she got up and crept to the window in the night, even opened it slowly and stood there, ready to leap to her death. It was the only way to be safe, it would free her from this fear. She stood, hands white from clutching the window frame, and stared into the night. But if she died, they would search her room, they would find it. They would take her aunt and uncle away. It wasn't very far down anyway, she probably wouldn't die. There was no escape.

Squat and black it crouched in her cabinet, the machine of her death. It was cursed, it had killed Alexander and it would kill her too. Had he not died after he got the machine and used it? Now it would kill them all. The hours dragged by and Aniela prayed and prayed for peace or just to be set free. A miracle, to make it go away. Finally she fell asleep in the small hours of morning.

She looked at herself in the mirror of their small washroom. Her eyes were red and dark circles showed around them. How she'd aged since she had married Aleš, not so many years before. But that was good. She looked awful; perhaps the soldiers would not notice her so much. She pulled a strand of hair down awkwardly under her scarf to look even more bedraggled.

Abel looked up from his diary when Aniela stepped out of the washroom. Thinking of her bathing in the little tub quickened his heart. She was a bit skinny and clearly had seen better days, but it had been months since he'd held a woman and Aniela looked every bit her namesake to him. Especially now, with her big dark eyes and her hair hanging down, like a disconsolate mouse. Clearly she was frightened of him and the others in the squad, a fact that brought a smile to Abel's face. *We are German soldiers, the entire world fears us, and well it should*, he thought. *But I could make you smile, too, and cry out.*

*****

Peter Klein knew a promotion would be coming his way soon but until that time he had to rely on his interim position as Commander of the Krakow Order Police to give him leverage over the other SS Lieutenants in the working at Silesian House. As soon as word that Sturmberg had been murdered, a few of the Poles and even some German soldiers had tried to test the 10:00 PM Curfew that night, but swift and decisive action had dealt with them.

He felt no pressure to deal with the death of his predecessor. Sturmberg's murder was strange, but he had been told that a special group had been sent to investigate directly on the Fuhrer's orders, and he was glad to let them handle it. As long as it went away, he was content to forget about the death of the Sturmbergs.

After four years with the the German police in Berlin before the invasion of Poland, Klein considered himself a policeman first and an SS officer second. Frustrated by a disorderly and chaotic world, he saw it his place to create order. When Reinhard Heydrich had set up the Einsatzgruppe to oversee occupied territory, Klein had signed on, seeing an incredible opportunity.

But the organization was primarily SS rather than police in structure, and Klein had to sit and watch the sloppy, rule-bending Sturmberg placed over him. A favorite of Heydrich, Sturmberg was untouchable, even when he would ignore the rules, and all the reports and comments sent back to command would not dislodge him. When Heydrich was appointed head of Interpol in 1940, Klein had hoped it would create a kinship between him and the man, but Heydrich used it as an arm of the SS to find and destroy anti-Nazi dissidents and spies. Heydrich was now busy in Czechoslovakia and had simply ignored Peter Klein.

But with his new position, Klein had the power to organize the Blue Police into a proper force, and use the local city police as an auxiliary to create order in Krakow. The Gestapo was busy with their own work in the Silesian House, but they had regular meetings with the Order Police and other Security Service agencies. And Ewald Lange was the liason the Order Police most often dealt with.

Lange and Klein sat at a rough wooden table in a white-painted office without any windows. Smoke hung in the air and cigarette butts were piled in an ashtray by papers, photos, and folders lying open on the table. Klein's throat was raw from smoke and coffee, but he barely noticed it.

"Surely you had some idea this was taking place?" asked Lange, but his tone was not accusatory, rather one of amazement.

"I knew Sturmberg was willing to bend the rules when it suited him," Klein's voice was clipped and controlled, as always, "but not that he would go this far."

Lange shook his head and crushed out his cigarette. "I understand the use of informants and maintaining order in a city like this but I would have never guessed. To ignore a direct order from the Fuhrer to round up and send all known Gypsies, especially their leadership, to camps, I can barely conceive of the treachery. Was it bribery?"

"We still aren't sure exactly who the leader of this Gypsy clan is," said Klein, indicating photos on the table. "It must be one of these four men, but the files are not precise enough. Sturmberg probably kept the bulk of his intelligence on this in his mind."

"We cannot move on these men directly, they are all too connected politically and too well established as loyal to the Reich," warned Lange.

"I agree. I cannot rely on the Blue Police for this. Their membership seems riddled with traitors. Sturmberg had to send the previous Polish commander..." Klein thought a moment "Kozielewski to Auschwitz for assisting the AK."

"Ach don't talk to me of the Armia Krajowa, I hear of them all day from my superiors, the 'underground' seem everywhere. But I thought the Blue Police were helping with regular collection of Jews?"

"They assist with rounding up the Jews, but will not kill them. They ignored a direct order and we had to have SS troops disable a group. The Poles stood and wept. I would have had them all executed, but Sturmberg refused. He may have been right there, though. We don't have enough men as it is, and every new recruit seems more likely to be a member of AK."

Ewald Lange leaned over the photos, arranging them in front of him. "Very well, we shall have to look into these men. But we must be subtle about it; these are all powerful businessmen and if they knew we were looking into them, they could bring uncomfortable pressure on us."

"Yes, well. Even worse, they could close up their operations and ruin any chance of catching their people." Klein looked up at Lange. "I have a few men I can trust, and I expect you do as well. We shall take two of these men at a time, and look into their true allegiances...subtly as you say."

Lange nodded. "I shall report to Obersturmbannführer Arlt about this. It is a pleasure to work with so professional and cooperative a commandant for a change."

Klein allowed himself a small, thin smile. It was good to finally be recognized.

Ritter, Czerny, Stoffel stood smoking on Jozef Pilsudski Bridge above the Vistula River. Built just over a decade earlier, the steel span had tracks for a street car but none had yet run across it. Cezar was disappointed about the location, but hoped it would serve.

"And what tale do you have for us of this location?" asked Stoffel.

"A suicide by a princess." Czerny replied.

Ritter gazed curiously at the Romanian. "That's it? Surely there is more of a tale than that."

"A sad one." Czerny started, reluctantly. "Long ago, Krakus was a great king. He founded Krakow and according to legend slew the dragon Smok Wawelski that lived in a cave under Wawel Castle. Krakus ruled the region for many years, apparently good years; there are many tales about him. When he died, he left only his daughter Princess Wanda behind, and she became queen. Wanda had the apparent misfortune of being very lovely and Krakow was a wealthy city by this point. So she drew the attention of an unnamed Germanic prince who demanded her hand in marriage."

Stoffel leaned on his forearms against the old railing and watched the river slide beneath him. It was wide and placid at this point, running from the Carpathian Mountains through Kakow and north to the ocean.

Ritter lit a cigarette and waited. He was in a better mood after a good lunch, and especially after Stoffel had apparently abandoned any argument with the Romanian. There was no point debating with the lesser races, they would soon enough be pushed aside for Aryan dominance. It was a matter of time; one could humor the less evolved like pets but it was fruitless to engage them any deeper. This one was a useful servant, not an academic to debate with. But the story about the alchemist and the giant rooster had amused him, reminding him of the tales he read his son Helmut when he was young.

"Wanda refused, wishing to find her own love," continued Czerny, "but the prince was not to be denied. Perhaps he'd always intended to invade and was only seeking an excuse."

He began to unpack his various odd implements on the brick paving of the bridge. Soldiers had blocked off the bridge on either end at Ritter's command. "The armies of the Germans reached Krakow and Princess Wanda met them not far from here, on an older bridge. She again refused to wed the prince, and knew that even should her people win this battle, her beauty and the riches of Krakow would mean an endless parade of suitors. Her people would never know peace while she was alive. In full sight of the city and the German armies, Princess Wanda leapt from the bridge to the waters of the Vistula. Her heavy clothing and jewelry quickly pulled her under and here she drowned.

Queen Wanda was buried..." he looked up and pointed into the distance "near the airport, under Wanda Mound, supposedly."

"Doesn't sound like much of an event," said Stoffel, flicking his cigarette into the river.

"Not in the great scheme of things, perhaps, although it is a sad tale. The German prince went back home, although they probably looted what they could, as armies often did back then. But it was a profound event for the people of Krakow and a self sacrifice that is of notable import."

"Could she have not found a suitable Pole to marry?" Asked Ritter.

"Perhaps," Czerny replied, without looking up. "Although some versions of the legend claim she was remaining chaste out of piety. Being married would not have necessarily stopped the claims to her hand in those days, in any case."

"Suicide to stop an advancing German army; I cannot help but think of Mayor Klimecki, riding out offering himself hostage to the Wehrmacht to save Krakow." Said Stoffel. "Perhaps it's in the Polish blood, the remnants of the nobility of the long forgotten Teutonic Knights."

"There is another version of the tale some tell," Said Czerny. "In that legend, Princess Wanda meets the German prince in the field of battle, and he is so overcome with her beauty and grace he kills himself instead."

"Ha! Sounds more French to me than German," scoffed Major Ritter.

Vladimir Czerny focused on his work. He had at first been worried at the location, since the bridge Princess Wanda had killed herself at was actually further down river, an old wooden structure called the Piedmont that had been destroyed long ago. This new bridge named after a recent dictator had been built when the old stone replacement had grown unstable and dangerous.

But unlike the old Rome Tavern, the iron bridge was rich with energy, as if it were regularly renewed. Perhaps young women came here to seek the guidance of Wanda's memory in their love lives. Maybe it was simply the way the people of Krakow held her in such high regard, but of all the versions of the tale, he knew that the river was the place where she had died. The supernatural ripples from that act of self-sacrifice for the sake of her people were still profound in the area. It would serve as a harness on the energy and spirit of the people of Krakow to find the outsider, the monster in their midst.

Czerny looked through the lens of a device at the river's smooth surface as it passed beneath the old bridge. Who would save them from the Germans this time?

CHAPTER SEVENTEEN

Rys Radescu put the phone back on its cradle and leaned back in his favorite chair by the fire. Lighting a cigarette fitted into a filter, he watched the flames leap and dance. His mind whirled and he barely heard the music playing behind him on the radio as he concentrated.

The game with the German telegraph had wrapped up with quite a lucrative haul. In fact, it was nearly as much as the amount tricked out of former Gestapo chief Bruno Müller's gullible wife Lette by Madame Dayana and her crystal ball. It had been incredibly risky, but all good games were. It helped that Lette didn't care for her husband's constant and blatant affairs with any woman he could reach.

But this telegraph scam had been brilliant, Rys admitted. Putting one of their number as the chief operator in Krakow to get information on wire shipments of cash and trimming off the amounts to whole numbers was a very small amount, but redirecting it to the Romani accounts in Switzerland had added up very rapidly.

It would have still been in place, had it not been for the other news. Rys frowned. Sturmburg had been a useful man, for a *gadjo*. Their arrangement had kept the clan from being targeted by the Germans, and it had kept the city safer to travel in and live in. Rys was frustrated by how he wasn't able to protect all his people, but there were far more that were safe and out of the camps than there would have been without his deal with the devil.

And now Sturmburg was dead. The reports had been very limited, which didn't surprise Rys. Probably the resistance, they'd managed to kill a few Gestapo and other German leaders in Poland already, and the Germans weren't fond of anyone learning about that. But he'd died so suddenly and Rys was concerned.

What had he written down? What had he told others and kept to himself? Surely not everyone in the Order Police would go along with this plan to use the Romani for inside information on smuggling and crime. It was too early to think about moving again, but perhaps it was time to start getting ready.

Rys looked up at the map above the mantelpiece, an ancient map of the known world from the 16th century. Originally he'd planned a move into the Ukraine, but the Germans had turned on their Soviet friends in 1941 and invaded that country. To the south it was no better, but at least the area was rugged enough and the people familiar enough that the Romani could blend in and hide. For as long as they had been a people, survival had required blending in and surviving, hiding in the lands they traveled through.

It was getting harder and harder to move around and seek shelter in the rural areas, though. There still were those who were friendly to the Romani, but in this new German world, he wasn't sure where they could be safe.

So far, the Germans had no official, systematic policy regarding the Romani as far as Rys knew of. They were certainly targeted and Germans despised his people as much as most Europeans, but they seemed to hate Jews even more. *Where had this all come from?* Rys wondered. *Was that darkness in all our hearts waiting to come out with the right circumstances?* He shook his head.

"Uncle Rys, what is wrong?" It was his hulking German guard Peter.

"Ah, Peter, it's just been a long day. How are your feet?"

Peter Fleischer crouched by the chair, still taller than Rys seated next to him. "Ach, these boots are no help. What can you do? I have such large feet, and they don't make the boots in my size, so they say."

Rys suppressed a grin. Another game, he knew, by another clan in Germany. In charge of one of the factories supplying the German army, they made all the boots very slightly too small. There was no money in this game; it was just a little joke on the Germans, but who knew what difference it might make in the war?

"Perhaps you should sit a while?"

Peter shook his head and stood. He took his job of protecting Rys Radescu very seriously. Crossing the room he turned over the record and started it playing again.

Rys watched the fire burn lower, and hoped he was wise enough to save his people.

*****

Major Ritter and Doctor Stoffel watched Czerny collect the devices not left at the site into his bag and prepared to move on. Closing off the Jozef Pilsudski was going to annoy at lot of people, but if it worked, Ritter was willing to give it a day. It was already late afternoon and both men were getting impatient with the slow progress.

The little Romanian claimed it would take a day to find the escaped Gypsy even after he had it all set up, and he still had two areas to visit.

A German soldier on a motorcycle was allowed through the barricade on the west end of the bridge and headed toward Ritter, who unsnapped the holster over his Luger. The soldiers guarding Czerny's devices on the bridge aimed their weapons at the motorcycle, but it pulled up short and the rider stepped off, holding a messenger's satchel.

"Sturmbannführer Ritter?"

Ritter saluted so the young man would stop doing so. "Yes, what is it?"

The messenger rummaged through his satchel and pulled out an envelope. "For you sir, from the Governor-General."

As soon as Ritter had taken it, the young man climbed on his motorcycle and sped away. Runners didn't wait for dismissal; their work was so critical they could ignore most protocol and many rules.

Ritter looked at the envelope. It looked genuine enough, but what would the Governor-General of the Occupied Polish Territories want with him? Stoffel inside the car sighed impatiently and the Romanian stood quietly without expression, waiting.

Inside the envelope was a simple card, inviting him and the doctor to dinner at Wawel Castle in two hours. Ritter grit his teeth and scowled at the city over the edge of the card. Wawel Castle stood over the river on a hill, a gray and red structure surrounded by trees, it was visible from the bridge. Two hours was not much warning for a formal dinner, and he was busy doing his duty.

For a moment, Ritter considered pretending he'd not gotten the message in time, but a request from Governor-General Hans Frank, friend and personal lawyer of the Fuhrer was not truly a request at all. And Ritter decided he could use a break from the mysticism of the Romanian.

"Professor Doctor, would you care to join me at the Castle for a dinner?"

Stoffel scooted along the bench seat and looked upward out of the car, expecting mockery. He blinked in confusion. "Of — of course, it would be an honor!"

Ritter nodded. "Very well, we shall need to prepare and dress for the occasion. Sturmscharführer Franz, take command of the project. You will need to escort the Romanian to the University and then the Church. Leave guards at each location to protect the work until they are relieved. Once his work is done, return the Romanian to my quarters. Understood?"

"Yes, Sturmbannführer!" The Sergeant-Major barked in reply with a quick salute and snap of the heels.

Ritter stepped into the Mercedes and slammed the door as it sped off. Czerny waited quietly as the sergeant turned and gave orders to his men. Sergeant-Major Franz liked Vladimir Czerny. The Romanian hadn't even flinched at first seeing his face, and the stories he told fascinated the soldier. Unable to advance in the Wehrmacht because of his hideous injuries, he was only allowed to remain in his position because of his iron will and great combat experience. He filled his little free time with a study of mythology and legends, and he knew little Polish history.

Franz sat with Czerny in the front seat of the Steyr Infantry Carrier, the top down and cold in the late afternoon. The sergeant preferred to drive, leaving eight men crammed into room for six in the back, two of them sitting on the backs of the rearmost seats as they bounced down the road. He drove more carefully than the orderly had in the Mercedes for Major Ritter, aware he was responsible for the vehicle's condition. Winding through the streets of Krakow, Franz wanted to talk to Czerny but knew it would be difficult with the engine noise and the wind, even though the man spoke perfect German with a slight Bavarian accent.

The truck pulled up in front of Jagiellonian University, one of Poland's oldest and most prestigious centers of higher learning. Once home to some of the finest minds in Europe, the university had fallen on hard times during the occupation.

When the Germans conquered Poland, the University had been assured it would continue operations, the Nazis claiming that education was very important to them. However in November, Lt Colonel Bruno Müller, Gestapo chief in Krakow at the time, issued an order to University rector Professor Tadeusz Lehr-Spławiński: all professors to attend a lecture about German plans for Polish education. The lecture never took place. Vladimir Czerny had been in Georgia at the time and only heard rumors and news reports about the seizure of the professors and several students and their incarceration in Sachsenhausen concentration camp. Eventually international pressure, including some from Mussolini himself had led to the older professors being released, but the rest were still in prison.

Now the University had been closed, and it lay quiet and empty after nearly six hundred years of operation. And it was to this place that Czerny came, for something far older than the University.

Krakow was in an area with many caves, pockets formed over the millennia in the rock of the hills and nearby mountains to the south. These caves featured significantly in many Polish legends. Caves filled with statues of soldiers who never came to life to save their country from the German invaders. Caves with dragons in them, caves with amazing treasures, caves that only opened once a year, and even caves where witches and wizards lived all featured in myths and fairy tales of the region.

And one cave under the university was of particular interest to Vladimir Czerny. It was likely few of the people there even knew it existed any longer, but Czerny knew.

"We will need to find a man named Adrian Byrk. He is a custodian at this institution, and he will know where we are headed if anyone does."

Sergeant Franz turned and issued orders to his men and they hopped down out of the truck and accompanied the Romanian through the gates. They were met by Jens Hauptmann of the Order Police who had been ordered to wait here earlier in the day.

"At last, I expected you hours ago!" Hauptman barked, then spotted the Master-Sergeant's face and paled, eyes widening.

"We are looking for a custodian, a groundskeeper by the name of..." Franz looked back at Czerny with a raised eyebrow, ignoring the policeman's reaction.

"Adrian Byrk."

"Yes, Byrk. You know of him?"

Hauptmann whistled for one of his men lounging on the broad stone steps of an old brick building.

"Yes my captain?" The young officer grinned. Hauptmann wasn't a captain in the force, but his last name translated as the word and the men tended to call him by it anyway.

"Where is the custodial staff today?"

"Last patrol we saw them working near ah" the officer consulted his notepad "Collegium Maius."

"Show these men to the location and get Adrian Byrk to talk to them."

"Byrk. Yes, my Captain."

"So, Herr Czerny, what tale do you have for us now?" Sergeant Franz asked.

Vladimir Czerny hesitated a moment, unused to his name being pronounced properly by a German.

"Like most nations, Poland has had its share of national heroes in legend. One of the most prominent was a scoundrel by the name of Juro Janosik. This fellow was a robber who would steal from the wealthy and burn their homes, then give the goods to the local poor, so it is said. "

"Like Robin Hood from England," said Sergeant Franz.

"Much the same, and likely in a similar time period, although some trace his origin to a highwayman in the 17th century named Juraj Jánošík from Hungary. The real Jansoik was from an earlier time according to my studies, and although the stories spread throughout the region south to as far as Romania, he was from this very city."

Crossing a well-tended green, the group found a trio of groundskeepers in humble clothing sitting on the grass eating cold meat and bread.

"Is one of you named Adrian Byrk?" the police officer asked.

Two of the three men recognized the name and looked at the eldest, a white haired man bent with age.

"I am he," replied the man, in accented German.

"Come with us. The rest of you get back to work," ordered the officer, kicking the food out of the hand of the nearest groundskeeper.

"We will take it from here," Franz directed the officer.

Adrian Byrk stood slowly and unevenly and walked behind the police officer to the porch of the Collegium Maius. Its brick walls and red roof were of the same construction and style as the Rome Tavern, complete with the raised balcony on the second floor.

"Mr Byrk, thank you for your assistance. I must ask you a question. This is the oldest college on the campus of Jagiellonian University, is it not?" Czerny asked.

"Yes, sir" replied Byrk, head down in deference. Or perhaps it was fear, Franz could not be sure.

"And you have been working here for quite a while, have you not?"

"Yes sir, for fifty years this August. Such a shame to see it so quiet this time of year." Byrk darted a look up at the soldiers, suddenly regretting his implied criticism of the Germans, but other than the sergeant, they were not paying much attention. The horrible-looking sergeant seemed almost sympathetic, but Adrian thought it could have just been how his scars made his face look.

"So you would know every inch of this campus then, all of its secrets and chambers, then." Czerny continued in German. It was awkward for the old caretaker, but he knew the Germans would not appreciate a conversation in Polish.

"I suppose so, sir."

"There is a certain place, under this building, a place not visited often. It is a cave, covered up by the college. You know of this place?"

Adrian Byrk was quiet a moment. "I suppose so," he admitted. The area had been closed off years ago, but it was once a place where some of the students once had snuck off to, and indeed a few of the faculty.

The old man led them down several flights of old stairs into the building, to a cellar filled with quiet boilers and furnaces. Against one wall was a set of shelves stacked with boxes, and Byrk indicated that there was an old door behind them. Sergeant Franz ordered the soldiers with him to empty the shelves and with the usual grumbling they set to work.

Czerny concentrated as he watched them work, focusing on the rest of the world around him. Slight spirits moved at the edges, but there was nothing special about the area.

"So what happened to this Janosic fellow?" asked Franz.

Byrk looked up slightly, recognizing the name.

"Many times the authorities tried to capture Janosic," said Czerny, "but he always eluded them, or easily escaped their traps. He was said to have three magical items given him by witches that would let him elude any sort of prison.

"The first was a belt that allowed him to move between places instantly. The second was a shirt which would protect him from any weapon, even bullets. And the third was an alpenstock which let him tunnel through solid rock. And if these treasures were not enough, he knew of an herb which could heal him from any injury. Clearly, all the king's men were outmatched by this bandit."

"Yes, I can see how that might make him difficult to capture," said Franz with a grin.

"I think I saw this movie, a few years back," said one of the soldiers as they finished stacking boxes. "It was some Czech movie with subtitles."

"You see too many foreign movies, Karl, you should watch something by Riefenstahl," said another. The soldiers continued talking quietly as they slid the shelf away from the wall. The exposed area was covered in plaster and stained with water that had run down it from above.

"Behind this, it was covered up in oh... '97 I think it was," Byrk said.

The soldiers began breaking the plaster away with their gun butts and eventually a doorway was revealed in the white dusty cloud.

"Check your weapons, see they are unharmed," ordered Sergeant Major Franz, and the men grumbled as they examined their rifles.

The door was plain wood, and it was nailed shut.

"Why is this so carefully covered up?" asked Franz.

Byrk shrugged. Franz Turned on Czerny. "Is there something about this tale we need to know?"

"Nothing dangerous. I wouldn't be surprised to find there are other legends about the cave, unrelated to Janosik." *And given what happened, it wouldn't be surprising if supernatural events took place in this area,* Czerny thought.

The door was forced open, revealing a rough passage leading downward with uneven, natural-appearing steps. Byrk picked up a heavy flashlight attached to a large square battery and turned it on. The yellowish light did not penetrate far into the depths. One of the soldiers pulled out a military-issue Daimon flashlight and turned it on. With the hood up on its square face, the more modern light reached further than the older one Byrk held.

Czerny led the way, followed by Byrk with his light held high. "Janosik seemed impossible to defeat, but the King had a clever advisor named Andre Mrozcka who set a trap for Janosik that even he could not escape."

"A girl," guessed Karl.

"Indeed. A girl named Anichka who caught Janosik's eye. A lovely peasant girl, she was promised a great deal of money if she could get the bandit's magical items away from him and destroy them. She brought him here, away from her father's watchful eye, and here she worked her feminine wiles on Janosik. While he was sleeping, she took his shirt, belt, and alpenstock away, and burned them," Czerny's voice became quieter in the echo, "in this cave."

The cave was small, but it clearly had been opened out and cleared by tools over the centuries. A small raised area in the rock near the wall opposite the entry was littered with dried flowers and other uncertain items that had withered over the years. On the walls were scrawled pictures in crude simple designs of women and men engaged in various sexual acts. A few of the soldiers chuckled and murmured together.

"And the police grabbed him then?" asked Franz.

"They tried, but even without his magical items, he eluded them. He was chased for weeks but finally was captured when an old woman supposedly threw peas at his feet in Slovakia, causing him to slip and fall. Janosik was tried and executed by hanging him from a hook thrust into his side."

"That's no way to die," said one of the soldiers.

"He was only a Pole," said another, and shrugged.

Vladimir Czerny began the ritual, carefully drawing in chalk on the cave floor, which was largely smooth and flat. The lights bent through his small lenses cast strange shapes on the walls and the shadows seemed to move slightly. The energy from those witch-crafted items still clung to the cave, as did significant erotic energy. *More than a few young couples must have come to this cave over the years,* Czerny mused. He doubted many were aware Janosik had been at the location. All of that power was the final key to finding the lycanthrope. It would shape the ritual to focus its energy on locating him and tracking him, hopefully.

Czerny had never actually attempted this before, something he did not care to explain to Major Ritter. He knew how it could be done, in theory, and had studied extensively on the subject, but had rarely attempted any such ritual in the past. He hesitated to call it magic, as it was not a spell as such. It was more an attempt to tap into supernatural energy of certain charged areas to seek a supernatural being. He had seen it done in Liverpool to find a ghost, many years before, but he was certain it would function for any specific creature.

"Tell me something," said sergeant Franz, and Czerny looked up. "How do you know all of this, Romanian?"

Czerny bent back to his work. "I have spent my whole life studying these tales and traveling."

"Yes, but this cave, buried under the university. The placque outside said this college had been built in the fourteenth century."

"Yes, under Casimir III. The first construction started in 1364."

"Yet you knew where it was."

"I knew where it was said to be," Czerny said. "Legends and myths always have some basis in reality, however slender the connection. All signs pointed to this location."

"And the other locations, the same thing? Legends you've researched?"

"Yes. I have been studying this a long time. I'm older than I look."

Master Sergeant Franz looked down at the small man's leather trilby covering his odd tattoos. He tried to guess how old Czerny was, but it was difficult. Younger than fifty, surely. He sat down against the cave wall to wait. The last two of these rituals had taken several hours to complete.

*****

The door to her home had a flag over it now, Aniela saw. Apparently the Germans had marked it, or one had insisted on the red, white, and black jagged cross being hung. She took a deep breath with her eyes closed and then stepped in, but there was no sign of the soldiers.

"Aniela, oh good you are home, hurry and change and help me with dinner, girl!" called aunt Joanna from the kitchen, looking around the doorway to the dining room.

"yes Aunt," Aniela said, hanging her hat and scarf by the door. "What happened to our... guests?"

Aniela crossed the room and leaned against the doorway to watch her aunt rolling out dough on the table.

Joanna Sawiki brushed her hands against her apron, smearing flour across the blue checked cloth. "Apparently they're all out on some mission or another. Some horrible looking ugly sergeant came in and yelled at them all in German and they dropped breakfast to run out not long after you left for work."

"When will they be back?"

"Who knows? That's why I need your help, to cook enough dinner in case they are back in time. They'll all want something to eat, boys at that age always do." Joanna said. "The one that speaks some Polish, he said they were hunting down some kind of gypsy that escaped from prison and he wasn't sure when they would be back."

Aniela's eyes widened and she ducked her head to stare at the floor so her aunt would not see her shock. *An escaped gypsy? In Krakow?*

Cezar?

Aniela rushed up the stairs and ran to her room, closing the door. She leaned against the wood and stared at her room, eyes focused at a point beyond the wall, thinking. Cezar was being hunted in the city, she was sure of it. He was all alone with the entire German army hunting for him, how could he escape? How could she help him?

The machine. She stared at the dresser. One last message to the British, and then she could dispose of it. She could work the door to the apartments next door open and hide it under rubble, nobody would look there. It would be out of her house. *Wipe it down and blow some dust into the hidden compartment of the dresser, then it's gone and out of the house.*

But first, one final message. The British always wanted her help, this time they could help her instead. Hands shaking, she opened up the cupboard and pulled the machine forward. Her back prickled with fear, even worse this time than usual. She listened so hard for footsteps in the hall her ears began to ring.

Typing as quickly as she could, she sent a message:

Escapee desired is eluding German hunters in city, is alone.

Shutting the machine's cover, she took a deep, shaky breath. Her hands were trembling so hard she wrung them together to try to control it. Peeling the pillowcase off, she set her pillow aside and worked the machine into it. She quickly gathered her laundry up into her arms and bundled it together with the machine. Stepping out in to the hall she felt the fear starting to drain out of her with each step she took the thing away from her room. Crossing the hall she reached the door at the other end that led to the adjacent building. Long closed and rarely ever opened, it was locked on her side with an old sliding bolt.

The front door opened then. Loud German voices rang below her as the soldiers returned, joking among each other. Aniela turned and flattened against the door, frozen in terror. She couldn't go into the other home, the door might make a lot of noise just opening. And then what if they saw her coming out or caught her in there? They would search, they would find the machine. She shook in place, unable to take a step. A quiet sound like a high pitched sigh slipped out of her lips and finally she was able to take a single step forward. Then another, as if she was so cold her limbs would not respond properly. The hallway stretched ahead of her, seeming longer than ever. She had to get back to her room. There were steps on the stairs now, boots creaking on the wood.

There was a legendary creature the Polish mothers told tales of to their children called the dusiołek. A nasty little goblin-like creature, it would come to people while they slept and sat on their chest, causing shortness of breath and nightmares, even strangulation. Aniela felt the dusiołek on her now.

When the first German reached the hallway, she was halfway back to her room. Tears formed in her eyes, and she ducked her head again, trying to ignore the men and move past them.

"Hey there, angel. Such a load of laundry! Here, let Jodl carry it, eh?" said Abel. He turned and said something about Jodl to the men with him and one shook his head and said something back.

"Jodl doesn't carry anything heavier than his hat tonight. Maybe I help you?"

Aniela pushed past and half of the laundry bushed loose onto the floor against Abel.

"Stop!" Abel commanded.

Aniela's teeth chattered slightly. The blocky square shape of the machine was visible half covered in laundry now, pushing against the pillowcase as if it wanted to be seen. *So stupid,* Aniela thought bitterly. *Why did I take the time to send that last message? What did I think the British would do about it? I could have had it buried and gone by now.*

"Here now, you dropped... well now."

Abel held up a pair of underpants, blue with lace at the top. One of the Germans said something and sniffed loudly. They chuckled with a feral tone.

"Well you want these back, eh?" Abel collected the rest of the clothes and piled them onto Aniela's bundle. "Careful now, angel. You can't trust these others but I'll never hurt you." He turned to go to the room he shared with one of the men. Turning at the door he winked at Aniela as she reached her room.

"Unless you want me to."

*****

Wawel Castle stood on a limestone outcrop overlooking the Vistula river. Like most of Krakow, it was reddish in color, but parts of the building had been first constructed in the ninth century. Although the centuries of additional construction and rebuilding had left the castle with several different architectural styles, it had retained its squat wide towers and outer wall long past the era of siege warfare. On the drive up, Major Ritter thought about how useless the walls were in a time of air combat, and was reminded of the Manginot line the French had built to stop invasion.

Inside, the castle was not as lush and gilded as some Ritter had seen, but it clearly was a wealthy center of government. Nazi flags hung from the walls like medieval tapestries but they did nothing to reduce the chill in the stone building. The ceiling of the dining room was made up of smaller squares, each gilded at the edges and painted with various religious images. The huge dark wooden table was piled with fineries and wines, and Hans Frank was a talkative and cheerful host.

"I see you have closed cultural institutions in the city; museums and such." said Dr Stoffel while they waited for the next course to arrive at the table.

"Naturally. This not only will serve to reduce national fervor and resistance in the future, but it is part of the elimination of lesser cultures. For the New Man to arise, the debris of the past, of failed, corrupt nations must be swept aside.

"I have spoken to the Fuhrer about this on several occasions. The Polish culture and people have no place in the future we are

108

building for humanity. I estimate that we should have all remnants of Polish culture and history eliminated by," Frank gestured with his knife, "1975. I have already issued orders to all schools to begin this process. The sole goal of this schooling is to teach them simple arithmetic, nothing above the number 500; writing one's name; and the doctrine that it is divine law to obey the Germans. I do not think that reading among Poles is desirable."

"And yet, I note that you have permitted the tradition of that trumpet song played from the basilica." said Ritter.

"Yes, I had a Gestapo officer just today in the church researching the tradition for me. It is my belief that this tradition dates from a pre-Polish era, to the proto-German aryans, and as such is not a part of Polish ethnic identity. In time, with the proper education, later generations will see it as such."

Konrad Stoffel stared at his food as he ate. Like many Germans, he admired the Polish culture and its people. Had they not been part of the Teutonic Knights in medieval history? Germans and Poles shared much of the same culture and heritage as well as a border. Governor Frank paused as the servants placed roast pheasant and truffles on the table. When they left, he continued.

"I see the Poles as useful workers for the Germans who settle the Wartheland, and here in the General Government."

"I understand Herr Himmler is relocating select Polish children in good German families, though." Stoffel finally said.

"Yes, perhaps. A few sufficiently Aryan children could be found in the population from the Danzig territory. But they will be raised as proper Germans." Frank shrugged. "In any case, to have a truly clean German empire, the Poles must be a people without a national identity, culture, religion, leadership, or education."

"This walled ghetto to the south, is this part of the plan?" Asked Ritter.

Frank frowned slightly, setting his wine down. "That is a different issue. The Jewish population of Krakow and the surrounding area is held in the ghetto. It was simply most efficient to gather them all in one place in the city, for later disposal.

"As we all know, a great Jewish migration was due to take place in the German empire. What should the Reich do with the Jews? They are a genetic blight and a cultural rot. Do you think they could be settled in Russia, in villages? I was told in Berlin, 'Why all this bother? We can do nothing with them either in Ostland or in the Reichskommissariat. So liquidate them yourselves.' And since the drive into Russia has slowed, I have gathered and segregated Jews into the ghetto. Once they have all been isolated, well... gentlemen, I must ask you to rid yourself of all feelings of pity. We must annihilate the Jews wherever we find them and whenever it is possible."

Stoffel moved the food around on his plate. He didn't feel much like eating.

"I have heard rumors that the locals are hiding out Jews still," offered Ritter, pouring himself another glass of wine.

"Unfortunately they seem to hold foolish sympathies for a dead race. We will find them all soon. With the new commander of the Order Police I expect the process to move more swiftly. I was never fond of Sturmburg but he had powerful allies."

"Politics. It continually gets in the way of carrying out the Fuhrer's wishes. I could tell you tales of delays and excuses you would scarcely credit." Ritter said with a scowl. The invasion of France had taken months to begin, with continuous resistance from Generals. It was true that ammunition was low and repairs were needed after defeating the Poles but France was unready and fearful. Thankfully even after the delays it had only taken two weeks to roll over France like a thunderstorm. Poland had put up almost a month's fight.

"It's not only politics," Frank said, rubbing his mouth with a napkin. "The clergy oppose me continuously. I have long despised the church and seen it as a hindrance to progress. Once the Jews are out of the way, perhaps I will have more time to deal with the Catholics here. I have already managed to send most of the troublesome and vocal members to Dachau."

"Religion is a corrosion of the third way," Stoffel agreed. Here he was on more comfortable ground. "Science has replaced god. We need no myths of Genesis, we have evolution. We need no schemes of sin and guilt, we have Freud. We need no savior; we have humanity's potential which the Fuhrer is unlocking. I understand the need to use religion to sway the masses but we have evolved past the need of deities."

"Have you read the writings of Friedrich Nietzsche?" Frank asked.

Stoffel nodded, his mouth full of buttered roll. He chewed quickly, trying to respond, but Frank went on. "By disposing of these myths and weak nonsense, the Fuhrer has become Nietzsche's superman. He sees that life only has the meaning we impose upon it, that there is no right and wrong, no truth or falsehood, only strength and will. The days of calling all to follow some bearded Hebrew in the sky and his alleged commandments are over.

"We now know as a modern, scientific people that right and wrong is what we choose, not what we are ordered to follow. And we know that as some are less evolved than the aryan race, then the path to the future is brought about by the cleansing of these corrupt and lesser races from the gene pool."

Ritter ate quietly. He had tried to keep up on the conversation but it had gone into uncomfortably vague and philosophical areas. He preferred hard reality and warfare, the rifle and the certainty of an enemy, not dreams and ideas.

Frank rapped out a rythm on the table with a finger as if to emphsize his speech. "I will have the cleanest area in Germany once my work here is done. Nothing to impede the progress of true humanity."

Stoffel tapped the table with his fork in agitation. Hitler's *Mein Kampf* had not so much been a revelation for him as the condensation of many of his thoughts into a coherent system. The true genius of fascism, as he saw it, was the blending of the best ideas from the communist left and the conservative right into a third way. Taking the respect for tradition and the heritage of Germany along with a love of military from the old and the economic systems of the new socialism and tying them together into a bundle would create a new path for humanity.

Providing government schools for youths to replace the superstition and religious nonsense of their parents would forge a new generation to lead the future. Controlling the production and regulating business to shut out wasted foolish old ideas was only proper. Good, scientific, proven methods could be imposed on businesses who did not care to wake up to the future, while stronger, more Germanic businesses such as I.G. Farben were encouraged to lead the way.

To make this all work, a strong central leader with a will of iron had to be given absolute power. The clear results would be order and a prosperous, strong future for humanity, guided by proper principles and scientific clarity. Of all this, Konrad Stoffel was sure.

But this business of racial cleansing, this Stoffel was deeply uncomfortable with. It was true he believed that the Fuhrer made good arguments for the weakness of the Jewish culture but Stoffel was unconvinced this was some innate genetic flaw of their ethnic stock. Under the skin, under the microscope, humanity was remarkably identical. What drove this hatred of races? He knew an undercurrent of resentment and dislike of Jews had always been in Germany, but to see it explode to these levels confused Stoffel. Where had it come from? Had such men always been among them, and given power had emphasized such hate?

"So Governor, do you miss your work as a lawyer?" Ritter asked in the lull, hoping to steer the conversation into less airy territory.

Frank shook his head, chewing a slice of pheasant. Swallowing hard he said "I did enjoy the courtroom work, especially when I defended Richard Scheringer, Hans Friedrich Wendt and Hanns Ludin in 1930; we made history. But now I am in a greater legal position, a sort of judge for the whole region, without any lawyers to make appeals or slow the process.

"The way I see it, a judge's role is to safeguard the concrete order of the racial community, to eliminate dangerous elements, to prosecute all acts harmful to the community, and to arbitrate in disagreements between members of the community. The National

Socialist ideology, especially as expressed in the Party program and in the speeches of our Fuhrer, is the basis for interpreting legal sources. And as the governor-general of this region, I can do just that... but without the restrictions a judge ordinarily faces."

A young, pretty girl entered the dining area, dressed in a short skirt and blouse that emphasized her generous breasts. She flashed Major Ritter a bold glance with her large blue eyes and then leaned to whisper something to Hans Frank. With another glance at Ritter, she turned and left, emphasizing her hips with a walk that swished her skirt back and forth.

"And I have been awaiting this all evening. Gentlemen, I asked you here not only for a fine meal and pleasant discussion, but I have the honor to welcome Reichsführer-SS, Chief of the German police, Reich Commissar for the Consolidation of the Ethnic German Nation, Reich Minister of the Interior and Commander of the Reserve Army... Heinrich Himmler."

And with that, Himmler entered the room, wearing the black uniform of the SS. All three men stood and saluted Hitler, as Himmler saluted back. When all had seated again, Frank spoke again.

"I was not sure when you would be able to arrive, but I had hoped it would be in time for dinner. Please, Reichsfürher, have something to eat, I am sure your trip has left you famished."

Himmler nodded. "I am quite hungry yes. And thank you for your hospitality. So. You have met, Herr Doktor and Sturmbannführer, hm?"

Stoffel and Ritter looked at each other across the table. Stoffel nodded slightly.

"Yes, Reichsfürher, yesterday evening Professor Stoffel introduced himself to me," said Ritter.

"Did he? Hm." Himmler stared at Stoffel a moment with his cold blue eyes. Then he nodded. "Please call me Heinrich, over dinner at least. Good, good. It was inevitable that you two should meet."

Hans Frank looked back and forth across the table. Stoffel sat on his left and Himmler on his right beside Ritter. He was confused and uncertain, there seemed to be a sort of tension. "Of course I was unaware of all this, ah, Heinrich. I do hope there is no trouble for my guests?"

Himmler looked up. He shook his head, chewing on roast beef.

"We discussed the situation over dinner two days ago, in fact." Ritter said.

"Well then we can discuss it further over dinner tonight," replied Himmler.

"I am... not sure what you are referring to, should I be aware of anything happening in my city?" Frank asked.

"It is a strange matter, one which has caught the attention of high command in Berlin," said Himmler. "This is quite excellent, I'm surprised you can find such quality food here."

"I have my contacts," said Frank with a grin. "It would not do to offer such an important guest anything but the best."

Himmler suspected that Frank always had the best; his rapacious greed was known all the way in the heart of Germany. But he was not inclined to criticize the friend and personal legal advisor of Adolph Hitler. Indeed, what was the point of power if not to benefit one's self? He turned to Ritter. "Have you had any success finding this... fugitive?"

"We tracked him from the camp to this city. He is somewhere inside, and I have squads searching for him. Herr Bormann assigned a strange little Romanian to my task and he has proved useful, if unorthodox."

Stoffel contemplated taking this opportunity to criticize the Romanian and his bizarre methods but he could sense a military kinship between Ritter and the smaller, slender Himmler. And it would not do to go against Bormann, a man of such power and sway over the Fuhrer.

"And you, Professor Doktor, what have you been able to accomplish?" Himmler asked.

"At a visit to the camp I was able to collect samples of the... fugitive... and have analyzed them. I have sent my results to your office but if you wish a summary?"

Himmler shook his head again. It would make little sense to him anyway, he guessed. "No, I shall read them later. What do you plan to do should you capture this creature?"

Hans Frank felt increasingly uncomfortable and excluded. His dinner party was becoming less a celebration of his power and wealth and more a meeting of people who knew and discussed things he had no understanding of. *What creature?* He wondered. *What is going on in my city?*

"I am developing an idea," said Stoffel quietly, "but it is contingent on the nature of the, ah, fugitive, and what the soldiers are able to do."

"I assure you we will be able to deal with whatever this gypsy thing is, professor," said Ritter.

"Gentlemen please; I must know what you are referring to, what has been let loose in the heart of my city?"

Himmler leaned back from his plate. The chair was more comfortable than it had looked at first, despite being carved wood with a simple cloth-covered seat. "It is difficult to explain, Governor. It seems that one of the gypsies sent to the Birkenau work camp was unusual in his nature and managed to escape. I have tasked the doctor to capture this fellow and analyze his nature. This is, of course, all very classified, you understand. I would have informed you more but even I am limited by the needs of the Reich."

"Of course, of course." Assured Frank, angry that Himmler had told him almost nothing, but unwilling to demand more.

"And yet you have been ordered to find and destroy this creature?" Himmler asked Ritter.

"Herr Bormann wanted it hunted down and killed, yes." Ritter replied.

"But he did not put a time limit on that, did he?" Stoffel offered. "Certainly he will die if that is the order but... some time to study and examine him first would be very useful to the future of the Reich."

Himmler and Ritter looked at each other. It couldn't be too obvious they were delaying orders but it took time for information to travel to Berlin. "A few days, I should think would be sufficient, yes?" asked Ritter.

Stoffel sighed. No, it would not be sufficient, but it would be the best he was likely to get. Although perhaps he could claim it had been destroyed and keep it sedated in the lab for more study. "As you wish."

CHAPTER EIGHTEEN

The morning broke with bright sunshine around the heavy curtain hanging on Aniela's window. She had managed to tuck the machine back into her dresser and none of the Germans had thought to ask why she was carrying dirty laundry back to her room. She hoped they'd been so distracted by her lingerie that they hadn't noticed it was unwashed. *What was it with men and underwear?* Aniela thought angrily.

Stretching, she climbed out of the warm covers and looked at herself in the mirror. Another day started, they always seemed more hopeful in the morning. Wrapping herself in a robe, she crossed to her window and slid the curtain aside, brushing her hair as she looked out on the city. *Krakow is a beautiful place, for a city*, she thought. *But I miss the country.*

Their little home was what she missed most, just Aleš and her on a little bit of land. She was a schoolteacher then, and he a writer. He hadn't sold much of his poetry, but it brought in a little and he was starting to get noticed outside Poland. They had two good years together. It was so hard to be alone after lying in his arms each night. Aniela flushed a little and grinned, *and in the day too, often.* All those times together and no baby, she wondered if it was something wrong in her or with Aleš? She couldn't visit the gypsy grandmothers for advice or a potion after marrying a gadjo, but the topic hadn't come up before the Germans invaded.

It was then that she learned he was working with the English to gather information. A full year before the invasion, Aleš had been sending information to England from his trips to Germany. They'd fought over it, over secrets, over how it endangered their home. But Aniela understood. She had tried to teach the children at her school about freedom and the dangers of a cold, heartless tyrant on their

115

border, but it was over now. The school had been closed, and she had fled south ahead of the armies.

Aniela wrapped her arms around herself, shoulders hunched. Just 22 years old, she had been so young and innocent when she married Alexander Wisznewski. His strong, gentle love had awoken something in her she'd never knew existed, a hunger that he had fed completely. At first, after he had died, Aniela could not imagine being with another man. She had simply missed her Aleš and his loving touch. She had avoided men, avoided thinking about it.

But recently, she had begun to long for that intimacy, and the hunger had grown again. She closed her eyes and saw Cezar's face, and wondered what he smelled like, up close. She wondered how hairy he was, Aleš had been so smooth. What was his touch like?

A knock sounded at her door. "Angel, you are awake?"

It was Abel, the german translator. Aniela clutched the robe around her closer.

"I am not fit for a visitor!" She almost shouted.

"Ach, too bad for me. I just want to say I will on a patrol again but I get back, we can spend a little watch together, yes? Only you and I."

Aniela shook her head but couldn't say a word. She wanted him to go away, to never enter her room.

"Until tonight, angel." Abels footsteps led away and down the stairs with a creak.

Aniela sat on her bed and stared at the window. Cezar was out there somewhere. She would never give herself to any other man.

*****

Nicolai Solonika was Greek, not Polish, but he spoke enough of the language to do business in the country. His business in wool did well, and he had been pragmatic and clever enough to work with the Germans even before the invasion. Now he provided most of the wool used in uniforms and other goods for Germans made in Poland. He was a member of the Nazi Party and wore a swastika pin not out of allegiance, but again out of pragmatism. Governments could come and go, but one always had to do business.

He sat patiently at the table with Ewald Lange and two other Gestapo officers whose names he did not recall. They had been very polite, introducing themselves and chatting, but there was a coldness under their demeanor that angered Solonika.

"You have done well working with the German army, Mr Solonika." Lange drawled around cigarette smoke. He prided himself in his excellent Polish, but Nicolai Solonika didn't know the German language well enough to sense undercurrents of meaning.

"It has been very profitable, for good reason. I supply the finest wool at the most reasonable prices. I have heard no complaints."

"No, of course not. High Command does not find fault with your product." Lange tapped a long ash off his cigarette and gestured with the filter. "We are here on another matter, simply a routine investigation. You know how it is, we get orders and have paperwork, and we have to follow through. It is all very routine."

"I am a very busy man, Lieutenant, if you will excuse my impatience, I have a meeting with Governor-General Frank later in the day and I must look at my inventory. There is an order for coats for the eastern front and that must not be delayed."

"Of course, I shall not delay any longer, for the sake of our boys in the east. I'm curious about your association with..." Lange checked his notepad. He knew the name but found theatrics to be useful in dealing with the powerful. "a man named Rys Radescu." Lange looked up, expectantly.

"Radescu. Perhaps, the name is familiar, but it doesn't sound Polish. Romanian?"

"I am not sure..." Lange scowled at his notes. "Well it doesn't matter, you do recall the name?"

"Radescu... it seems to me he helps me with labor, supplying strong backs for unloading shipments. I don't deal with him directly, that would be the work of Krystian Zero, he handles personnel and hiring. I met with Radescu once, in '40 to set up the hiring."

"In 1940, very good. Yes, that makes sense."

Lange wasn't actually sure what it meant but he thought it useful for the German authorities to always sound informed, one step ahead.

"I've not had any trouble with the men he supplied, they show up on time and do their work, as far as I know. I could bring Zero in here for you to question?" Solonika offered.

"No, no that won't be necessary. So you have not had occasion to spend any time with Mr Radescu socially?"

"Its possible he has been at some of the dinner parties I have attended, but I would not have noticed him. My time is spent with more influential and powerful members of society."

Lange noted the threat and decided to let it pass. Mr Solonika did not seem to be associated with the gypsies, but he bore looking at for his attitude toward the Gestapo. Perhaps a midnight raid on his home; there was bound to be contraband. A few nights in a cell would teach him the meaning of respect.

"Very well, thank you for your time, Mr Solonika, and I trust you will not be late for your meeting with the Governor-General?"

"No, but I must go. Miss Bialek will show you out."

Lange put on his gloves and overcoat offered him by the buxom, blocky Miss Bialek. Her hands shook slightly as she gave Lange his hat and he smirked. At least she knew what she was dealing with.

Neither of the men on the list he had dealt with were directly tied to the gypsies, although Solonika's work with the laborers put him close. But the name Radescu kept coming up. Neither of the other four men, Antol and Katula, were significant to Radescu, and Lange had crossed them off his list. It was time to examine these laborers he had heard rumors about.

Tonight he would have to speak with Klein again, and compare notes, but it looked like Radescu was their man. He would be a tough one, though. Very closely tied in with the high command in Poland, and by most accounts a personal friend of Hans Frank, somehow. Klein had said he was suspected of smuggling, but since he provided goods for the Governor-General and other important figures – including Lange's own commander Obersturmbannführer Arlt – he enjoyed a certain immunity from the Order Police.

It seemed that was about to change.

Inside, Nikolai Solonika fumed, puffing on a cigar in his office. The Gestapo, interrogating him. True, it wasn't inside some dank cell at the Silesian House but still. He hadn't been fooled by the lieutenant's polite attitude. Solonika could see the cold contempt in Lange's blue eyes when he looked at him.

More importantly, his friend Rys Radescu was in danger. Solonika had long known that Rys was a gypsy, someone important to their people. For decades, Solonika had worked with the Gypsies in moving and protecting his supplies. It was better and cheaper to work with them and accept some losses in delivery than have them prey on him and scam his shipments. And he felt a sort of kinship with their wandering, homeless life. From the start of his business, Nikolai Solonika had been so often between nations and without a regular, long-term home he felt without a land as well.

He stared at his phone for a long moment. They would find out if he called Radescu directly, it was too easy to simply question a switchboard operator at the apartment. Solonika dialed another number instead and waited for the answer.

"Yes, this is Nikolai at Solonika Wooliers. I need a special order of wine, something particularly fine for tonight. Yes, tonight, I will pick it up. And this order, have it at the counter. I think that Chateau Gruaud Larose Red Bordeaux Blend St. Julien '20 you've been saving."

He listened to the receiver a moment. "Broken? Yes, well someone should be warned about that. It would be a shame if your shop was condemned for poor safety practices. What else do you have? Hospices De Beaune Cuvée Estienne '30? Are you sure, most of the '30 wines were miserable. Very well, I'll trust you on that. Tonight, at 5:00. Very well."

Solonika hung up the phone and puffed a thick cloud of cigar smoke around him. That was the signal they had agreed on. It was too bad they didn't have the bordeaux for real, but it was a miracle they had the Cuvée Estienne in stock. Someone at Krakus Cellars must have a hidden closet to keep that from the Germans. He'd done his best, now it was up to Radescu to save himself, and perhaps his people. If it were possible.

*****

Vladimir Czerny, Konrad Stoffel, and Heinrich Ritter stood around the altar inside St Mary's Basilica. The altar was a solid stone piece fronted with gold in front of a bare section of wall. Before 1939 the Viet Stoss altarpiece had stood there, a magnificent screen made of gilded statuary standing several times the height of a man. It had been taken apart and hidden in crates when the Germans neared Krakow, but the Sonderkommando Paulsen had found it and shipped it off to Nuremberg.

In the pews sat several soldiers with Sergeant-Major Martin Franz. The altar had been cleared of religious articles and now had a brass device on it that looked like a cross between an astrolabe and a model of the solar system. Czerny adjusted one of the lenses slightly, sighting along a chalk line drawn on the top of the altar.

Major Ritter watched with his arms crossed. Each day that went by since he had seen direct evidence of the creature's existence he became more skeptical and felt more idiotic for working with this Romanian. He could almost hear the men laughing at him behind his back, although they mostly looked bored.

"No story for us today, Czerny?" asked Stoffel.

Czerny pushed his glasses back on his face with a finger. "No, this location is simply more central and not likely to be disturbed; it has no special significance for the ritual."

"Nothing about the golem or the dragon living under the castle?"

"The golem was created in Warsaw, not Krakow," said Czerny. "I am skeptical of its validity in any case. Jewish legends are filled with the alleged magical power of the name of God, but no real evidence."

Stoffel snorted. "I thought you were the religious type."

"Whatever power the name of God has, it is not something you can conjure by."

Czerny stood back. All three looked at the apparatus, Stoffel with a barely patient look on his face, smoking a cigarette, and Ritter standing still with his arms crossed, a slight scowl on his face.

The apparatus moved. It turned slightly, the lenses refracting colored light from the windows onto the altar. Stoffel's eyes narrowed. Sgt-Major Franz leaned forward in his seat and rubbed the ruined half of his face. One of the soldiers nudged another and nodded at the altar.

The apparatus slowly swung a few centimeters and one of the lenses lowered slightly, focusing light along one of the lines.

"Good. It is working." Czerny said in the quiet. "Within the hour we should have a direction the creature is most often found and by the end of the day the distance to where it is most often. It cannot give

119

exact location because the creature moves about as we all do and tracking its energy at this range is beyond my skills."

Ritter turned his head slightly to stare at Vladimir Czerny. "A day. We must wait another day."

"Yes, that is as swiftly as it can be done. Assuming the other devices are not tampered with."

"I assure you, no one will touch them or there will be hell to pay," said Franz.

Ritter looked at the device on the altar. He didn't see any springs or magnets, and the altar was made of stone. Yet it had moved. He'd seen it move, hadn't he? He looked at Stoffel, who was crouching, staring at the apparatus. He too was looking for some mechanism but it was only brass and lenses. It still felt as if the thing was in motion, but so slowly it could not be watched.

Ritter looked around him, but the soldiers were chatting quietly and looking at the altar. He stared at the colorful, painted ceiling of the basilica. It was more garish than he preferred. Every single surface of the building was covered with patterns, gold leaf, inlaid stone, and paint. There were more colors than he was used to in a church, especially compared to the relatively austere German cathedrals. The lens moved again slightly, turning a small amount away from the chalk line, but still pointed toward the hidden cave beneath Jagiellonian University.

"How is it done?" asked Stoffel. "Brass is not a ferrous metal, and there is nowhere for magnets to be hidden. I see no springs or other form of machine."

"The energy from the three locations is focused here, each for a different purpose. This device simply uses that energy to direct it to one use: the location of our quarry."

"Our quarry." Stoffel said, crushing his cigarette under a shoe on the stone floor. "Why do you seek the, ah, fugitive?"

"For the same reason as Sturmbannführer Ritter. To destroy it."

"I should think you would want this thing to be free, it is killing only German soldiers. Is your land not occupied by the Reich?"

"I have lived a long time, Professor Stoffel. Many armies have occupied many lands I have lived in, and life goes on. No empire lasts forever."

"That is where you are wrong, Romanian," snapped Ritter. "The third Reich will last a thousand years or more. We will eclipse the Persians the Greeks, the Romans, and the English. The iron will of the Aryan people is absolute."

Czerny said nothing, his face completely blank.

Ritter turned toward the soldiers in the pews, who sat back and stiffed under his gaze.

"Franz, stay here with the remaining men and guard the location. I will oversee the patrols on the streets. Perhaps we can find this escaped gypsy in less than a day."

The major stopped and glanced at the device once more. "Perhaps we shall focus a bit more on the university district."

*****

Cezar sat on the edge of Aniela's bed. The whole room smelled of her like a flower garden and he closed his eyes a moment just taking her in. One of the first changes he noticed with his senses was that few things actually smelled *bad* any more. Some scents were too strong to be comfortable, but even things that used to smell horrible now were merely informative and interesting. Sweat and tears took on their own special character, like a signature to each person's life. Dust and other scents were layered in the room along with food from between the floor boards, rising up from the kitchen beneath. Smoke from the uncle's pipe and the hearth mingled in the air as well.

It smelled like home, like love, and like comfort and safety. But there were other scents as well. There were Germans staying in the building now. Cezar hadn't been to any rooms other than Aneila's, entering through her window. But their scent was there, with gun oil and the smells of soldiery. And under the homely scents of the building there was acrid fear and pain, the adrenaline-driven smells of people living in nearly continuous stress. Cezar scowled at the bedspread. Somewhere in the world people were living normal lives. Perhaps he could reach them.

And then you could teach them the true meaning of terror, growled the thing inside him.

Below him, he heard the door open, light steps on the wooden floor. Aniela's smell reached him and he took a deep breath, his eyes closed. He listened as she chatted with her aunt and then heard her climb the stairs. He rose and stood by the dresser, hands crossed at his waist, holding his wrist.

Aniela was uncomfortable. She'd had the most vivid dreams in her life about Cezar the night before and all day long felt that heat and awareness of her body beneath her clothes. It felt like her heart was beating harder all day, but not faster like she'd been running, just... stronger. When she opened the door to her room, she didn't notice him at first, but turned and kicked her shoes off next to the door, closing it. She imagined Cezar being in her room, with no shirt on...

"Good evening," Cezar said quietly.

Aniela jumped and squeaked, covering her mouth. Spinning, she saw him standing there, leaned against the dresser. She blushed, feeling silly like she'd been caught stealing cookies as a little girl.

"What, what are you doing here?" She asked.

Cezar smiled slightly. "I came to see you. To be with you."

Aniela felt a thrill through her body as nerves jumped. She was breathing with her mouth open, unaware of it. "I – I have to talk to my aunt, please don't go anywhere."

Cezar nodded.

Turning, she fumbled with the doorknob, angry at herself. She was acting like an idiot, like a nervous child. *Men are nothing new to me,* thought Aniela. *I was married for two years. Grow up.*

"Aunt Joanna?" Aniela said, standing in the kitchen door. "I am not feeling very well, its been a very difficult week. I think I shall lie down, I don't think I could eat a bite."

Joanna set a bowl of cabbage on the counter and crossed to Aniela. Taking her in her arms, she held Aniela against her soft rounded body in a gentle hug. "You poor dear, it has been so hard, and with your work and helping me, I am not at all surprised you should be so worn down. Oh, your forehead is flushed and quite warm, yes you should lie down. Do you want me to bring you something after dinner?"

"No. Oh no I... I am sure I won't be hungry at all."

"Very well then, dear girl, you lie down and rest, I won't bother you until morning."

Aniela nodded and feeling slightly guilty turned away. Joanna watched her climb the steps with a deep sigh. It would mean more work for her getting the dinner ready but Aniela had been through so much these last few years. Some rest would do her good.

The candle in Aniela's room flickered and wavered as she closed the door behind her. Cezar leaned against her dresser, watching her with a confidence and ease so powerful she felt slightly dizzy. She could not see him very clearly in the candle light yet but as her eyes adjusted, she could see the amber color of his eyes.

"I knew you would come," Aniela said.

CHAPTER NINETEEN

Awakening suddenly, Aniela looked around her. Her single candle had guttered out sometime in the night, forgotten, and no light peeked around the heavy dark covering over her window but a sliver of light showed under her door. She could not see her clock but knew her uncle and aunt must be awake still; a thin light showed under her door from the lights downstairs.

Aniela looked beside her at Cezar's strong form in the small bed, heavy and warm beside her. He had almost none of the covers on him and she felt a small thrill at his form exposed beside her, barely visible in the heavy, cold darkness, until her gaze reached his face and saw the slight glint of his eyes. The thrill slid into foolish guilt at peeking at him.

"I could smell something in your room that didn't seem to fit," Cezar said without moving. "A sort of mechanical scent, like a typewriter or an adding machine."

Aniela lay silent, brain still somewhat in a half-sleeping state, confused. She felt she'd missed something he'd said earlier that would make sense of his statement.

"So while you slept I looked around a bit, trying to find out what it was. It was not easy to find, but I did find it; an unusual device, something no Polish girl should have hidden away in the back of a cabinet. I thought perhaps you didn't know it was there, but it wasn't dusty and everything around it was. And it was too new, too modern a machine to have been hidden away in some secret compartment for years.

"It smelled slightly of you as well: you didn't just know it was there, you used it. Who are you talking to with this strange machine?"

Aniela stared with wide eyes at Cezar. She thought she should be outraged at him snooping around the room, she tried to be tender thinking of his concern, but all she felt was fear. All she could hear was the sound of Uncle Rys' voice, how genuinely frightened and anxious he was.

*"You must not seek this man, you must listen to me. You must stay away from him. This man is dangerous, he is unspeakably dangerous, you **must not see him again.**"*

Cezar looked at her a long time, he could sense her fear, she was almost trembling like a leaf. "You must answer me, Aniela. I must trust you or I cannot see you again." The beast snarled inside him, *oh we'll make sure of that.*

Still Aniela did not speak. She knew the longer she said nothing, the less believable a lie would be - indeed the less believable anything she said would be. What would he do? How would he react? She wanted to back away on the little bed but there was no room. Finally she found her voice, choked and small like a child's.

"I ... you cannot tell anyone, please Cezar, you have to promise." She waited for the promise yet Cezar was silent in the darkness. Finally she plunged on. "It—it is the British; they contacted me before the invasion. They wanted information on the Germans, on the invasion."

Cezar's hostility faded to a distant, patient look, and Aniela turned onto her back, feeling a weight of secrecy lifted from her shoulders by sharing it with another. Her shoulder pressed against Cezar's warm skin and she felt a thrill through her at the contact.

"Alexander... my husband, he was part of a group that worked with the British academic societies, and he sometimes helped them move materials through Poland that had come from Germany before the invasion, I never asked how it all started. I wasn't even supposed to know, but how could he hide it from his wife? When Aleš died, a man spoke to me at the library, then again in a little cafe, asking if I could work with my husband, help with his fight for liberty.

"He spoke of freedom and civilization, of the growing darkness and the need for all of us to fight against the Nazis. All I knew was that it was good enough for Aleš, that the Germans were threatening my home, that they had killed my husband so I wanted to be a part of what he had been. They gave me a contact, a place to drop letters off that I wrote and a place to look when they wanted to talk to me. For months there as no sign, then the scarf was hung on the lightpost like they had said and I met with a man in the basement of an apartment building. He gave me a little book and told me to memorize it, to learn it, and that they would be delivering something.

"I learned that book; it was what kept me sane as the bombs fell and the guns fired and I sat alone in a room full of strangers, screaming at God for taking away my Aleš. I learned the book so that I could quote the entire thing - my memory has always been good with that kind of thing. I suppose that's why they chose me. I learned the book and burned it, gone forever except in my mind."

Aniela squirmed on the small portion of her mattress to face Cezar, trying to see his expression in the darkness.

"When I moved to Krakow to live with my uncle and aunt, along with my other supplies a passerby – a man I'd never seen before – helped me carry my furniture to my room, and with it was this new dresser, carefully made, and in the back was the machine. They have a name for it, but I just call it the machine. I turn it on for short moments to recieve messages and send them. I don't know if I'm any help at all, but I know that it feels like I'm doing *something* to fight back."

Aniela looked in Cezar's eyes a long time, hoping he would understand, that she could trust him, looking for some sign she had not made a ghastly mistake. Cezar lay there a while looking annoyed, then his eyes closed and he began to chuckle, a deep rumble that forced a nervous smile from her as well.

"Well. Every man has enough ego to think that, at least some moments, he is irresistible, that he is so virile and handsome that a woman cannot resist his advances. So." He paused a moment fighting his grin. "Well humility is, they say, a virtue. You bedded me for information to send to your British friends, still, I am in bed with a beautiful, exciting woman, how much can I complain? You wish to know something, ask."

Aniela shared a giggle with him and blushed. "It wasn't *just* for information."

He acknowledged the compliment with a raised eyebrow and a grunt, tipping his head slightly.

"You are not angry with me?" Aniela asked with more than a little concern in her voice.

"Oh, not so much I could not be convinced to forget it, but first, ask your questions."

Aniela nodded. Now that she had an opportunity, she wasn't sure what to ask. What *did* they want to know? What did she want to know?

"Cezar, my ... I call him my Uncle, he said you were *marime*, could... could you tell me? What happened?" Aniela's voice became quieter and softer as she spoke, as if she was asking a lion to show her how hard it can bite.

Cezar backed his head away a moment to look at her again. She never went where he expected. How much had she learned? He had hinted to her about his nature and she did not react, was it because she already knew?

"Hm. Well perhaps the best way to answer is to say that it is the same reason I am alive today."

"You were in ..." she whispered, as if Germans might be listening "one of the camps, you escaped. It was you."

He nodded. "They tried to gas me. The poison killed dozens of people around me, mostly Jews. They all died. I lived, because gas cannot harm me. It smelled awful though."

Aniela just stared at him, hearing Rys' warnings in her head again:

...he is unspeakably dangerous.

"When they opened the door, I left."

They lay in bed, facing each other in the darkness, the cold air causing Aniela to snuggle into the covers a bit more. Then she opened them up, a gust of the chill washing over her as she threw them over Cezar as well.

"Aren't you cold?" She asked as she moved close against him.

"No, Aniela."

"Well as hairy as you are I'm not surprised." It was true, he had hair on his chest and legs almost like a beast, but a magnificent, wild hunting beast; fierce, exciting, and virile, she thought.

Aniela kissed him then backed up a bit and watched him, waiting for him to speak. *He has something to say, something awful and yet I just don't care*, she thought, amazed at herself.

It was Cezar's turn to roll on his back. He stared at the ceiling, one shoulder partly off the side of the bed. Only once before had he spoken to anyone about his curse, and Marisol had not been a clever, lithe bitch like this one. He swore silently at himself. *This one is no bitch to mount, show her respect*, Cezar thought angrily. *She spread her legs just like the others,* the beast growled within him. Cezar shook his head, trying to shake loose the angry thoughts.

"Aniela, I'm not like any man you have met."

She grinned "I know."

"No, you don't."

The flat finality of his voice stopped her smile and the chill of Rys' words caught at her again. It was getting harder to push that voice back. How had he "smelled" her machine? How did he know she was Romani back at the market? Why were the British so interested in him?

"I knew where you lived because I followed your scent, out of sight. I can smell you now, you are a little afraid. You should be.

"Aniela, I have been cursed, something horrible lies within me. Sometimes it gets out, and when it gets out, blood and screams and death are unleashed."

Aniela started to speak and he touched her face.

"I don't mean metaphorically, angel. I am not cursed in some philosophical way, like a man with bad luck. I mean *cursed*. Long ago, too long now, I betrayed someone and paid a horrible price that I carry with me still."

Aniela felt very small and very vulnerable in her little bed, like a mouse lying next to a lion. Her skin crawled where he'd touched her, the little thrill gone. The words "curse" and "betray" like spikes driven into her heart. *Dear God what have I done?*

"Let me tell you my story," Cezar said.

Cezar looked into Aniela's dark eyes, the pupils so large in the dark there was almost no color showing. He could see her full lips and soft skin clearly in the darkness, her blankets clutched up to her chin by fists. Aniela could barely see a glint on Cezar's eyes and his vague form. *If you tell her and she doesn't like it*, the beast snarled within him, *you know what you'll have to do.* Cezar closed his eyes and, feeling unworthy and blasphemous, uttered a little prayer. Then he told his story.

CHAPTER TWENTY

"Before there were cars in Romania, before the new century, life was simpler there. A new king, Carol I, had been installed by the government and the newly reformed   country of Romania seemed destined for growth and prosperity to match the other European countries to the west. Yet, it still was a troubled place. Troubled by old hostilities, old traditions...old fears.

"I was young, in my teens when I met an old man who lived near my village of Brejoi in the mountains. He had a hut in the forest, away from the village; I only found him by hunting in a valley the others avoided as too rugged, a place that never had game. I didn't catch any deer that day but I found someone who became a friend."

Cezar's eyes looked into the distance, into the past through Aniela's eyes.

"He was a strange man, he did not look so terribly old, but he *seemed* ancient, like he was as old as the rocks around him. The old man of the mountains we called him. The village knew about him, sort of. He taught me about the forest, about the history of the area, he taught me the stars and the winds. I knew much about life in the mountains, but he taught me more than I thought possible. For years I visited him, although the villagers thought it odd. He gave me a cloak of wolf's skin that would mask my smell from the animals, help me blend in and keep warm. It became my favorite clothing, I always wore it to visit him and to hunt.

"A sorcerer he was called, a warlock. Dangerous, satanic. He never seemed it to me, only a wise old man who knew much and was a friend. He knew much of medicines that even the midwives were unaware of, what herbs would heal and harm and perhaps that was why they called him warlock. At least that was what I thought. The priest would often talk with me, warning me away from the old man, telling me he was wicked, that I should stay home. That he would corrupt my soul.

"Yet for years, it was an..." Cezar thought a moment, "an academic topic. Something to mutter about and warn a young man over, but nothing of terrible concern in the timeless repetition of seasons in a small mountain village. They thought me odd and perhaps bewitched, but still were friendly enough as I was the best hunter in the region by this point and brought food in even the coldest of winters.

"At first, they were distant and worried, but as time went on, they began to accept my skills and I grew in favor in the village. The girls started to flirt with me, thinking me 'a fine catch.'" His voice was bitter. "I was happy and proud and told no one my secret, but they all knew: it was the old man's influence. Still, as long as it helped them, they were content to enjoy my bounty."

Aniela lay still listening. Cezar looked younger than thirty, yet he was talking of a king dead for decades now; of times before her father was born. She felt slightly sick inside, *was he a madman?*

"Then the drought struck. It was dry one winter," Cezar continued, "with little snow. The spring had almost no rain, the creeks dried up. The wells dried up. The game moved to lower ground, the crops would not grow. Children began to die. The town began to look for reasons; they turned to the priest for guidance. 'A judgment from God,' Father Lacusta declared, for the people's turning away. Too rarely did they come to Holy Eucharist, too little did they teach the children, too often were they clinging to the old superstitions. Return to God, he said, perhaps He may show mercy.

"The people didn't care for that answer. They liked the old ways, they didn't care for teaching of God, they preferred to sleep on Sunday mornings. It must be something else. So they looked for another reason, and they saw me. That Cezar, he is practicing deviltry with the old man of the mountain, they said. He is with the sorcerer, in league with the Devil! Father Lacusta tried to tell them that Satan was no match for God; he told them that they needed faith and prayers, but the people preferred torches and billhooks. I came home with a hind after a hunt of many days, and met angry, accusing eyes.

"They seized me and beat me. They burned the deer I'd brought claiming it was the result of witchcraft, for how else could I have caught game in this drought? How could I be so good at hunting? I must have bewitched the animals, used dark magic to find them. Maybe if I died, there would be rain. The old man was using his evil sorcery to curse the land and cause drought so the village would depend on me more, and be under his power, they cried."

Cezar could still see the mob in the village square, his former friends angry and filled with hate. He could see in their eyes the accusations, hear their bitter cries. He remembered the beatings, the spit, and the hatred. 'It is your fault it all went wrong!' they cried. *Even papa.*

He was silent a while, remembering, and catching a small scent of fear and revulsion from Aniela. But it was too late to turn back now.

"The seized me, and the priest alone would defend me; father Lacusta, my only friend left in the village. He thought me wrong, he thought me probably lost, but he also thought me one of his sheep. He argued with the crowd, called them to be merciful, appealed to the Word. They rejected him until my father finally argued that the priest was right-we should not cut off the fruit of witchcraft, but the heart of it. Kill the sorcerer and the boy might be saved.

"All eyes turned on me. Everyone I knew in the world other than the old man of the mountain was there, eager to kill me, perhaps burn me alive. They all had hate and fear in their hollowed, hungry eyes. They would kill me, I knew it. I recognized the look in their eyes, I'd seen in the eyes of predators. They saw me no longer as a fellow man, no longer as a villager. They saw me as the enemy, as the source of their suffering. Better that I die than them. The priest had returned to his little chapel to pray, for no one would listen to him, and I was alone against everyone in my home.

"I feared them, formerly the ones I loved and laughed with. A girl there, Camelia, she was my first fumbling love in a meadow of flowers just that summer. She looked at me with hate and accusation along with the rest. All of the girls who promised me such sweetness if I would choose their hand threw rocks at me now. They would kill me, and I could not escape. They would hang me at the very least, burn me almost certainly. I would find no mercy from them. I wanted to live.

"I was a coward.

"I formed a plan: I could lead them to the old man and they would exile me, far away from their village, never to return. I could tell them where the old man of the mountain lived, I keep the old man busy while they seized him. I could live.

"I presented a scheme to my former friends and family. All I had to do was keep the old man from using his magics. 'Take him by surprise and he cannot turn the forces of evil against you,' I argued; 'do this and you may live!' they screamed. My plan was to lead them into the forest I knew so well and use my skills to escape. Once away, their best hunters would be hard pressed to find me, if they even tried.

"So we set out into the mountains, but the biggest men of the village held me. One on each arm, one behind me. They had dogs with them, and the dogs snapped and snarled at me, sensing their master's hate. I looked for a way out, I tried to think of a way to escape. I feigned thirst, and was ignored - they all were thirsty. I pointed out game that was not there, and they said there would be meat for everyone once they were done. I said I was tired, and they snarled I'd find eternal rest if I stopped. They were pitiless, relentless, fists clenching my arms so tightly I lost feeling in my hands.

"We reached the valley of the old man, and after a superstitious pause, forged on. Only the priest stayed behind, for he would not join this procession. What became of him I know not, whether he remained in the village afterward and tried to win them away from their anger and fear or if he left them to their damnation, I never learned."

Aniela's heart beat hard in her breast as she listened. Despite herself she felt the tension, the anxiety. This was too close to home, the betrayal of loved ones, the sudden brutal sense of violence. Every day she lived in fear of having those she knew turn on her, of being captured and disappearing on a train like the others.

Cezar's voice was sad now, thick with emotion. "I was sent ahead, the men of the village armed with their hunting weapons pointed at me. 'Betray us and be cut down,' they warned me, and their eyes said *we hope you do.* How they could have turned so completely on me I still cannot understand. Fear makes us do horrible, evil things, that is the only answer I can think of. I was strange, and they were desperate. The hate awoke in them so easily, the desperate need to save themselves. Yet I was no better.

"Alone I approached the old man's hut as the others crouched out of sight, weapons trained on my back. When I knocked on his old wooden door, the old man welcomed me in as always. He saw my anxiety, yet I suppose he thought it was because of the drought. He began to teach me how to find water, showing me a barrel of clear spring water he had. Then the shout came from outside: 'In the name of God you shall burn, warlock! Try not your wicked sorcery upon us!' Torches were hurled onto the thatched roof, against the wooden walls. I fled out the door and shots tore into the wood, perhaps aimed at me, perhaps to keep the old man from following.

"The old man... I can hear his voice still." Cezar's voice was ragged now, "he called me Judas. He called me betrayer, and in his voice I could hear the same confusion and hurt that I felt against the villagers: *what did I do to you? How could you turn on me so?*

"I ran to join the villagers, hoping they would forgive me, that they would take me back, that it would all be like it was before the drought. In my heart I knew it was not so, I would always remind them of this day, of when they went mad. As I ran, though, I heard the old man, speaking in a voice I'd never heard from him. It was clear and strong like a slamming coffin lid, thundering over the wind and the flames and the villagers' voices, over the gunshots.

"'Betrayer!' he cried, 'Cursed shall you be! Forever more, you shall wear the wolf's hide! You took gifts from me and repaid me with death! You shall never find death, yet always long for it!!'

"The voice seemed to echo off the valley's walls and into my soul. I felt as if acid had formed around my guts, eating away in terror. Something black and horrible clawed its way into my soul. The villagers began to scream, backing away from me. They scrambled to reload their guns as they stared at me. I could feel what they could see: the wolf skin was *moving* on my back, crawling upon me, digging into me. It sank into my flesh and I could feel every awful moment, making me scream in fear and revulsion. I felt the hairs of the wolf's pelt wiggling and piercing through my skin, digging into my body and merging with me. The dogs cried and cowered and fled.

"The wolf's pelt was gone from my back, for it became a part of me, and that day I felt... I felt the beast, within my soul."

And I shall never leave you, it purred within Cezar.

"The villagers forgot the old man, forgot the burning building, forgot their hunger and began to chase me. I felt their bullets hit my flesh, I heard their cries and calls for death. The bullets struck me and caused pain but did not penetrate my flesh. I fled the villagers, running as I had never before, swift and tireless. I left them and my life far behind me.

"Nothing stopped me, nothing slowed me. I ran, and ran and ran. I kept running that day, that night, for days, without stopping. I ran until I reached a river and swam across it. The horror on my back was still there, behind me. I ran from it, feeling the wolf behind me. I ran until I realized I could not escape it again, ever. It was not at my back... it was *in* my back, it was in my soul. I wandered for days, until the moon was full.

"That was when the terror truly began," he said, and the beast within laughed, echoing off of Cezar's bones.

Aniela felt paralyzed. It couldn't be true. She mouthed the word "no" again and again, saying nothing. Cezar ignored her, staring at the ceiling but seeing the past.

"I was near Timișoara then, not far from Hungary. I feared everyone, half mad. Hiding from people, I had slept in barns and ate what I could steal. Each night the moon became fuller, the nightmares grew within me, matching the pregnant moon's progression. Finally, the night came. I tried sleeping in a pile of leaves so close to Timișoara I could see the steeple of the cathedral mocking me. But the heat within me grew, and pain arose, like I'd not felt for weeks. I burst out of the leaves and snow, screaming in the bright clear moonlight of a cloudless sky, my skin silver where I tore my tunic away. The scream grew louder and deeper and then became a howl."

Cezar clenched his fists under the blankets. He wanted to reach out to Aniela, but could smell her horror; cold sweat mixed with bile on her breath. She would not be like Marisol. She understood too well what he was and what he did, she would not embrace him.

She's too smart, growled the beast.

"I woke. When it happens, I never remember, only dreams later on with scattered images and sensations. The joy of slaughter, the rising blood fever, the screams. I was in the wreckage of a home and blood was everywhere. Pieces of..." Cezar choked off, and was quiet a moment. It was too late to win her approval. He had never told this part of his past to anyone, but he had to tell someone, to share it. Perhaps it would weigh less if someone else knew.

"I had awoken happy, for it had been a night without the dreams and I'd slept well for the first time in nearly a month. Then I looked around me. There were pieces of children scattered in the room like doll parts. A mother was dead, her throat torn out draped over the table like a slaughtered hog. The furniture was broken, the windows shattered, and I lay in a pool of blood in the ruins.

"Outside, I heard angry voices and weapons being readied. I could see them peering in at me, eyes huge and filled with anger. I was naked and so covered with blood it was as if I'd been dipped in it. Flashes, brief images of what had happened flickered at the edge of my mind. I had done this. But it wasn't me it was... what I had become."

"I don't remember exactly what they said, but I suppose you can guess. I lay there and did nothing. They beat me with clubs and gun butts and fists and boots, but it did not hurt very much. Then they hauled me to a prison. I was tried and yet I said nothing. What could I say? I had killed a family, slaughtered them. I didn't care what happened then; I had run far enough and had given up. Apparently I had killed a swath through the city and ended it at that home. Dozens were dead, torn to pieces. I was sentenced to die; it was all quite fast. They wanted to know how I could possibly have done it with my bare hands, but I said nothing. They put me on the scaffolding and covered my head and when I felt the noose around my throat I thanked the God I knew had damned me it was finally going to be over.

"I felt the fall, I felt the tug at my throat, and I hung there. It wasn't even hard to breathe. I cried out in frustration and rage, ripping my hands free to pull at the rope, trying to drag it tighter, but I could not. People in the crowd screamed and a shot rang out; I do not know what it hit, for I did not feel a bullet.

"After a time, they cut me down and put me back in prison. I could hear them discussing the problem in fear and frustration outside my cell. After a few days, they decided. A firing squad was to be assembled, a dozen men with rifles. But by then it was too late; the moon was full once more. I cried at them to flee, but they laughed at me. I was chained to the wall, the prison door was solid. I prayed that perhaps they would be safe.

"I awoke the next morning in a hay loft. I was miles from Timişoara, almost to Hungary. Over the next few weeks I dreamed memories of what had happened. The chains bursting, the door crashing aside, the guards dying, the streets of screaming and fleeing people. Gunshots. Leaping over carriages and out into the fields. I would never be free. The old man of the mountains was right. I longed for death and could not have it."

Aniela lay quieter now. The fear and revulsion had faded, leaving only a quiet emptiness in her. Cezar was as dead to her as Aleš, no longer part of her life. If only she had shown more strength and told him to leave instead of... but that was past, and she knew she could not change the past. She could only act on the present.

Yet some of her felt pity, a sadness at his story. Born gypsy, she knew the stories of the vârcolac and the curse it put upon a man. His story rang all too true to her childhood memories of tales told around the fire. Aleš would have scoffed at it, but she was more ready to believe. Whatever the truth, clearly Cezar was deeply wounded by what he had done, a kind of long-carried sorrow. She felt some small sadness and empathy for this strange, compelling, frightening man.

"Did they not hunt you?" Aniela asked.

"Yes. But in those days it was easier to run and hide. There were no telephones or telegraphs over most of the region. There were no cars and people did not travel much. I could stay for a time in an area and move before... before the moon was full. I would try to stay in the mountains away from people, but I found the beast inside me was able to twist my rage, fill me with contempt and hate and I would lash out too easily. I would kill for what another man would shout over. And then I would have to flee again."

"Why?" asked Aniela, impatient.

"Why did I run?" Cezar seemed annoyed.

"No, why do you kill?"

He was quiet a while. He knew but he wasn't sure how to answer.

"The beast I turn into kills because it loves to spread terror and death. If there is a hell, it surely came from such a place. It is evil, pure hate and evil. And it seems to most want to kill the things that will horrify and shock me; at least it used to. I am beyond shock now. It's not really me at all when I change, I am gone, only the wolf remains.

"But... I kill, too. My temper is awful, I used to be so calm and quiet, long ago. I was a good boy. But the slightest thing can make me so angry now. And when I get angry, people just don't mean much to me, life doesn't matter so much anymore. I've killed a lot of Germans, Aniela. Many, many soldiers. Many people of many nations.

"And I can force the change, now. For years it would only happen in the full moon, or when I was especially afraid or angry, when I was in great danger. But I learned to control it, and keep it inside"

The beast laughed and laughed, loud and almost hysterical. Cezar turned away from Aniela, facing the window as if she might see its mockery in his face.

"I can keep it from changing now, except during the full moon, then it is in charge. Each night it takes over until morning during the full moon. Other times, I can control it, I can... I--" A screaming face flashed before his memory; the police captain, and a splash of blood. "Most of the time I can. Sometimes I wonder if I am not simply putting it off until later. But I only change when I choose to now. Then I lose control completely for hours. It doesn't like to come out during the day, but I can make it happen."

"I... I only know the legends." Aniela said, "but does not the bite of the varcolac cause others to become one?"

Cezar nodded, then realized Aniela could not see him. "Yes, it can, if they live. The wolf does not seem to want them to live." Inside him the beast growled softly. "There was one, once but... but she died."

Cezar was quiet a moment. The beast *did* want more of his kind, but it almost never left anyone alive, only when the sun was rising, as if it had run out of time. Cezar pushed the bleak thoughts away.

"But why do you kill?" Aniela asked again, quietly.

Cezar stared at the old ceiling, his eyes tracing a long crack in the paint. "I don't want to. I don't like to kill, its like a madness... no, I cannot blame it on insanity. I do not want to kill and yet I do. I hate it, but when I'm doing it I love it, like the evil inside me corrupts my soul, a cancer inside me. I tried for a long time to live peacefully and then I had to kill the one I cared for the most."

Cezar was silent a while. He didn't want to talk about Katyushia, and yet he wanted to finally share the tale with someone. "I do the opposite of what I want, and when I'm doing it I like it. It's no excuse, I can't explain why. I only..." He trailed off into silence, wretched and alone beside a beautiful woman.

Cezar was silent a time, struggling to find a way to explain the war that went on inside him every day to someone who did not carry that burden. The evil in his soul that reached out trying to poison everything and twist all he did to its horrible will. How could she understand the fight to keep it back, to never turn again? And then the sheer soaring glee at destroying and killing, at hearing the screams; who could understand it?

"For a time I sought a cure, and it brought me to the Romani in Hungary. Surely if anyone knew it would be the old wise women of the People. I visited an encampment and begged their help, but they threw me out, threatened to kill me, for they said they knew how. By then I'd given up seeking death and only wanted to be free of the curse. So I found another encampment near Poznan here in Poland and did not share my secret yet. There I lived with the Romani, and learned their language and their ways. Each month I would travel, taking any excuse to be away from when it was... time. I would gather herbs for the women, I would carry messages to another camp, and I would go for supplies. I would hunt, for I still was a very capable hunter, and now I needed no gun.

"I think they suspected something, but for seventeen years I lived with different camps, but I finally found one that became my home. My best friend was a young man named Rys, barely a man, then. I am sure he knew something because his mother was the one I turned to finally for a cure. By then I had grown cold to the killing and the monster in me. I just wanted it away, to have a chance to sleep at night without the memories. Rys Radescu, he was a good man."

Aniela lay on her side staring with wide eyes at Cezar. Uncle Rys when he was young, that was long before she had been born. Yet with the curse, it could be... he would not age any more. She thought back, trying to calculate his real age if his story were true. Perhaps eighty years.

"Mama Radescu said she had heard of a cure, and perhaps it might work. I had to gather herbs from the Transylvanian Alps, in Romania and she could prepare a potion. I had to drink it when the change started, in a chapel. So I gathered the herbs. It took me two months to make the trip to Romania and back to Poland on foot. Horses were terrified of me. I did not know how to drive a car, although by that time I would see one at times.

"Finally I returned, and presented Mama Radescu with the herbs. She mixed her potion and I went to the chapel with Rys and his mother and a few of the men of the camp. I knew they were armed with weapons they thought would kill me, if the cure did not work.

"Kneeling in the chapel, I was prayed over by the little old priest. I do not recall his name, I'm sure he's dead now. I stayed there a full day before the full moon, reading prayers from a book he gave me. They meant nothing to me, but I thought the words might help with the cure. A wooden, painted Christ looked down at me from his cross on the wall and I saw no pity in his eyes. I could be free of this curse, but there was no redemption for me, not after what I had done.

"The little priest told me something about a man in the Bible named Paul, but I understood almost none of it. Latin I could read with effort but I still do not speak Polish well. I suppose he was telling me it was never too late, that no one could sin more than Jesus could save, but had Paul ever done what I had?"

Aniela touched Cezar's face. She could feel no love for him again, she knew, but she felt compassion for him.

"The night came. The priest refused to leave, and prayed over me. He put some water on my head from the font, and held his hand on my head praying as I knelt. I could feel the change coming as the moon rose, and I drank the potion as quickly as I could. I..."

Cezar lay quietly and swallowed his tears away.

"I did not change, then. Rys rejoiced, for by then we had become friends. I tried to stay distant but he was so easy to speak to and I felt almost like family. There was even a girl... but no matter. We went back to the camp and celebrated. Rys went to his trailer and I slept outside to guard as I usually did, near mama Radescu's trailer.

"But I could still feel it inside me. It was there, but it felt like it was, I suppose the best way to think of it was that the best was asleep. I still was strong and I still did not feel the cold of the night. I could still hear them talking in their trailers and smell everything. But I hoped it was over and would fade away. I told myself that was what it was."

But you knew, growled the beast. *You knew and stayed anyway.*

"God help me, I did!" sobbed Cezar. He wept lying on his back, the bed convulsing with his sobs, silent in the darkness. It had been a long time since he had cried, more than a decade. Downstairs Aniela heard her aunt and uncle talking, it sounded like she was going to bed. He would probably wait up for the soldiers.

Cezar cleared his throat, angrily rubbing his eyes. "I woke the next morning above the camp, on a hill. Three of the wagons were overturned, one smashed. I could see the bodies lying on the ground. Blood was over my face and hands. I was naked again, and I could hear the wailing and shouting below.

"Lying on the ground by the ruins of her wagon, I could see Mama Radescu in a pool of blood. I could see at least ten dead. Her potion had failed. I had failed. I had two choices: flee, knowing they would never catch me, or return to the only family I had left. They had never betrayed me, I had them. I walked slowly down the hillside, my head low.

"They were shocked to see me return, I'm sure they thought I was miles away. Immediately they beat me down to my knees, and I fell more out of sorrow than because of their attacks. Rys stood over me and shouted condemnation. I had murdered his entire family. I had betrayed the People. I had killed the ones who loved me. I was to die. I nodded. It was the only answer. Silver bullets were made from some jewelry and prepared while I sat outside the camp tied in ropes that only held me because I had given up.

"Yet none wanted to shoot me in cold blood, just kneeling there. Even after what I had done, they remembered me as their friend and family for years. I had played and sang and danced with them, I had brought them food. Finally one man volunteered. His name was Tomas, and he had hated me for how Rachel had flirted with me, for he wanted her for himself. He had hated me for so easily beating him when we had fought. He was a rough, angry man that was feared and disliked, but he was family and you know how it is. You put up with that. At least, *they* did.

"He held the gun to my face and stared down the barrel. Silver bullet, he said, it would kill the evil in my soul as it killed the spirit in my body. He sneered at me how Rachel wouldn't like me so much with a hole in my face. And then he pulled the trigger, as I leaned my forehead against the barrel."

Aniela stared at Cezar. Everyone knew silver bullets killed werewolves.

"I don't know why it didn't work. It hurt a lot, and it knocked me over, but I did not die. I bled but the bullet did not break my skull. Nobody understood what had happened. David reloaded and shot me again, but the bullet would not kill me.

"The men of the camp met in council and finally Rys declared that I was *marime,* banned from the camp and accursed. I could not be allowed to travel with them any longer, and I was never to associate with the People again, anywhere. He said he would spread the word, and I would never be welcome in any camp. He put a curse on me for how I had killed his family and the others, but apparently it was only talk. My life has not gotten any worse. Perhaps it cannot, it is as bad as possible."

"I should have nothing to do with you." Aniela said. There was no judgment in her voice, it was flat and without emotion. *I should have listened to Uncle Rys*, she thought.

"Perhaps no one should have anything to do with me," said Cezar. "I feel more distant from humanity each year. I had friends, once, not only the Romani. During the Great War, I signed on to fight.

"I had spent decades wandering, trying to find others of my kind or at least a cure. I lived in Germany for years and learned their language well. I even met with an alienist in Austria who tried to convince me it was all in my head and somehow my mother was involved. I almost killed him when he said I had lusted after her; I didn't even remember her, she died when I was very young. But I was trying to stop the killing, then. I made my way to France then, seeking a scientific answer. The men at the Académie des Sciences did not take me seriously, but they were willing to poke and prod and take samples of my blood."

Tell her about when you all went out for a demonstration, hissed the beast inside him. *Tell her how they all died.* Cezar ignored the voice.

"When the war started, I joined with the French to fight. Here I thought was a good use for my abilities. I feared no bullet or cannon; I could use my abilities without anyone caring. At first it went well. I volunteered for everything; I was a scout for my battalion. I went into the worst of the fighting and tore the enemy to pieces. When the full moon came, I managed to always be deep in enemy territory scouting and then made it back eventually to my men.

"Most of the other soldiers feared and despised me for my luck and glee at killing. They hated the war, hated to kill, they hated the fear they always felt. Some though, a few liked me. My squad thought of me as their good luck charm. I never got hurt bad, I could face anything. Poison gas angered me, grenades knocked me down, bullets stung but did not harm me much."

Cezar smelled Germans nearby. A foot patrol, out to find those out past curfew. This one had found some vodka, by the smell of their breath. He paused to listen to them pass by, one in the middle of a story about a milk maid's hands.

"But I grew bored and restless. And the war did not feel like I hoped it would. Killing Germans and their allies did not feel like I was using my abilities properly. It was just killing, still. I could not hate them, these Germans. They were just soldiers like my friends. And I could speak German well enough by then that they even sounded just like my squad. The same jokes, the same hopes, the same fears.

"I left one day on patrol. I just kept running east. Anyone who stopped me died, and I expect the soldiers all thought their good luck charm finally ran out of good luck. I don't know, and I don't especially care. I'd heard stories out of Russia, about a revolution there. They were fighting to defeat the Czar and his family, for freedom, to overthrow the rich and powerful. That sounded good to me."

Aniela had heard tales. Some of her Polish friends spoke fondly of the Russian revolution, hoping it could happen there. The ones most in favor of Lenin's ideas were the ones she suspected were in the resistance. She had no contact with the AK but everyone suspected they knew some.

"I joined in the revolution, although I could speak no Russian. Enough spoke French that I could get by, and we flew the red flag with pride, for a time. And then after a while I noticed that the only ones fighting were the upper class educated people.

"The peasants didn't seem to care one way or another who was in charge. They were almost completely ignorant of life outside their village, so simple they could barely add small sums. They liked the idea of not having lords and ladies rule over them, but freedom didn't even make sense to most of them. And for the poorest, nothing much really changed, only who gave them orders. Someone would show up and tell them about their freedom and how everything was changed, then they would leave and it would be the same as before.

"And the speeches and claims of the revolutionaries seemed to only apply to words, not practice. Everything was to be put off until later, and until then, they would be the same as the aristocrats before them. It would be years, they said, before the people were ready to be free and equal. But they wanted to rule now.

"It was in Russia that I met Katyushia. Katarina Borisovna, a lovely girl who served some duke near Riga. The revolutionaries called me 'Stalnivolk', the steel wolf. They didn't know exactly what I was, but they knew I could be sent into the worst traps and toughest fights and I would rip through them all.

"This duke had a veritable army protecting his summer palace and his family was hiding there. The local people loved and protected him and the revolutionaries could get no help from them. So they sent me, and I went in alone, in the evening of the full moon. I entered the palace and painted it with blood, killing everyone. Everyone but this handmaiden; for some reason the wolf let this pretty blonde girl live, barely. She was in her late teens, and skinny as a stick but so beautiful.

"I nursed her back to health, entranced by her huge blue eyes. They had a tilt in them almost like an oriental, perhaps some Mongol blood from generations past."

Aniela felt a thrum of jealousy run through her and felt foolish for it. Why was she jealous over a dead girl for man she didn't even want any more?

"Katyushia, she called herself. How she lived I do not know. But I cared for her and forgot the revolution. We left for the mountains and lived there off my hunting in an old cabin someone had abandoned.

She taught me Russian and I taught her French. I thought perhaps I'd found a new life, and somewhere deep down I knew what she would become. But then, she would be like me, and I would not be alone.

"When the full moon came again, she changed. By then she had fully healed and I knew she was like me. We hunted together, and I did not care who died. She was beside me, my she-wolf to share my life. But Katyushia was different than me. She wanted to be the wolf constantly; she loved the power and the freedom. Perhaps it was growing up a servant, perhaps it was just her age, I do not know.

"She became more and more unstable, attacking me for the slightest disagreement, going out every day to hunt people. I had to go after her and make sure her targets were dead; whether she was leaving them alive on purpose or not I could not tell and she would only smile at me when I asked. I tried to teach her to control her beast, but she only wanted to know how to force the change.

"The last time we fought, she changed in the middle and tore my guts out. I healed rapidly, lying on the cabin floor and knew I had to hunt her down. I tracked her across Russia into Ukraine, across the forests and finally caught her. She was still the wolf; somehow she had never changed back. Perhaps that's what eventually happens, when you finally give in. She never fought it, she embraced the beast. We fought for more than a day, a battle across miles of forest, through villages and into lakes.

"Somehow, we could hurt each other more than mere weapons. Perhaps the beast is vulnerable to its self, perhaps there's something supernatural about our attacks, I can't say. Finally I caught her and... I managed to — to kill her."

You tore her head off, growled the beast. *Tell your little angel about how you did that to the child.*

"And so I found my way to Poland and lived in the west for years, hiding out and living on my own. Then the Germans invaded."

"But what were you doing in the prison camp?" Aniela asked.

Before Cezar could answer, the door opened.

CHAPTER TWENTY-ONE

Cezar winced. He'd been so wrapped up in his story and his memories he had not even noticed anyone in the hall outside. The figure in the door wore a German uniform, a thin young man huge dark eyes trying to see into the blackness of the room.

"Angel, is that you in the bed?" Asked Abel. "I've come like I promised! It was a very long day, the patrol was much later than I hoped."

Cezar slid out of the bed and walked to the window. Aniela pulled the covers around her like a little girl hiding from the monster in the closet. Abel entered the room and closed the door behind him. There was a click as he turned on the little rectangular light issued soldiers by the German military. The beam swept over Aniela in the bed and Abel smiled.

"Ah you are awake, how nice."

"Go away, please." Said Aniela. "You don't know what you're doing."

"Ah you can show me, yes? Show me what you like best." Abel knelt on the bed and leaned over Aniela, one hand on the wall.

"Junge," said Cezar quietly "raus, während Sie können."

Aniela looked at Cezar wondering what he'd said.

Abel froze at the sound of the voice.

"So, you have a lover do you?" he said, slipping the bayonet at his side out of its sheath. "Wie war sein Name?"

"Cezar Alexandru."

Abel turned his flashlight at the sound of the voice and his eyes widened. The figure was tall, almost half a head taller than him. He was broad shouldered and muscular like a circus strong man, with thick body hair over his chest and down his legs, and completely nude. His

141

hair hung past his shoulders, black as night and slightly wavy, with part of it hanging in his dark eyes. *Cezar Alexandru...*

"Du? Der Flüchtling!"

Cezar grinned through his dark beard, showing teeth that seemed sharper than an ordinary man's.

Abel started to take a breath to shout and Cezar crossed the room in a single leap, seizing the soldier around the throat with one hand and by the crotch with the other. Lifting Abel off the floor like he was made of straw, Cezar held him a moment as the soldier uttered a strangled cry of pain, then slammed him against the brass railing at the foot of the bed, straight across his lower back. Abel rolled to the floor, stunned. In a flash of pain his legs had gone numb yet his groin felt as if it had been crushed in a car door. His flashlight spun on the floor, dropped and forgotten, its light pointed at the ceiling. Huge shadows at an extreme angle from the light bore into the wall, and Cezar's seemed darker than the rest to Aniela as she sat curled up against the wall against the head of her bed.

Cezar bent over him and whispered something Aniela could not hear, then his hand flashed down. A crunching, rending wet sound slid through the darkness and Cezar stood with something in his fist dangling wet, torn pieces. Liquid splashed on the floor and spread, some of it spattering the flashlight and turning the room reddish.

"Abel, wie geht's?" Said a voice outside the closed door.

"Kommen Sie und sehen." Said Cezar, voice deep and rough like a growl. He dropped something to the floor with a thud.

"Was ist —?" The door opened suddenly and another soldier stood there. Jodl, Aniela remembered from the hallway. Cezar laughed as Jodl stared at the body on the floor. It was lying in a widening spread of blood which had begun to widen under the door and was pooling around his boots. It was the body of Abel. It had no head.

Jodl tore at his waist, fumbling with the leather pouch holding his luger. Cezar patiently waited until he started to pull it free, smiling at the German like a patient schoolmaster. Then he lunged, his momentum carrying the soldier down the stairs with a crashing of bodies against wood. Aniela stared at the hallway, hearing them tumbling down the stairs.

He heard a masculine scream suddenly cut off, and more shouting in German. Beneath her there were footsteps, boots on the wooden floor rushing to see what the commotion was. Aniela heard her uncle cry out to stop fighting, wondering who this intruder was. She heard another cry and a horrible crunching noise as if a human body was being crushed in a giant press.

A gunshot, incredibly loud and sharp, rang Aniela's ears, shocking her free of her pose clutching the sheets against her. She swept her clothes off the floor, worried that they would get dirty from the blood without realizing what she was thinking. Pulling her clothes on as quickly as she could, Aniela stared at the head on the floor. It stared back at her, Abel's dead face frozen with a look of confused amazement and spattered with his own blood. Her slippers were sodden with blood and she left them, stepping bare footed carefully around the red pool to the stairs.

Several more shots rang out, then something hit the wall below so hard it shook the entire house, dust falling from small cracks in the ceiling. There was a tearing sound accompanied by a bellowing scream. The screaming went on as Aniela carefully picked her way down the stairs, avoiding the blood smeared on the wall.

A body slid across the floor on a loose rug, twisted so the head and upper body was facing completely backward, hands clenched into claws of agony. Cezar's laugh bounced off the wooden walls to Aniela, almost to the bottom of the stairs now.

"What have you done??" Demanded uncle Aleksy.

"My dear God, who are you?" Said aunt Joanna.

Cezar said nothing, only chuckled. Aniela stepped into the room carefully over the German soldier. A hand gripped her leg and she shrieked, looking down. The twisted German was looking up at her with one bloodshot eye, tears streaming from it.

"Bit— bitte, Mädchen. Bitte..." his voice trailed off and his hand slipped free, lifeless.

Uncle Aleksy followed Cezar into the kitchen. "Who are you? Do you know what you have done? You have killed us all!"

"Grow some eggs, old man," growled Cezar in heavily accented Polish.

"The Germans will come, they will take us away! Who are you? What are you doing here??"

Aunt Joanna stared at the kitchen then at Aniela. "You, Aniela, who is this man?"

Aniela stared at Joanna helplessly.

"You, you brought him into our home, didn't you? What is he?" asked Joanna

Aniela shook her head. She had only half believed his story before, but now.... Aniela slid a hand across her belly. What if he had planted a seed in her? What would a baby from a vârcolac be like? Would it claw its way out of her instead of being born? Would it have a tail and ears like the wolf-man in that movie? Would she have to brush all its fur? She giggled a little, feeling dizzy and unsteady. Joanna looked at Aniela closely. She seemed hysterical, in shock.

"Aniela, what is wrong with you?" Joanna crossed the room to her. "You're so pale! What did he do to you?"

"Oh, *everything*." Aniela said, blushing deeply at her boldness and the memory.

"Aniusa, little one, what have you done?"

Outside, Private Erich Meier ran. He was sure the man had seen him slip out the door and was chasing him down the dark street. Behind him lay his bayonet and knapsack, his helmet and various tools and implements he had throw aside. They were all slowing him down. He could hear nothing but his feet on the bricks, but the huge man's bare feet would be quiet on the street. There were no cars, no people talking, no radios playing this time of night. All the windows were darkened and lights off. He didn't even see a patrol as he ran.

Finally, exhausted, he staggered into a shop entry, sunken between two windowed show spaces with drawn shades. He slid down the glass window lettered carefully in crazy Polish letters with lines and strange marks on the words. He saw no sign of the man, but whoever it was probably was in the shadows. The Sergeant had shot him three times with his luger, and it had done nothing. He had torn poor Marcus Liefeld's arm completely off and hit Marcus with it as he fell to the floor spraying blood. He was unstoppable.

Erich shook helplessly against the door, wondering how, if he was so tired, that he still had the energy to shiver in fear. His legs ached as if they were dipped in acid, throbbing with the exertion of his flight. Still no one came for him. *Perhaps he did not see me*, thought Erich.

After his heart calmed and his legs stopped burning, Erich lit a cigarette. No patrol had driven or walked by yet. He thought the patrols would more thorough, but they probably were drinking in some bar. His hands still shook as he held the cigarette. He had to tell someone. But what could he say? Everyone in his squad was dead save himself. He had no rank or connections to be heard.

But that SS major, he had listened to the Romanian's stories and seemed interested. This was connected with whatever they were doing, he was sure of it. It had to be the fugitive. Nobody in the squad understood why so many soldiers had been pulled in to search for one missing gypsy. Erich understood now. He had to find the major.

*****

"You, big man," said Sergeant-Major Franz. He lay awkwardly against the floor, his head at an angle against the wainscoting at the base of the wall. Cezar had broken his neck and pelvis along with several ribs, but he felt no pain.

Cezar walked back in, still nude but so confident and powerful-seeming nobody seemed to notice or care. He had washed the blood off his face and hands, but his body was still spattered and smeared, like some ancient berserker.

"You're who we are hunting, eh?" asked Franz in German, voice weak and rough.

"Are you hunting me?" asked Cezar, crouching close to the sergeant to peer at him curiously.

"A lot of us are. We'll find you."

Cezar looked around the room, littered with bodies, and said "You did."

"No, the military will find you. There are more looking... looking for you. It's too bad, I won't get to see you meet the Romanian."

Cezar looked down into his eyes. "I've met a lot of Romanians."

"Not like this one. I guess he was right all along."

"You look familiar. The part of your face that is not damaged, at least. From the war."

"You don't."

"I doubt you ever saw me. I was in Lille when the German armies invaded from Belgium. When you crossed the Deûle I was there, I saw how you ordered Belgian civilians to cross in front of you to protect you."

Franz thought a while. "I didn't make that order; it was given to me by my Hauptmann. But they were franc-tireurs, resistance."

"Even the children?"

"No one forced the French to open fire. They could have let us advance."

"You forced the civilians forward at gunpoint. Some tried to run and your troops shot them."

Franz closed his eyes.

"We all did horrible things in that war, Sergeant. But war didn't make us evil."

"Maybe its inside us, waiting for an opportunity," Franz said very quietly.

"Some of us more than others," Cezar said even quieter.

Cezar grasped his head in both hands, but Franz had already died from his injuries. Cezar wiped his hands on the sergeant's clothes and headed up the stairs.

"Aniela, what is this? Who is he??" Aleksy asked in a whisper.

Aniela shook her head. "Uncle Rys warned me but... I couldn't... I don't know Uncle, please don't."

"Please don't what? They will drag us to Pomorska! We're all going to a camp now! That man, he murdered all these soldiers in our house, don't you understand? We are Romani, they will find out and no one listens to us, they won't believe some crazy man killed them all!"

Joanna stared up the steps. "What did Uncle Rys say? About the man."

"Marime." She said. *Werewolf*, she thought.

"Oh, *Aniusa*. You never could listen to anyone. Oh Aleksy what will we do?"

"We must get Aniela away. She can hide, send her to the bookstore."

"Now? After curfew? Alesky, we are not Armia Krajowa, we do not have a way to move people around the city! The Blue Police are probably already on their way!"

"What about next door, she could hide there, no one goes there anymore."

"And her room? All of her things, what will they say when they find it? You have someone else here, that's what they'll say. They will beat us when they find her. All of those men are corrupt." She whispered the last words, looking at the front door.

Cezar came down the stairs from Aniela's room, dressed again.

"Aniela, come with me."

She shook her head and leaned against her uncle Alesky.

"She's right. Stay here and they'll take you all. Come with me and I can keep you safe"

Yes, like Marisol, she'll be safe with you, won't she? The beast sneered.

"She is going nowhere with you, monster!" Aleksy yelled at Cezar, striding across the room. He was a foot shorter than Cezar, and had a middle aged belly he could rest a glass of Tatanka on, but he was fierce in his protection of Aniela. "You are a destroyer, you will stay away from her and from us. Get out. GET OUT!!"

Cezar looked down at Aleksy, head tilted slightly. For a moment he considered backhanding the old man into a crumpled heap at the feet of his trembling wife who stood kneading her night robe in her fists.

Aniela's voice was strangely cheerful but calm. "Cezar. You don't have to be the monster."

Cezar flashed angry eyes over at her, daring her to continue. She stood quietly with an almost hysterical look in her dark eyes. Cezar hung his head. *I am a destroyer. All I ever bring is death.* He looked up with tired eyes. "Good bye, Aniela."

Turning, he walked out of the room, tracking blood in his footsteps. Joanna slid down against the wall, wailing in fear and despair.

CHAPTER TWENTY-TWO

Rys Radescu rode toward Wawel Castle in the back of his Cadillac Series 61 sedan. Just getting the car to him from America had cost more money than the purchase price, but it was such a status symbol that people stared and scattered away from it. Rys thought of riding in the Cadillac as being like riding in a tank; people assumed you were so important they didn't want to bother you. Four meters long and black as night, the chrome gleamed like starlight and the huge German driver in front sent another warning to anyone who looked closely.

They were driving past curfew, but Rys had managed to buy a special pass allowing him to travel when others could not. They were not even stopped by a patrol; everyone knew his car and feared his connections. That was all coming to an end. He could almost feel the Gestapo closing in, grim hunters in black coats like a murder of crows.

At the gates of the castle, he was let in mostly out of reputation and his paperwork. It was too late to be dropping by, and rumor had it that Himmler was in town staying at the castle. But these were desperate times, and Rys was going to call in all his favors for the final great game.

At first Hans Frank refused to see Rys. He was sleeping, indisposed, the officious German aide insisted. But Rys would not be refused.

"Ask him if he is interested in the Sanzio 'Portrait of a Young Man.'"

The aide looked uncertain, and Rys just waited, the hulking German bodyguard standing behind him. After a few moments of indecision, the aide turned away and left the room, muttering to himself.

"Do you think he will come?" asked Peter Fleischer.

147

"For the painting yes. But it will take more to calm him down."

The bodyguard looked at the boxes he'd brought in. "You won't have much left."

"All of this I collected only for just such an occasion."

Peter had smoked two cigarettes before the governor-general arrived. He was dressed for bed and his hair was askew, making him look confused and surprised.

"Yes, what is it, Radescu? It is eleven at night!"

"My apologies, but this could not wait. Might we sit down?"

Hans Frank looked impatient, glancing back the direction he'd come. The girl in his room had been particularly athletic and enthusiastic even if she didn't have the blonde hair he preferred. In the dark it wouldn't matter but she wanted the lights on.

"Very well, Rys. But be quick about it."

Rys unrolled the painting on the small table between their seats. The edges draped over the sides, but the identity of the image was unmistakable. Frank leaned over the painting, staring.

"It was you?"

Rys nodded. "You must forgive me this little joke, I knew you wanted it but I had to play a little prank and picked it up first."

"I thought the black market underground had stolen it!"

They had, but Rys was not about to admit that to the governor-general.

"No, I had a friend pick it up, he's been useful to me in the past at... acquiring items."

Frank and Radescu shared a grin. Both were fond of collecting valuables by any means. The position of governor over the General Government region had given Frank many opportunities to loot and gather treasures as far away as Sophia.

"So, the joke is over. Here, it is yours. I trust you hold no grudge over this?"

Hans Frank shook his head. Adolph Hitler had expressed an interest in hanging the painting in the Berghof. Being able to produce it now would charm the Fuhrer. Despite their friendship, Hitler had always distrusted and disliked lawyers, and Frank always sought to ease that rift.

"But that is not why I came. I have a request to ask of you." Said Rys.

"Yes?" Frank was distracted, looking at the painting. It was in magnificent shape still. "What was it you wanted?"

"I must leave the city soon, and I was hoping you could help me with two problems."

Frank looked up. Leaving? Why would Radescu wish to leave the city that he had become so wealthy in?

"First, I have a concern with some... enemies of mine. I have long been troubled by people that have despised my success. They say horrible things about me, and my association with the Germans. As you know I have tried to reach out to the people here, finding them work and helping them with homes and such."

Frank nodded. Several times Rys had come to his office asking for assistance and bringing gifts. Usually it was for people the Gestapo suspected of being Gyspies.

"I have had no success, and I fear that if I try to move, they will attack me when I am out of my home, and vulnerable. You understand."

"Indeed I do. I have been a target of these resistance fighters since I arrived."

"There you have it. I have been able to arrange a train to be brought to Krakow, I was hoping you could find a way to have some soldiers escort these... people to the train for, shall we say, relocation?"

Frank glanced up at Rys from the painting.

"A bit of work for them in a camp, then?"

Rys shrugged. "I tried to make friends, but what can I do? I would need all the proper paperwork and authorizations. Peter here has them filled out, all they need is your signature."

"Perhaps it can be done."

"I understand, this requires some thought. Yet I have a second problem that only you can help me with. As you know over the years here I have managed to acquire a few items, nothing like your superb collection of course, but a few items of value. I cannot take them all with me on a trip. The Cadillac, for instance."

Hans Frank leaned forward slightly, despite his attempt to seem disinterested and calm.

"I cannot take it with me on an aeroplane, and of course, I have other items. If you could be so kind as to oversee them, to keep them for me, should I have a chance to come and collect them again in perhaps a year or two?"

Peter opened up one of the boxes. In it were several Dárer etchings and beneath it he could see the glitter of gold and jewels. Other rolled up paintings and ancient books were stacked in boxes, and Hans Frank's eyes glittered.

"These will of course all be registered and cataloged."

"Naturally," Rys nodded. "I know I can trust you to care for them as you do the other art treasures of this land."

Frank eyed 'Portrait of a Young Man.' The Fuhrer had seized Frank's DaVinci for the Fuhrermuseum several years earlier, perhaps this could take its place on his wall for a few months. He reached for the stack of forms and selected a fountain pen from a nearby desk.

*****

Officer Pryczing of the Blue Police stood in the doorway of the Sawiki residence looking at the carnage. He was glad someone had called the police instead of the Germans, although they were sure to be

149

on their way. His men were picking through the bodies, removing evidence from their pockets and wrists. One of the Germans had a valuable ring as well. By law, 10% of all evidence collected went directly into the pockets of the Blue Police, and his men were well trained in collecting everything from a crime scene. The Germans in command had found it useful in motivating and corrupting the Polish officers.

Pryczing stepped carefully into the room, trying to avoid the blood. The gore was like a scene out of a Stefan Grabiński novel.

"Doesn't look like they have much... evidence here to collect." Officer Syring said quietly as he passed by. Pryczing nodded. He would find out. He walked to the young woman in the heavy coat sitting at a chair. Tipping her face up to him, he could see through the tears and fear that she was attractive, in her twenties.

"Young lady we'll need to know the whole story. But first, you will tell us where everything of value is in this house. All of you will be detained and questioned, and we cannot leave the house to be looted while you are away. All will be taken and cataloged for later. If you leave anything out, it will just encourage looting."

Aniela shook her head. She felt like she was numb and floating instead of in the room. That strange giddy feeling had gone away and she felt sick inside.

Officer Pryczing rolled his eyes, then backhanded Aniela off her chair. She landed without a sound staring up at him with tears welling in her eyes.

"Leave her alone!" shouted Aleksy, and officer Syring punched him in the belly. Aleksy doubled over as Joanne bent over him, crying again.

"Tell us where it all is, now. We are not wasting any more time." Pryczing said with a bored tone as he drove a boot into Aniela's side. "I will break a bone for each time you refuse."

Aniela lay on the floor silently, tears sliding down her face. Cezar was a monster, not just a werewolf, but an uncaring killer. He could have stayed and protected them, he could have taken them all away. He cared nothing for anyone but himself, all those sad stories about how bad he felt. What about his victims? What about the families of the people he murdered? How did they feel?

She barely felt as Pryczing kicked her again. He shook his head and ordered his men to take her to a room. She'd wake up after a few of them had their rounds with her. Until then he could work on the old woman. Break a few of her fingers and the old man would tell her where his grandmother buried the family jewels.

"What is happening here?" A commanding voice demanded in German.

So soon? Officer Pryczing thought. Turning he stepped back a pace and swallowed. It was an SS Major, with a cluster of SS soldiers behind him. And this one looked very capable.

"Ah, um," Pryczing thought furiously, trying to translate into German "Herr Major, we, ah..."

The Major turned to a soldier and the young man stepped into the room.

"I am corporal Sankt, I will translate for you." He said in accented Polish. Pryczing felt a small level of relief.

"Good, thank you, corporal. We have just arrived, having received reports of gunfire. I have not had time to interrogate the people here, but there appear to be four dead here and perhaps more upstairs."

"Yes murdered by a man," Sankt translated the Major. "I am referring to your stealing from the bodies of my men."

Pryczing froze in place staring at the Major, his mouth opening and closing without any sound. The look on Ritter's face was ice cold and merciless. Major Ritter saw the men lying mangled on the floor in all that blood with vultures picking over them and could only remember the fields of Belgium and France.

"Who are you?" Asked a clipped German voice behind Ritter.

Ritter spun, furious at the interruption, to face a lieutenant in the SS.

"I am SS-Sturmbannführer Heirich Wolfgang Ritter, here in Krakow on special assignment, upon Deputy Fuhrer Martin Bormann's personal orders. And who are you, *Untersturmführer?*"

Peter Klein once again felt disappointment that his promotion had not come through yet from Berlin, but was not intimidated. "I am Head of the Order Police for the General Government and I was alerted to a murder here of SS troops. Were they your men?"

Ritter eyed the young lieutenant, his anger fading rapidly as it always did. "Yes. They were murdered, by what I believe to be a fugitive we have been tasked with tracking down."

"You have my sympathies, Sturmbannführer. My men will handle the investigation so you may continue your work for the Reich on behalf of Herr Bormann."

"I will turn over the investigation to you once I have examined the scene," Ritter said quietly and stepped into the room.

Peter Klein seethed inside. Politically, he was in a more powerful position than Ritter, but he was outranked, and special orders from Bormann himself would probably counter his position as temporary head of the Order Police. He was determined to not let the first major case he would oversee be taken away from him, but he felt cautious. It was not absolutely certain that he would be given the command of the Order Police, and he wanted to demonstrate speed and efficiency in solving the case. Antagonizing a superior officer working for such a powerful man would not help certify his promotion.

Inside, Ritter looked around the room. There were five bodies of SS troops and the sergeant with his heroically ruined features lying on the floor. They had died horribly, but swiftly, just as most of the men in the forest had. He tried to remember how many it had been, how many were on the escaped monster's account. Dozens, at least that he knew of. Good German men, soldiers with families, heroes fighting for the Reich and slaughtered by something that ought not exist.

One of the Blue Police officers came down the steps, laughing. "Hey, Syring, the girl had some jewelry in her room, let's pick out our ten percen—" his voice tailed off when he saw Ritter standing in the room with a face like a tombstone; chiseled with death and finality.

Ritter pushed past him up into the upper floor, and Peter Klein began giving orders to his men. They took over from the Blue Police, who were pushed outside and told to go report to their superiors. Syring and Pryczing looked at each other in relief, hoping the SS Major would forget them, and never find out their names.

Aniela, Joanna, and Aleksy stood holding each other like an island of family in a sea of contradictory brutality and cold indifference. At first the police moved around them as if they were furniture, taking pictures and measurements, collecting evidence. Foot prints were measured, fingerprints taken, and everything modern and scientific that Peter Klein could find in a book was done to the crime scene. Finally, the family was shuffled off to a truck and driven away to the Silesian House.

Aniela watched the small patch of light from their home slide away as the truck rumbled over the rough street and could only think of those thorough, efficient policemen finding the machine in her room. Aniela knew it was a sin to kill herself, but she was certain that under questioning she would let something slip and doom them all. Father Gorski would tell her it meant a certain trip to hell and that she could never be buried in sanctified ground but surely it would be worth it to save her aunt and uncle? Aniela touched her stomach again. And perhaps it would prevent another monster from entering the earth as well.

*****

Vladimir Czerny watched the device in St Mary's Basilica. The candles were the only light source in the room now, but the thing was still reacting to the energies it was fed and focusing their soft light onto the altar's surface. A German map of the city had been laid on the wooden surface as precisely arranged as Czerny could manage.

Two of the lenses showing the werewolf's abode were still adjusting, moving the light more toward an area Northwest of Wawel Castle, near Park Krakowski. Czerny's attention was upon something else, though.

The third lens was directing attention northeast of the castle, and it had been almost immediately as soon as the device had started working. Vladimir had intended the energies from Princess Wanda's suicide to be harnessed for the spirit of the Polish People to protect

152

them from the monster in their midst, to give the ritual force and swiftness. But all of it was being directed toward that one indicator.

Czerny betrayed no emotion or reaction, his face bland. Already the soldiers guarding him and the location had become bored and were sleeping. Only three remained from the troop that had brought him here, the rest returning home with the hideously scarred sergeant. But Czerny watched the lens closely as it focused on one point on the map.

Someone in that location was being indicated by Wanda's spirit and nature. And the lens had recently started moving, toward the area noted by the others.

CHAPTER TWENTY-THREE

It was an hour earlier in Bletchley, England. The mansion Bletchley Park stood in all its victorian splendor with the curved drive and well-manicured lawns hiding a hive of secret activity inside. Inside the stately building, Paul Connelly sat at the table with a man from SIS in London whose name he had not been told, his commander Josh Cooper, and Alan Turing from decryption.

Connelly had been Watch Commander when the first werewolf message had come in from BANGLE in Poland. He had been very hesitant to contact his superiors on the information, but as different sources and reports, some from ENIGMA had begun to support her report, it had been impossible to keep quiet.

"See here now," began Cooper, "I still say this is preposterous."

Turing was a quiet man who preferred solitude and was squirming slightly in his seat from discomfort. "I am only reporting what the cyphers are giving us."

"We don't even know the full ENIGMA code yet, you must be mistaken!"

The man from London cleared his throat and the others fell silent. "As astonishing as it may seem to you, there have been quite a few reports on this from many sources. And were I to tell you what the Germans have been up to in Egypt, you would call it wild fiction. We have to consider this information part of ULTRA."

The table was quiet a while. The men looked at their paperwork as if it would hold answers they prefered.

"Gentlemen, BANGLE has recently sent us another communication," said Connelly.

The other men at the table looked up at him in unison, as if they had practiced. Connelly suddenly felt less confident.

"She reports that the, ah, the escapee is being hunted through Krakow by the Germans."

"Anything else?" asked the SIS man.

"There has been no contact since then, sir. BANGLE does not report in very often, but... has been very reliable and accurate." Connelly struggled to avoid mentioning her gender. *All these secrets, so hard to keep track.*

"Well then, I suppose the question is what our response should be." said Cooper. "If this chap is some sort of prodigy, it seems like it is in our interest to keep him out causing as much mischief for Jerry as possible, as long as we can."

"All well and good, but our assets are very limited in Krakow," responded the SIS man.

"What about the resistance?" said Connelly, feeling more confident.

"Which resistance?" asked Cooper. "There's the Armia Krajowa, and the ZOB."

Connelly wracked his memory. ŻOB, Polish: Żydowska Organizacja Bojowa. The Jewish Fighting Organziation. He recalled a few reports of successful strikes against SS and Gestapo leaders by their group.

"Churchill doesn't trust the AK," said the SIS man. "They are far too cozy with the Soviet Union for his liking, and mine as well."

"How significant a presence do we know the ZOB have in Krakow?" asked Cooper.

"Very little, they are primarily in Warsaw."

"What are our other options?" Connelly asked.

The man from SIS looked up and frowned. He didn't care for the other options. It would require approval from INTREPID and a call to London to activate their only asset in Krakow. Was it worth it? He decided that was outside his authority to decide.

"I will contact London and see what we can do. Keep me appraised with any new developments."

The men nodded and went back to work. Today was their long day, a 16 hour shift at the end of the week before a day off.

*****

Major Ritter rode in the front of the old Mercedes truck, bumping along the rough streets. The investigation last night had gone so late he'd barely had time to go to sleep before his orderly woke him. In a bad enough mood after last night's clash with Peter Klein, his mood had not improved upon finding the Romanian's device was not yet focused on one point.

However it had shown a distinct enough area to allow a full scale search. And while Klein had been annoyingly territorial, he had returned all of the soldier's personal effects to the bodies. More importantly, because the killer in Klein's case was very likely the camp escapee, that meant more men were on the street looking for him and Ritter welcomed the manpower, as unprofessional as it may be. If the weird Romanian and his experiments had not shown any promise, Ritter had planned on commandeering officers from the Order Police to assist with the search in any case.

He had left Czerny at the basilica with the device with orders to the men guarding him to send word of any new developments or information. The little man was even less talkative than normal; just getting those stories about Polish history had been surprising from him. Ritter guessed it was nerves, he had to know what he would face if his efforts failed. Czerny had made it clear he expected to be executed once the work was done in any case, but Ritter was not sure. The Fuhrer loved mysticism and word of success from this little man might ensure him a place in Berlin as an advisor. He certainly seemed well informed.

The truck stopped at the first building in the grid that he had laid out on the map. House to house searches were usually boring and time consuming, but one never knew what they might find. After all, Peter Klein had reported to Himmler weeks ago that there were still Jews hiding in the city. Ritter approved of Governor-General Frank's ghetto scheme. When the time came to "disable" the Jewish population it would be considerably easier in a controlled area.

As the men hopped out of the back of the truck and lined up by the house, Ritter glanced up and spotted a figure on the rooftop, then it was gone. He climbed out of the truck, slamming the heavy metal door. They would head to the top floor first.

*****

Cezar grinned, leaping to another rooftop. He wasn't certain the SS troops were after him, but it seemed likely after his slaughter the night before. He didn't regret killing the men, he almost never did and these were only German SS. The German regular army was made up of men fighting for their country for the most part. But the SS were the most loyal, most fascist, and most inhuman, Cezar thought.

You'd know about being inhuman, the beast snarled.

Cezar ignored it. It was fairly quiet after the killings and the night with Aniela, as if it had been sated by sex and slaughter. At least she didn't seem to hate him as much by the time that German had stepped in. He wasn't sure what Aniela thought of him now, she'd been in such shock that he couldn't even smell her mood.

He stood on a balcony of an empty building and watched the city pass by. The castle and St Mary's was visible from the balcony, and the street was busy beneath him. He had come to this location several times before and sat to watch the people. He felt less lonely this time, less abandoned. Talking to Aniela had taken a great load off his heart, even if nothing had changed.

"I would have expected you to keep moving," said a voice behind him in Romanian.

Cezar spun, angry at himself. Twice now someone had intruded on him without his being aware of them. The interior of the building was lit well in the morning sun, but the only one standing there was a short, slim man in a black coat and leather trilby wearing round spectacles.

"You're lost, little man. Run along while you can." Cezar responded in the same language, and then realized he had been speaking Romanian. "Who are you?"

Vladimir Czerny turned a nearby crate on its side and sat on it.

"The only one in this city who can help you."

"I don't need any help." Cezar said and turned back to watch the city.

"You can be killed, you know. It's not easy, but it can be done."

Cezar turned back to the little man.

"Enough damage at once," Czerny said, "and you could not heal fast enough from it all. It's been done before."

"There's no one else like me."

"No, not any more. Your kind used to be less unique, long ago."

"Who are you?" Cezar asked again.

"If you would like to know, I suggest traveling with me somewhere else, somewhere different from here. There is a store called 'Under the Eagle' in the Jewish Ghetto. It's a pharmacy, we can get a soda there and chat a bit away from here."

"No one is here."

"No one will bother us there, either." Czerny turned and walked down the steps quietly. "But here may be very busy, soon."

*****

They were clearing the third building when a runner arrived. He was still out of breath when he finally found Major Ritter.

"Sir, I have news, from the church." The young man leaned against the wall and took deep breaths.

"Report." Ritter snapped.

"The Romanian, he has gone."

"Gone? Gone how?"

"He stepped out with a guard to the facilities and when ten minutes had passed, the guard checked and no one was in the room."

"Climbed out a window? Sloppy, the guard should have accompanied him into the room."

"The windows don't open sir. They are too small for someone to climb out of. He seems to have just...vanished."

Ritter glared at the messenger until the young man began to shake. It wasn't his fault, but the men should have kept a closer eye on the little man. The guard probably went out to smoke and came up

157

with this idiotic story. Some time on the Eastern Front would remind him of his duty.

Ritter dismissed the messenger to get a drink and rest a moment then scowled in thought. Why would the Romanian leave now? Had the machine finalized where the beast would be found and he was avoiding the shooting he feared? Or had it shown him something else?

"Round up the men and the prisoners. Schultz, take a squad of Order Police and deliver the prisoners to the Silesian House. The rest load up and tell Heinz that we're heading to the basilica." The wizened old sergeant was not much of a soldier but he drove well enough.

*****

Aniela sat in the small stone cell in the wet basement of Silesian House and stared at the wooden door. It had been built in a diamond pattern, with planks set at 45 degree angles forming a design like some other doors she'd seen in older Krakow buildings. It would have been attractive in another setting. A long iron latch reached halfway across the door, securely anchored outside. A small circular porthole in the door was covered by a heavy iron shutter.

The only light in the cell came from a single bulb covered by an iron cage. The room had no bench, bed, or facilities and the floor was wet. One corner of the room had a small pool of water in it. The walls and floor were concrete and on the wall nearest Aniela someone had written a bar of music, and the words "I too was here." Aniela wondered what the music was.

Somewhere a man screamed, crying out love for his wife, then nothing. Aniela leaned against the wall, arms around herself. She was cold in the simple striped prison smock and the wall was wet where she leaned, making her colder. It didn't matter now if they found the machine, it was over. No one left this place free. There wasn't even any way to kill herself in here. The Poles knew this place as Pomorska, and the very word filled them with dread.

The shutter swung open with a creak and a face showed in it momentarily.

"Step back from the door!" the voice commanded and the shutter slammed shut. Aniela stood still against the far wall and waited.

The door nosily unlocked and a man entered with a small desk and chair, setting them up in the middle of the room. He turned and stood by the door, and then a man in a crisp black suit entered holding a wooden box. From the box he took out a sheaf of papers, a small leather-bound book, a stamp, a bottle of ink, and a cloth pad imbued with ink. Setting them up carefully on the table in a method that suggested hundreds of repeated performances, the man sat down at the desk.

He was a handsome man, Aniela decided, with bright blue eyes and soft blond hair. He looked around thirty years old but not getting soft around the middle. His suit looked very expensive, down to the golden swastika pin on the lapel. That little pin made him ugly in her eyes.

"I am Alfred Schneider, Gestapo." He said in a voice that rang uncomfortably loud in the small cell. "I am here to ask you questions. You will answer directly and simply to each question. Tell the truth and you have nothing to fear. Do not waste my time; I have many prisoners to interrogate."

Aniela nodded.

"Your name?"

"Aniela Maryla Wisznewski."

Schneider wrote on a form. "Marital status?"

"I am a widow."

"Husband's name and date of death?"

"Alexander Wisnzewski. He died September 14, 1939."

"Location of birth?"

"Piła."

"'Pilwa,' that is in Reichsgau Wartheland?"

"Yes." It had been known as Posen, before the Germans invaded. A beautiful wooded area.

"Height?"

Aniela blinked. "Excuse me?" *Was he still talking about Alexander?*

"Your height."

"165 centimeters."

"Weight?"

"52 kilos."

"Eyes brown, hair blonde... occupation?"

"Hair dresser."

"Religious affiliation?"

"Catholic."

Schneider stared at Aniela's features. She didn't appear Jewish, although she had a darker complexion than most Poles.

"Have you any Jewish ancestors or relatives?"

"I know of none."

"Are your people originally from Poland?"

Aniela swallowed. "Yes."

"How many generations back?"

"I do not know. At least back to my great-grandparents." That much was true. "My people had moved to Poland from Romania during a famine many years before."

"Tell me about the events of last night, as clearly as you can."

Aniela had been thinking about this all night long, and had not slept. They would not believe her story of a werewolf. They would not care to know she had been sleeping with the man who slaughtered the soldiers. She did not know what her aunt and uncle would say.

"A man came into my room; I think he entered the empty adjoining house. There is a door that connects the two buildings and I believe he entered through that."

"I do not want speculation. I told you not to waste my time."

Aniela nodded. That made it easier.

"He entered my room while I was sleeping. He was a big man, very strong. He forced himself on me in my bed. I cried out once, when his hand slipped away and one of the German soldiers staying at our house came to check on him. Abel, I think was his name, he was a translator."

Schneider wrote in his book. He showed no reaction to the story.

"They fought, but it was very dark and I could not see what was happening. The soldier had a flashlight but it was in my eyes part of the time. I heard the soldier cry out and then a terrible sound. Another of the soldiers came to check on the noise and the man left my room to attack him on the stairs. I stayed in my room and hid and heard fighting downstairs. There was shooting and fighting. Then the man left. I looked downstairs and found my aunt and uncle in the room with all the bodies and...and then the police came."

Schneider finished writing. "Did you know this man?"

Aniela shook her head.

"Had you seen him before?"

"I do not remember. Maybe at the salon, I saw a man in the window yesterday that could have been him."

"What was his name?"

"He did not say." Aniela tried to tell the truth as much as she could, safely. Cezar had never said his name that night.

"Describe him please."

"He is tall, more than six feet, but I was lying down and it was very dark, so I cannot be sure. He is very broad and muscular and very hairy. He has a beard and hair to his shoulders, all very dark. I think his eyes were brown. I am sorry I did not see him very well."

Schneider wrote more.

"There were fingerprints and foot prints we could not identify on the windowsill of your room. They matched boot prints in your room. How do you account for that?"

"On my sill? But there's no ledge, my window is five meters from the street."

"What is your connection to the Armia Krajowa?" Schneider asked suddenly, not looking at Aniela. She was tired, how will she react?

"I have no connection to them." She sounded tired.

"What do you think about the German occupation of Poland?"

"I wish they would go home and leave us in peace."

Schneider looked up at Aniela, but he did not seem angry. "You are part of the Reich now. This *is* our home. One last question; why did this man not attack your aunt and uncle?"

Aniela thought a moment. "I don't know. When I came down stairs, he was gone. I heard my uncle shout at him."

Schneider wrote in his book and looked up at Aniela. When it was clear she had no more to say, he closed the book and packed up all his materials.

When the Gestapo man had left Aniela stared at the door. They had not asked about the machine, were they just leaving it out to see how she would react? She had expected a beating, tortures. Instead it was just business, cold and efficient, but not brutal. The Polish Blue Policemen had been worse to her. She felt terribly tired and knew she must sleep but did not think she could. Her nerves were so jumpy she was trembling and her stomach cramped. Had they not found the machine? Had she looked nervous? She supposed everyone looked nervous in a Gestapo cell; being too relaxed would probably make them more suspicious.

Later, Alfred Schneider stood in front of the desk of Ewald Lange, checking his notes.

"I doubt she's slept much tonight, although if her story is true she got a little before being attacked. She did not show any clear signs of dissembling, and her story was consistent with what the others said. Perhaps a few more days without sleep may get us to the truth."

Lange looked over his reading glasses at Schneider. "People find it harder to keep their lies straight when they go without sleep long enough, but they can find it hard to keep the truth straight as well. Have Frau Keppler examine the girl and question her again while she's under examination. It should disorient and upset her enough to stumble with any stories.

"Oh, one last thing. This rapist, she says. Why did he get undressed?"

"Untersturmführer?"

"According to her account, the rapist crept into her room at night to attack her. Why would he disrobe entirely? Its not unheard of but it is unusual."

"I see, a possible inconsistency in her story." Schneider marked it down in his notebook. "Very good, I shall ask her about that."

"See that you do. You are coming along well but have much to learn about interrogation. This case is meaningless for the Gestapo, but it is good practice for you."

Lange did not mention that he was doing Peter Klein a favor as well. With the SS-Major taking so many of his Order Police forces on a search for this fugitive killer he was understaffed and would not have gotten to these prisoners for a week or more. Klein hated the delay and the deviation from routine and regulation, a notion Lange shared. Order and system were the Aryan way.

161

The girl's story was plausible, but the killings disturbed all of the men involved. It was inconceivable that a single man could possibly have done the damage those men suffered, but Major Ritter had not been concerned by it. In fact, he acted as if it confirmed something. Had it not been for the orders shown Klein coming directly from Martin Bormann, Lange would have pulled Ritter in for questioning; there were too many unanswered questions for his liking. But this was a special case, it was lofty company the Major kept, if rumors of his dinner with Himmler at the castle were true. The Gestapo had wide-reaching powers that could ignore the usual chain of rank, but in this case Lange felt it was best to let him alone.

For the time being, at least.

CHAPTER TWENTY-FOUR

Cezar sat at a table in the back of the Pharmacy Under the Eagle. Owner Tadeusz Pankiewicz had offered him a place to sit when he had requested some soda. Getting into the ghetto had been a simple task, leaping from a rooftop to the wall to the street below. Once inside, no one paid him any mind; no one tried to break *into* the ghetto. Tadeusz had been nervous about the huge, rugged looking man in ill fitting clothes, but he would turn away no one in need.

"Here you are, sir, a bicarbonate of soda."

"Could you mix up a drink? Something sweet?"

"Perhaps a few years ago, but I have no syrup left even for medicine. Sugar is very difficult to find even for a pharmacist."

Cezar shrugged.

"Was there anything else I could do for you?" Tadeusz asked.

"I'm meeting someone here, supposedly," Cezar replied.

Tadeusz nodded and pulled the curtain separating the back area from the store front. When the Germans had closed off the Podgorze district, Tadeusz had been offered a pharmacy in the city to run. All non-Jews living in the area had been allowed to leave, even encouraged. He had refused, and still lived in the building. He was allowed to leave and pick up supplies and his family could stay in the ghetto where they had lived almost a decade.

Vladimir Czerny stepped into the pharmacy and removed his leather trilby. Pankiewicz stared a moment at his tattooed bald head then blinked the surprise away.

"How may I help you, sir?"

"I wonder if you could help me find a certain old medicine."

"Old is about all I have here these days, what are you looking for?"

"*Aconitum Napellus.*"

Tadeusz blinked again. "Ah, well I believe I have some from a while back, its dried and probably decades old. The man I bought this shop from was a bit more old fashioned in his remedies, and I still have some of his...yes here it is."

"That should be sufficient."

"Just take it, but please be careful, it can be very dangerous. Aconite is a poison."

Czerny nodded. "There is one other thing. I am here to speak to a large fellow, behind the curtain, I suspect?"

Tadeusz nodded and gestured toward the back. Czerny bowed his head once and let a folded stack of złotych on the counter.

"How did you manage to get past the guards?" Cezar asked as Czerny sat down at the table.

"I have astonishingly high-ranking orders, and guards do not look very closely at paperwork signed by the Reichsminister of the Third Reich."

Cezar sipped some of the bicarbonate. In truth his stomach did not hurt, but he'd paid for it. It was salty and fizzy and did not taste very good. "Where did you come by that kind of document?"

"He gave it to me in his office. I was summoned and ordered to find you."

"And who do you believe I am?"

"Cezar Alexandru, Romanian, recently escaped from Birkenau."

"Well here I am."

"The Germans are very anxious to find you. They gave me quite a few SS and a very impressive major to do the job. And keep an eye on me, of course."

"They might not like what they discover."

"That depends. Do you wonder why I wanted to talk to you here?"

"You needed headache powders?"

Czerny removed his glasses and cleaned them. His eyes seemed softer and sadder without the thick circular lenses covering them.

"This pharmacy is run by a Roman Catholic Pole, a graduate of the local university. He took over the business in 1933 and has stayed here in the ghetto. Do you know what he does?"

"I imagine he sells chemicals and medicines."

"Not very many. Most of the people moved into this area have had their riches stolen by the Nazis and the Blue Police. When they were relocated their riches were confiscated. Some have managed to hide jewelry and cash but most are destitute."

"Hard to stay open as a business when nobody pays."

"Mr Pankiewicz gives away a lot of his medicines. Aspirin, rubbing alcohol, bandages, Iodine; various goods for the people here. Hair dye is popular, from what I understand. The Nazis will run the elderly off to camps immediately but if you look younger, you can avoid their attention. And if you need to hide a child, a little bit of tranquilizer makes them sleep and not fuss."

Cezar leaned back in his chair, the wood creaking.

"He runs his business," said the Romanian, "and helps people in need with what he has at hand."

"How do you know about this?" Asked Cezar.

"I lived here a few months last year. When there was a gathering of Jews in the city, I had no papers and was with a Jewish family. They packed me into a home for 4 along with 10 other people. There are more than ten thousand Jews living in this small walled in section of the city."

"Cozy."

"Not especially. Malnutrition is common, and some Jews have turned against their people to save themselves. I know one boy named George who seems especially gleeful at pointing out and enriching himself off of his fellow Jews in Hungary. The Germans call the betrayers "Judenrat." They seek to live another day by turning in their fellow Jews. Fear makes us all do strange, terrible things. If we grow old we have to live with those deeds."

"I assume you have a point to your rambling nonsense?"

"This little building is the only gentile-owned business in the ghetto. While Judenrat betray their own kind, this man is an outsider, but helps them. His family is alone in the ghetto, not part of the religion and culture of the Jews. But he does what he can to help the people here, more than I'm willing to say."

"You're a strange Nazi."

"I am no Nazi at all. I subscribe neither to German nationalism nor socialism."

Cezar and Vladimir stared at each other a long quiet moment.

"And yet Martin Bormann hired you to track me down."

"I have a certain reputation in some circles."

"What circles would those be?"

"I am a spiritualist, a specialist in supernatural and mystical matters."

Cezar's golden eyes focused on Vladimir Czerny with quiet intensity.

"The reason I was able to track you," Continued Czerny, "was because your nature leaves a very significant spiritual... 'scent' for lack of a better term. The rage inside you, the monster you hide is quite disruptive to its surroundings in a spiritual sense."

"Sometimes it gets disruptive in a physical sense."

"Often lately, it seems."

"People should leave me alone."

"But that will not happen now, you know it."

"People get dead when they do not leave me alone."

"If you wish." Vladimir Czerny shrugged slightly. "And you will die as well. But there is another choice."

"I don't die."

"You die, everyone dies, eventually. Some take longer than others, but it is the fate of all man."

"Many have tried."

"Yes, of course. As I said before, though, enough trauma swiftly enough and you will die. And of course, there is silver."

"That has been tried."

"I would be surprised if it had not. You have not been very secretive."

"The silver bullet did not harm me much."

"Do you know why silver is supposed to harm the supernatural?"

Cezar finished off his bicarbonate. It tasted awful all the way to the end, but he was determined to not show his distaste. This strange little man was not afraid of him, nor was he prey. He was a rival of some sort, a threat that made Cezar feel wary and aggressive.

"I haven't given it any thought."

"It represents purity, among other things. A flexible sort of strength and lack of corruption."

"Silver tarnishes like anything else."

"Indeed, it does – badly in modern air – but long ago there was less sulfur in the air and it would last longer without showing decay. In any case, silver is a symbol of purity. Symbolism and spiritual imagery is very powerful in the supernatural realm. But silver is not enough in its self. The person wielding the symbol must be pure as well, lacking hate and cruelty."

Cezar looked at Vladimir Czerny a long moment. "So if the shooter hated me, or was a cruel and brutal man..."

"The silver would be of little more efficacy than any other bullet. Still, as I said, enough of any sort of bullet would do the deed. You are very resistant to ordinary weapons, particularly in your wolf form, but you are harmed by them. You simply heal very quickly."

"So a few bombs might tear me up so badly I could not heal, you think?"

"Or a few thousand bullets from a large enough gun."

Cezar leaned back in his seat and kept a level gaze on the little Romanian.

"How did you get out of the ghetto?"

"For some time now I have been hunting creatures such as yourself. I am known in some rare circles as an expert in supernatural and occult history and events. Adolph Hitler is fascinated by the occult, and believes it may be harnessed for his power and personal protection. He is not a young man, and he does not wish to die. For him, the vision of a thousand-year Reich includes him permanently as fuehrer, life extended by curiosities from lost cultures and mystical artifacts. The chief of the SS, Himmler, has teams searching all around the world, from Egypt to India."

"My experience with that kind of thing did not turn out well."

"It rarely does for us; there's a reason those civilizations were lost. When Hitler learned of my location and talents, he had me recalled. He convinced himself I was not Jewish, and since my past is... obscure, that was not difficult to do."

"So you're Hitler's pet monster hunter. Well you found one."

"I'm surrounded by monsters, or have you not been paying attention?"

"They're just men."

Vladimir Czerny thought a moment. "And you are more than a man? Is the monster in you worse than these men?"

"Ask those soldiers last night who was worse, them or me?"

"A mushroom can kill a man; does that make it impressive or monstrous?"

"So murder isn't evil to you?" Cezar smiled. "I can see how you get along with the Nazis so well."

"Murder is evil, it simply isn't *special*. Anyone can do it, lycanthrope or not. And you weren't the wolf when you did it, were you?"

Cezar said nothing.

"You've been in one of the camps. There are hundreds of them scattered all through German territory. I have seen maps, heard reports from Berlin's high command. From Norway to Italy, Croatia to Spain and the Channel Islands, these prison and work camps have been built to systematically obliterate entire cultures and peoples. You have killed a few hundred people, impressive for a single man. They have killed millions *in Poland alone*. You terrorize people in a town, they terrorize an entire planet. You are cruel and murderous, they are cold and ruthless. I have heard tales that you would call fantasy – rumors of lampshades made of human skin, piles of teeth taller than a man, mined for their gold."

Cezar felt the beast inside him stirring. He did not fight it.

"The evil that you do," continued Czerny, "and it is evil, you do because of a corruption inside you. Where does theirs come from? You have a name for the demon inside you, the wolf that rots your soul. What is their excuse?"

"So these men are greater monsters than ever before?" Cezar asked.

"No. There have always been evil men, always been wicked men who do horrible things. The past have always had these monsters. What has changed is the reach of their arm. What man was once able to reach by his sword, he now reaches with planes. What he was once able to travel on a horse he can travel on a train. A man could kill another with with a bowshot, now he can kill hundreds with a bomb. This was the lesson of the Great War, a lesson no one seems to have learned.

"Our technology, our devices, our cleverness have given us great cures and advancements, but along with them it has given evil greater reach than ever before. One man could kill a few in the past, now he can kill millions. One man could terrorize a town, a nation in the past, now he can terrorize a planet. It takes no special training to use a machine gun, you can kill with a bomb as easily whether a moron or a genius.

"But that is not my point here. The wickedness in these men's hearts is not new, but it is different from you. Ask yourself a question. You've been very careful to stop more of your kind from spreading. Why?"

"Maybe I just like to be the only one." Cezar answered.

Vladimir Czerny waited, his face calmly betraying no emotion.

"Maybe I don't want to have to deal with any of my 'children' in the future."

"The beast wants more, doesn't it?"

"Yes." Cezar said quietly.

Fill the world, snarled the wolf.

"And you do not. Yet when it takes over and you lose control, it kills; it does not wound and leave them to change. Why do you suppose it does not act on its desires?"

Cezar looked at his hands. There was still rust-colored dried blood under his fingernails from the previous night. He knew. He had long known but did not want to say it. It wanted his soul to be so corrupted and lost and dark that he finally gave in entirely and agreed with its whims. And each year that went by he felt closer to that abyss, felt pulled toward it.

"You resist the evil that is inside you. You know what you do is wrong."

"What does it matter? I do it anyway."

"You do not do all you could, and you fight against it. All man faces this battle; the darkness within us that we fight and lose to far too often. You fall, but you rise again. These "new men," these Nazis, they do not fight it at all. They consider the fight to be weak, they believe there is no real good or evil, only what they are able to force upon the world by their will. They believe the world is what they make of it, and they will make it with whatever tools are necessary. They fall and wallow in the filth of their own making.

"Each of us fights that darkness within us in our own way, but some give up that fight. We all make excuses for when we do not fight or we lose a battle. We tell ourselves that it was for some greater good. It was the fault of someone else. It was actually the right decision, somehow. But we all know, deep down, what is right and what is wrong at some level.

"But if you deny that fight long enough, it can be like a burning coal that sears our nerves away, leaving us numb, *spiritually* numb. I know; I have lived a long life with many evils in my past. I have done much wrong and for a long time lost my way. I too was fool enough to believe the power of mysticism and supernatural could make me a greater man than I was. It made me less than a man. It made me a beast."

"What of those of us who had no choice?"

"Truly? Do you believe you had no choice?"

Cezar thought back to the echoing voice in the forest, damning him for his betrayal.

"Perhaps."

"This pharmacy represents an island of normal life for the Jews trapped in this ghetto. It gives them medical care and even a connection to the outside world. Because of a man who owes them nothing save the duty to do good and fight the evil within and without us. We are in a time when we are surrounded by those who do not fight, who even assist the evil. Each of us has a responsibility to do what is right, and to fight what is wrong with whatever opportunity is allowed us."

"Is that why you are helping the Nazis? Working for Adolph Hitler?"

"I am working to find you, with the opportunities given me by the Nazis. I do not work for Adolph Hitler. I do work that he presents me the chance to do, without serving him."

"What's the difference?" Cezar asked. "Is that how you make it seem alright in your mind? How you convince yourself that what you do is acceptable?"

"The difference is motive and result. I cannot overthrow this regime, but I can work within it to accomplish goals different than they desire. I have seen tyrants come and go, and each seems more invincible and more terrible than the last. They all fail. Empires arise and crumble. What matters is what each of us do where we are, when we are.

"I led the Nazis to this city. One faction wishes to capture and study you, to make more of your kind." Cezar glanced up in horror. "No, they do not understand what they are doing. The other seeks to simply destroy you for your defiance of German might, and I suspect they are led by a man who considers you a very personal enemy for the destruction of his troops."

"Perhaps I should let him succeed." Cezar felt the wolf rebel with in him, twisting in fury. *That Aniela bitch kept your nuts, weakling. The only way to get them back is to deal with her.*

"Perhaps you could find a way to use your opportunities to do what you know is right."

"I am to fight the entire German army? I thought you said they can kill me."

"Indeed. There may be other things you can do. I offer you two choices. The first is simple. I have this pistol," Czerny laid a luger on the table "It is loaded with silver bullets, and I assure you I hold no hate toward you. You would die, if that is what you wish.

"Or, perhaps, I can help you rid yourself of the monster within you."

He lies; take the gun away, snarled the wolf.

"I have tried both paths before. Neither ended the way I had hoped." Said Cezar.

"Life rarely goes the way we hope. I only offer you choices."

"So I should fight the Germans as a normal man? Join the underground?"

"I will give you time to consider your choices. Either way, I cannot allow the monster within you to continue. It must die one way or another; that is my task. In this Major Ritter and I agree: a werewolf cannot be allowed to live."

"So you would kill me, then? And I should stand by and let it happen?"

"You wish to continue this life? It is called a curse for a reason."

"Some days, sometimes. It is not all bad."

"You must think about it, but we should go. By now the SS troops should have a pretty good idea where I have gone. I need to return to the basilica, and you should go wherever it is you go to be alone."

Cezar stood and leaned over the table, towering over Czerny's small figure. The light behind him cast a deep shadow over the Romanian, seeming darker than was natural. "I could destroy you as easily as this glass." He said, and crushed the glass in his hand with a loud pop and tinkle of shattered pieces. "You would break that easily."

"We will talk again," said Czerny, and he walked past Cezar's hulking, powerful form. Cezar stared at the chair where Czerny had sat. He was a rival to the wolf's power, Cezar could sense it. The Romanian was so small and weak-appearing but something about him held terrible potency, and a calm sense of inevitable purpose.

Vladimir Czerny was stopped by a patrol of German soldiers who drove him to the gate upon seeing his papers. There stood Major Ritter and several SS troops talking to very uncomfortable-looking guards.

"And you let him walk past you based on a glimpse at a signature? You did not bother reading the orders at all, did you?" Ritter was quiet but fury was etched on his face.

"But Sturmbannführer, we are not told to keep out anyone without proper orders, only those who are suspicious or without paperwork. Surely orders from Bormann are enough to establish someone's credentials!"

"This man was not given credentials to wander wherever he chooses, he is..." Ritter recognized Czerny as he stepped out of the Opel.

"Tzerny! Take him to the truck," he snarled to the men with him. "We have much to discuss."

CHAPTER TWENTY-FIVE

Vladimir Czerny sat in the first pew facing the altar. Major Ritter paced back and forth in front of the altar with barely restrained rage.

"Explain to me what you were doing in the ghetto." His tone warned of the price of a poor explanation.

"While you were away I noticed something in the ritual, an energy that could be tapped into in that area." Czerny quietly replied. "You were clearly displeased with the speed at which the ritual was concluding, and were not available to speak to. Your troops here, while doubtless capable fighters, did not seem like the kind who would take liberties with your orders to restrain me to this location. I slipped away while a private was distracted and headed to the area to gather an object from the ghetto area. If you would like I can tell you the story behind it and how I am using it?"

"No. No more stories. Continue."

Czerny watched Ritter calm slightly. He seemed to alternate between barely-restrained rages and calm dedication to duty and orders. Vladimir had expected the story to be rejected; he had a tale ready but the truth was there was no such device in the ghetto or energy. He had simply taken a new lens from his kit and finished the device.

"With this new input, the ritual has moved much more swiftly. It is directly pinpointing one area." Czerny looked at the altar.

All four lenses were now focusing light from the sun through colored windows onto the map of Krakow at a point just north of Park Krakowski. Ritter looked at the map. The sun was not directed on the map like a tilted flashlight, but in a small point which was heating the paper slightly.

Ritter stared at the location. "This is the headquarters for the Gestapo in Krakow. It is the home of the Order Police, Silesian House."

"Apparently our quarry is clever. Who would search for him there? Who would dare search the Gestapo?"

Ritter stared out the open doors at the end of the church. "I would." *But I must be certain.* Ritter was one of the highest ranking SS officers in the city, but Fritz Arlt was an SS lieutenant colonel and head of the Gestapo in the region, he outranked Ritter significantly in not only military status but political power. The Gestapo were given almost unlimited power to find treachery, spies, and resistance movements. Ritter feared their power. *But,* he thought, *there might be a way.*

"Tell me how to kill this monster." *There, I said it. He is a monster, not an escapee, not a fugitive. I must admit the truth to face him,* Ritter thought bitterly.

Czerny closed his eyes. "You asked me of silver bullets. They can harm him, usually. If you do sufficient damage in a short enough time period, you can overwhelm him, while he is human. When he is a wolf, I do not know."

Ritter's rational side sneered at the thought of a man becoming a wolf, but his memory haunted him. No ordinary man could do what this man had, and the Birkenau guards may have been unfit for service with real soldiers, but they were not making up stories about the monster they saw.

"Fire probably will not harm him especially. If you have some sort of supernatural weapon from Berlin, it would very probably do him significant harm."

"I regret to say we were not issued Mjölnir or Gungnir" Ritter was proud he remembered the name of Odin's spear.

"I doubt they exist. But no matter, you cannot fight this man as if he is a soldier. He will tear through your troops the way you've seen twice now."

Ritter nodded. "I have obtained silver bullets for the men, and my sidearm is loaded with them. Are you sure they will work?"

Czerny looked up at Ritter. "I cannot answer with any certainty."

The trip to the Silesian House was silent. The men in the back had some idea where they were going and believed there was no good end to this mission. The consensus was that at best they would survive and be sent to the eastern front. Following orders would only protect a soldier so far, but searching the Gestapo headquarters?

In the cab Heinz could sense the major's mood and tried to be as invisible as possible. Ritter seethed. He had only a vague plan as to how to handle the mission and he had felt ridiculous having silver bullets made and handing them out. The more he thought about the entire mission the more he felt the Romanian was making sport of him. He always had a calm answer that seemed plausible despite being ridiculous. In real combat against a real enemy, the missions and goals had always been clear, even if it wasn't exactly clear how to get there. This entire episode reminded Ritter of his aborted attempt at learning French. Everyone in the class seemed to be laughing at him for not understanding what was so easy for them.

The truck stopped in front of the Silesian House. Passersby scattered as unobtrusively and subtly as they could, leaving Królewska and Pomorska streets empty at the corner. The rounded five-story building stood quiet in the afternoon sun, twin flags scribed with swastikas flapping over the corner entry. Ritter sat in the truck glaring at the dashboard a moment then took a deep breath and stepped out of the truck, slamming the door. Sergeant Heinz pounded the back of the cab twice and stepped out as the men started to hop down from the truck.

Ritter entered the building first, pulling his cap off. Erma Leser was at the front desk, typing a form. She was a pretty girl in her twenties with her dark hair in a braid around her head like a halo, and Ritter felt uncomfortable as he always did around women other than his wife and mother.

"I am here on orders from Martin Bormann, I need to speak to Peter Klein."

Ritter had considered initially going straight to Lieutenant Colonel Arlt, but had decided he might find a better reception if he requested assistance from Klein first. They had at least met before.

Erma smiled at the tall, handsome soldier. She could sense the major felt awkward and out of place in the building; almost everyone did. "I'll see if he's in, please have a seat."

Major Ritter remained standing as she called Klein's office. The room looked so ordinary. He knew that prisoners were taken in the back and down stairs to the cells beneath, but this office broke up the building into two wings, the Gestapo to the north and the Order Police to the west. And if the Romanian was right, somewhere in this building was the fugitive. The building was much bigger than he remembered from driving past.

"Hauptsturmführer Klein will see you now, sir." Erma smiled again.

Ritter wondered if she was really that friendly and as interested as she seemed or if that was why she was working the front desk: a pretty face to greet people and make them feel welcome. Captain Klein; apparently he'd been promoted. An SS lieutenant stepped into the reception area and saluted, clicking his heels.

"Untersturmführer Bedel, sir. If you would follow me?"

Ritter replaced his cap and followed the young man through corridors and up stairs. Klein's office was as orderly and neat as the man had seemed in person. Everything was lined up and squared off as carefully as if it was sculpted into place. There were no personal items, no photos or keepsakes on his desk.

"Sturmbannführer Ritter. Please, have a seat. You wished to see me?" Klein said.

Ritter removed his cap again as he sat and scratched his short hair. "I have a problem that I believe we can work together to solve, Hauptsturmführer. Congratulations on your promotion, by the way."

Klein nodded in acknowledgment. "I received the news this morning by telegram. I hope that by the month's end I will be confirmed as head of Order Police."

"The promotion seems encouraging," suggested Ritter.

"Indeed. What did you have in mind?"

"As you know I have been searching for a fugitive, an escapee from the Birkenau work camp. I have reliable intelligence that he has been hiding somewhere in this building."

Peter stared at the major, waiting for some sign of a joke.

"I know that sounds outrageous, but this is no ordinary prisoner, " Ritter continued. "He is very resourceful and very capable. He is the one who killed my soldiers in that home last night, you have seen some of his work. This is no wretched, broken Jew or hopeless Pole. "

"In this building?" Klein thought about it. He supposed that it wasn't impossible, there were several entrances and the building was not completely occupied. If someone were careful, they could get lost in the hundreds of workers. And if there was ever a place in Krakow where no one wanted to ask questions of anyone else or draw attention to themselves, it was Silesian House. The more he thought about it, the more plausible it became.

"You understand my concern. I do not care to march my troops through your offices as if you were some Polish suspect. But perhaps if we work together, we can do a more respectful search."

"And you would need to search the Gestapo wing as well."

"Indeed, and I have no contacts with the Gestapo. I was hoping you might accompany me to Obersturmbannführer Arlt's office."

"Arlt is not here, he was called north on some business. I know a good officer in the Gestapo, we can visit him." Klein stood and straightened his crisp uniform. This would be a feather in his cap. They could not deny him the position if he brought in a dangerous fugitive under the nose of the Gestapo.

*****

Aniela was curled in the corner of the cell, arms around her knees. She was still sore from the examination that morning. The same questions again, and she was so tired she could barely focus on seeing what was in front of her. Aniela had tried to sleep but was so weary she couldn't even relax. She barely remembered the interview, or what she had answered. She hoped she had said the same things. She hoped

Joanna and Aleksy would be set free. She hoped Cezar would burst through the door and carry her away.

He was a monster, a horrible killer, but he had been so kind to her. And who did he kill? The occupiers of her home, the monsters who had crushed Poland, the ones who had imprisoned her for being nearby when their soldiers died. She remembered the cries and screams of the Kowalski family next door as they had been dragged off in the night for the crime of being Jewish. The old grandfather had refused to go and had simply been shot and left lying in the doorway.

It had happened out of nowhere, not long after the Germans had occupied Krakow. The Governor General had issued a decree that all Jews were to be gathered in Podgorze district in 1941 and walled off. Aniela remembered that night too well.

From early morning until late at night she had witnessed almost indescribable events. Armed SS soldiers and Blue Police scoured through the city looking for Jews. The Jews were taken from their houses, barns, cellars, attics, and other hiding places. The sharp sound of gunfire was loud throughout the entire day, like fireworks on New Years. Sometimes there was a deeper, louder sound as hand grenades were thrown into cellars. Jews were beaten and kicked; it made no difference whether they were men, women, or small children. The Germans assembled the Jews in the marketplace and questioned them, categorizing them as useful to the Reich and not. Only those who were capable and skilled at physical or factory labor were considered useful.

By afternoon of the first day Aniela guessed that a thousand Jews had been assembled. The Germans began moving them to the outskirts of the city. All had to walk except for members of the Judenrat and the Jewish police; they were allowed to use horse-drawn wagons. Aniela remembered the signs placed on the walls, tatters of some were still in place. The penalty for hiding Jews was declared to be death, but special rewards were offered for showing their hiding places to the authorities.

The world seemed to have forgotten. Britain had declared war on Germany in 1939, but had not fired a single shot to help the Poles. No one had fought back against the Germans until the Poles. Nations like Austria had practically welcomed the Nazis. Others had simply capitulated out of fear or the memories of the horrors of the Great War, a desire to not repeat them. Poland had held out longer than the French, who had considered it a great victory that Paris had been spared.

Krakow had been spared. No bomb had fallen on the city. Spared, that is, to the hands of the Nazi regime. *Better I had died in Aleš' arms*, Aniela thought. He had not been as exciting and strong as Cezar, but he was loving and romantic and tender. Cezar had been rough, it was thrilling but it would be uncomfortable very often like that. So rough the German nurse had apparently believed rape could

176

have been possible. The Gestapo man had lost interest in Aniela. She wasn't sure if that was good or not.

Suddenly she heard gunfire. It was close by, overhead, as if it was inside the building. How was it possible? Her heart thrilled to a fantasy of British soldiers parachuting into the city. The Soviets might have invaded again; although like manhy of her fellow Poles, she had no love of Russians after their decades of occupation in the previous century. Then she heard the crashing sound and the men's screams, and her eyes widened with recent memory.

*****

"Absolutely not." SS-Captain Kurt Frowein said. "Under no circumstances are my men to be treated as collaborators. No one here is harboring a fugitive from the Third Reich."

Major Ritter and Captain Klein sat in the office of the Gestapo's second in command. Ewald Lange was standing by the captain at his desk, arms crossed. Ritter could sense they were putting up a strong front of Gestapo strength, trying to impose their authority. But Doctor Stoffel was standing on the other side of Captain Frowein with his hands clasped at his waist, looking patient, and Ritter could not think of what he was doing there.

"Of course no one is harboring a fugitive," said Peter Klein. "Your men are above suspicion, as are all of the Gestapo. But this is a large building, and I understand not all of your rooms are occupied?"

"Perhaps he could be here posing as some menial laborer," suggested Ritter.

Frowein leaned back in his chair. His office was well decorated with photographs of family and friends. The walls had pictures of the captain with various party officials such as Goebbels and Himmler, and images of him in battle scenes. Ritter wondered if Frowein had a personal photographer that followed him.

"This fugitive is of great interest to the Reich," Ritter said, hoping the man's ambition would be sparked. "Dr Stoffel has been commissioned by Himmler himself and I have am under orders directly from Bormann's office."

"Lange?" Frowein prompted.

"I am not responsible for hiring laborers," Lange said. "Heidi Volstadt is in charge of personnel."

"He may be hiding here without having been hired," suggested Klein. "There are so many people here."

Frowein thought of buxom Hedi and how she had rebuffed his advances. "Very well, we shall take a look, but this job seems fit for the cat."

Ritter feared it was the waste of time Frowein had suggested. He handed Klein and Lange the copies of the description and camp information on the fugitive. They were already on file in the building for both departments but he did not want to wait for the information to be dug up. Each took a small group of men and split up to search. Stoffel remained in the office to speak to Frowein, and when Ritter glanced back as the door closed, Stoffel paid him no heed.

"Hauptsturmführer Frowein, I understand a prisoner is being held here regarding the massacre at..." Stoffel looked at his notes and squinted slightly, "Josefitow street?"

Frowein looked blankly at Stoffel. There were dozens of prisoners in the cells below and it was Lange's job to keep track of them and the 'interviews.'

"A young woman, named Aniela?"

Frowein leaned back in his chair. He remembered that young beauty. "Yes, what of her?"

"I beleive she might be key to my orders from Reichsführer Himmel. If I could ask her a few questions, that would be very rewarding, I expect." Stoffel said carefully.

Frowein nodded and pulled a form out of his desk. Filling the form out with practiced, aggressive strokes of the pen, he handed it to the professor.

"Thank you for your time. I will remember your assistance in this matter."

Stoffel turned and left the room to ask the secretary for directions to Aniela's cell.

*****

The workers at Silesian House were annoyed at the intrusion and offended that anyone would suggest a criminal hid among them, but kept their annoyance to themselves. An SS major, a state police captain, and a Gestapo lieutenant were not to be denied, even by other lieutenants.

Lange and his five men climbed to the top of the stairs to the fifth floor. A man stood at the top holding the door open.

"Looking for me?" He said in slightly accented German.

Lange glared at the man in annoyance. He was slightly winded from the climb but did not want to show it. He was taunted enough about his belly by other officers.

"Move aside, idiot –" he began when sergeant Kopfel grabbed his arm.

"Sir. That's him, I'm sure of it."

Lange looked at the paperwork then up at the man leaning against the doorway. He was tall enough to almost brush the top of the door frame, with long jet black hair that became wavy as it lay on his shoulders. He had a beard at several inches long, black as night, with a very slight curl. The beard had grown up to his cheekbones, giving him a wild, ancient look. His eyes were almost golden yellow and his eyebrows met in the middle under a very low widow's peak. The man was broad-shouldered and thick-necked, like a circus strong man and wearing clothes that did not fit him well, cuffs high on his forearm and above his ankle.

"In the name of the Third Reich –"

Lange did not finish this sentence either.

Ritter heard it first, working the third floor offices between the two sections where the L-shaped building's wings met. Gunfire and screams, the sounds of something hitting the wall or floor very hard. Racing to the stairs, he was brushed by a hand as a body fell past down the hollow center of the stairwell that the steps formed in a square as they rose above and dropped beneath the third floor. The body hit the floor with a grunt and a sound like a sack of flour dropped out a window.

"Men, load your rifles and follow me!" he cried, pulling his luger out. "We will have revenge for our fallen brothers!"

When Klein heard the shots, he was opening the first door on the fifth floor. Most of the floor was unused, and he had not paid much mind to the areas on the first two floors he worked on regularly; he would have remembered anyone as distinctive looking as the way the escapee was described.

Uttering an especially foul curse, he urged his men toward the sound. *The shot had been close, on this or the fourth floor*, he thought. But the shooting kept going on. Was the prisoner barricaded behind something? Had he somehow managed to sneak Armia Krajowa into the building?

He rounded the corner and threw the door open to the stairs. Something slammed into his body, hurling Klein backward and into his men. A horrible scream echoed through the stairwell, amplified by its hollow shape.

*****

Aniela crouched at the door, listening. The sounds were above her, distant but somewhere in the building. The stone hallways and cells in the basement distorted the sounds with echoes, making them even more eerie. A machinegun fired, then more screaming. There were so many gunshots, could it possibly be him?

She turned and leaned her back against the door. Did she really want to see Cezar covered with men's blood again? He had seemed so wild and fierce, so heartless. It was like something else rose up inside him. Something else. Aniela bowed her head and prayed. Maybe he really was damned like he said, but could not Mary intercede for him as well?

Her cell door abruptly slammed open, surprising Aniela. Every time before, she had been ordered against the wall through the little window before the door was opened, and for a moment she had a hope that Cezar would be there, filling up the door in dark fury at her captors. Instead it was a middle-aged man in a well-tailored suit with thinning blond hair and cold gray eyes. Behind him was the interpreter from before and another of the huge blond SS soldiers, holding a chair.

Markus Kohler set the chair down and stepped back to stand against the door, arms crossed. The interpeter stood next to him, while Dr Stoffel sat down and crossed his legs after straightening his cuff. He lit a cigarette and looked at Aniela. She was dark for a Pole, but would be lovely cleaned up and in better circumstances. The prison smock barely covered her, showing enticing glances of slim thighs high on her legs. Aniela felt his gaze and tugged at the front of the striped smock, feeling it lift behind her against the cold, wet stone wall. Dr Stoffel spoke through the interpeter, hoping his tone and mood would carry through a third party.

"Aniela, I understand you entertained a certain Cezar Alexandru recently."

Aniela stared at the man, trying to remember if she'd ever said his name or the interrogators indicated that they knew it. Had they brought it up?

"He didn't say his name," she said finally.

"Of course, you say that he took advantage of you?"

"Yes."

"And then he went berserk and attacked the soldiers, killing them all?"

"I only saw him kill the one in my room. I guess so."

Stoffel smoked a moment, watching Aniela. She seemed tired and sad and scared, but not crafty. The best liars never did, and she certainly was in a situation to lie her best. It was not outside the realm of possibility that someone would rape her, but to break into her house to do so?

"Why do you suppose he killed so many of them?"

"I think he was angry at, at... Abel... for interrupting him."

Stoffel held his breath a moment. Aniela had cringed slightly and had to force herself to say the name, Abel. He looked through the notes of the interrogation that Lange's office had given him. Aniela stared at the wet stone floor of her cell, waiting. The man seemed to read a long time, but she wasn't even sure if it was day or night any more, let alone how many minutes passed. All sense of time had faded into a memory.

"Rottenführer Abel, ah yes, the interpreter. Hmm, tell me about him."

"About him?" Aniela was confused.

"Yes, yes, humor me," Stoffel smiled.

"I — I didn't know him well. He spoke some Polish for the other soldiers."

Stoffel watched her cringe slightly against the wall. *Perhaps there was rape involved but was it by Cezar?* He thought.

"This Abel, a young soldier in a home with such a pretty girl, did he make any unwelcome advances toward you?"

Aniela shook her head over and over, saying nothing, staring at the floor. But what was she saying 'no' to? Stoffel wondered.

*****

Ritter reached the fifth floor at a run, skipping steps. His rage and need for revenge drove him, tireless, determined that the man who butchered his men would pay. Lange lay in the doorway at the top, his chest caved in as if a train had hit him. Splintered pieces of rib jutted through his wet jacket and his blood flowed to the steps and began to run down them. Two other Gestapo men were strewn down the steps like dolls, crushed and mangled.

Major Ritter slowed as he stepped into the corridor at the top of the stairs. Bloody bootprints led to the left and ahead down the hallway. Each floor was laid out the same; a rectangular hallway with rooms on either side and a stair at each end of the wing leading to the other floors. He had left six men outside, to cover the exits from the building, and taken ten with him into the building.

Ritter cocked his luger, the sound loud in the empty hallway. He sent half his men to the left and went ahead. The bloody prints here showed regulation German military boots and another pair of more worn, non-military boots. It was time to stalk the beast.

"Sturmbannführer Ritter," started one of the men.

"Hans," Said Ritter. Discipline wasn't as important as morale now.

"...Hans," continued the soldier. "Is this truly just one man?"

Ritter glanced at him. "Sturmmann Beckenbauer, yes?"

"Dieter," grinned the lance-corporal.

"Dieter. Yes, we face one man, but not just a man. You have probably overheard some of what the Romanian said. I do not know how seriously to take his stories but it is best to be sure, yes?"

Dieter and the other four men nodded.

"Then we'll act like he's an unkillable werewolf and stalk him like a monster. Stay back, move and shoot, keep him moving and away from you. Use silver bullets, and pray to God if you have faith."

They reached the first corner, checking to see if each door was locked. Ritter crouched low and spoke quietly.

"If he's just an ordinary man, then we feel a bit silly. If he's not, then we're ready."

"Yes, Hans."

Ritter glanced back at his men. They looked determined and fierce, and afraid, just as he felt. He nodded at them and turned toward the corner again.

*****

Stoffel smiled his most charming smile, the one that got them into his room at night, and crushed his cigarette under a polished leather shoe.

"Aniela, why would this man stalk all the way into your house and accost you in your room?" The interpeter repeated his question.

"I don't know," she said, staring at the floor. Her hair hung over her face, obscuring it.

"Come now, look up, I'm not so ugly eh?"

Aniela looked up. She had gotten only three hours of sleep in the last two days and felt like she was floating. It was true, he was a handsome man, if a bit old. Aniela thought he had nice hands and wondered why she cared.

"There we are. He could have attacked you anywhere, on the street, going to the store, coming home from work, yes?"

"I guess so."

Stoffel closed his folder with all the notes. He had known women who had been raped before, one a student of his that came for him for help against the professor. Dr Stoffel felt disgust at rapists, so pathetic they could not win a woman's affections and so afraid they had to take one by stealth and force. But none of them had reacted to the man who attacked them with calm disregard. They had tended to react in the way this girl had when the name Abel came up.

There were no obvious signs of physical torture on her and she seemed capable of movement. She would do for his purposes. Nodding to the interpeter he turned and left, and the soldiers shoved Aniela in front of them, her bare feet making little slapping noises on the cold stone floor.

Aniela prayed silently, her lips moving as she felt herself being marched to her death.

Dr Stoffel didn't notice, his mind busy planning. In his mind the city spread out like a map, at least what he could remember of its layout. The men assigned to him would be useful; they would know where troops are stationed through town, who has telephones. There was too much to do and not much time.

*****

Peter Klein crouched at the corner of the hall. One man, Horst Waechter, had fled and the killer had chased after him down the hall, so Klein had taken what remained of his men around the other corridor. Around this corner he'd heard something moving, perhaps heading to the stairs. Waechter had cried out once then a window had shattered, and there had been no sound after that.

Klein was breathing hard, his heart hammering. His military career had always been well behind combat, in headquarters. He was skilled at administration and organization, and even as a police officer he'd been mostly at work in the office, not the streets. He was afraid, more afraid that he'd ever been in his life. His hand shook violently when he wiped his palm on his pants then gripped his pistol again. It still felt slick despite the textured grip.

Nothing in his life had prepared him for the shocking violence and strength of the fugitive. As Klein had watched, the huge man had rammed his hand completely through the chest of Unterscharführer Ehrlich right in front of him. Peter glanced down at his chest, still glistening with the life blood of the soldier. He knew he should lead the men around the corner, and he knew to do so would be his death. He felt paralyzed. Klein could hear the men behind him, and believed he could feel their stares of contempt for his cowardice boring into his back. To run would mean being shot for cowardice and abandoning his men. To move forward was to die at the hands of that creature, for it could be no ordinary man.

Suddenly a figure loomed in front of him, and Peter shot at it. The hallway rang with loud gunfire, the muzzle flashes unnaturally bright, and then it ended. In front of him lay an SS soldier, clutching his abdomen, and behind him he could barely hear one of his men crying out in pain through the keening ring in his ears.

"Cease fire!" roared Ritter.

Three men were down, one certainly dead with a hole in the back of his head in a sudden blaze of violence as they had turned the corner. He sighted down his luger at the cringing Peter Klein, shaking with fury, then lowered his pistol. He could see his second squad trotting down the hall with rifles out, and gestured for them to stop and crouch. They lined up along the wall and watched him.

"Klein. Get up." Ritter said.

Klein looked up at Ritter in horror. He had shot German soldiers, SS troops. He had opened fire on his countrymen. Klein began shaking his head over and over, saying nothing.

Ritter sighed, looking at the other men. "You, Unterscharführer, what is your name?" The Sergeant was the highest ranking Gestapo he could see.

"Ehrich Schreiber, herr Sturmbannführer."

"You are in command of these troops now. The quarry has left this floor, we must resume our search."

"Yes, sir." Schreiber was clearly torn between joy at his effective promotion and dread at his task.

"Beckenbauer, have the men share out some of your ammunition to the Gestapo troops."

Beckenbauer saluted and started gathering ammunition, starting with Jens Kohler lying dead on the floor.

CHAPTER TWENTY-SIX

"We must hurry, my dear. You will have to leave that behind," said Rys.

His wife Marta had loved their expensive home in Krakow, the most permanent place they had lived in their lives. She had missed the caravan and the camps, but missed them less each year as her rheumatism had worsened and the cold had soaked into her bones more and more. Now at sixty-eight, she had hoped to never have to move again.

Rys glanced in frustration at Peter Fleischer, looming in the doorway. Every minute counted; they had to move before the Gestapo closed in, but Marta kept finding something else that had to be packed. Peter raised his eyebrows at Rys. Rys closed his eyes and nodded.

Crossing the room, Peter began gathering luggage and boxes, shutting them. Marta protested loudly, even hitting him, but her little fist bounced off his muscles harmlessly. She turned her fury on Rys.

"This is all your fault! We would never have had to leave if you had kept that gadje-loving Aniela out of our home! You know I foresaw disaster coming from her marriage!"

Rys knew, it was a common theme in their arguments, rare as they were. Marta had the gift, she would have glimpses of hazy future possibilities. They always came true, although rarely the way she interpreted them. Was the bombing of Aniela's home and the death of her husband not disaster enough?

"We must go, Marta. We must go *now* while we can." He could almost feel the Gestapo closing in like a gathering darkness around the building.

"We must go because you would not listen to me! And now look at us, fleeing again, when we finally had a place to call our own! I am too old to travel any longer, and you force me to! That girl bats her eyelashes and wiggles her skinny butt and you can't say no!"

184

Rys glowered at her. Aniela was a daughter to him, beloved and treasured. Marta looked away, stammering. She knew she had gone too far. Rys took a deep breath, then walked to her and put his hands on her shoulders gently.

"Marta I am sorry for forcing you to move again. I know this is terribly hard, and I know that I should always listen to you more. But did you not also *see* that Aniela would bring safety to our people?"

Marta nodded slightly.

"We must trust God and see to ourselves, for no one else will."

Marta nodded again and sadly picked up a suitcase. She did not look up, loathe to see all she was leaving behind. Her shoes felt heavy, with the gems hidden in the soles, and she hoped it didn't show but it felt awkward walking in them. Taking a deep breath, she looked up and smiled at Rys. It was just another role to play, the happy traveler and wife. She would miss her life in Krakow, but she would get used to it in time. And they could rebuild with what Rys had hidden away, somewhere far away from the Nazis and their cruelty. If there was such a place left in the world.

The three hurried to the ground floor and out the back of the building where an old, battered Model T truck waited. Rys checked his papers one more time to make sure he had them all and climbed in the back as Peter loaded the luggage and covered it with a tarp. Pulling the creaking front door open, Peter climbed into the truck which tilted on its leaf springs with his weight. The truck looked as decrepit and old as it was, but it ran well; Rys knew it had been used for many smuggling runs by his people. And he knew that an old truck drew less attention than a shiny Cadillac, which now was parked at the Wawel Castle in any case.

Peter drove the rumbling truck over the streets, jarring over missing bricks and potholes. The Governor-General had done well taking care of Krakow and rebuilding his portion of Poland using the strong backs of Polish men as slave labor, but the streets always seemed to be rough somewhere.

Rys looked over his paperwork one more time to make sure it was all in order and present. He knew it was from the last five checks, but if there was one thing the Germans were sure to want, it was papers. He could have gotten forged papers made; back at the book store old Fonso's son Dragomir was a genius at creating German documents. But having Hans Frank sign them personally meant the Governor-General was in on it to a slight degree, and that gave him one more layer of protection.

A pistol swung across his face and fired, deafening Rys temporarily. He felt a splash on the side of his head and saw red spray against the side window. Peter stopped the truck as Rys stared at his dead wife slumped against the side of the truck. The German gestured at Rys with the pistol as he stepped out of the truck. Rys stared in horror at the huge soldier's slight grin. He said something but Rys could only hear his ears ringing after the gunshot in the cab of the truck.

Peter felt it too, rubbing one ear with his free hand.

"Loud eh? Come on old man, out of the truck."

Rys stumbled out in a daze.

"It seems Governor Frank has changed his mind. Not about *everything*," Peter said. "He'll gladly transport those gypsies to the camp as you arranged. But you'll not be carrying these riches out of the city."

Through the ringing, Rys could just hear Peter's mocking tone. Gone was the simple stupidity that he'd sounded like in the months guarding him. He sounded very educated and precise, but still with that German accent. Stumbling before Peter, Rys fell to his knees on the empty street. In his preocupation with his papers, Rys had not been watching where they were going, but the loom of Wawel Castle was above them, the gate open with Governor-General Frank walking toward them through it.

"Rys, you seem surprised!" Frank said with a broad smile.

"Did she have to die?"

"Your wife? Rys, you're all going to die, it is the inevitable movement of man toward the future. Lesser races are being left behind. The New Man will conquer this world; superior cultural movements are replacing weaker, inferior ones. The old and corrupt is being destroyed to make way for the superior. It is the future. You won't be needing all those riches you are trying to smuggle out."

"He promised me half, but I think it was more like a tenth of what they really have hidden away. There are even gems hidden in the hubcaps." Peter said. "It breaks my heart to have him betray me after so many months of dedicated service."

"You have done well, Peter. No one else could have kept such a close watch over him. And without Captain Sturmberg in the way to interfere, well..."

Rys looked down at the pavement. It didn't matter any longer. Not with Marta gone. She was his treasure, not the gems and banknotes. He had never trusted Peter but he had underestimated the big German. He felt the barrel of the pistol against the back of his head and sighed.

"You were quite useful for a time, Rys, but now, well. Welcome to the future." Frank nodded. Peter pulled the trigger of his luger.

*****

Major Ritter and his men carefully moved down the stairs from the top floor of the Silesian House. They felt better with the additional six Gestapo SS with them, but still cautious about what lay ahead.

Peter Klein was still kneeling in the hall next to the corner. He felt as if staying still was what kept him alive, but the body of the soldier he'd shot lay in front of him, eyes staring blankly at a space just above Klein's head. He had died quietly, in a pool of spreading blood, staring straight at Klein the whole time. Two soldiers were behind him, one bandaging and caring for another shot by one of the Major's men. He tried to remember the name of the lieutenant behind him but could not. The wounded soldier had stopped making so much noise but Klein could not look back at him because that meant turning his back on the hall with the monster in it.

The glass of the side window was shadowed by the building in the late afternoon sun, and reflected the hallway around the corner. Klein stared at it like a crystal ball, showing his future. One of the windows near the door leading to the stairs was broken out, what he'd heard just a few moments ago before it had all gone so wrong. And through that window in the reflection, he saw a dark figure climb into the building, a huge man with long hair. Peter shook as he stared at the figure glance down the hall and grin. The monster glanced up at the reflection, put a finger to his lips to shush Peter, and quietly opened the door to the steps, slipping through. Klein's mouth formed a shout of warning but no sound came out.

Cezar walked down the steps with the other men, mimicking their cautious movements. One of the soldiers glanced back and saw him, but for a moment didn't notice who it was, only seeing a figure moving carefully with them. It was Lance Corporal Beckenbauer, against the wall and carefully moving down the steps to the next landing that glanced up and saw him. Cezar grinned, his teeth slightly sharper and longer than a normal man's and his amber eyes almost lit up in the shadows of the stairwell.

"My God, its him! For Franz!" Beckenbauer cried out and fired a burst from his MP38. Cezar was pushed against the wall opposite the Lance Corporal and slumped onto the steps, shocked. The bullets had burned into his skin, slamming into his chest like hammer blows and he could feel blood running down his torso. No one moved as Cezar looked down. The bullets had not penetrated far, but they had wounded him. It had been a long time since he'd felt this kind of pain.

"Shoot!" yelled Beckenbauer as he fired another burst, hitting Cezar on the shoulder, then along the wall up toward the ceiling in his excitement. Cezar growled, a sound unlike a man should make, and leapt over the railing between the two stair sections. He landed on the opposite run of stairs across the open center as a pistol rang out, gouging across his other shoulder. Backhanding Ritter and his luger out of the way, he bounded over the railing and plunged down to the ground floor.

"After him! The bullets work, move, move!" Ritter commanded and the men ran down the stairs. Their fear had been changed into jittery adrenaline-charged energy now, driving them on without tiring or caution. The monster could be killed. Their friends could be avenged.

Cezar crouched at the ground floor, grimacing in pain. The bleeding had already stopped but the pain was intense, like fire surrounding each wound. His blood roared in his ears, and he could hear the beast inside him growling louder and louder, overpowering the sounds around him. Fighting for control, Cezar swung open and staggered through the door in front of him and out onto the street. Three soldiers stood there, one examining the body of Horst Waechter crumpled in a pool of blood. Cezar looked at them a moment and they looked back. In his soul he felt the beast tearing at its chains, and the whole world seemed to slide into redness.

The soldiers stared at the figure in the doorway. He was streaked with blood in a shirt torn with bullet holes. His eyes seemed almost orange in color and he was hunching over, growling. They grasped at their rifles but were distracted, hands artless and confused as they stared in horror.

The man fell to his hands and knees on the bloody sidewalk, head down. Popping and rending noises came from his body as he shook, his clothes tearing away. Hair grew from his body at an astounding rate, then deep red fire engulfed him, burning away his clothes as it seemed to burn away his skin. The fire died down and in the place of the strange figure was a wolf, a huge wolf as long as the man was tall with black fur tipped in rusty red like old dried blood.

The wolf looked up at them, red burning in its eyes from an eternal fire within. With a roaring growl, it sprung at them. Private Mastricht wet himself.

Ritter and the other men had slowed slightly on the stairs, discipline and caution overtaking their excitement. The sound of rifle fire outside spurred them on, with Major Ritter leading the way. At the ground floor, the door to the outside was closed and the window coated with what looked like blood and pieces of meat. Ritter started to reach for the knob when a body crashed through it, smashing him back against his men and showering them with glass from the window.

Swearing furiously, Ritter pushed the door and the body off of him, afraid the monster would be on him while he was pinned to the floor. Outside he could see a car tipped on its side, the undercarriage facing him. Against it was the body of one of his soldiers, the rifle still in his hands, but his face missing, the bones and skin bitten away to reveal the layers of tissue, brain, and skull beneath. There was no sign of the monster.

Slumped against the wall by the door was a soldier, barely alive. Ritter knelt by him as the others spread out, looking for Cezar. It was corporal Jenson, one of the men who had come with him from Birkenau. Jenson was staring at Major Ritter with no pain or distress on his young face, but his hands were working to push the slimy pile of intestines that poured from his torn midsection back into his body. Each handful he pushed up slid away and he tried again and again as he spoke.

"He... he changed, Sturmbannführer." His voice was so quiet Ritter had to lean closer to listen. "He turned into a gigantic wolf, it had to be four feet tall."

Ritter nodded, listening. The young man did not have long to live. He was sitting in a pool of his own blood, it had stained his pants and jacket dark with his ebbing life. It seemed terribly important to him to tell his tale and Ritter wanted to give him this last wish.

"He changed, it was... it was horrible. It was so fast, the wolf. We shot it and it cried out but it kept moving. So fast. And then when we were all down, it...it ran... it ran up the wall, Sturmbannführer. You have to believe me. I, I am not making this up."

"After what I've seen lately, I am not going to challenge you, soldier."

"It ran right up the wall and over the roof. I saw it leap into Sergeant Heinz and drive him through the door, then it just ran...right up...I...Sir, could you help me, I can't seem to put it all back. Its..."

Then he was gone, his lifeless hands sliding to the bloody sidewalk. Ritter looked up the building rising above them. Maybe it was true. There were huge bloody paw prints trailing up the wall. Maybe it was all true, and that Romanian had been the only one who really knew.

Then he heard it.

All of Krakow heard it; a challenging, furious roaring howl, loud as if it were in the same room, echoing off the stone buildings. The howl went on and on, building in power with a tone that shook the souls of all who heard it. Some crossed themselves, some clung to each other in fear, and some reached for a weapon. The entire city was alerted to something unnatural among them. Even the sun seemed afraid, hiding behind a layer of clouds that slid across it as the howl ended.

And every dog in the city cowered, whining and digging at the ground, seeking a place to hide. Then the city was silent.

CHAPTER TWENTY-SEVEN

Aniela walked beside the huge soldiers. One seemed like he stepped off a German recruitment poster, a tall broad-shouldered blonde man who had movie-star good looks and arms that strained at his SS uniform. She could not tell what his rank was, could not understand German to hear their conversation, but the other soldiers seemed to respect and obey him. He towered over the man they called doctor, who was in turn was taller than Aniela. In her bare feet she felt like a girl, surrounded by huge men.

She wasn't sure where they were going, because she did not know this part of Krakow very well and she was so tired the world seemed sort of dream-like and fuzzy in any case. The streets felt very cold under her feet, but she was aware of this only in a distant, theoretical sense. She was cold all over in the rough cotton prison smock, so tired she forgot how short it was.

The slim, shorter soldier who spoke accented Polish had hold of Aniela's right arm and the huge tall blond one had her right. The translator at her left pulled her to a stop and the big soldier walked away. They were standing in front of some army truck with canvas over the bed like a covered wagon from some American movie. Aniela grinned thinking of the truck that way and tried not to laugh. Everything seemed so funny.

"Get up, into the truck, girl. Schnell." Said the translator.

Aniela clambered into the truck trying to keep her dress down around her legs; they hadn't let her keep any underwear. It was itchy on her skin, but at least it was something against the cold. In the truck the breeze didn't bother her but it smelled bad, like some animal. The floor of the truck was metal and it had iron bars nearly all the way to the top. Aniela looked around her, confused.

The doctor said something in German and the big man climbed into the truck, rocking it on creaking springs. He said something quietly to her in a soothing voice rather than the bored contempt the other Germans spoke to her with. But he took out old hand manacles and chained her to the bars in the front of the truck bed, facing the back gate. Then he climbed out and dropped the canvas, leaving her in the darkness. The men outside started talking in German and Aniela wondered where Cezar was.

"Where did you find that cage?" asked Lieutenant Markus Kohler.

"There used to be a zoo in Krakow Park around the turn of the century." said Dr Stoffel. "This one held a bear I think they said." It had taken half a day to get the cage and bolt it to the floor of the truck.

"Big enough" said Sergeant Berndt Gerber.

"She seems tired enough to just sleep through it all," said Kohler, looking at the truck.

Stoffel nodded, reaching into his satchel. "Yes, but she might warn him. I should give her a mild sedative, enough to keep her from becoming alarmed."

"Was that really a wolf? I've never heard one that sounded like that." asked Gerber.

Stoffel looked up from his bag and frowned slightly, his brow furrowed. "Not a true wolf, I'd say. More likely the subject believes he is one, I should think. Some psychosis would likely be associated with the syndrome. Dr Freud would be fascinated in the case. If there were only more time, I could take him for analysis.

"Freud, isn't he the one that writes about that Jew Science?" asked Gerber.

"Psychiatrics is not Jewish science. Freud's associate Carl Jung has spoken extensively on the subject and he is a German in good standing."

"But Freud himself is a Jew."

"Yes, I believe he is. Please focus on watching for the subject and leave the thinking to me." Stoffel sounded frustrated.

Gerber rolled his eyes at Kohler, who shrugged as Dr Stoffel climbed into the back of the truck holding a hypodermic.

*****

Vladimir Czerny heard the howl and looked at the soldiers sitting near him in the basilica. They stared back at him, picking up their rifles.

"Was that... him?" Asked one of the soldiers.

"Let us hope not." Said Czerny.

*****

191

Ritter and his men ran along the street. The howl had echoed off of the walls and stones of Krakow, but it sounded as if it has come from the north. One of the men was in the truck driving behind them on the radio. Ritter had assumed all authority and told him to demand all available troops for a search, and any mechanized equipment available. There were no tanks in the area, as they had been moved to the front in Russia, but there were some halftracks available and he thought he'd seen an armored car in the Wawel castle courtyard, probably left over from the Polish invasion. Lets see him bite through *that*, thought Ritter.

Screams echoed off the walls now, and a roaring sound. It was close. The men ducked down instinctively in their trot and spread out against the walls. Ritter let his Sergeants take over and watched as the men moved up in covering formation. Even the camp guards he'd been given remembered their training, even if they were a bit rusty. Ritter felt proud of his men. These were no mere Wehrmacht Heer, they were SS, the elite of the German forces.

The man on point signaled and the others moved up, crouching against walls and watching in all directions. Ritter walked down the middle of the street. It was bad tactics, but they were only after one man; even the AK would be hiding with this many troops on the streets. He believed the act would project strength and confidence for the men, and they could use it.

The man on point was aiming his rifle down an alley and the sergeant was standing in the entry, staring the same direction. When Ritter came up to him he saw that there were two women lying on the filthy stones of the street, torn open and bleeding. They looked like they had been young and pretty, but now they were twisted with pain and terror. The plump one had a bag in her hands that had spilled pieces of dirty clothes into the alley. Huge bloody paw prints were in the alley and smears of blood spelled a short phrase:

Sie sterben letzte, Ritter.

Ritter felt a chill as his eyes darted around the alleyway.
You die last, Ritter.
The thing had written words? With ... its paws? Major Ritter crouched low, mind reeling.

The paw prints led down the alley a few feet, then up a wall, fading as they climbed and the blood wore off. Ritter felt a prickling at his spine, *its behind me*, he thought but resisted the urge to spin in fear. If it was back there, the men would be firing at it. He turned and looked around, seeing only his eager men and a face briefly peeking out a window across the street, then curtains falling into place. Then he looked up. On the roof of the buildings across the street stood a huge black wolf, its red eyes lit up even at that distance, staring at him. Its jaws were open slightly showing a deep reddish glow from within making the wolf appear to be grinning with hellish fire in its maw. Ritter clawed at his luger but by the time he leveled it at the rooftop, the figure was gone.

"Across the street, it is on the rooftops again!" he shouted, louder than he meant to. The soldiers immediately turned and started moving down the alley across the way.

"Stop!" ordered Sergeant Müller. "First squad circle around the building. Remember the bullets hurt it but do not immediately kill. Shoot on sight."

Müller watched the first squad move around the buildings and counted, then said, "Second squad move down the alley; covering formation."

Ritter walked to the old Mercedes truck that was following the troops. "Anything?" he asked over the rumble of its diesel engine.

The private shrugged. "Command says they're sending available troops and a halftrack. Doesn't sound like much."

"Shitheads. Call them up again and give me the handset."

"Yes, my Major." The private called up the base again and waited, then handed the headset to Ritter.

"Yes? Who is this speaking? Hauptmann Kohnstadt? This is *SS-Sturmbannführer* Heinrich Ritter working on special orders from Reichsleiter Bormann and I expect complete obedience and cooperation, do I make myself clear? You will immediately make all your forces available to me and at once deliver a platoon and that Panzerspähwagen I saw at the castle to ..." He looked around.

"Grottgera, Nowa Weis," said the private.

"Grottgera... I don't care if Frank requires the vehicle, you leave that to me. Make it fast if you don't want to be in on the attack on Stalingrad." Ritter handed the headphones back. He looked at the private and remembered his name. "Stay in contact, Färber."

"Yes sir." Private Färber put the headphones back on his nearly bald head.

Ritter looked down the street. *30,000 troops in Krakow and he thinks he can't spare but a handful to hunt this thing down,* Ritter thought angrily.

The squads moved around the building but saw nothing. Müller was about to send a team into the building to search it to the roof when one of the men spotted the wolf.

"Unterscharführer! I see it!" the private pointed at the rooftops to the east. The dark form of the wolf paused a moment, then ran on, leaping out of sight.

"Mount up, men, into the truck."

Private Färber in the cab radioed their movements to direct the reinforcements ahead of them. The wolf seemed to be leading them on a chase, visible every so often ahead of the troops as they drove through the streets of Krakow. Ritter swore bitterly as he watched it move, running and leaping from roof to roof as fast as they could drive the truck on the rough, narrow streets.

The driver was now Lance Corporal Beckenbauer and he was content. He loved to drive as much as he hated Poles and took special glee in chasing pedestrians as the truck sped through the city. Twice he crashed along the side of small cars not swift enough to move aside and at least once he was certain he'd hit an old Polish woman. Beckenbauer let the others guide him, ignoring the rooftops and concentrating on the streets. A boy half his age glanced off the side of the truck and Beckenbauer couldn't help grinning. It was like a game, and Germans would always win.

The truck slowed as they lost track of the wolf. Ritter and Färber stared at the rooftops and alleys, but saw nothing. Then they heard shouting and screams ahead and Ritter knew it had to be the wolf. The truck came to a halt near an old church with white walls and a copper roof corroded into green. The front door was open and people were running out of the building. Ritter leapt out of the truck and grabbed an old man in priestly robes.

"What is going on?" he demanded in one of the few Polish phrases he knew.

The Priest looked around him nervously at the door then took a deep breath. He stumbled to respond in German, "a monster, a devil has invaded the church, I was, I was... helping the others get free."

Ritter sneered at the old man for his lie and cowardice. Pushing him to the street, he ran along the truck and slapped the side twice to signal the men. Luger drawn, he carefully looked into the church, but it seemed empty save for one priest who was near the altar holding his chest.

"Beckenbauer, stay with Färber and direct any reinforcements when they arrive. Färber stay in contact with command and direct the men here." Ritter ordered.

Sergeant Müller brushed past Ritter with a glance and a nod, followed by a squad. The men entered the church and spread out, kneeling behind objects and aiming at the empty building. Ritter stepped in and walked down to the priest with Müller and another private, Janson, who was the Company translator now that Corporal Hoffman was dead.

"Where did it go?" asked Ritter, and Janson translated.

The priest said something in Polish, and Janson looked to the side door. "He says down to the catacombs. Under the church."

"Catacombs? What is this place?" Ritter asked.

Janson spoke with the priest a moment. "The Church of St Casimir the Prince, apparently."

"Too many churches in this city." Ritter grumbled.

Sergeant Müller ordered second squad to the catacombs entrance and one spread out around the building. "Ask him if there is more than one way into them," he ordered Private Janson.

Janson asked the priest, who shook his head.

"Then we have him trapped," said Ritter. "We have him."

Müller didn't look at the Major. *A cornered gigantic wolf that climbs walls and shrugs off bullets,* he thought. *How many more men will we lose?* He pushed the thought aside and steeled himself for the task at hand, leading the men to the crypt.

Janson stood before the ruined door. Stone steps led down into the earth from the crypt, carved from the rock Krakow stood on. The thick wood of the door lay shattered and strewn down the steps and the men looked at each other.

"We're hunting a wolf?" asked Private Klaus quietly.

"Not just a wolf. What do you think the silver bullets are for?" snapped Müller in the same low tones.

Klaus stared into the darkness at the bottom of the stairs. *Hunting a werewolf into a crypt.* His hand shook as he pulled his boxy flashlight out.

Janson grinned "Killed plenty of wolves on my grandfather's place in the Rhine Valley."

"How many of them could smash through a door like this?" asked Klaus, aiming his light down into the catacombs. The beam seemed to dim and die in the darkness, like it was consumed.

Staninud by the truck outside the church, Ritter heard shots and imagined how loud they were in the underground area. *How many caves are there under this city?* He wondered. The sound was muffled, distant but he still could hear shouting and gunfire. The gunfire became more sporatic and finally ended but the ending scream he heard was loud enough to reach the street. *Could that possibly be the creature?*

Ritter ran to through the church down to the catacombs. There was no sign of his men at the entrance, and he peered into the darkness with his luger ready. There were no wires leading into the area, and no switch. *Apparently this church has not reached the 20th century,* Ritter thought angrily. By the door someone had posted a sign designating the catacombs as an official air raid shelter in German, but it seemed that was all that had been done to prepare them.

From a nearby shelf, he pulled out a lantern and lit it with a match. Stepping slowly down into the catacomb he felt a sort of religious awe at the history of where he was. But the lantern revealed a cave smaller than he'd expected. Catacomb conjured images in Ritter's mind of a long series of complex corridors and chambers, but these were quite small. Built of a series of rounded, arched rooms, the catacombs held hundreds of bodies, but was clearly not the vast system under Rome.

The rooms were painted white, Ritter could not tell. But even with the lantern and the light colored paint, the entire area seemed shadowy and cramped, with low ceilings that the major's hair almost brushed. There was no sound except his footsteps, then a skittering noise as he kicked something on the ground.

Looking down, Ritter saw what his foot had bumped against. It was a hand, holding a flashlight. The light was still on, face down. He crouched, looking around him carefully and picked up the light, hand still attached. It was a struggle to get the hand to let go, as if even in death it clutched to the light in terror of the darkness.

There was no blood except a smear where the hand had been, there were no spent casings from the men's rifles. It was as if nothing had happened here at all, had it not been for the single detatched hand. Where had the bodies gone? Ritter carefully stepped through the catacombs. The ancient bodies were set up almost as if on display in a museum. Some were seated in chairs. One was a Napoleonic era soldier, sitting stiffly without weapons, although his hand was clutched as if he once held a rifle.

All of the bodies were strangely preserved, almost unchanged in mummification. Some were more shriveled and decayed than others, but many seemed recently dead, if very dry. Most were partly buried in sand, with a block of wood under their heads. Some strange atmospheric condition of the area preserved them, Ritter decided. But where were his men? And where was the creature?

Further in, the paint on the bricks that made up interior walls was flaking off and the slate tiles covering the stone floor were more uneven and smooth, as if the area was even more ancient. Back in this area, he saw a few scrolls and books tucked into and behind coffins, as if to bury them with their owners. There still was no sign of the soldiers.

Then he found them. It was a drag mark in blood that drew his attention, and he found them lying side by side in coffins on top of the original residents. Each one was mangled and killed horribly, slashed by sharp teeth and rending claws. Piles of shells lay in the coffins with them. Bloody paw prints, each bigger than Ritter's fist, led away from the bodies, deeper into the catacombs.

Ritter followed, crouched low and pistol leveled ahead in one hand while he carried the lantern in the other. The flashlight he'd clipped to his belt, and it shone at the floor showing the paw prints. The prints led back and faded away as the blood dried and rubbed off, turning a corner and then were too light to see. Ritter carefully rounded the corner and saw that the steps that led to the entrance. Cursing under his breath, he moved more swiftly, and then stopped.

At the top of the stairs, the wolf stood, huge in the doorway. It was black as night and the shadows around it seemed to be gathered deeper and darker, as if the light feared drawing near. It growled, a deep sound that resonated with the stones in the cave causing a humming sound that echoed deep into the catacombs and back. Ritter felt his knees giving out and fell to them on the stone, staring in growing fear at the monster. That deep growl seemed to reach into his soul and suck away all courage and hope.

Still, he raised his pistol, determined to avenge all the men that had died under his command before he died but his arms felt slow and ice cold, muscles aching and unresponsive. The wolf laughed. It was a chilling sound, deep and resonant, a huffing part of the growling. Then the monster turned and vanished up the stairs. Ritter fired, finally, the bullet ricocheting off a wall somewhere in the crypt.

Upstairs he heard shouts and cries of dismay, and a few gunshots, but Ritter stayed on his knees with the dried husks of long-dead monks. Finally he holstered his pistol and stood, eyes feeling dry but still unable to blink for fear of what might happen in that split second when he could not see.

That must be what it wants, Ritter thought. *For me to fear, for me to see my failure and the men dead around me. To despair.* Setting his jaw with grim determination he slowly, stiffly marched up the steps. *I am an Aryan soldier, I am German. I will fear no creature out of myth or reality. No monster is more fearsome than the forces of the Nazis.*

The priest met him as he left the crypts, saying something urgent and demanding in Polish. Ritter stopped and stared at the priest, who ignored his glare. He gibbered on nonsensically, gesturing at the crypt. Ritter pulled his luger and shot the man in the face, and walked away as the priest fell dead to the floor. *Governor Frank is right*, he thought. *We need to eliminate these Catholics.*

Outside, Beckenbauer was dead on the street dozens of meters from the truck, as if he had been dragged by his intestines. Farber was crouched in the cab of the truck shouting into the radio for reinforcements.

The Romanian had lied about at least one thing, Ritter was certain. That wolf had to have been shot dozens of times with silver bullets and yet it still seemed to be unharmed. Ritter decided to keep one last silver bullet for when he met the Romanian again.

*****

The wolf ran along the street, ignoring the terrified people it passed. It hated the daylight and the sun, and the day was so bright and hot and clear again. The city was scattered with children of the enemy but he did not have time to slaughter them all. It was enough to terrify them and fill them with doubt. Weakening faith was more important to the monster than killing.

The crypt had been a frustration for the wolf. It had been a fine, frightening place for an ambush and the men had been pleasing to slaughter, but there was no exit. Years before Cezar had heard about the place, and heard the tales of the catacomb, but the fool who told the tale said it exited in the graveyard. It was perfect, a place that filled men with idiot fear of the rotting dead. But it was just a cave, and the wolf had almost been trapped.

The bullets had burned like silver fire in his body, piercing his skin. Yet the hate of the soldiers and the darkness in their hearts had overwhelmed their righteous vengeance, preventing the bullets from taking full effect. They had hurt nevertheless and it had been many, many decades since the wolf had felt that kind of pain.

It knew no fear, only frustration and fury. It wanted to make the ones who had hurt it to feel fear, to feel pain. The soldiers were meaningless, they were mere puppets of the ones truly in power. Those were the ones it wanted to feel pain and fear, the leaders, the men who thought they were conquerors. It heard a gun, felt the impacts, but they were only ordinary bullets. The wolf leaped up and ran along a wall to a rooftop, peering around.

Then it saw what it wanted in Cezar's memory and flashed a sharp-fanged grin, eyes blazing red.

CHAPTER TWENTY-EIGHT

Huddled in their homes, the people of Krakow peeked out of windows and wondered what was happening. The radio shows were no help, they gave no news of events in the city. Official word on the radio had gone out that everyone was to stay in their homes and not go outside, and now trucks full of soldiers, heavy machinery, and German shouts could be heard on the old brick streets. It felt like back in September of '39 again when the Germans had invaded.

Some saw the wolf, a huge black figure moving at unnatural speed through the street and over rooftops, leaping over obstacles almost as if it could fly. As it passed, shadows seemed to deepen and the air felt colder. Pets cringed and cried as it drew near, children screamed and thrashed as it passed. It was heading east, into the old Kazimirez suburb and the Germans seemed to be chasing it. Something had gone very wrong, but no one in their homes knew what it had been. They only knew it couldn't be good for them. Nothing was good for them.

Major Ritter had lost command. A Colonel named Hans Procter had taken over, and he was directing the hunt with the help of air support in the form of an old Ar-68 circling the city. Ritter was still in charge of his SS, but the Heer were out of his hands. He was glad of the change in command; things were turning out much worse than he had anticipated. So far his company had been nearly obliterated, and the silver bullets did not seem to have much effect on the beast.

He had thought about trying to explain what they were after but kept silent. They would find out soon enough, and would think him demented if he told them to use silver bullets. It would take Governor Frank's treasury to melt enough silver down anyway. If the Romanian was right, enough concentrated conventional weaponry would suffice.

"The wolf is running neck over head south and east toward the river. They think it is a lion or something," said Private Färber, listening to the radio as Ritter himself drove the truck.

Ritter took some comfort in the monster's rush. Perhaps that meant it was afraid or at least rethinking its rash attack on German soldiers. Now that the full might of the Reich was arrayed against it, this farce could come to a proper end. He only had five men left, four whom were guarding the Romanian. He had ordered the men that had been attached to Dr Stoffel to join him, but he had not seen or heard of them yet. There was nothing left of the men from the gestapo.

It bothered Ritter slightly that they were able to track the wolf so easily. It was as if it was trying to stay in sight, but perhaps it was not used to the airplane. *How intelligent was the thing in that form?* He wondered. It seemed to be as intelligent as the man had been. Dangerously clever. It had been moving in apparently random directions, as if afraid or confused, but now it was running full speed directly toward the river in the southeast. Perhaps it hoped to vanish in the river. *Did such a monster need to breathe?*

In the Arado biplane, Karl Stompf watched the black form streak through the streets. It was difficult to track, fly the plane, and report in, but the twin wings of the biplane gave so much lift he could drop his airspeed to nearly the same rate as the wolf. The bulky radio jammed in behind his seat made the cockpit uncomfortably tight, but he found that it did help balance the plane better since it had been stripped of ammo and guns. The plane was so old and outdated that most of its kind had been scrapped, but Stompf had flown one in the Spanish Civil War and loved it. A few had remained in Poland as reconnaisance because they could fly slow and were very maneuverable, and the skies were clear of enemies.

The beast had turned a corner and was out of view, so Stompf turned almost on a wingtip and swooped around to catch another glimpse. He was not very familiar with Krakow so he was having a hard time identifying areas and landmarks. Stompf saw the black form again, moving slowly across a churned up grassy area behind a blocky building with copper and tile roofs over different sections. He didn't recognize the building or the streets, but the building was large and had German flags flying over it.

"The target has slowed, it is moving toward... a large building, ah, it has our flag over it and what looks like military vehicles around it near a graveyard. A few guards."

The guards looked up at the circling biplane buzzing overhead. It had German markings but they were surprised to see the old thing in the air. It had been a dull day like always, but this was a change of pace. One waved at the plane, then was struck in the side by a black form and collapsed under it, making horrible sounds as the beast chewed through his chest. The other guard swore and pointed his Mauser 98k at the huge black form. The rifle refused to fire, and with

200

more profanity, he levered the safety off and fired into the body in front of him repeatedly, working the bolt action as quickly as he could. The huge form turned slowly to face him apparently ignoring the bullets, then lunged forward, biting through the laminated stock of the rifle and ripping it out of the guard's hands. As the guard died, he stared into the face of the enormous wolf in confusion and pain. *What was a wolf doing in the city?*

The first troops sped up to the building, an old synagogue now turned into a German facility. They spotted the wolf and opened fire, bullets hitting the walls and street all around it throwing brick dust into the air. The wolf turned to face the soldiers, fur jumping and twitching as bullets struck it, then spun and dove through the doors of the Synagogue crashing through them as if they were made of cardboard.

More trucks arrived, as word of the target's location spread. Ritter slid his truck to a stop and jumped out, ordering Färber to follow. The radio was pointless now.

The monster was inside. Ritter saw no higher ranking officer in the area and ordered men to surround the building. He was determined that it would not escape this time, if the building had to be turned into a crater. Whatever was inside didn't matter as much as killing this thing.

The Romanian had been right about one thing, Ritter thought. There was no way he was going to allow Stoffel to fill the world with more of these horrors. Looking around, Ritter saw that there were squads with machine guns arriving, so he set one up facing the door out the front window of an empty shop across the street and prepared to take one inside personally. More soldiers arrived and gathered by the building. Inside were the sounds of shooting and screaming and horrible low growling. Ritter ignored them but many of the men were staring at the building in confusion and dismay.

Then the armored car rumbled up. The Panzerspähwagen shook with the power of its 8 cylinder engine as Ritter yelled a conversation with the driver.

"I need you to point that cannon at the building. When I give the word...how fast can you fire that thing?"

"Fritz can put 280 rounds a minute from the 20mm cannon into whatever you point at."

Ritter grinned. "Excellent."

The Panzerspähwagen looked something like a small tank with eight wheels rather than tracks. The cannon was on a turret at the top, but as it was designed to carry soldiers, its armor was too light to face other tanks. It would stop small arms fire, but not any sort of shell or grenade. Still, it was the heaviest thing Ritter had and it made him feel better for the sheer power of it. To fit any men inside he guessed it probably wouldn't even carry 280 shells but it surely would not take that many to soften up the beast.

Ritter walked to the gathering of officers waiting for his word.

"Men, we're going to soften up the building a bit with that cannon then move in, hard and fast. Shoot everything and anything you see not wearing a german uniform."

One of the young army lieutenants spoke up. "Sir, I am not sure we should do that."

"Nobody in there is alive except our target, I can assure you."

"If you say so, sir but that building is..."

Ritter cut him off angrily. "That building is expendable. You have no idea what we're after here. This entire *city* is expendable, do I make myself clear?"

The lieutenant swallowed and nodded, hoping he would not go on record. Angering an SS officer was not a profitable career move. Besides, if he was only following orders, who could condemn him? He began moving surreptitiously around the Panzerspähwagen to get behind it. A handful of other soldiers crawled behind heavy objects and crouched, hands over their ears.

Ritter gave the order. The 20mm cannon began firing at a rapid rate, like an anti-aircraft weapon, punching holes in the bricks and exploding inside with rumbling firey roars. Smoke billowed out of windows that shattered and Ritter smiled more. *It might not be dead, but it cannot be very happy in there*, he thought. He was being reckless, he knew. It was unlike his character, but the past few days had been insane and he was feeling crazy himself. Ritter was grimly determined that his men would be avenged if it was the last thing he ever did on this planet. The monster must die, at all costs.

Bricks crumbled from the side of the building to the sidewalk with a clatter and the men crouched near the building, hands over their ears. More troops arrived and set up as close to the building as they dared while the shelling continued. The cannon was not firing at its maximum rate, only in bursts as the gunner tried to deliver rounds into the building in a useful pattern. Ritter hoped none of the shells would penetrate the far side, leaving an exit or harming the soldiers surrounding the building. The might of German engineering and modern weaponry was going to turn that monster into a bloody smear, Ritter was certain.

But the wolf knew something that Ritter did not. Cezar had been to Krakow before and knew that the old synagogue was something else now. The Old Synagogue had been destroyed in the early 1500s by fire and rebuilt, but the Germans had been far more destructive, as they had been to most of the Jewish quarter. All the furnishings and silver had been stripped out, the Rabbis and staff shipped off to the camp at Plaszow. Governor-General Frank ate his dinners lit by silver candlesticks taken from the synagogue. The German occupying forces had even emptied the nearby Jewish cemetery and burned the bodies. The various buildings of the Old Synagogue had been converted into warehouses, the main structure turned into a magazine.

The synagogue's interior brick walls offered no more resistance to the 20mm rounds than eggshells and one of the exploding shells set off a stockpile of TNT stored within an interior room. As the TNT exploded, it set off other munitions and explosives, including rockets and grenades filling the interior with death and flame. Bullets began to ignite in the flames, ricocheting off walls and through holes in the sides. The building erupted, flames blossoming out around the rising and shattering bricks, throwing debris as far away as the river over a mile distant.

The explosions continued for several minutes as superheated ammunition rained around the old Jewish quarter, firing in all directions as it fell. The blast wave had launched bullets blocks away, raining down from above like an aerial assault. Grenades fell from the sky into buildings and streets. Rounds of ammunition fired from the remains of the building as the heat cooked off bullets from their storage as if a platoon of soldiers were inside firing in all directions.

The Ar-68 was struck several times, and its pilot looked down at his thigh which had started bleeding like a tipped wine bottle. The old plane still flew despite being pushed up and jerked around on the blast wave like a cork in a river, but it was smoking and had several holes through it. Stompf turned the Arado toward the airbase and hoped he would survive long enough to put her back on the ground. She had served well and he wanted to honor the old bird, even as he could feel his life ebbing away from the severed artery.

When the explosions finally ended and the smoke began to clear away, only a handful of soldiers survived, crawling in the rubble bleeding from the ears and nose. Some were naked and burned slightly, clothing ripped away in the force of the blast. The Panzerspähwagen was on its side, the gun crumpled under the weight of the vehicle when it rolled. Trucks were on fire and toppled all around and the Old Synagogue was the crater Ritter had desired. Bricks and pieces of the building hit the ground for almost a minute after the initial blast.

The wolf crawled out of the rubble of a side building and shook the dust off its fur. Howling again, it shook the rubble and pieces of glass scattered around the building with the fury of its victory song. Inside their homes, the people of Krakow prayed and looked at each other in fear. Was this good? Were the Germans losing a fight?

The Polish people began to care for their wounded and move the dead from the catastrophic explosion of the magazine. For blocks in all directions the bullets and debris had maimed and killed, rending apart buildings. Not a single window was intact for blocks. Dying and wounded people lay on the sidewalks.

When the building had exploded, it had sounded like war, the kind of war that had not reached Krakow for generations. Then all was quiet, and even the buzzing sound of the plane had stopped. A hand-cranked siren began to sing out in the distance.

CHAPTER TWENTY-NINE

The Germans were in disarray. Stompf had passed out landing his plane which had skidded sideways to a stop before colliding with the control tower. There were a few scattered survivors at the Old Synagogue but they were either too wounded or too dazed and stunned to make sense of what had happened. The only one in town who still knew what was going on was Konrad Stoffel who sat in the cab of a rumbling army truck with a cage in the back containing Aniela Wisznewski.

Over the radio he received reports of the fugitive's movement from spotters he'd placed around the city. It was headed to the castle or the river, they couldn't be sure. It was less obvious now, harder to spot. When it passed through shadows it was very difficult to see, and it seemed to be avoiding people and busy areas. The sirens playing around the city and Germans moving through the streets on heavy patrols had kept most people in their homes, particularly after the huge explosions, and the wolf was able to move through alleys and back yards without encountering many people.

The spotters were not sure what had happened at the Old Synagogue. Some thought the plane had dropped a bomb, some thought the Germans had called in artillery. Stoffel was shocked at how loud the explosions had been and how long they had lasted. He shook his head, determined to never come as close to a battlefield again. Even worse, it had been difficult to rely on the spotters, who kept referring to the escapee as a "giant wolf."

For the first time Dr Stoffel wished he had the Romanian with him. *He might have some idea where the thing was probably headed*, the doctor thought. Or at least a story to tell. The fugitive seemed to know the city very well, as if it had been here before, and Stoffel guessed that perhaps Cezar Alexandru had been.

When he'd heard the reports of the thing turning into a wolf, Stoffel had been scornful and annoyed, but the information was too consistent and repeated. The escapee had definitely changed somehow, apparently gaining fur and moving like an animal. His mind spun with the possibilites, how the biology and physiognamy worked. How much was still human inside it? Did it retain Cezar's personality and memories? How much energy would it take to change in that manner, and how could it possibly do so?

Stoffel knew that certain creatures could change their shapes, such as octopi and squid, perhaps it was along those lines. And to make the information more confusing, everyone was reporting that the wolf was enormous, even bigger than a human. *Where could that extra mass come from? Perhaps it was just the fur, or some psychological effect on the viewers*, Stoffel pondered.

Another report crackled in over his headphones. They were delayed by each scout needing to use a telephone to call a private at Stoffel's lab, who then radioed him in the truck. The wolf was down by the river, running along the cliff under Castle Wawel. To a cave. That had to be its destination, unless the thing wanted to dogpaddle somewhere.

"Move, we're headed to the base of the castle, along the river." Stoffel ordered his driver, Sargent Gerber.

Gerber put the truck into gear and rumbled over the bricks of the street. He knew the city well enough to drive comfortably through it, and with Stoffel's paperwork, there was nowhere they could not go. No one wanted to make an enemy of Reichsfuhrer Himmler. Gerber enjoyed the job, even if it was more suited to a corporal or private.

"Maybe we should get those prison clothes off the girl. It might upset our target." Gerber suggested.

Stoffel glared at him from the corner of his eyes.

The cave had several names. Most called it *Smocza Jama*, The Dragon's Den. Stoffel didn't know anything about it, and the placque telling about the cave had been ripped out by Gestapo to eliminate that part of Polish heritage. It wasn't a very impressive cave entrance, although there was a paved section up against the base of the cliff face and railings by the Vistula River. The cliff wasn't tall, only about thirty feet at this point, but the red brick-lined walls of Wawel castle rose another twenty feet above that.

In the rough rock cliff wall was an opening that had a black wrought iron gate across it, wide open. Dr Stoffel had Gerber park the truck out on the paving stones with the back toward the gate. The nearest spotter arrived on a bicycle, a bit red in the face from the ride around and down from the castle.

"I saw it go inside, but I don't know if it is still there, Professor Doctor. It took a few minutes to ride down to here and meet you, so I lost contact."

"He probably is still there," Stoffel replied. "I expect he was wounded in the attack on the Old Synagogue. Gerber, stay in the truck on the radio and maintain contact. If you hear differently let us know."

Stoffel looked at the cave entrance. A few small steps led down to the gate, and a guard lay in a pool of blood at the base of the steps. Stoffel thought about checking on the guard, then decided against it. He could not do his research if he put himself in danger, he had to stay back. Even if it wasn't truly a wolf, canines had extraordinary senses, and he did not want to tip it off, and without more data, he had to assume the escapee was not simply somewhat canine in appearance. The wind was blowing from the direction of the castle and out over the river, which he hoped would help prevent their scent from reaching the cave. He reached a decision.

"Everyone back behind the truck, down near the river. You too Gerber," he ordered. Then Dr Stoffel unlocked the cage and swung it open with great effort against the spring that had been rigged on the door and climbed inside. The girl was slumped against the back of the cage, barely awake. He pulled her up into a sitting position and pondered her a moment. Stoffel thought a moment. *Perhaps Gerber had a point about the prison clothes, they would smell like a jail cell, but would the wolf recognize that?* They only smelled of unwashed girl to Stoffel. Slapping Aniela to dazed semi-consciousness, Konrad Stoffel steeled himself to the task at hand, telling himself it was for the good of the Reich and scientific study.

The wolf lay in the cave, glaring at the door. He could smell traces of the truck and had heard it drive up. It hadn't sounded like very many soldiers, but they were still on his trail. The silver bullets had been very painful and had damaged him, but the explosion and all the shrapnel from the building and ordnance had been even worse. The wounds were healing rapidly, but it had suffered greatly and wanted to stay out of sight a bit longer. That guard at the door hadn't died immediately, which was a source of annoyance to the wolf. It was weaker than normal, and Cezar was fighting hard from inside.

Without a full moon and in the daytime it was harder to stay in control, but the wolf was determined to stay in power. Cezar was weakening and even intended to 'cure' himself; this could not be. At the very least the wolf had to make sure he was so hated and such a fugitive he wouldn't have a chance to try, and if that Romanian could be killed, so much the better. There was something very dangerous and wrong about that man, it was certain.

Then the wolf heard a scream. It was used to screams in the way an alcoholic is used to the satisfying taste of liquor, but this was different. When this scream had echoed off the pocked and rough interior of the Dragon's Den, it had been a very familiar sound, a tone and voice that the wolf knew, and more importantly, that Cezar knew.

Cezar fought harder for control, pushing against the wolf's will with desperate strength. The wolf growled, a deep sound that rung off the cave walls. One of the lights wired inside fell over with a crash of glass. Aniela. The bitch that had caused all this. If it wasn't for that bitch, Cezar would have never cared about being cured, never been caught in this trouble. The wolf knew just what to do. Without that final light in his life, Cezar would give up hope.

Stoffel climbed out of the truck and pushed the door against the spring until it stopped in a catch, holding the door open. Just someone climbing into the back of the truck might shake the vehicle enough to release the door to slam shut, but the pad of cardboard on the floorboards hid a trigger back near Aniela, and just in case Stoffel had led a rope from the latch under the truck to where the men were waiting.

Lieutenant Kohler pushed the safety off his Luger. Stoffel looked at him and shook his head as he walked around the side of the truck but Kohler ignored him.

They waited, staring at the truck. From where they were crouched, they could see under the truck a few feet, and that was how they first spotted the wolf. Its huge paws moved over the paving stone with nail clicks that sounded unusually chilling in the quiet. Even the sirens had stopped, and only the distant sound of shouts and trucks driving through town were in the background. That and the constant sound of the Vistula behind them. Stoffel squinted, staring at the paws. *How could the man's hands and feet change so completely? Was it even the same person?*

The truck shifted slightly, as the wolf moved around to the back, two paws on the bumper.

It looked inside, staring at Aniela, who sat up facing the entrance. She was staring, half-lidded, with tears on her face and one arm was twisted in an unnatural position. Aniela whimpered slightly in her dazed state. The wolf stared at her with hate and hunger to kill, and inside, Cezar stared as well.

It was his fault. If it hadn't been for him chasing after Aniela, she never would have been in this situation. Whoever had hurt her had done so to get at him. She was in prison clothes, chained to the truck because of him.

The wolf hesitated. It could clearly see the bars of the cage and the spring; this was so plainly a trap it almost laughed. The idea that it could possibly hold him was not even a remote concern but it didn't want to just fall prey to a trap when it would be so much more frightening and eerie to avoid it. If it could get one of the men who tried to trap him caught in the cage as well, that would be even better. It puzzled over the situation and was unready when Cezar made one last, frenzied attempt to break free. Surprised, the wolf reeled, stumbling to the pavement, and lost control.

Cezar rose from the burning ashes of the wolf's form, shaking from the effort. Stoffel crouched at the river's edge staring with his jaw hanging open. From his vantage point the entire transformation had been clear under the truck and his mind spun as if he'd downed an entire bottle of schnapps.

Cezar Alexandru felt weak and wracked with pain, bleeding and bruised. He could not remember feeling this awful ever before and looked down at himself, breathing hard. Looking around, he saw the rope tied to the cage door, and anger overtook his weariness and pain.

"So," said a voice behind him. "You were right, he may be found here."

Cezar turned slowly to face Major Ritter and Vladimir Czerny. Ritter was bleeding and burnt, one eye closed with a terrible gash across his face. His crisp black uniform was torn and charred, and his left arm dangled useless at his side, red and black from burns. Vladimir Czerny looked unchanged, face emotionless and black leather trilby in place on his bald, tattooed head, a black doctor's bag in his hand. He seemed small beside the SS officer, calm beside a barely contained madman.

"The Romanian here told me you probably were headed to this cave, when I asked him. I told him that you were reported to be running toward the castle by the river, and he told me the strangest story."

"What story is that?" asked Cezar, staring at Vladimir. *An agent for the Nazis all along?* He wondered.

"He would tell it better, but if he talks or moves again I will shoot him first. Then you." Ritter raised his luger and aimed it at Cezar.

"It seems when this city was founded, there was a dragon living here. It had six legs and no wings, supposedly, and it was eating all the farmers. The prince called on all the people to find a way to kill it, and it took a cobbler's apprentice...?" he glanced at Czerny. "Yes, it was a cobbler's apprentice to defeat the creature. This clever young fellow took a quantity of sulfur and hid it in some meat, then left it at the cave entry. When the dragon came out to eat it, it got a terrible belly ache, and dove into the Vistula to cool off. It exploded from the sulfur, for some reason, and died.

"A day or two ago, when I heard stories like this, I chuckled at the fairy tales and the credulity of those people in the past. Believing in dragons, what else will they fall for, eh? Werewolves?"

Ritter and Cezar stared at each other.

Ritter fired his luger at Cezar, and the silver bullet struck him in the forehead. Cezar collapsed backward, bouncing off the back of the truck. The spring-loaded door slammed shut with a loud bang, and Ritter fired again, startled.

Dr Stoffel and his men ran around the truck. Stoffel looked from Cezar on the ground to Ritter still holding his pistol on the body, his head tilted slightly.

"What have you done??" demanded Dr Stoffel.

"Be silent, doctor." Major Ritter said through gritted teeth. "You are not so important you cannot be taken to Silesian House for the Gestapo to question."

"Herr Sturmbannführer, what shall we do?" asked Sergeant Gerber.

Ritter slumped slightly, lowering his gun. He looked over at Czerny. "I wasted my last bullet on the truck. You must live a charmed life."

Vladimir Czerny said nothing.

"Take the prisoner back to her cell, burn that body, and call a medic. I seem to have been wounded a short time ago." Ritter looked at his arm. *This is not going to help me get any promotions*, he thought. *Perhaps it is time to retire from the battlefield.*

Lieutentant Kohler began to climb up to the back of the truck and open the cage when Cezar grabbed his foot. Stoffel swore and backed away, bumping into Sergeant Gerber. Cezar swung Kohler to the ground, knocking the breath from him, and stood up. He was still battered and bleeding and had a hole in his forehead that oozed blood but Cezar stood tall and furious, veins standing out on his muscles and neck.

"Everyone here is about to die," he said quietly.

Doctor Stoffel ran.

Ritter stared at Cezar, his mouth slightly open. He swayed slightly on his feet, unable to believe what he was seeing. He groped for Czerny, but the Romanian had moved away. Sergeant Gerber pulled his luger and fired, but missed and Cezar backhanded him, sending Gerber rolling on the pavement almost to the railing at the riverside, stunned. Cezar casually reached down and picked up Kohler by a leg as he scrambled for his pistol that had skittered away when he fell. The gun was almost in his grasp, but then Cezar swung him through the air like a club and struck Ritter. Cezar let go of the lieutenant, sending him spinning toward the cave entry.

Ritter lay on the paving stones in a daze, pain overwhelming him as barely-scabbed-over wounds reopened and he began bleeding heavily again. He could not see from all the blood on his face. He felt terribly cold, as if his whole body had been drained of heat and strength.

"Enough. No cure. No running. No mercy. Everyone dies." Cezar growled and the beast within him soared with joy. *Now fill the world with our kind,* it growled.

Gerber fired at him again, and the bullets hurt like fist blows against his naked skin. Cezar leaped across to the sergeant who had half risen against the railing, and hurled him into mid-river dozens of yards away.

"Cezar..." Aniela's weak voice reached him from the truck. Cezar stopped and stared out over the water. "Please, Cezar."

He closed his eyes, and hung his head a moment. The beast inside raged.

Crossing over to the truck again, he held the bars in his hands and rested his head between two of them.

"Cezar you have to stop, please." She sounded so weak and tired. Cezar's heart hurt listening to Aniela's voice. "You have to stop... stop the killing. You cannot let ...it ...win."

And as if that had taken all of her strength, she fell silent, her eyes closed.

Cezar fell to his knees against the truck. Behind him he heard Czerny walk closer.

"The dragon story. Is it true?" Cezar asked.

"No, its just a legend," said the Romanian.

Cezar felt confused but brushed it aside. "What must I do?"

Vladimir Czerny rummaged through his satchel. "How long has it been, since you became the wolf?"

"Longer than you've been alive. The last half of the 1800s."

Czerny was silent a moment. "I had hoped, at first, that we could save you. To remove the curse, and leave you free. But...you have been too long the monster, and it has grown far too strong. I do not know exactly the process, but the beast seems weak when it first ... when it takes someone. Then as the years go by, it grows into its full strength. Even silver bullets do not harm it very much. You should... you should not have survived all this."

Czerny nodded. He thought of the faces of the dead, the screams that haunted his dreams. All the people, all the fear and torment, the pain and death he had caused. And he was so close to giving in completely to it. He shook, thinking of what would come from that final surrender. How much horror had Aniela saved them all from with her simple plea?

"I am sorry, Cezar. I believe you could be a friend, in other circumstances. But there is no cure for you," the Romanian paused a long moment, "save one."

Cezar looked around at Czerny, who was holding a dagger. He looked down at the wooden blade.

Czerny rubbed the blade with an oil speckled with greenish brown crumbled material. "Hawthorn, with wolfsbane. It has been blessed. You must do it, or it will not die."

Cezar stared at the blade. The light colored wood was stained darker where the oil had been rubbed. He looked up at Czerny. "One last thing."

Rising, he walked over to Ritter who lay on the cobblestones. Blood trickled from him between the stones paving the ground, and his breathing was labored. Bubbles formed at his lips.

"You are dying, Major Ritter." Cezar said in German.

"Oh no, I'm healthy as a fish in the water," Ritter groaned and coughed, spattering the stones with blood.

"I suppose I'll be joining you soon," Cezar said quietly, crouching close to Ritter.

Ritter turned his head, trying to look up, but the blood on his one good eye blocked his vision. "Do you know... I always had hoped?" He said, coughing wetly. "My father was a colonel... I had hoped to surpass his rank." Ritter's head fell to the paving stones and he breathed one last misting of blood.

Cezar stood and walked back to Vladimir Czerny.

"What about her?" he asked, nodding toward Aniela in the truck.

"She will live or die, as we all do."

"Make sure she is safe."

"I will do what I can," said Czerny.

Cezar sighed. Taking the dagger from the Romanian's hand he looked at it again. "The priests say if you kill yourself, God cannot save you. But then, I am already damned."

"I try not to tell God what He can and cannot do," said Czerny.

Cezar shrugged. "I'm absolutely sure that there's a devil, I've lived with something like him for years. But God? Look around you. Look at this world."

"You've lived long enough to know that tyrants come and go," said Czerny, "and that good people come and go. What seems insurmountable one day is forgotten the next. I believe everything is moving forward to something in the end, and that is guided by someone. Even today."

Cezar stared at the knife then shrugged, and pushed it against his chest. He strained against the blade, feeling it against his skin with a searing coldness unlike anything he had ever felt.

Darkness slid in from the edges of his vision like tendrils of smoke and he felt an awful presence inside him.

You shall not escape so easily, the wolf murmured.

Cezar closed his eyes and tried to ignore it, but he felt his arms getting weaker, shaking. The creature was weakened after its long time in the sun but furiously pushing its will against his. When had he ever won, really, against it? It was hopeless, pointless to try.

Stop this and I can give you all the power you need to satisfy every hunger you have.

Cezar shook his head. He knew what the cost of that power would be. His hands drooped slightly.

Give me control and you will heal, the pain will stop and you will fill your enemies with dread.

The dread already filled the world, and Cezar did not want to add to it any longer. The knife point lifted from his chest.

You could rule this world, nothing can stop you with me to give you power.

Cezar was tired of this world. He almost dropped the knife.

"Cezar. You want me to care for Aniela, yes? What happens to her, if the beast takes you?" Vladimir Czerny said quietly.

Cezar opened his eyes, their amber color wavering with tears. He could feel his will weakening, and he knew this would be the last time. In his mind he felt as if he were standing on the end of an endless chasm, the ground crumbling beneath him. If he gave in this time, there would be no coming back. All that would be left would be the wolf, there would be nothing left of him but a screaming prisoner in an eternal hell within the demon. The beast was quiet inside him; confident, waiting.

Czerny put his hand on Cezar's and the contact gave him new strength, as if the little man was feeding his considerable willpower into the much larger one.

"Aniela," Cezar said, and pushed the blade into his chest with all of his strength. For a moment he stared at the hilt jutting from his chest, felt a darkness shred away from him, the hairs pulling from his back and a light he'd not felt for seventy years return.

Then he fell to the pavement, lifeless.

CHAPTER THIRTY

Aniela sat in the truck between Lieutenant Kohler and a man she did not know the name of. He was very fat and smelled heavily of beer and sweat, the most unattractive and heavy SS man she'd ever seen. She felt small and crushed between the men, both of whom were at least a head taller than she was sitting down. She felt like a child again, and the drug was wearing off leaving her with a headache and ringing in her ears, but her arm didn't hurt as much as it had earlier. Aniela kept her eyes down and said nothing. There was nothing to say.

The truck did not stop at the Silesian House, however. They kept going. She watched the building as they drove by on Pomorska street and wondered where they were going to kill her.

When Kohler had stood up, swearing in German, Aniela had been awake. She couldn't tell what was going on outside, only that she seemed to be alone. Then she heard men talking in German and the back of the truck rocked as someone climbed up on the bumper. Kohler had opened the cell and unshackled her, but he seemed gentle and his manner had been concern, not cold indifference.

He had helped Aniela walk out of the truck, her knees like a newborn deer, and held her up by her good arm when she stepped down onto the pavement. The stones had been so cold on her bare feet. Aniela felt dizzy and heard the sounds around her coming in pulses or waves like the surf at the ocean.

There were several German officers there and another truck arrived with more soldiers. A group was working its way along the Vistula downriver, looking for something, and the rest were looking around the area with weapons out as if they expected an attack. There was no sign of Dr Stoffel. She saw them carrying the bodies of an SS officer and Cezar's huge nude form, putting them in a truck. Could Cezar really be dead? She didn't understand what had happened.

Eventually, Kohler was given some sort of orders, and he took Aniela to a big green truck like the one she'd been caged in and squeezed between himself and the driver in the cab. Along the way, the two had spoken in German, and at one point it sounded almost like an argument, but apparently Kohler had won.

The truck bumped along the streets through Krakow to a train yard, and Aniela was taken out of the truck roughly by the driver. Kohler went off to speak to some men near a train car. She was put in line behind a lot of other people guarded by soldiers and the fat driver walked away and got back into the truck.

Lieutenant Kohler looked back at Sargeant Kranz. It had been good to get out of the cab away from the man. He could not understand how that sort of man had even been able to even earn SS status, but politics and patronage can do strange things, even in the elite of a military. Kohler knew too well how someone can be where they didn't belong.

"Are you sure she's Gyspy?" Asked the man next to him, dressed in a train engineer's clothes.

Kohler nodded. "The Gestapo say so."

The man grunted. "No guarantees, you understand. I don't know what happens down the road here. But then, who does?"

"The paperwork is in order?" asked Kohler.

"Of course, our best man worked on it. It would fool Aldolph Hitler," said the engineer.

"I'm not sure that's such a challenge," grumbled Kohler.

The engineer chuckled. "Well, then it will fool Hans Frank. He even signed some of it."

Kohler nodded. He'd done his best. "Give me the paperwork, and I'll make sure you get out of the country. From there you are on your own."

"This won't hurt you?" asked the engineer.

"It shouldn't. I am being transferred tomorrow in any case. I was only here to work with Dr Stoffel. Then its back to France again."

"Tell the French ladies hello for us," said the engineer, handing him the packet.

"They don't seem to care for me very much over there for some reason."

The train was loaded up, three boxcars filled with men, women, and children. It was tight and uncomfortable inside, and there was little room to sit. Aniela didn't mind standing, but she felt an emptiness inside her like the mouse being carried away by an owl. It was all over with but how she would die. She had heard what happened to the people put in cattle cars.

The car lurched and everyone inside stumbled, pushing against the ones pinned against the back wall of the car. Aniela winced and held her arm against her. The young man who fell against her apologized. He was wearing ordinary street clothing and seemed a bit shy.

"I'm sorry miss. Are you all right?"

Aniela shook her head silently.

"Oh, I'm so sorry, did I step on... oh, I see."

After a few minutes of the train slowly gaining speed, he said "Please here, have my coat, I'm not cold at all but you must be in just that smock." He peeled off his coat and wrapped it around Aniela's shoulders, bumping other people. "Is your arm...?"

"Broken," Aniela said. "By a doctor." It would have made her laugh, not so long ago.

Aniela stared at her bare feet on the floor. They were very dirty. She remembered coming into her home with dirty feet and her mother being so upset at the footprints she left on the wooden floor. After that she had tried to make sure her feet were clean before entering the caravan. What had it all been for? Why did she try to live a good life for so long? It was all ashes, it was empty. None of it had any meaning.

"Here now, don't cry," said the man quietly.

"Give her some water," said a nearby woman. "It will be all right" said another.

Someone passed a tin cup full of water to her. Aneila looked up and around her in disbelief.

"Don't you know where we're going??" She demanded, angry. "Don't you know why we are put in this car? Did you think the passenger cars were too full for us, or something? This is how the Germans send us to camps! Have you not heard? Have you not see the cars full of Jews? We're going to a camp to disappear, to die! How can you act like this??"

One of the nearby women put a hand on her shoulder and chuckled a little.

"Oh my, dear. You weren't told?"

Aniela stared at her. She was mad, they were all crazed, or stupid.

"Sweety, this train isn't going to a camp. Uncle Rys played one last wonderful game. He gave up everything so we could get out. We're going to a port in Turkey, and then to Oran, and from there to Morocco, and passage to America."

Aniela stared at her. *Could anyone be this gullible?*

"We were loaded by German soldiers, this is a German train. We're going to a German camp to die at the hands of German bastards."

"No, dear. This train has German markings but it belongs... belonged to Uncle Rys. The whole train is run by the Romani. Its all one grand trick on the Germans, and the Polish for that matter. The Germans think we're headed to Płaszów. They don't put water on *those* cars."

Aniela shook her head and closed her eyes. She felt sad for them all and their idiot hope. Even the Gyspies could not fool the Germans. They were too careful, too clever, too organized.

Oh Aleš I will see you again, my love, she thought, and the thought warmed her slightly.

*****

The truck rumbled across the paving stones back to the German military base outside Krakow, with Sergeant Kranz still driving. Kranz stopped the truck on the bridge over the Vistula and leaned against his door.

"So, I want in." He said with a sneer.

Kohler looked at Kranz in confusion.

"Don't give me that, you think I'm dumb as a bundle of bean straw, eh? That engineer, he gave you some cash. I don't care what you're into or what this is about, but I want my cut. I drove you and that girl here, I want a piece."

Kohler sighed. *I should have guessed this was coming,* he thought. "I have to split this with several other people, you realize," he said after a moment.

"I don't get where that's my problem."

"I guess I understand where you would see things that way. Very well." Kohler reached into his coat and pulled out Major Ritter's wallet. When the werewolf had killed himself, Kohler had just laid in a heap hoping that popping sound in his side had not been ribs cracking. He was afraid, and didn't want to move. Nothing human should be that strong or that fast, and he was afraid if he got up, the huge naked man would kill him, or worse, beat in him more like he had before. He'd heard it all, stunned and disbelieving and had even watched the monster kill its self through slitted eyes.

After the strange Romanian had left, Kohler got up painfully and stumbled over to check on the SS Major. He was dead in a puddle of blood that had trickled between the stones like red mortar between black bricks. Kohler hadn't known who the major was, but his wallet said he was Hans Ritter.

Kohler had pocketed the wallet and gone to hesitantly check on the monster. He was not moving and seemed dead, but even so he seemed huge and dangerous. His heart wasn't beating and the body had already started cooling but there was very little blood. Kohler looked around and wondered what to do next when a staff car and a truck rounded the road to the riverside and pulled up, full of soldiers. None of them seemed to outrank him, so he took charge.

It had been easy enough to get the girl away, clearly she was a prisoner who had been brought here. Kohler answered a few questions and insisted he had to report to Silesian House before he could explain any more. Comandeering the truck and the reeking sargeant had been a matter of a few orders; none of the regular Heer soldiers wanted to question an SS officer.

He handed half the wad of cash from Ritter's wallet to Sergeant Kranz. Kranz counted the money out with a smile that got wider as the numbers got bigger.

"Good operation eh? You ever need help again, you let me know."

Kohler nodded and put the wallet away. He hadn't checked how much money was in it, but it looked like it had been quite a bit. Ritter apparently had been a very wealthy man, for all it bought him.

The trip to the base was quiet. Kohler went over in his mind how he'd handle his officers, and Ritter's cash would help. He would turn in the wallet when he got to his commanding officer, keeping most of the money. Leaving some in the wallet would look good, but leaving too much in would seem suspicious.

He kept the paperwork in his jacket. Apparently the sergeant had thought the transfer had been money, not papers, and Kohler was fine with that.

Later, deep in the night after debriefing, Lieutenant Kohler looked over the paperwork. The documents were solid, it would get the train out of Poland. It looked genuine, down to the official stamp and the signature from Hans Frank; almost too genuine. Maybe the gypsies really *had* been able to trick the governor-general into signing them.

Kohler held is head in his hands and stared at the papers lying on the desk. There were no authorizations for letters of transit among them, so he wasn't sure how the trainload would get out of Africa, but they just might make it as far as Morocco. From there, they would have to wait, and wait, and wait. Maybe they would make it to America, maybe they would die in some wretched little town. It was still better than the camp the train was supposed to take them to.

He closed his eyes and thought of all the other people who did not make it. All of the train loads of Jews and Gypsies and Slavs and epileptics and all the rest who were declared unworthy of life by the third reich. This one train load was such a small number to save, of the hundreds of thousands being sent to camps for efficient slaughter. It was Płaszów they were sent to from Krakow, usually. Even the SS murmured in amazement at how brutal and horrific the camp was. The average life expectancy was less than a month in that place. The SS were amazed at how inefficient it was to get so little work out of the prisoners.

When Kohler had gotten the brief message from England, he was confused. His position was dangerous enough as it was, deep inside SS ranks, but to ask him to work to prolong the life of a monster, to assist him in causing chaos and death had confused him. What had this war become? And when he saw what the creature really was and what it could do he had wondered at the sanity of the English.

Markus Kohler's father had died in the Great War in the trenches, leading his men to fight for Germany, and he felt proud to be a soldier. He loved his homeland and his fellow people, but when the Nazis had taken over, it was like a horrific cancer had infected his beloved Germany. He felt sick to his stomach being in the military and fighting for this government.

Like all Germans, he'd been enraged and humiliated by the Versailles Treaty and how Germany was treated. And when Adolph Hitler had spoken, he felt his heart stir in patriotism and fierce indignation at their state. When all Hitler seemed to want was to reclaim land stolen from them by greedy European leaders at the table in 1919, Kohler felt only slightly nervous. It was true the Nazis had ended the violence in the streets, and the economy was doing better. And Kohler felt that Germans should take back what was theirs. He had signed up to be in the SS, since it was the finest and best of the military, and no one questioned Kohler's patriotic fervor.

But once in that black uniform with the unnerving skulls, he began to learn more than he cared to about what was really going on. And when Poland had been invaded, he had given up his brief allegiance to Hitler, secretly. Sitting in a bombed house for hours in the rain, he was wondering how he could possibly go on serving monsters and demons when he overheard a meeting in the basement below him. It had been a resistance movement meeting, and they were in contact with the English. They wanted to fight the Nazis.

It had taken weeks to convince the resistance that he was geniuine, and over a year before England would talk to him. But after several months of feeding them information, undertaking operations to gain data and undermine German operations, and putting himself at risk, they had named him BARREN as an operative, and he had gone to work for the British Intelligence. It hurt him to think he was betraying his country, but he thought of it as betraying Nazis, not Germans. They did not represent his country or his people. They were a disease infesting the real Germany. And there were Germans on the throne of England, after all.

It had been much easier in France when he had been part of the invasion there. That had been a real war, Germans against French, and this time the Germans won. It had been for his father, and for all the men who died with him, to right the wrongs of the Great War. And service there had been easier and safer for him. Back in Poland he had not thought they would ever try to contact him, until Leopold Okulicki from Armia Krajowa had met him with a message from the British.

Kohler hoped he had succeeded. The thing had torn a bloody path through Krakow and managed to get the magazine destroyed. It had to have killed a batallion of soldiers including many officers before killing its self. And whoever that girl was, she had saved them all. He could not understand her or even hear her clearly, but whatever she had said to the thing had made it stop. Kohler doubted anything else could have.

Later in his room, Kohler thought about the girl. The train had been a last minute decision. Kohler had heard from his reistance contacts that the Gypsies had managed to work out some kind of deal and were getting a train out of the country, but Kohler knew they would not make it. Their paperwork was brilliant, it was true, but it was too high level for an engineer and a bunch of prisoners to have. It would be like a bum using a king's signet ring for passage through a castle gate; nobody would believe him.

Aniela, the girl was named. His decision to take her to the train instead of Silesian House was just a whim. She seemed so sweet and harmless in her prison dress, all confused and sad. He couldn't put her under the Gestapo again. After this mess, they'd simply have her put to death just to avoid anyone involved being able to tell the tale. His own commander had been insistent that no one speak of the episode when he'd returned to base.

So many Gestapo and SS slaughtered, in their own headquarters. Shelling their own magazine and destroying a city block, if word got back to Berlin what really had happened, Hitler would be enraged. Heads would roll. A different story was being concocted, he knew. Probably Jews would be blamed, an excuse to do something horrible to them. The Nazis were brilliant at that, from the Reichstag fire on through Poland, the lieutenant knew. Kohler took a deep breath and held it a while, letting it out only when his lungs started to ache.

Taking Aniela to the train had worked out well. By arriving when he had, Kolher was able to transfer their paperwork to the correct authorities. Word would get to the checkpoints and the guards, proper documentation would reach them. The train would be let through, it wouldn't even be questioned. No one would even wonder what had happened to it, why it never got to the camp. The right people had filled out the right paperwork and filed it in the right place. With the chaos of covering up the werewolf and its destruction, it would be forgotten.

Kohler turned out his light and laid on his cot. He wasn't sure he would get much sleep, but at least he felt as if he'd managed to do some good. In the hell he lived in, a little was all he could hope for.

*****

Allistair Dennison sat with Captain Edmund Rushbrooke in a small room under Downing Street. The pipes rattled slightly as someone flushed upstairs and the light flickered when a truck drove by, but at least it wasn't as cold this evening. Captain Rushbrooke had been appointed Director of Naval Intelligence just the year before and still was not comfortable with the job.

"I understand that situation in Krakow has been resolved," Rushbrooke said.

Dennison nodded. "I'm told that the Germans are working hard to paint the whole thing as the work of the Armia Krajowa. I'm surprised they didn't pin it on the Jews."

"Jews don't have much of a presence in Krakow; its Hans Frank's capital, for lack of a better word. From what our psychological profiles say of the man, he wants to make it a model city and would never admit Jews caused him that kind of problem."

Dennison looked through the paperwork in front of him. "ULTRA intercepts indicate that the thing killed an awful lot of people. Mostly German soldiers. I can't get reliable confirmation but there's a claim that it killed quite a few of the chaps inside the Gestapo HQ."

"How very tragic," Rushbrooke grinned.

"Quite. More reliable information from the Russians about the explosion here. Apparently almost a whole city block was wiped out, no one seems to know what happened, but there were scores of German casualties from that as well."

"But the thing is dead?"

"That everyone seems to agree on. I have no contact with BANGLE, just dropped off the planet far as I can tell. Pity about the thing dying, we could use a chap like that."

Rushbrooke shook his head. "No, not from what I've heard. We don't want that."

Dennison looked up a moment, then back to his papers. "As you say. Finally, I have an unusual note here from Diplomatic Section. Some specialist from Berlin wants to cross the lines and join us. Details are sketchy at the moment, but apparently he got word to us through Czech resistance, wants to be part of the Allies now."

"Any explanation why?"

"It seems..." Dennison shuffled through pages and read one breifly. "It seems he is dismayed at how Jerry is using, ah, mystical items. Claims he is some sort of expert on the subject, a Romanian."

Rushbrooke looked bland as always. "I see. Yes, I've read of this Romanian. I'll see if Alexander can't send a sub over to pick him up somewhere. Thank you for bringing this to my attention."

"Important?" asked Dennison.

"Oh, he might be useful to us, yes. You would scarcely credit what the Germans are up to."

"At this point, sir, I doubt anything would surprise me."

Rushbrooke gathered up his paperwork and carefully arranged it in his attache case. So, the Romanian had his fill of Berlin? This war might all work out after all.

He didn't know where he was. The countryside looked like it always did this time of year in Poland; green and beautiful. There was no snow on the ground even in the shadows of trees, but Doctor Stoffel was not paying attention to the scenery. He barely was aware of what was around him, feeling only a numb shock.

Everything had happened so fast, he could scarcely understand it all. Over and over in his mind the events replayed, the sounds like spikes in his ears, assaulting him.

Nothing made sense any more. There was no way he could go back to his work, back to Berlin. He had failed in his task and he wasn't sure how the Reichsführer would react to that failure. And now he wasn't sure what his theories could possibly mean any more.

He turned into a wolf. They shot it in the head. It got back up.

Stumbling over the rough dirt of a field, Stoffel stared into the past. Everything he'd been so certain about, so confident in, the stability and certainty of the world in exact scientific order with predictable, absolute results from proper technique seemed like a cruel joke. What had that philosopher said?

"Wenn du lange in einen Abgrund blickst, dann blickt der Abgrund auch in dich hinein"

When you gaze into the abyss, the abyss also gazes into you. Had Nietzsche been right all along? Was there no meaning, no purpose, no order to the universe, just some cruel random joke that only the strong could force sense into?

They shot it in the head.

Stoffel kept running, his mind crumbling under the strain.

HISTORICAL NOTES:

When Germany invaded Poland in 1939, they had already either taken over or turned several other nations into puppet states. Nobody wanted to fight another war so soon after WWI (referred to as the Great War in this book) and they tended to give in rather than get bloody. The Poles refused to give in, and they were the first to fight the Germans. It took the Germans an entire month to conquer Poland despite having superior weapons, tactics, and leadership. The Poles were fighting tanks and bombers with largely 19th century technology and still held off the German armies for almost all of September.

By contrast, for example, it took about two weeks for the Germans to defeat the entrenched, advanced militaries of the French and capture Paris. In some ways, they Polish never did give up the fight.

The time period this book is set in has so many events and statistics that they seem almost more unbelievable than a werewolf. The numbers roll off a litany of evil and horror that becomes numbing; a human can only take so much before they can't pay attention any longer.

It is well known that more than six million Jews were murdered in the holocaust, but what is not generaly known is that about half of that number came from Poland alone. In total more than six million people were murdered in Poland by the Nazi occupation. More than 1 in five Poles were killed by the Germans during their occupation of the country. Not all of these victims died in prison camps, either. Many were summarily shot where they stood or up against walls. In Krakow alone, the entire patient population in Chelmo mental hospital was shot by soldiers with machine guns.

The movie *Schindler's List* shows much of what took place in Krakow, but the cleansing of the ghettos did not take place until shortly after the events in this book. The owner of the Under the Eagle Pharmacy survived, having aided and saved many Jews while working in the ghetto.

And aside from the deaths, there were the destroyed families. Between 50,000 and up to 200,000 Polish children were taken from their families during the war. They were sent to the farms and families in the Reich never to return, permanently becoming part of Germany.

Some of the actions by the Nazis in this book might seem unbelievable, but I have kept to the exact historical record as much as possible. Where possible, I have used historical figures and used as accurate a portrayal of their personalities and even their precise words where I could. Although Major Ritter, Dr Stoffel, and many others were invented, there were men like them in the war.

Jagiellonian university was cleared out by the Gestapo Commander in the manner I described. The professors were sent to prison camps around Europe and even Mousollini was outraged by their treatment. Eventually all of the prisoners over the age of 40 were set free but most died from malnutrition and disease shortly after their release.

There was a mass murder of Catholic clergy and leaders as well. Hans Frank, despite later allegedly renewing a childhood allegiance to Catholicism, seemed to have a particular dislike for Roman Catholics.

Hans Frank was a slippery sort. Transcripts of his trial after the war show how clever a lawyer and how intelligent he was. He admits to small wrongdoings to show good faith and cooperation and cleverly argues how he's not guilty of anything major. He was careful to not document any wrongdoing, and on paper seemed to be carefully protecting and cataloging Polish art treasures, while hording them. Most historians agree that it was Hans Frank who invented the rumor that Adolph Hitler had a Jewish grandmother, possibly to muddy the water and confuse prosecutors. It didn't save him. Hans Frank was executed for his many, many crimes.

There was a deliberate, systematic effort to obliterate Polish culture and eliminate any Poles deemed insufficiently Aryan. There seemed to be a conflicted mindset in the Nazi party regarding Poland. Some seemed to love the land and many of its people, certainly its ancient history. On the other hand, some seemed to hate the Poles as a people. The Nazis were so successful at destroying Polish culture and achievement that to this day few know anything of their history, art, music, poetry, or other great works.

In the late 19th and early 20th century, Krakow became a center of culture and art, with famous painters, poets, and writers worked in the city. Few are even aware of the names like Paderewski and Jan Matejko, or that men such as Chopin were Polish.

Operation Tannenberg in late 1939 was meant to solidify German control of the nation by eliminating potential troublemakers, and more than 700 mass executions were carried out to remove prominent Polish citizens and leaders.

In the following year, 1940, tens of thousands of Poles were arrested by the Germans and killed. Over 30,000 university professors, teachers, priests and other academics were shot to death outside Warsaw in the Kampinos forest near Palmiry. Most of the remainder were sent to various concentration camps to die.

And that wasn't the end of it. When the Soviets took over, Poland didn't face the kind of organized slaughter that the Germans were engaged in, but many many more died. For an example of Soviet atrocities against Poles, do a search on "Katyn Forest Massacre" some time. When the Soviets returned to Poland, Stalin officially gave orders to the Red Army to rape, pillage, and massacre, telling them "everything is allowed!" In terms of plunder, soldiers were allowed ten pounds weight of loot from the Poles, while generals could fill several boxcars.

The nightmare didn't really end until 1991 when the Soviet Union was finally dissolved and the Eastern Bloc countries were independent for the first time since the Nazi invasions.

Writing this book was a challenge in many ways. I have strived to be as accurate to history and Polish geography as I could. I relied heavily on internet research for much of the book's information, and any errors that you find in this book are my fault, for which I apologize; I intend no disrespect.

One particular glaring historical innacuracy is Mengele's presence at Birkenau. He did not arrive there until 1943, but he was such a pivotal personality and bizarre character I had to include him to interact with Dr Stoffel. And yes, its common in German, particularly at this time period, to refer to learned men by all their titles. Its a sort of honorary and a matter of pride to the men who achieved that level of academic success.

I do not speak Polish, and I have no idea how to pronounce most of the Polish terms and locations in the book. I grew to love Polish culture and history through writing this book and would love to one day visit the nation and see it for myself.

One thing I want to apologize specifically for is the way I used the story of Janosik in the book. The main details and myths are accurate as written, but I took him out of his primary location in the Czech area and pushed him back in time a few centuries to fit the story better. The story of the bandit Janosik is pretty fascinating, and has been made into several movies over the years.

Because of the tone and characters of the book, I do not give much attention to the Polish resistance, which was very impressive given their situation and resources. The AK was responsible for the death of several key German leaders, and so was the Jewish resistance forces, but it was only formed a few months before this story is told. And yes, it was Polish intelligence that first captured and analyzed an ENIGMA coder and managed to get it to the English even before the invasion of Poland. They were critical in the decoding process as well, working with the English.

Something readers may notice is that I've tried to use Polish names for locations as much as I can, although the Germans renamed most of it when they took over. I also played with language a lot, and I apologize for any confusion. When a German speaks his language, I've retained the German words for unique SS officer names such as "Sturmbannführer" for major. Most of the time, when someone speaks another language, I either leave the listener confused or translate it, because I don't speak Polish as I noted earlier, and speak too little German for complex dialog. That way I didn't have to put footnotes or translations in either.

Many of the main characters in this book are Gypsies, or Romani as they prefer to be called. The Romani are a fascinating culture and people, and they were also considered unworthy of living by the Germans. While there was no official specific policy for dealing with the Romani like with the Jews by German officials, they were generally despised and the camps were filled with Gypsies. I've tried to retain some of the interesting culture of the Romani and give them credit for their part in the war as well, but I confess Uncle Rys and his train of escapees is entirely fictional.

In closing, I want to give my respect and honor to the men and women who lived through this horror, and I hope that my story has in no way belittled your experiences, heroism, and the eventual triumph over evil that all of you were part of.

If you enjoyed this book, try *Snowberry's Veil* by Christopher Taylor, also available in paperback and e-book formats. Following is Chapter One of *Snowberry's Veil:*

The leaves were wet and dragged on my skin like cold hands trying to slow me as I ran. The chill was so bad that my feet were like blocks of wood -- I couldn't feel them at all, which was good because without any covering they were torn and bruised and bloody. The only clothing I had left was a nearly shredded pair of breeches that barely covered me, the rough cloth tattered and bloody from the scratches and bites on my legs. I ran as best I could through the forest, through a land unknown to me at the base of huge mountains.

Behind me I could hear the baying of the beasts, and distant shouts. How much of a lead I had, I could not guess, I only knew I needed speed and to stay away from their tearing jaws and spears. There were at least five different voices, with a number of those great wolves that I could not count. My mind was focused on the pathway ahead of me, trying to follow an animal trail through the woods as the underbrush lashed and pulled and slapped at me. The cold was all through me like I could never again be warm, and I knew that each step I took marked my path like a fire for the wolves to follow.

From what I knew of their kind, these beastmen were able to track by scent nearly as well as the wolves with them, but they preferred to use their companions. I had seen no shaman in the tribe, which was at least some small comfort. I had been separated from a caravan headed into the wilderness to settle, I had hoped to draw off the wolf clan's attention so that they could pass unmolested. I could only hope that my efforts had succeeded, that this pain and cold and fear was not a complete waste. In my mind's eye I could see my bones lying on this forest floor, scattered and gnawed by the jaws of the wolves, but I had to try my best to survive and return to the caravan, to see if they were safe.

I had been scouting ahead of the caravan, a few hundred strides ahead of the main body when I smelled smoke mixed in with the usual scents of forest and earth and mountain. If the caravan had been further off, I would have been less concerned, but I knew they wouldn't be quiet enough to pass by safely at this distance. With a last look back through the trees to where I knew the road was, I slipped through the forest with the skill that years of training and experience lent me, and closed on the fire downwind. My senses are not keen as an elf much less a wolf, but I could smell dog-smell even before I reached the rocky outcropping above the meadow where their fire was lit. Around it sat half a dozen beastmen: rough tribal creatures; part man, part animal.

These were wolf-like, with a wolf's head but man's keen eyes. Their hands were almost like a dog's paws, but with longer, more agile fingers. Their legs were bent like a hound's as well, with bare paws, and from under leathern kilts made from multiple layers of uncured hide a tail jutted. They were adorned with feathers and strips of leather, leaves, and white chalk in patterns on the short fur that covered their bodies. Standing upright like men, they held spears and they had fire.

With them were an equal number of huge wolves, bigger than I'd seen before. They were not wargs, lacking the malevolence and exaggerated features, but they seemed larger and fiercer than ordinary wolves. Feral wolves, perhaps, enchanted to give strength and cunning beyond their ordinary kin. The beastmen seemed unaware of the caravan and certainly of myself. I saw no ranged weapons unless the spears were intended to be thrown; each had three spears with razor-sharp stone heads in addition to what looked to be stone daggers. They were roasting some small creature over the fire and speaking in a tongue I did not know when a seventh arrived from the forest, so stealthy I had not seen him until he stepped into the clearing.

He spoke and pointed out of the clearing, toward where I knew the caravan was passing. The others seemed excited, and the fire was rapidly put out. Weapons were readied, and I knew that the scout had spotted the caravan just as I'd spotted their fire. They would attack soon, and in the caravan there were hardly four men who could fight, the others ill or injured from a previous attack by goblins. I thought of the families in the caravan, especially Thealea, and knew what I must do.

There was a stack of rocks, each as big as my head on the edge of the short cliff above the meadow, and I pushed against it, grunting as it rattled and collapsed, raining the stones down in to the clearing in a roar. I stood up as the beastmen scattered unharmed, and saw the wolves already spreading out like water to find a way up the cliff and to my flesh. I slung my cloak back and tucked it behind my quiver to give easy access and prevent it from snagging and then I ran. Would the others follow, or would they leave me to the wolves? I heard voices behind me; at least some were following, and some would be enough for the caravan to fight off the ones who stayed behind.

I slipped through the forest with practiced ease. I did not know this exact area, but I knew forests like this and the patterns were burned in my brain from years of experience. As one of the King's Rangers, I served my king scouting and mapping and cataloging, and I did it well. I studied the animals, the plants, the races, the monsters, and the natural resources, mapping and keeping notes so that others would know what I'd seen and found. When travelers, huntsmen, woodsmen and others needed aid, I was there to lend whatever help I could. Yet this trip I was not acting for the king, I was just a man helping a friend, yes and helping the daughter of one of the caravaners, lovely Thealea with the red hair and smart mouth. She'd had little good to say of me yet with that full-lipped mouth, but her bright gray eyes told another story when no one else was looking.

The feral wolves and beastmen followed me and I led them on a merry chase, fast and light on my feet. It would be simple, I thought, to lead them away like a mother quail then lose them – wolves and all – in the forest and rejoin the caravan while they searched hopelessly for me. I should have known better.

I was doing well, just slow enough to keep them sighting me on occasion and to keep the wolves on my path, but fast enough to stay safely away when I ran into a second group of them. The second group was decorated the same way as the first, Wolf Clan beastmen with the same patterns of chalk and the same kind of equipment. They were ready for me, of course, with all the clamor the hunt was raising, but they had not been exactly sure what was being chased. So when I ran between two large rocky sections like a low ridge broken in half, I nearly ran into their spears and everyone was caught by surprise. This group had no wolves, but they were in front of me and their allies behind, and I was caught with the gap behind me between a stone escarpment tall as a castle wall and only one path through that led straight to the rest of their tribe.

I froze, and the beastmen laughed, their spears pointed at my chest. I was not wearing my armor today; only the outdoor clothing I favored and my fenen cloak. The bow at my back was no use, nor the long knives I wore at either side, for they would run me through with those wicked-looking stone spear points if I reached for obvious weapons. Their equipment was crude and simple, but clearly serviceable and a man can die from a flint spear point just as well as a mithril one.

I raised my hands to shoulder level and behind me I could hear the wolves drawing very close, almost to the gap in the ridge. I took in my surroundings; the ridge dropped off rapidly to the right, into a very deep valley with what looked like a lake at the bottom hundreds of spans beneath us. The beastmen ahead of me had been following a trail that led between the sections of ridge, a trail ahead of me and behind them that rose almost steep as a cliff on one side and dropped rapidly on the other. I had but one chance to take or die to these creatures, and likely a hard death as well – I knew many of the beastmen clans preferred torture before they feasted, and these looked merciless.

Around my neck I wore a little pouch, like the ones some shaman I'd seen among the beastmen and goblins wore. Yet mine was no spirit pouch, it was a strange enchanted item I'd found in my travels. Within it was a magical surprise, one I could use but once a day. I reached carefully to the pouch and pulled the top open. The beastmen looked suspicious and pushed their spears against my chest painfully. Make no sudden moves I understood that action to be saying. With two fingers I reached into the pouch, trying to look innocent and harmless and pulled out a little ball of fluff the size of a dandelion's head. The beastmen relaxed some, not seeing some terrible spell or weapon. They seemed curious and amused, perhaps thinking I was hoping to bribe them for my freedom. I dropped the ball, as if accidentally, and the magic ran its course.

As the little ball fell, it began to change. The pouch was unpredictable; I never knew what would come out of it. The little pouch could produce anything from a butterfly to some monstrosity I'd never seen before, always some creature or creatures I could – for a short time – command. The fluff darkened and split and multiplied, shredding into a cloud of small flying objects. It became a swarm of bees. Thanking whoever made the item, I commanded the bees to attack everyone but me, and spun to escape as their spear points tore my thin leather tunic and cut my chest. The beastmen pulled back, dismayed at the sudden appearance of an angry swarm diving at their faces. They were brave enough, yet even the bravest can be daunted by thousands of tiny stingers.

The feral wolves behind me were not so concerned. They leapt at me, slamming into my body and tearing at my legs, shredding the legs of my breeches, and biting painfully into my flesh. They clawed at me with short, hard nails and I could smell the fetid breath of rotted meat on their jaws.

I fled, diving to the side. I had planned to roll and get cover, commanding the bees for the short time I could and using arrows to cause mayhem, perhaps taking a few of the creatures out. Yet the land betrayed me. What looked like solid ground was instead a fallen tree's ancient roots, rotted and supporting Merin, leaves, and shrubs on a thin crust of crumbling earth. It caved away as I landed, and the slope to the lake below was much, much steeper than I'd thought. Two wolves went with me, slewing to the sides as I fell.

Down I went, uncontrolled, rolling and crashing through underbrush and against trees, painfully slamming into unyielding wood as I rolled. I lost my quiver, my bow, and my knives. I lost my fine fenen cloak and the enchanted pouch from around my neck. A hard rock gouged into my back, knocking the breath from me and preventing me from grabbing anything to slow the descent. In the long, tumbling fall, I lost my boots and the dagger tucked into one, the backup knives from behind my neck, and the pouch at my side containing some food and my steel and flint. By the time I finally rolled to a stop in a shallow creek, I'd lost my cap and my gloves and my shirt was in tatters when finally I rolled to a stop in a creek. Above me the two wolves who'd joined my fall had stopped halfway down the ravine's slope, thanks to four legs and a better sense of balance.

I lay stunned a moment, sputtering in the cold shallow water and trying to gather my senses. Above me I could hear the wolves and the wolf clan crying out and working their way down the steep slope. Stripping off the wet tatters of my tunic, I tied the rags around my waist and had to flee – nearly naked and without weapons.

Now at the bottom of the valley, I had run around the lake I'd seen and into a fan of smaller valleys, picking one at random and following it. I kept to a small animal trail, knowing that the creatures that made it used it so often that it formed a visible trail did so because it was a good path to follow, leading somewhere useful. Leaving the pathway might be a good way to travel, and it might not: there was usually a reason that animals kept to the trails they did. A likely enough looking way might lead straight to a cliff. And there were worse things than terrain in the wilderness.

It was late afternoon then and I knew I needed to find shelter soon. This part of the wood did not look like it was traveled much by anything but smaller game, and I was hoping the wolf clan on my trail would not follow me too deeply into unknown territory. A single target might not be attractive enough to follow, but then I'd made them angry with the bees from my little pouch now lost on the mountainside. I would have cursed but I needed to save my strength and my breath.

I kept a steady pace up, long used to travel by running, trying to ignore the pain in my legs and in my back. I also tried to ignore the numbness of my feet and nose and fingers. Fully dressed it hadn't been so cold, but now I was shivering with the chill. The little trail led along a ridge and my eyes caught a hint of a path leading up the side. What was more important was a plant that I saw by that path. It was a small shrub that I'd been hoping to spot, with waxy blue leaves and yellow stems, each stem ending in sets of six willow-long leaves. The plant never flowered, but did produce string-like sticky appendages that attracted bees and other pollen-carrying creatures. But it wasn't the leaves or the sticky growths I was after, it was the root.

I had bare seconds to spare, yet if I could get at the roots, I could perhaps save my life and shake the feral wolves off my trail, and if I was clever, the beastmen as well. Digging furiously with my hands I revealed a thick, yellowish root and picking up a sharp looking stone I hacked at it viciously. The root finally gave way, and I could hear my pursuers growing closer. They were not cautious, so perhaps this area was known better to them than I'd hoped. With the root in hand, I crushed the end using the stone and rubbed the mangled, wet end on my feet. I shuddered looking at the torn flesh and battered soles of my feet and the root coming away smeared with blood. Through the numbness somewhere deep in my feet I felt stabbing pain as I jammed the root mercilessly against them. The thick, wet sap coated my feet and swiftly dried, leaving a glossy surface.

That surface would protect my feet slightly, but what's more it would staunch the bleeding and most importantly the mild enchantment of the eads herb would negate the ability of the wolves to track me. I would leave no scent, no track at all, for as long as an hour. Throwing dirt over the roots, I tied the eads root into the rags of my tunic around my waist as I fled. That root could serve me again for a few days, if I lived that long. I left the path I was on, following a faint trail rising along the ridge, and kept low, moving slower now, trying to make as little noise as possible. Moving carefully, I avoided stepping on

231

anything that would break or rattle and tried to avoid brushing up against any plants. Speed was less important than being undiscovered at this point. A cold wind blew along the ridge, reminding me of how bare I was against the elements of the mountains.

Below me I could hear the wolves and beastmen reach the point I left the animal track. The feral wolves growled and whined, sounding frustrated, confused, and less confident in a new meal. I heard what sounded like the wolf clan discussing the matter in their language, and I continued moving as swiftly as I could without revealing myself. They could still smell me on the air if the wind shifted; at present it was blowing past the wolves toward me, but it might swirl or back and the lack of a trail would become meaningless as they would follow the scent of my body.

I climbed the ridge, higher and higher, until it became rough and rocky, with few trees. Among the boulders there were shrubs and small plants, but the trees could not find a foothold in this rough terrain. My footing was smoother on the rocks, but between them it was treacherous footing of sharp and broken stones. I tried to move carefully, not letting any rocks move against each other, yet sometimes a few pebbles rattled, sounding like thunder in my ears. I hoped I was high enough now that they would not hear, but was not confident. Those peaked canine ears on both beastman and feral wolf looked to be very keen, and sound traveled well in the mountain air.

Finally I crouched behind a large boulder and hazarded a look around the stones, through a sparse dry shrub with wicked looking spines on it that I'd not seen before. My ranger's subconscious cataloged the type of bush; its pattern of growth, where I found it, what kind of leaves it seemed to have in life, and so on. But my conscious mind was hyper aware, staring down the mountainside at the forest, trying to pick out any slightest movement. I heard the sound of the wolves growling and whining, complaining at the loss of my trail, and I heard the beastmen talking. It sounded like they were arguing, or at least upset. Perhaps some wanted to go back, but by now the caravan would be miles away and we were even further from the roadway, such as it was even if the wolf clan had ever noticed it.

The caravan had set out from the westermark along the south road four days, heading to the wilderness to settle in new lands. Originally there were seven wagons, each one representing a family and their hopes, containing the goods they thought they'd need and supplies to begin a settlement. There were already some small villages started in the south as the King had begun to grant land to worthy people and sell land cheap to others. Expand into the unsettled areas and one could have their own territory, and what riches might you earn? Free from the city life and control of barons and dukes, the frontier would one day be under the same system of hierarchy and government but for now it was open and wild.

One of the wagons broke down early on and the family gave up on the journey, heading back after repairs while and the rest kept going. One of the wagons had been destroyed in a raid by goblins almost two days ago, killing two men and a child, leaving the grieving widow to return home with a rider who'd decided he didn't really want to explore all that much. The last five wagons kept going down the trail and to the east, skirting around wild Wrenland to the south to the rich frontier lands further inland from the ocean. This area was little known, and all that was there in the way of roads was a pair of ruts that previous wagons and riders had left. No patrols watched this land and no soldiers kept the monsters at bay. The road had the stink of man on it enough to keep many creatures away, but was remote enough that it was prey to groups like the goblins, and these beastmen, at least to the unwary.

The settlers didn't know exactly where they wanted to go, only that they were going to the frontier, to the new lands. There was word of a keep that had been built in the frontier, an attempt to provide some security and regular trade as an outpost in the wilderness. Some wanted to find land near there, to cluster near the remnants of civilization. Others, including the wagon with Thealea, wanted to go deeper to untamed lands to test their mettle.

Leading the caravan was a man that I did not care for, but I could not give a reason other than that he was richer, more handsome and powerful than I, and interested in Thealea. He was a lord, and to me seemed untrustworthy, as if he had some other reason for taking this trip in his fine clothes and on his fine horse, but I could not explain why I thought so.

Long ago the elves had kept these areas patrolled and secured; there were ruins yet of old roads, markers, towers, strange statues and structures as if in the middle of the forest, they thought even greater beauty was needed. Other, stranger structures were sometimes found. Some were the ruins of a forgotten human kingdom from centuries past and some were the work of other creatures and races. Dwarves had colonies in the mountains that no one knew about save their own kind, and they were not keen on visitors. Yet to man, it was wilderness; untracked, unknown.

By now the caravan should be far enough on the road that they would be safe from these creatures, and I would need to rejoin the when I could. They had fighting men, but few, and none with my experience and woodcraft. Yet I could not reach them this day, I had to find shelter, food, and water. Everywhere man goes he is in need of these things. The thin boundaries of civilization are around him like paper walls, keeping these needs at bay with ready homes, food, and drink. It takes only a disaster, a sudden catastrophe to reveal the basic need we all still share – and I'd had my disaster.

The sounds of the wolves became quieter and the wolf clan had stopped arguing, but I could sense they were not heading up my trail.

They had turned back for now at least as I confirmed by a glimpse of them moving away through the trees. I breathed easier, now and closed my eyes a moment to try to calm my nerves. I could not rest, not yet, but at least I could move without open pursuit.

Shelter was my first need; I could go a few days without water and a week or more without food, but shelter... I'd die overnight naked in the mountains. Fire and something to keep the elements off me, that was what I needed most to begin with. The ridge top I was near looked too exposed and the stones too unstable. They were heavy and seemed solid right now, but if one were to start moving no force I could bring to bear would stop one from its course.

I knew a few minor magics, elemental tricks to make life easier, but I was no mage. I'd seen them summon entire keeps out of nothing to stay in comfort. I couldn't even summon a bedroll. I knew this was going to be one uncomfortable night, but there was no way to avoid it. I tore off part of my tattered tunic and tied the remnants around my poor battered and bloody feet to provide some semblance of covering for them. Somewhere along the way I'd lost my Eads root, but there was more about. In fact, I'd spotted several other useful herbs that I could take advantage of, if I could only find some shelter.

I looked around at the dying afternoon and saw the mountains about me. Huge snow-capped peaks lay in the distance to the west: the Dawnspires. To the north, the mountains I was in fell to rolling hills repeating into the gray distance beyond one huge peak whose name I did not know. Around me were ridges like roots of a tree, tangled and long with valleys between them. Tall firs, pines, and a few mixed ash and aspen covered these ridges and valleys in a green coat of varied shades. The sound of the wind in the trees filled me with pleasure, again, like it always did. Except for the forest sigh and my own breathing, it was silent now.

Overhead the sky was a deep blue with massive clouds drifting in some distant wind. I felt the awesome aloneness of being in the wilds, and reveled in it.

In truth, although Thealea was beautiful and fascinating, and seemed bright and exciting, I knew deep down that I could have no woman – for the wilderness would not share. The wilds were an exacting wife already, jealous of any other love. I could not leave a beloved behind for weeks, even months at a time as I cataloged and mapped and explored. That she might come with me seemed absurd as well; how could I move and work with someone else, someone I had to care for even if somehow I could find a woman who would do so? I knew a few female rangers were active, but they were rare and a special, strange breed. Yet, I felt attracted to Thealea at the same time, an irrational pull that I could not deny.

I moved along the ridge, looking for a useful place. My needs were simple: some coverage with a fairly open front that would allow me to see anything drawing close. Even a few fallen trees or a rock formation would work, although a cave or pocket in the stone would be better. The longer I went, the less picky I became. Night fell fast in the mountains and by sunbloom I'd be chilled to an eternal sleep if I didn't find shelter soon. I had maybe three hours before it became too dark – and too cold – to properly prepare and bed down. Yet even in this dire predicament in which I found myself, the smell of the forest was rich and comforting, like an old home remembered and loved. Wild scents of pinesap and earth, flowers and leaves, musk from animals and the smell of the clean, crisp air were perfume to me.

I found a huge fallen tree, roots forming a barrier of earth and torn up rocks against a stone formation rising up the side of a ridge. This wedge shape gave me shelter from the wind and sight except from directly above or ahead. Some of the branches of the tree were still in place, forming the beginning of a roof, and I worked quickly to clean out beneath them. Breaking branches off nearby firs, I built a rough thatch over the wedge shape in the back, weaving through and using the same foliage of the original tree and nearby bushes. From a distance it would look normal and natural, yet it would keep all but the most driving rain out when combined with the canopy further overhead from the huge pines. I gathered wood; piling dry branches and old sticks near the back of the wedge, out of sight. When I thought I'd gotten enough, I went and gathered more, then did it again. I knew from bitter experience that wood had a strange way of being used up faster than expected, and there was a plentiful supply.

The light was fading already when I had the shelter in rough form and I went out one more time to gather bark and soft boughs. By this time the birds were singing their night songs and it was so cold my hands were shaking almost uncontrollably. Once I'd collected a pile of leaves, bark, and boughs, I dug out a trench using stones and branches, then laid a bed of the softest stuff I could manage. With clumsy, numb hands I used boughs to form a blanket of sorts that would lie over me, then set about to make a fire. By now my mind was wandering, I had to force myself by willpower to stay on a task. I was so cold I'd stopped shivering; my whole body felt oddly numb and disconnected, like it wasn't really me. Only continuous action was keeping me warm enough to function at any level.

Often I did without a fire as my clothing was usually warm enough and this crude shelter would provide enough protection in this weather to make do. The fenen cloak I'd left behind on that slope was enchanted, it would have kept me comfortable down to freezing temperatures if I wrapped it around me. Unfortunately it was at least a mile away and I wanted the beastmen even further away before I headed back to try to recover it. I was sure they'd found and kept everything for themselves by this point, but as soon as I could I planned to go back and search for myself. I lacked their keen senses to find man-smell and items, but I could at least try. My lost bow was of elfin make and I was very loath to lose it. Those supplies had gotten me through many years of wilderness travel and work for the king.

Now, however, I needed a fire; I was too cold, too bare, and too wounded. This was not a terrible challenge, as I had learned long ago how to make a fire without any flint or steel. There were several mechanical methods that could be used, each tedious and frustrating. I could use one or another herb to heat and begin a fire. Yet it was one of the little spells I'd learned that was most useful here, and I hoped I wasn't so tired and cold that I was unable to work this simple magic. I piled the tinder together in a pit, lined with stones, and set a large slab of bark from the fallen tree propped up with dirt behind it to act as a reflector, pushing more of the heat back to me and again off the stone wall beside my bed. Piling larger sticks over the tinder in a pyramid, I then sat by it carefully. I wasn't very good at this, and it took concentration to work any magic. Over time, apparently, study and technique made this a lot easier, but I didn't have the time or inclination to learn magic that well. I concentrated, eyes closed, focusing on the training I had.

Then I jerked myself awake, somehow. It was dark now, pitch black and at some point I had drifted to sleep in the cold without even realizing it. Another little nap and I would not wake up again. I had to make a fire now or die.

Concentrating as hard as I could, talking to myself with each step, I thought of the words and the movements then made them real with voice and hands, the power flowing through me and from me tracing bluish white strips of light in the air from my fingertips that faded quickly; then I forced the elemental energy to focus on the tinder, and a flame lit up, rapidly growing and finally a fire was started. I took a deep breath and stacked the fire into a larger blaze, big enough to stay warm and burning into the night. The spell was minor, yet after the day's exertions and pains, it was wearying. All I needed then was sleep, for sleep would bring healing and it was already later than I cared for. This would be enough heat to bring some warmth back into my poor abused body and with the bark and the stone to reflect the heat I knew I should be able to survive the night. The air was becoming quite frosty, but the fire pushed the cold back as it hungrily devoured the wood I fed it, casting light in my rough shelter and heat over my chilled, aching body. Pulling the boughs and leaves over me in a cold, scratchy blanket, I settled in to sleep.

Somewhere, a wolf howled.

ALSO FROM KESTREL ARTS

FANTASY ROLE PLAYING ADVENTURE:

THE LOST CASTLE: Lurking in the wilderness is an old dilapidated castle and the ruins of the nearby village. This castle has been taken over by the creatures of the wilds, but what lies beneath these crumbling walls, and why are they being rebuilt? Officially licensed by Hero Games! The Lost Castle is a complete Fantasy Hero adventure with maps, locations, treasures, and all the information you need to run your game!

ELENTHAR'S TOWER: The great mage and mystic experimenter Elenthar has vanished, his tower in the city gone silent and locked tight. What has happened? His home stands still save for mysterious moaning sounds at night. What strange wonders may be found in the archmage's home? Do you dare explore, or even more daring, loot this manor? A complete Fantasy Hero adventure for 4-6 characters of no more than 750 total points, combined.

THE FANTASY CODEX: A massive set of spells for fantasy role playing. Designed for Fantasy Hero, but adaptable for any game system, with almost 1000 unique spells. Includes a fully designed magic system, tips on building spells, an alternate random side effects system, unique creatures, and much more. From Necromancy to War magic, from Shamanism to Illusions, the Fantasy Codex has you covered.

THE JOLRHOS BESTIARY: A tome packed with unique, special, and interesting monsters. No goblins or dragons are in this book, only the unusual and unique to the Jolrhos Fantasy Hero campaign. Nearly 300 creatures of all sorts from the Accursed to the Zhar, plus indices to make finding just what you need and an intro filled with useful tips, ideas, and information.

FANTASY FICTION:

SNOWBERRY'S VEIL: The tale of King's Ranger Erkenbrand facing a deadly wilderness, fearsome monsters, and the evil in the heart of man to rejoin his love Thealea. Found on Amazon Kindle in e-book form and on Lulu in print!

OLD HABITS: Street thief Stoce burgled a fortune in gems for the Brotherhood, but now the jewels have been lost and before he can recover them, Stoce will face assassins, sorcerers, holy knights, and a castle torn by a deadly conspiracy. In the end, will Stoce find his gems, or will he find a far greater treasure?